# The Sleeper Wakes

## HARLEM RENAISSANCE STORIES BY WOMEN

*Edited and with an introduction by*

## Marcy Knopf

### FOREWORD BY NELLIE Y. McKAY

SERPENT'S TAIL

*London*

First published in the United States by Rutgers University Press, New Brunswick, New Jersey
First published in the United Kingdom by Serpent's Tail, 4 Blackstock Mews, London

A catalogue record of this book is available from the British Library on request.

*To the memory of my mother, Jane Gibbons Knopf*
*and for Lisa Maria Hogeland*

*Two women who have inspired and shaped my life*

# CONTENTS

# FOREWORD

NELLIE Y. McKAY

The Harlem Renaissance! When and how did it begin? When and why did it come to an end? Was it a period when black arts flourished or one in which the most creative of the race sold their talents for the proverbial mess of pottage? Was it really a renaissance of black expressive culture, another time when black was beautiful, or merely an interlude when rich white people, bored with their own lives, indulged their fancies and fantasies with the perceived exoticism of people of African heritage? These and other questions interrogating the value of the most talked-about movement in black culture persist for scholars of African-American history, literature, arts, and politics. Most critics agree there are no definitive opening or ending dates for the period, while debates on the whys of its existence are not altogether settled either. Most critics also agree that *something* different from what had previously existed happened in black arts between the last years of the second decade of this century and the beginning of its fourth. And it was a renaissance, for there was a time in the nineteenth century when black writing flourished, at least in America.[1]

In our time, the intellectual study of the Harlem Renaissance as a phenomenon in African-American culture has now been around for many decades, yet the subject remains inexhaustible. This, in spite of the many perspectives from which it has been approached. "Here is *The New Negro* (1925)!" exclaimed Alain Locke's anthology that introduced the work, critical and artistic, of the principal players on a newly unveiled stage, while James Weldon Johnson's *Black Manhattan* (1930) documented the development of the black capital of America. For Arna

---

[1]See William L. Andrews, "The 1850s: The First Afro-American Literary Renaissance," in *Literary Romanticism in America*, ed. William L. Andrews (Baton Rouge: Louisiana State University Press, 1981), pp. 38–60.

Bontemps, who was there when it happened, *The Harlem Renaissance Remembered* (1972) framed his nostalgia in his edited collection of scholarly essays on those larger-than-life characters who were there too. *Harlem Renaissance* (1971), unembellished, was Nathan Huggins's excellent historical evaluation of the period, followed by Jervis Anderson's *This Was Harlem* (1981) and David Levering Lewis's swift-moving rendition, *When Harlem Was in Vogue* (1981). A list of books on the subject could be many times as long as that given here: bibliographies, dictionaries, histories, and literary and historical criticism; and the essays on the actors in this play and the reviews of its failures and successes are legion. The Harlem Renaissance continues to engage the imagination of many, with the multiplicity of viewpoints their interests generate.

In the early 1970s, when I was a graduate student and knew very little about the Harlem Renaissance, I discovered and became enamored with the *Crisis* and *Opportunity* magazines—journals deserving enormous credit for the stupendous job they accomplished in preserving the history and achievements of black America in the 1920s and 1930s. Although the *Crisis* came into being in 1910 and continues to exist, and *Opportunity* had a life span of more than two-and-a-half decades (1923–1949), the 1920s and early 1930s were their most successful years. I recall the long hours I spent in window seats in the musty bowels of the library, reading, no, drinking in the story recorded in these publications. The information that came to me pleased, horrified, and fascinated me: from the accounts of white atrocities against black people to the pictures and stories that celebrated black successes; the rallying calls for black action against their oppressors—the poems, short stories, book reviews, and dramatic pieces; photographs of paintings and sculpture by black artists; accounts of weddings, funerals, college and high school graduations; and from a black perspective, reports and editorials on current events that had meaning to the lives of everyone in our country. These journals represented diaries of a race—a running group history recorded as events unfolded. They were full of the kind of information that neither my high school, or undergraduate, or graduate school educations had bothered to fill me in on: information about me.

At the time, despite the demands of a graduate program to complete and my need to tend to the myriad anxieties I had about the future I faced, I made mental note of a project I hoped someday to return to and engage: work on a collection of *Crisis* and *Opportunity* short fiction of the Harlem Renaissance. Looking back on that moment in my life now, I think of how swiftly the years have slipped by, and that the time was never right for me to return to the note—until now—not to fulfill it as I once anticipated I would, but to observe the significance of the step that a new researcher has taken in a direction I could not have imagined in the early 1970s. Marcy Knopf's *The Sleeper Wakes: Harlem Renaissance Stories by Women*, a far advance from the project I envisioned then, marks another landmark in the study of Afro-American writings, of Afro-American women's writings, and of the Harlem Renaissance.

*The Sleeper Wakes*, a selection of twenty-eight stories by fourteen women who published not only in the *Crisis* and *Opportunity* (the major black journals of their day), but also in much less well known black magazines, is the first book of its kind. For these women there were both the courage to write and the courage to make sure they published wherever they could.[2] Why did we have to wait so long for this anthology? Although by the early 1970s a generation of black feminist scholars, newly entering literary studies, were beginning to raise the banner for the writings of black women, in the context of the times, with Black Studies and [white] Women's Studies struggling to claim legitimacy as intellectual fields of endeavor, the position of black women's writings was marginal to group concerns of gender and race. Throughout much of that decade their writings (past and contemporary) were difficult to come by, not for want of a corpus, but because they were victims of the flagrant disregard of those works by the sources with the power to make them available. Not until its closing years, as a result of the pressing agitation of black women writers and critics, did publishers and others begin to change their attitudes toward black women's writings. As strange as it might seem today, because of the place some of these writers now occupy in the public consciousness, Zora Neale Hurston's novels, including *Their Eyes Were Watching God*, were out of print until well into the mid 1970s. In 1979, even after the publication of and the acclaim she had won for *Song of Solomon* and *Tar Baby*, Toni Morrison's *The Bluest Eye* and *Sula* were out of print, and remained so until the early 1980s. In the earliest university courses on black women writers almost all of the materials available to students and faculty were photocopies of long out-of-print texts. After all that has happened, it is difficult not to conclude that black women's texts disappeared from publishers' lists

----

[2]In her "Introduction" to this collection, Marcy Knopf notes that the young Dorothy West published in the local black Boston literary magazine, *The Saturday Evening Quill*, and that Gwendolyn Bennett's "Wedding Day" first appeared in the short-lived *Fire!!*. On the one hand, placing their work in these magazines indicates the difficulties these women faced in finding suitable publication outlets, on the other, it suggests their determination to be published writers, and their self-confidence on that issue.

because of a perception by marketing departments of a general lack of interest in books by and about black women and girls. The long struggle for recognition of the value of black women's writings, especially on black women's lives and experiences, until recently, is the story of the persistence that characterizes a tradition that enabled black women of the nineteenth century and the first half of the twentieth to disregard the absence or presence of an audience for their works, and to find in the process of writing itself the rewards for the task.

Black women in America, we now know, have been writing for a long time: from the often maligned "Bars Fight" by Lucy Terry in 1746,[3] to the women in the 1980s and 1990s who earn Pulitzer prizes and Mac-Arthur grants and other national and international awards. During the summer of 1992, journalists and others observed in wonder the strange phenomenon of books by three black women on national best-seller lists. More significant for many of us in black women's literature, however, is our knowledge of the determined consistency that over the span of two centuries produced this group. For a long time this was not known, but the recent Schomburg Library of Nineteenth Century Black Women's Writings, another landmark event in publication history, makes it impossible for anyone unwillingly to remain ignorant of this body of literature.

But if the Schomburg Library opened up a general awareness of black women's writings of the nineteenth century, there is still much to be learned of their literary productiveness during the early part of this century. *The Sleeper Wakes* takes a valuable step in that direction. Standard histories of the Harlem Renaissance, such as those mentioned at the beginning of this Foreword, do little to inform readers of the special contributions of women to the period. Although it is true that individual writers like Zora Neale Hurston, Jessie Fauset, Nella Larsen, Dorothy West, and others have received respectable critical attention within the past ten years, not enough has yet been done on how women artists as a group contributed to the movement as a whole. Toward that end, Daphne Duval Harrison's *Black Pearls: Blues Queens of the 1920s* (1988), which throws light on more than a hundred "lost" women blues singers

---

[3]Lucy Terry, a slave in Deerfield, Massachusetts, authored the oldest extant writing by a person of African origin in this country. In 1746, when she was sixteen years old, an Indian raid on her village inspired her to write a poem describing the massacre. Her account is the most complete historical document of that incident. Preposterously, some critics dismiss this eighteenth-century slave women's writing for her shortcomings as a poet.

of the era; Maureen Honey's *Shadowed Dreams: Women's Poetry of the Harlem Renaissance* (1989); and Gloria T. Hull's *Color, Sex, and Poetry: Three Women Writers of the Harlem Renaissance* (1987) are immensely important. A good source for identification of women of the time is *Harlem Renaissance and Beyond: Literary Biographies of 100 Black Women Writers, 1900–1945* (1990) by Lorraine Elena Roses and Ruth Elizabeth Randolf.[4]

*The Sleeper Wakes*, a carefully balanced anthology, truly enhances efforts to bring the lives and experiences of black women writers into our lives and classrooms and to the consciousness of today's readers. Some of the authors included, like Hurston, Fauset, and Larsen, are already well known to those familiar with black women writers of the earlier part of this century. They are like familiar old friends to us. Some of their stories in this collection are already anthologized and may be known to some readers; the others will be like pleasant secrets in their lives we are only now discovering. But several of these writers have not appeared other than in the journals in which they were first published, and their names and works are virtually unknown to most people. This mixture of the known and unknown is an excellent menu for giving us a new look at the Harlem Renaissance.

The stories cover the variety of experiences that over time have defined the identities of black women in America. The majority explore events and ideas in the domestic sphere where the survival of individuals and the group occurs amidst an entanglement of intraracial relationships that are not always nurturing or supportive. To a large extent, literally and figuratively, the women represented here wrote to address the struggles of women and sometimes men at the intersection of race and gender, even when this does not always seem apparent in their narratives. Themes range from the problems that skin color and/or "passing" raise, and how they affect some people, topics that were popular during the Renaissance, to the reaction of a mother who, like Toni Morrison's Sethe in her renowned novel *Beloved*, decides to kill her child rather than have him live only to suffer the horrors of America's system of racial injustice. The deadendedness and despair of poverty in the lives of lower-class blacks in such stories as Dorothy West's prize-winning "The Typewriter" is balanced by others like Leila Amos Pendleton's "The Foolish and the Wise," in which a domestic servant

---

[4]A number of books focussing on black women in the Harlem Renaissance are currently in progress. These include Cheryl Wall's study of women of letters of the Harlem Renaissance, forthcoming from Indiana University Press.

named Sallie refuses even to consider that Cleopatra and Socrates might be white since she will not permit whites to rob blacks of ownership of intelligence and accomplishments. Knopf observes too that many of these narratives appear to be trial runs of the early ideas of some authors who also wrote novels, as many of the themes in their stories reappear in their long fiction.

But *The Sleeper Wakes* and the studies of women in the Renaissance cited above are only the beginning of the work that must be done if black women in the arts during the Harlem Renaissance and later, including writers, are to receive their just due in the critical literature of our time. *The Sleeper Wakes* reinforces the urgency of the need for books such as this one. These stories reveal a great deal at the intersection of life and art in the lives of black women: on one hand, they give us a cross-section of the social and sociological concerns of urban black women in America during the 1920s and 1930s; and on the other, they provide insight into black women's efforts to develop an aesthetic which, that historical time, would accommodate, without compromise, the artistic productions of a group that was neither white nor male. How much of their goal they achieved and how well they accomplished it is left to the critics to decide, but our literature is certainly richer because of this new and exciting anthology.

# PREFACE

I first came into contact with the Harlem Renaissance when I was assigned the novel *Plum Bun* to read for a course in American women writers. Three hundred and seventy-nine pages later, I was a changed person. Jessie Redmon Fauset touched me inside and gave birth to my interest in the period and, later, to my preparation of this book. When I went to New York the following summer, I found my way to the Schomburg Center for Research in Black Culture to see what more I could learn about Fauset. There was so much information at the Schomburg that I made a habit of going there on weekends, searching through periodicals. It was not long before I realized that Fauset wrote a great deal more than just her four novels. I became equally interested in other women whose names kept appearing as authors of short fiction in *The Crisis*, *Opportunity*, and other publications. I soon realized that most of the stories by women, both the well known and the relatively obscure, had never been reprinted in book form. Maureen Honey's *Shadowed Dreams*, a volume of women poets of the Harlem Renaissance, served as a model for my work. This collection, like hers, is the first of its kind.

Most of the stories that appear in this anthology were originally printed in African-American magazines during the Harlem Renaissance. And with the exception of the stories by Zora Neale Hurston, Alice Dunbar-Nelson, and Marita Bonner, none has been reprinted since its original magazine publication. I chose the material for *The Sleeper Wakes* after spending several months reading stories on microfilm at the Schomburg Library. There were many stories to choose from, both by well-known writers and virtually unknown ones. I decided to include here only the work of women writers, because most of the writing by male authors of the Harlem Renaissance is available in reprint form and widely anthologized. The stories in this volume are by women who were as prolific during the Renaissance as their male coun-terparts, yet have been forgotten and overshadowed by them.

I initially decided to prepare this anthology because there is not much information available about the women writers of the Harlem Renais-sance, except for Zora Neale Hurston, Jessie Fauset, and Nella Larsen. Though there are many historical studies of the period, they focus primarily on the accomplishments of the male writers, artists, and polit-ical figures, such as Langston Hughes, Jean Toomer, Countee Cullen, and Claude McKay. The revival of Hurston's works within the past few years has led to an increased curiosity about other women writers of the Renaissance. However, women's accomplishments have been mar-ginalized, devalued, and ignored in many of the historical texts. The present anthology corrects this bias by devoting itself entirely to women writers of the Harlem Renaissance.

I researched hundreds of stories, from which I have tried to select the most compelling, readable, and representative. These particular fic-tions fit together as a cohesive unit because they share such com-monalities as links to slavery, a recognition of the double and sometimes triple oppression of black women, and issues involving the conflicts of color. Many of the women here use a male voice or protagonist to tell their stories, which make them similar to those written by African-American men. By using a male voice, the female writer was able to access the wider audience and readership of the periodicals in which they were published.

The publication of this book will enable readers to finally view a more complete literary and artistic history of the Renaissance, one that in-cludes women as prominent participants and leaders in the develop-ment of contemporary African-American literary culture.

# ACKNOWLEDGMENTS

There are so many people who have made this book possible for me, I hope that in my thanks I am able to remember them all. First of all, I would like to give my never-ending thanks to the one person who has inspired me from the beginning, Lisa Maria Hogeland. She introduced me to the Harlem Renaissance with Jessie Redmon Fauset's novel *Plum Bun*, which ignited the fire inside me to further research this period. I would also like to thank Elizabeth McCord for her constant support both academically and emotionally, during this project and in every other part of my life.

During my research at the Schomburg Center for Research in Black Culture I was helped by so many dedicated people. I would like to extend my special thanks to the following people: Helen L. Roberts, Genette McLaurin, Ernest Blackwell, Jim Huffman, Lisa Henry, and Terrance Johnson. I would also like to express my appreciation to Julie Hotton for continuing to spread the Harlem Renaissance art work throughout the artistic community by displaying her wonderful photographs by Carl Van Vechten in her home gallery. I feel a special debt to Gloria Roberts at the Planned Parenthood Federation of America for helping me locate Angelina Weld Grimké's story. I would like to thank Janet Sims-Wood for helping me with my research at Howard University's Moorland-Spingarn Research Center and Dorothy Porter Wesley for sharing her stories with me about women during the Harlem Renaissance in Washington, D.C. I would like to express my gratitude to Nancy Glassman, Maria Aragon, and Paul Tremer for allowing me to stay with them while I researched the material for this book.

I would like to thank the University of Cincinnati Taft Grant Committee for financially assisting me through my research. Also, thanks to Elaine Hughes at the University of Cincinnati Langsam Library for her research help. I would also like to express my gratitude to Amy Elder for her academic support and guidance through this project. Also thanks to Elisabeth Patch for her editorial advice.

This project would never have been possible if it had not been for the faith Leslie Mitchner and Nellie McKay had in me. Additionally, I would like to thank Akasha (Gloria) Hull for sharing information with me on Georgia Douglas Johnson and Alice Dunbar-Nelson. Her support of this project helped to inspire me. Also, I extend my deep gratitude to Dorothy West for telling me anecdotes about her life and for sharing with me what it was like to be a part of the Harlem Renaissance. It means so much to me to know that they believed in me.

Never the least, I would like to thank my father, David, my sister Leah, my husband, Tom, and the rest of my family and friends who have given me support throughout this entire project. Most of all I would like to express my never-ending gratitude to my mother, Jane, who inspired me through her own achievements in journalism and who helped me to make this project a reality. I only wish she had lived long enough to see it through to its completion.

# INTRODUCTION

On February 17, 1919, the 369th African-American Regiment marched up New York's Fifth Avenue from downtown to Harlem, a symbol of the dawning Harlem Renaissance and the advent of the "New Negro."[1] The name "Harlem Renaissance" identifies a period of resurgence in black arts and letters and the emergence of a new kind of black: the New Negro, who was part of the first substantial group of college-educated African Americans. In 1917, 2,132 African Americans had graduated from college, but by 1927, at the height of the Renaissance, 13,580 African Americans held college degrees and 39 African Americans held doctorates. Educated African Americans were having careers not only in the arts but in the professions as well, as teachers, nurses, librarians, lawyers, and doctors. The "Talented Tenth," as W.E.B. DuBois called this segment of the population, were able to educate themselves and had enough economic security to form a new class of African Americans throughout the United States.

However, even among the educated and middle-class, all African Americans still experienced racial violence and racism and lived with the threat of poverty. At the same time that the more affluent especially felt an upsurge in pride for their race, they grappled with racism and fought against atrocities like lynchings. This was also the period of the Great Urban Migration from the South, partly in response to the formation of the new Ku Klux Klan in 1915 and partly in response to other kinds of economic and social oppression. Blacks moved to New York in large numbers, but also to other cities in the North, including Pittsburgh, Chicago, Philadelphia, Cincinnati, and Detroit. The head of the Chicago Urban League remarked, " 'Every time a lynching takes place in a community down South you can depend on it that colored people will arrive in Chicago within two weeks.' "[2] For the most part, those from the rural South were primarily farmers and unskilled laborers, not members of the "Talented Tenth."

While blacks worked to gain equality and end discrimination, there were opposing political views among them on how this change would be achieved. Notable among these oppositions were the different political philosophies of W.E.B. DuBois and Booker T. Washington. While Washington, an accommodationist to white Southern interests, was the most prominent black leader from the late nineteenth through the early twentieth century, DuBois began to speak out against his position and to assume a leadership role in the 1870s. His book, *The Souls of Black Folk* (1903), advocating social equality between blacks and whites, made clear his opposition to Washington's policies. By the end of the nineteenth century, DuBois was the acknowledged leader of most black intellectuals. When DuBois became director of publicity and research for the National Association for the Advancement of Colored People (NAACP), he launched the Association's magazine, *The Crisis*, a social and literary journal. DuBois also conceived the idea of the Pan African Congresses, which brought together blacks from all over the world to discuss ways to give people of African heritage more opportunities and greater freedoms. Congresses convened four times during the Harlem Renaissance—in 1919, 19213 1923, and 1927—and then again in 1947. Although no real changes evolved from these meetings, the dialogue was important in keeping issues in the public eye.

Also in contrast to DuBois's political philosophy was Jamaican Marcus Garvey's Universal Negro Improvement Association (UNIA). Garvey called for African Americans to reclaim Africa for themselves rather than to focus on racism and terrorism in the United States. Similar to DuBois's Pan African Congresses, Garvey sought to unite all African people from nations around the world, but unlike DuBois, he called for "the creation of a black economy within the white capitalist world, that would both liberate blacks in America from the oppression of discrimination and redeem the peoples of Africa from the oppression of colonialism."[3]

Before and during the Harlem Renaissance, literary magazines served as forums for writers and artists to voice their opinions on current racial violence, including lynchings, and to arouse racial consciousness. The community of African-American writers and artists helped to promote each other's work through these magazines and by developing connections with the white publishing world. They shared a concern for their race and were aware of the impact they were having not only on the African-American community but also on the literary and creative world at large.

As editor of *The Crisis*, DuBois wrote constantly against racial prejudice and lynching. At its peak, *The Crisis* sold close to 116,000 copies per month all across the United States. David Levering Lewis claims that "[i]n an era of rampant illiteracy, when hard labor left Afro-Americans little time or inclination for reading Harvard-accented editorials, the magazine found its way into kerosene-lit sharecroppers' cabins and cramped factory workers' tenements."[4] After 1919, DuBois hired Jessie Fauset as literary editor and together they published the literature of the "Talented Tenth." In fact, Fauset was most responsible for this, although DuBois received most of the credit.

In January 1923, the Urban League, another organization that fought for black rights, launched its magazine, *Opportunity*. The Urban League's director of research and investigation, sociologist Charles S. Johnson, served as the editor. Johnson believed strongly that African Americans' artistic creativity could bridge the gap between whites and blacks and thus help to create racial equality. He used every piece of literature he published as a "weapon against the old racial stereotypes."[5] In conjunction with *Opportunity*, Johnson organized the Civic Club Dinner on March 21, 1924 to honor Fauset's first novel, *There Is Confusion*. The dinner was one of the early events that sparked significant interest in African-American literature on the part of white publishers, including Paul Kellogg. Editor of *Survey Graphic* magazine, Kellogg was so impressed he decided to devote an entire issue to African-American writings and writers. Kellogg worked with Howard University professor Alain Locke on the March 1925 issue of *Survey Graphic*, which was subtitled "Harlem: Mecca for the New Negro."

In May 1925 *Opportunity* held its first annual literary award ceremony. The judges for the contest included white and black writers, and the event contributed to bringing the winners into the spotlight of the white publishing establishment. Award winners included essayists Sterling Brown and E. Franklin Frazier, short story writer Zora Neale Hurston (for "Spunk"), and poets Countee Cullen and Langston Hughes. Langston Hughes's award-winning poem "The Weary Blues" was read aloud at the banquet, and Carl Van Vechten, who acted as a liaison between the black community and publisher Alfred Knopf, encouraged Knopf to publish Hughes's first book of poetry. *The Crisis* soon followed suit and held its first literary competition in November 1925.

Witnessing the flourishing of these publications, groups of African-American writers joined forces to publish their own magazine. One such was a group that included Wallace Thurman, Langston Hughes, and Zora Neale Hurston, who together launched *Fire!!* in November

1926, although this was the only issue ever published. Also involved with the project were Gwendolyn Bennett, who assisted with editorial work, and Aaron Douglas and Richard Bruce Nugent, who supplied the art. This group of artists intended to set the literary community "ablaze" by breaking away from Harlem's literary establishment. But many of the black intelligentsia were put off by the offensiveness of *Fire!!*'s contents. David Levering Lewis claims that "Thurman had meant to shock," and critics noted that the offensive qualities were direct influences from Carl Van Vechten's recent novel, *Nigger Heaven*.[6] The magazine contained work by Countee Cullen, Arna Bontemps, and Helene Johnson, as well as material from the editorial staff. Ironically, after its first and only issue, most of the original copies burned up in a fire in the warehouse where they were stored.[7]

The black literary community of Philadelphia also published a magazine, *Black Opals*, from 1927 to 1928. Writers involved in this project included Philadelphians as well as contributors from outside of the area. Materials consisted mostly of short sketches, poetry, and portraits by Nellie Bright, Mae V. Cowdery, Jessie Fauset, Marita Bonner, and Arthur Huff Fauset. Boston's black intellectual community developed its own magazine, *The Saturday Evening Quill*, published from 1928 to 1930. Edited by Eugene Gordon, it included stories and poetry from writers such as Helene Johnson and Dorothy West. The more radical socialist publication, *The Messenger*, was edited by A. Philip Randolph and Chandler Owen from 1917 to 1925, when George Schuyler took over until its final issue in 1928. *The Messenger* initially opposed the political views of DuBois and Garvey by attacking the capitalist system and calling for a socialist revolution, but when its readership declined, it began to support African-American economic advancement in business.

Clearly, the Harlem Renaissance was defined not only by the political struggles of African Americans but by their artistic expression as well. Looking at the period, we get the impression that the most prominent artists and politicians were male; yet there were many women who achieved similar success, especially in the arts. Perhaps the best-known artists of the period were its musicians, as part of the larger phenomenon dubbed the Jazz Age. African Americans dominated (but did not necessarily control) the music industry before, during, and after the Renaissance, but they achieved success in all of the popular genres of the 1920s and 1930s, including the blues, opera, and jazz. Jazz artists such as Duke Ellington and Louis Armstrong flourished and became household names in both white and black communities. Many women achieved success also, primarily as singers and dancers, through the avenues of Harlem nightclubs, traveling shows, and musical recordings, as participants in choruses, as leads in Broadway musicals, or as solo performers in prominent theaters.

Many white performers attended the popular Harlem nightclubs where black blues artists performed and then popularized the music through their own recordings; it was important, therefore, for African Americans working in the tradition of the blues to feel some sense of ownership over their careers. Some women, including Ma Rainey, Bessie Smith, Ethel Waters, and Gladys Bentley attempted to maintain some control over their music, insofar as this was possible in an industry controlled by white men. Despite the claims of some white artists to the materials, many blues compositions were originally written, composed, and sung by African Americans. Ma Rainey was known as the Mother of Blues because of the pervasive influence of her unique style. "Ma Rainey developed a blues style that bridged the never entirely congenial gap between the early, primitive, rural blues and the later, more sophisticated, urban blues."[8] Although Bessie Smith performed primarily in African-American theaters, she sometimes performed for white audiences, reaching a national level of success when she starred in such films as the 1929 "St. Louis Blues." Through exposure to a dual audience, Smith taught white America about African-American music. Owning her own career and life in ways that influenced future generations of African-American women artists, Gladys Bentley accompanied herself on the piano while singing her own compositions, and created her own outrageous versions of popular songs. Ethel Waters made approximately 259 recordings, which she promoted by touring, primarily in the South.

Unlike the popular performers and singers, entertainers with a training in classical music, like Marion Anderson, Minto Cato, and Lillian Evanti, went abroad and gained international recognition, then returned to perform in the United States. Marion Anderson was one of many artists who went to Europe to develop her career and later became the first black singer to appear with the Metropolitan Opera Company. She is perhaps best remembered for the controversy that developed over her scheduled performance at Washington, D.C.'s Constitution Hall in 1939. When the Daughters of the American Revolution, who owned the Hall, refused to let her sing there, Eleanor Roosevelt, on behalf of the White House, arranged to have the concert moved to the Lincoln Memorial, where Anderson sang to an audience of seventy-five thousand people. Also finding it difficult to build a career in America,

Lillian Evanti toured Europe, later returned to the United States, and founded the National Negro Opera Company in 1943. Minto Cato opened her own music studio in Detroit and performed with her company. She dedicated herself to teaching in order to foster future African-American efforts in classical music.

African-American actresses contributed greatly to the Harlem Renaissance, both on the stage and in the new medium of film. Yet it was still very difficult for dark-skinned women to get roles, although dark-skinned men, such as Paul Robeson, were accepted as actors. When women did get parts, these were almost always as stereotypes. Light-skinned women like Nina Mae McKinney and Freddi Washington fared somewhat better, but still, like many singers, found it necessary to travel to Paris to gain recognition and acceptance as serious performers. Jessie Fauset's novel *There Is Confusion* portrays a talented singer who faces similar obstacles in her career.

Like so many writers and other artists of the Renaissance, actresses turned to Europe because their career opportunities were limited in America. At the same time some African-American actresses broke out of the boundaries set by white theater and film and joined black-owned theater groups, where they performed in plays or films that depicted the African-American experience.[9] There were also some African Americans who reacted against what was produced for white audiences with their own work and the beginnings of black film production. In 1917 Oscar Micheaux produced *The Homesteader*, starring actress Evelyn Preer, the first silent film produced by an African American.

Other African-American actresses were seduced by the temptations of Hollywood. When Freddi Washington played a mulatto in the first film version of Fannie Hurst's *Imitation of Life*, her light skin and the theme of "passing" showed that such parts, too, would arouse controversy and fear. Many African Americans believed that Washington's depiction of the tragic life of a mulatto passing for white represented her personal opposition to the goals African Americans were fighting for, while others were not even sure if she was in fact an African American. Bothered by this questioning of her identity, Washington took out advertisements in newspapers around the country to publicize the fact that she was an African American. She made it clear that she took the part in the film because she saw it as a black role. Her outspokenness scared those whites who feared the publicity would encourage passing even more. Although the outcry over *Imitation of Life* ended Washington's career in Hollywood, the position she took on the issue was important, because she did not lose sight of her identity and stood up for it courageously. In order to help African Americans in the performing arts, she founded the Negro Actors Guild in New York.

Probably the best known actress and dancer from the Harlem Renaissance is Josephine Baker.[10] Color was a factor here, too, of course: Baker was typecast as a comedienne in the United States, and to achieve recognition for the full range of her abilities she had to follow the path of other Harlem artists and move to Paris. While Baker was frustrated by being typecast as a comedienne Jackie "Moms" Mabley did not find this a problem, and she flourished in Harlem at Connie's Inn and the Cotton Club. Mabley began in vaudeville, gradually developing a stage character for herself as a "world-weary old woman"[11] through the use of her tattered and mismatched clothing, and performed for thirty years as the headliner at the Apollo Theater. Mabley also played a serious role in Harlem's literary community by collaborating with Zora Neale Hurston on sketches for a revue entitled *Fast and Furious;* together they played cheerleaders in the sketch "Football Teams." As one of the first African-American comediennes, "Moms" Mabley was an important figure. Rather than accepting the designation comedienne as a limitation, she made it her calling.

Rose McClendon fought diligently throughout her career against discrimination in the entertainment industry. Although she worked primarily as an actress, she also directed plays at the Negro Experimental Theatre. She believed deeply in the idea of establishing a theater to train African-American actors and produce plays by African-American writers, and to this end she established the Negro People's Theatre in 1935 with actor Dick Campbell. When she died, he formed the Rose McClendon Players, as a tribute to her commitment to the training of African Americans in all aspects of the theater and performing arts. Of the African-American theater group that she envisioned, McClendon stated, "Such a theatre could . . . create a tradition that would equal the tradition of any national group," developing "not an isolated Paul Robeson, or an occasional Bledsoe, or Gilpin, but a long line of first-rate actors."[12]

Although the performing artists of the Renaissance were the best known, there were a number of important African-Americans in the visual arts as well. In the aftermath of the Renaissance, in 1937, the Federal Arts Project of the Works Progress Administration (WPA) helped to establish the Harlem Community Art Center. The first director of the Center was sculptor Augusta Savage, well known in Renaissance circles, who was followed in that position by writer Gwendolyn Bennett. The Center assisted artists financially and promoted new talent in the community by offering classes taught by established figures in the African-American art world.

Paving the way for others, Augusta Savage played a vital role in the African-American arts by her mentoring of younger artists. Even before the Center was started, she established her own studio, the Savage Studio of Arts and Crafts, for young artists and opened the Salon of Contemporary Negro Art, which was committed to exhibiting and selling work by blacks. Artists Savage nurtured and influenced include Gwendolyn Knight, Norman Lewis, and Elba Lightfoot. In 1923, when Savage was rejected from a summer art program in Paris because of her African-American heritage, she brought the issue of discrimination against African-American artists out into the open by going public with her story.[13]

Boston sculptor Meta Vaux Warrick Fuller was one of the first artists to focus specifically on African themes. As David Driskell has noted, "She looked to the songs of Black America and to African folktales for inspirational themes that focused on pathos and joy in the human condition."[14] She was also revolutionary in refusing to cater to white American art patrons, as her predecessors had done. "Until Fuller, the aesthetic of the black visual artist seemed inextricably tied to the taste of White America, more particularly, perhaps, to subject matter and definitions of form derived from European art."[15] Her sculpture was one of the first art forms by an African American to have an Afrocentric subject and aesthetic. Unusual for a woman of her generation, Fuller built a studio and continued to produce her sculptures in spite of her husband's opposition. She was probably also the first African-American theater designer. "[I]nspired by W.E.B. DuBois' Pan-Africanist philosophy, which emphasized Black Americans' common heritage,"[16] Fuller created art works that employed all facets of the African-American experience. In conjunction with Savage, she laid an important foundation for future African-American women artists by proving to them that they could overcome racial discrimination, economic restraints, and the inhibiting effects of marriage.

During the Renaissance all visual and performing artists, both women and men, found it difficult to support their artistic careers without help from patrons. Carl Van Vechten with his wife, Fania Marinoff, Charlotte Osgood Mason, Fannie Hurst, and Amy and Arthur Spingarn were important white promoters for many black writers and artists.[17] Among African-American patrons, three women, in particular, made a notable difference in the lives of their fellow artists through their support.

A'Lelia Walker's Dark Tower salon in Harlem served as a place for intellectuals to meet. Ironically, Walker was able to afford these gatherings for black and white artists because of an inheritance from her mother, Madame C. J. Walker, who had a thriving business in hair-straightening for African-American women. A'Lelia Walker was a vital supporter of the artists of the Harlem Renaissance, and her death, which occurred toward the end of the period, dealt a blow to Harlem intellectuals. "When A'Lelia Walker died, the young writers and artists of the Harlem Renaissance lost one of their steadfast admirers and benefactors. Not only had she always invited them to her parties, but in the late twenties she had converted a ground-floor section of her town house on West 136th Street into a meeting place for them."[18] Although Walker acted as a hostess, she did not financially support any artists. She invited the right people and let them make their own contacts with promoters such as Carl Van Vechten. Her contribution, however, was essential to the flourishing of the artistic environment of the Harlem Renaissance.

In Washington, D.C., Georgia Douglas Johnson played a similar role. A writer herself, Johnson opened her home on S Street to other writers on Saturday evenings so that they could read and discuss their works. Among the writers who attended these sessions were Marita Bonner, Jessie Fauset, Angelina Weld Grimké, Alice Dunbar-Nelson, and Gwendolyn Bennett. All were welcomed at her home, both the established writers and the younger generation on the threshold of their careers. These evenings helped young writers make contacts and share their work, as well as to receive advice from more prominent figures. All those who attended agreed that Saturday evenings at Johnson's helped foster writing careers.[19]

Finally, there was Jessie Fauset. Until recently, historians and literary critics have neglected her instrumental role in promoting the work of others, especially as editor of *The Crisis* and *The Brownie's Book*. According to David Levering Lewis, when Fauset left her position at *The Crisis*, which she edited from 1918 to 1926, the literary quality of the periodical deteriorated, and tensions developed between the magazine and its writers.[20] When Fauset believed that particular writers had a valuable contribution to make, she published them and helped nurture their literary careers by championing their work. Her "correspondence show[s] her deep personal support and concern as well as her professional regard and backing" for many literary figures during the Harlem Renaissance.[21] The support was mutual: those writers Fauset published and encouraged through her letters and literary reviews gave her equal support by including her work in their anthologies and maintaining a stimulating correspondence with her.[22]

Although Langston Hughes is the best-known writer of the period, few know about Fauset's role in promoting his work. It was her discovery and subsequent publication in *The Crisis* of Hughes's poem "The Negro Speaks of Rivers" that sparked his long-lived career, one that far overshadowed her own. In addition to publishing his work, she introduced him to other important writers and artists. She also encouraged Jean Toomer and Countee Cullen through her correspondence and published Toomer's first two poems. In recognition of her constant personal and literary support, Cullen published her poems in his anthology *Caroling Dusk*. Through her own literary achievements and her encouragement of others, Fauset played as crucial a role in the literary community of the Harlem Renaissance as did Charles Johnson, W.E.B. DuBois, and Alain Locke. Fauset should be remembered not only as a distinguished and prolific writer but as an instrumental champion of the Harlem Renaissance.

The promoters of the Harlem Renaissance worked to bring a wide range of artists together to discuss, publicize, and display each other's work. Walker, Johnson, and Fauset enabled artists of the 1920s and 1930s to cross racial lines. Artists and writers were together breaking through boundaries, whether sexual, racial, stylistic, or geographical. There was at the time an interconnectedness among the arts that extended beyond the limits of Harlem and Greenwich Village and indeed beyond the United States. In this period of Modernism and experimentalism, creative artists of all kinds gathered to discuss the latest trends in writing, painting, music, and theater. Harlem Renaissance and white Modernist writers and artists were drawn to Paris as a place to achieve the acceptance not easily attained in the United States. Gertrude Stein's atelier in Paris, for example, like Walker's salon in Harlem, served as a meeting place for a wide range of writers and artists, thus furthering artistic interchanges. Historians and literary scholars are only now beginning to explore these connections between the black and white artistic movements of the early twentieth century.[23]

Beginning with the Great Depression there was a steady decline in the outpouring of artistic creativity from Harlem. Although African Americans continued to create and to publish during the 1930s, the overall level of activity decreased each year. In times of economic hardship for whites and blacks, it became increasingly difficult for white promoters to commit finances to projects by African Americans. The closely knit community of Harlem became disjointed when various members of the community relocated; Jessie Fauset moved to New Jersey, Alain Locke became busier with activities at Howard University, and Charles S. Johnson became absorbed in his teaching at Fisk University. The death of A'Lelia Walker in 1931, followed by those of both Rudolph Fisher and Wallace Thurman in 1934, further eroded Harlem's literary circle, and in that same year DuBois resigned from the NAACP and *The Crisis*. Finally on March 19, 1935, the Harlem Riot, provoked by deteriorating urban conditions and joblessness (over half of the Harlem work force was unemployed), broke down the remnants of the artistic community. As scholars disagree as to when the Renaissance began, so they disagree as to when it ended; most, however, agree that it was precipitated by the Great Depression and ended sometime in the 1930s.

Black women played a large role in shaping the Renaissance. With innovations rooted in African-American folklore, Meta Vaux Warrick Fuller and Ma Rainey made huge strides in their media, as did Zora Neale Hurston in her creative use of African-American folklore. All black women artists also shared the same adversities, the same struggle against oppression. Although the male artists faced racial and sometimes economic oppression, these women were oppressed because of their race, class, and sex. Aside from the discrimination they encountered in the white world, African-American women artists were oppressed by their male counterparts. The writers included in this anthology, especially Jessie Fauset and Angelina Weld Grimké, record experiences of triple oppression.

Many of the stories explore the legacy of slavery as a means connected to the search for freedom from racial and sexual oppression. Most of these writers were second or third-generation free African Americans who write of traditions and themes similar to those of Harriet Wilson's *Our Nig* and Harriet Jacob's *Incidents in the Life of a Slave Girl*. The experiences of slavery were handed down through family histories and genealogy, and many of the writers used these experiences to examine their own contemporary racial oppression. Throughout the stories in this collection themes of slavery, tension between North and South, and between urban and rural prevail.

The three stories by Jessie Fauset all explore black women's triple oppression. In "The Sleeper Wakes," Amy, the beautiful, fair-skinned protagonist, although uncertain of her racial heritage, passes for white and marries an extremely wealthy Southerner. He loves her dearly, but the marriage falls apart when she takes the side of the black servants whom he constantly abuses, and announces that she too is black. For a while she lets him support her, but when he invites her to return to him as his mistress, the insult is too great for her. Her disentanglement from him includes working to repay the money he had spent on her and a reunion with the black family with whom she had lived as a child. Fauset's story is set at the crossroad of race, class, and gender oppression, and offers a preview of the themes of passing, interracial marriage, and the search for economic security that dominate in her novel *Plum Bun*.

Similar to Fauset's novel *The Chinaberry Tree* and like her main character in "The Sleeper Wakes," Angélique in "Double Trouble" knows nothing about her father, although her racial identity is not in question. However, because of her mother's affair with one of the town's most prominent black men, which resulted in her birth and the breakup of his marriage, the town treats her as a pariah. Angélique only learns the cause of her ostracism after the young man with whom she is in love discovers they are sister and brother. On the other side of the story, Angélique's aunt, whose chances for a good marriage were limited because she (Angélique's mother's sister) was the daughter of a slave master and a slave woman, hates the young girl for the further disgrace (double trouble) her sister brought on the family through her behavior. Focusing more on intraracial than interracial conflicts and problems, "Double Trouble" is still a story of women as victims in a man's world.

Fauset's third story in the anthology, "Mary Elizabeth," is unusual for her in its use of Southern dialect and first-person narration; it is also one of the few stories she did not later develop into a novel. A black household worker in the home of an urban middle-class black couple, Mary Elizabeth, using her own family as an illustration, gives her employer a useful lesson on how difficult it was to hold black families together in slavery. Her father had been sold down the river after her birth, and had thus lost his family; returning twenty-six years later (with his fourth wife), he discovered that his first wife had remarried and had several children by her second husband. The lesson is well taken by the young urban wife, who realizes two important things: first, how easily elements of black history are lost through time and distance and second, how much she and her husband have to be thankful for.

Gwendolyn Bennett's "Wedding Day" is her only short story and first appeared in *Fire!!*. The locale is Paris, where both Bennett and Fauset traveled frequently, as is evident in most of their writing.[24] The action explores the pervasiveness of white American racism against blacks, even in Europe. In spite of his determination to repulse associations with all whites in Paris, Paul Watson, a black American, falls in love with a white American woman whom he befriended when she was in financial straits, only to be jilted by her on their wedding day.[25]

Only three short stories written by Georgia Douglas Johnson survived her. "Free" is a psychological study about two women's economic and sexual oppression. In contrast to her plays and poetry, Johnson does not identify or discuss the race of the characters in this sketch. Johnson's biographer, Gloria Hull, explains this by stating that "[Johnson] clearly intended that issues independent of race focus the work."[26]

The Renaissance did not occur only in New York, as we can see from the literary efforts of Dorothy West in Boston and Marita Bonner in Washington, D.C. and later (after 1930) in Chicago. Bonner brought to the movement the most experimental of styles and techniques among women writing in that period, and was clearly a high Modernist. Not only did she experiment with style but also with content: in contrast with most other Renaissance writers, she wrote of working-class African Americans.

As a young girl in the Boston area during the Harlem Renaissance, Dorothy West joined The Saturday Evening Quill Club, which produced the magazine, the *Saturday Evening Quill.* The club was formed for African-American men and women who wanted to write and share their work with the flourishing literary communities in Boston and Harlem, and much of her early work, including "Funeral" and "Prologue to a Life," were published in their magazine. At the age of seventeen, with "The Typewriter," West won second prize in *Opportunity* magazine's short story competition, and as a result, Harlem's literary community began to hold great expectations for her. "The Typewriter" illustrates the tensions between North and South through one man's hope that his urban migration will lead to the prosperous future and increased self-respect that he desires for himself and his family.

In "One Boy's Story," published under the male pseudonym of Joseph Maree Andrew, the paternity of the protagonist, Donald Gage, is kept a secret from him. Reared in an all-white community, where his mother works as a seamstress for the wealthy women of the town, he knows no black men and most admires the town's white doctor, who is his father. Bonner invokes the Greek myths of Oedipus and Orestes and the biblical legend of David and Goliath to structure her story as well as parallel it. "The story's denouement is a paradigm of literary silencing and the dangerous truth that cannot be spoken: Donald, having unknowingly killed his real father, is wounded by his mother in a strange accident that results in the amputation of his tongue."[27]

In contrast to the more conventional and Eurocentric style of "One Boy's Story," Bonner's "Drab Rambles" adopts a more Afrocentric and experimental style. The story took a first-place award in *The Crisis* 1927 literary contest. Exploring the relationship between race and economics, Bonner divides the piece into two portraits. In the first, a hardworking, uneducated black man faces racist attitudes both on the job and in his attempt to find medical attention; in the second, a working single black mother discovers the harsh realities of race, gender, and economic oppression. In "Nothing New" Bonner returns to interracial relationships as the focus of racial antagonism. Refusing to stay on the "black" side of the world, even as a child, art student Denny Jackson eventually ends up a murderer because of his love for a classmate, who happens to be a white woman.

Historically, black women have had to face the question of what happens to black children who are born into a racist world. Angelina Weld Grimké's only extant story, "The Closing Door," which was written for Margaret Sanger's journal, the *Birth Control Review*, considers this dilemma. The story takes place during the age when lynching was rampant in both the North and the South. Although she lives in the North, after pregnant Agnes Milton's brother is lynched in the South she reconsiders the wisdom of having her own child to grow up in the existing society. Her dark brooding on the subject leads her to smother her infant, to save him from a worse fate. Agnes's predicament and her solution to it are similar to the themes explored in Toni Morrison's novel *Beloved*. Although much of Grimké's poetry and drama reflects her lesbian identity, in "The Closing Door" she does not make this a central issue.[28] However, there is on scene in which Agnes and the story's narrator, Lucy, have a very intimate and affectionate moment that indicates a probable lesbian relationship between the two women.

While many of the writers who appear in this anthology have come to public knowledge in the last two decades (they were of course very well known in the literary circles of their time), there were other gifted writers of the Renaissance who have dropped almost completely from sight, and I have included some of their work here in order to give more breadth to the collection. One of these writers, Maude Irwin Owens, deals with oppression, but most specifically white religious oppression, in her story "Bathesda of Sinners Run." Because of good recordkeeping on the part of the slave owners, Bathesda's maternal lineage can be traced back seven generations, beginning with Jezebel, the slave of

Richard Thornton. Bathesda, however, whose father was part African, part white, and part Indian, was born twenty years after slavery was abolished, and thus enjoyed a freedom her female ancestors did not. From her father, who was not a convert to Christianity, she learned a reverence for nature, which became her religion. She also is different from the other blacks in her community because she can earn an independent living through sewing and Indian artistry and because she rejects the men who want to marry her. This brings out hostility in the other women of the community, and on one occasion they attack her physically in an attempt to humiliate her. Saved by the falling of a tree that woodsmen had been in the process of removing, she suddenly discovers the gift of healing in herself, something that had been present in all of her female forebears, but which had been widely held to have come from the power of Christianity.

"The Foolish and the Wise," Leila Amos Pendleton's stories of black Sallie Runner's reactions to accounts of Socrates and Cleopatra, inform us that the debate over the racial identity of such historical figures has been ongoing for at least most of this century. Through her two portraits, Pendleton shows how whites have claimed ownership of African accomplishments. Sallie believes that Cleopatra and Socrates are black and appropriates for her own race the intelligence that the white world deny black people. Through Sallie, Pendleton shows how white people have presumed to "own," not only human beings, but all significant human attainments, and have complacently assumed that anyone who achieves a great deal must, as a matter of course, be white.

Anita Scott Coleman's "Three Dogs and a Rabbit" reminds us of how strange were the circumstances of black life in the South, while "Cross Crossings Cautiously" is a cautionary tale about race. In "To A Wild Rose" and "Blue Aloes," Ottie Graham, like Zora Neale Hurston, evokes black American folktale and folklore with links to the African past.

The two stories by Alice Dunbar-Nelson included here are not the best representatives of her short fiction, but I chose them because they were written during the Harlem Renaissance.[29] "His Great Career" and "Summer Session," not published until the 1980s, are important because they are examples of Dunbar-Nelson's detective fiction. Like her predecessor, Frances E. W. Harper, who wrote in many different forms in the course of her literary career, Dunbar-Nelson tried her hand at nearly every publishable genre. I felt it was important to include some of the work of that she produced during the Renaissance because she was a vital figure in that movement. Her better and earlier work in short fiction, *The Goodness of St. Rocque and Other Stories* and *Violets and Other Tales*, was published before the turn of the century. The stories in these two collections primarily center around Creole characters and are similar to those by Eloise Bibb Thompson, who, though years older than Dunbar-Nelson, was, like her, born in a middle-class family in New Orleans and wrote in several genres. Thompson's stories in this volume, like so much of Dunbar-Nelson's work, focus on color prejudices among the Creoles of New Orleans. Gloria Hull has noted the thematic similarity between Dunbar-Nelson's early work and Angelina Grimké's 1919 story "The Closing Door."[30]

From the myriad of stories Zora Neale Hurston wrote during the Harlem Renaissance, I chose two that mark milestones in her life and are relatively unfamiliar to the public. Much of Hurston's best work has by now been heavily anthologized, appearing both in mainstream collections and in those focused on African-American or women writers. Here I have included one of her earliest works, the little-known "John Redding Goes to Sea," which she wrote as a student at Howard University for the university magazine, the *Stylus*. It tells the story of a young man born with an urge to wander, who gets his wish only in death. "The Bone of Contention," altogether different in style and mood, was developed by Hurston from an animal folktale. In both of these stories, as in much of the rest of her work, Hurston uses her knowledge of Southern folklore and Southern black dialect to tell of African-American life in the South. Nella Larsen's "Sanctuary" similarly uses Southern black dialect and folklore, in contrast with the styles characteristic of her novels. Best known for her two novels, *Quicksand* and *Passing*, Larsen's short stories have been overlooked.[31] "Freedom" and "The Wrong Man" were both written for *Young's Magazine*, where she published under the anagrammatic pseudonym of her married name "Allen Semi."

The stories by Hurston and Larsen appear at the end of this anthology because they marked in some important way the closing of the Harlem Renaissance. Hurston's "The Bone of Contention" was a sketch that she planned to develop into the play "Mule Bone," in collaboration with Langston Hughes. This play itself became the bone of contention between them. It is known that Hurston and Hughes worked together on at least two acts of the play and that Hurston pulled out of the venture, and later denied that Hughes had any part in the writing. It is not known, however, what motivated Hurston to end their collaboration and friendship, although efforts to reconstruct the events have been attempted through piecing together letters and portions of biographies.[32] Larsen's "Sanctuary" was also surrounded by controversy. After it appeared in *Forum* in January 1930, an anonymous person alerted the magazine editor to its striking similarity to the story "Mrs. Adis" by Sheila Kaye-Smith, published in *Century* magazine in 1922, and accused Larsen of plagiarism. The editor gave her a chance to refute this charge, which Larsen did by submitting working drafts of her story and by writing a letter to *Forum* in her defense. She argued that "Sanctuary" was based on an African-American folktale told to her by a patient while she was a nurse at Lincoln Hospital. In the April edition of *Forum*, the editor acknowledged Larsen's innocence and dismissed the charge, concluding that the likeness of the stories was a coincidence. Nevertheless, the scandal was so painful to Larsen that she never published again. The "Mule Bone" controversy and the accusation of Larsen's plagiarism, both of which occurred in the early 1930s, were almost simultaneous with the decline of the Harlem Renaissance.

The writers that appear in this anthology come from a long line of African-American women writers and together form a literary tradition. This tradition consists of black women speaking to their own conditions even when no one else was listening. There is a continuity of black women writers in America over a long period of time, connecting the anonymous narrators of slavery days to Toni Morrison and Alice Walker. With the aid of Henry Louis Gates's Schomburg Library of Nineteenth-Century Black Women Writers series, we have been able to piece together this tradition.[33] Until this series was created, there was no proof of the huge volume of black women's literary activity in the nineteenth century. The stories I have included here stand as a link between twentieth-century African-American women writers and their nineteenth-century predecessors thematically, stylistically, and historically. African-American women writers share a common bond in their writings of their triple oppression as well as in their search for autonomy and control over their own work.

In the decades following the Harlem Renaissance, the African-American women's literary tradition continued to grow and to speak of their sexual, racial, and economic oppression, nurturing such important works as Ann Petry's *The Street* (1946), Gwendolyn Brooks's *Maud Martha* (1954), Margaret Walker's *Jubilee* (1965), Paule Marshall's *Chosen Place, Timeless People* (1969), Toni Morrison's *The Bluest Eye* (1970), and Alice Walker's *The Third Life of Grange Copeland* (1970). These titles only begin to suggest the richness and variety of the literary tradition of black women. Common themes unite black women writers across the generations, giving the tradition a cyclical quality that we can see clearly, for example, in Toni Morrison's *Jazz* (1992), a novel set in the Harlem Renaissance. It is hoped that *The Sleeper Wakes* will likewise help us better to understand, not only the Harlem Renaissance itself, but also the various traditions these stories represent, including African, African-American, American, and women's literary traditions.

# NOTES

1. Historians disagree slightly as to the specific dates that mark the beginning and end of the Harlem Renaissance, although they basically concur that it spanned the years between World War I and World War II. Nathan Irvin Huggins and David Levering Lewis agree that 1919 was the year the Harlem Renaissance began; Bruce Kellner cites 1917 as the opening year. Nathan Irvin Huggins, *Harlem Renaissance* (New York: Oxford University Press, 1971); David Levering Lewis, *When Harlem Was in Vogue* (New York: Oxford University Press, 1979); Bruce Kellner, ed., *The Harlem Renaissance: A Historical Dictionary for the Era* (New York: Methuen, 1984).

2. Lewis, *When Harlem Was in Vogue*, 20.

3. Cary D. Wintz, *Black Culture and the Harlem Renaissance* (Houston: Rice University Press, 1988), 46.

4. Lewis, *When Harlem Was in Vogue*, 7.

5. Lewis, *When Harlem Was in Vogue*, 48.

6. Lewis, *When Harlem Was in Vogue*, 194.

7. Copies of this magazine are available in facsimile form: Wallace Thurman, *Fire!!* (Metuchen, N.J.: Fire!! Press, 1982).

8. Kellner, *The Harlem Renaissance*, 293.

9. Jessie Fauset and Gwendolyn Bennett also achieved success in Paris, as well as in the United States. See Michel Fabre, *From Harlem to Paris: Black American Writers in France, 1840–1980* (Urbana: University of Illinois Press, 1991).

10. A recent biography (Phyllis Rose, *Jazz Cleopatra: Josephine Baker in Her Time* [New York: Vintage, 1989]) and a movie about her life (John Kemeny, *The Josephine Baker Story* [New York: Home Box Office and Anglia Television, 1991]) have given Baker even more prominence today. The movie, produced for HBO viewers, is now available from video rental stores.

11. Kellner, *The Harlem Renaissance*, 227.

12. Jervis Anderson, *This Was Harlem 1900–1950* (New York: Farrar Straus & Giroux, 1981), 276.

13. Information regarding Augusta Savage is taken from Kellner, *The Harlem Renaissance*, 315.

14. David Driskell, "The Flowering of the Harlem Renaissance," in the Studio Museum in Harlem's *Harlem Renaissance Art of Black America* (New York: Abrams, 1987), 108. Subsequent information regarding Meta Warrick Fuller in this introduction is drawn largely from this source.

15. Driskell, *Harlem Renaissance Art of Black America*, 108.

16. Mary Schmidt Campbell, Introduction to the Studio Museum in Harlem's *Harlem Renaissance Art of Black America*, 27.

17. Although this book dwells mostly on the male promoters, Cary Wintz's *Black Culture and the Harlem Renaissance* shows the relationship several of these women had to both male and female Renaissance writers. He also includes several useful charts that show which companies published specific works.

18. Anderson, *This Was Harlem*, 231.

19. Gloria Hull documents the importance and impact of these literary evenings with quotes from various writers who profited from them. *Color Sex and Poetry* (Bloomington: Indiana University Press, 1987), 165–166.

20. David Levering Lewis attributes Fauset's resignation from *The Crisis* to a financial dispute, arising out of a twenty-five hundred dollar loan made by Fauset and her sister to W.E.B. DuBois. Lewis also discusses the deterioration of *The Crisis* as a consequence of Fauset's departure in *When Harlem Was in Vogue*, 199.

21. Carolyn Wedin Sylvander, *Jessie Redmon Fauset: Black American Writer*, (Troy, N.Y.: Whitson, 1981), 60.

22. Carolyn Sylvander credits Fauset with discovering and encouraging Jean Toomer, Countee Cullen, Langston Hughes, and Claude McKay. Sylvander, *Jessie Redmon Fauset*, 59.

23. For a discussion of Modernism in relationship to the Harlem Renaissance, see Houston A. Baker, Jr., *Modernism in the Harlem Renaissance* (Chicago: University of Chicago Press, 1987); and Bonnie Kime Scott, ed., *The Gender of Modernism* (Bloomington: Indiana University Press, 1990).

24. For more information on Bennett's and Fauset's relationship with Paris, see Fabre, *From Harlem to Paris*.

25. James Baldwin's story "Stranger in the Village" is a later example of a text which explores this theme.

26. Hull, *Color Sex and Poetry*, 197.

27. Joyce Flynn, Introduction, *Frye Street and Environs: The Collected Works of Marita Bonner* (Boston: Beacon Press, 1987), xvi.

28. Grimké's poetry which appears in Maureen Honey, *Shadowed Dreams* (New Brunswick, N.J.: Rutgers University Press, 1989) provides clearer evidence of her lesbian identity.

29. For the publication dates of these stories I have followed Gloria Hull, the editor of Dunbar-Nelson's collected works. These stories were reprinted for the first time in volume 3 of *The Works of Alice Dunbar-Nelson*, 3 vols., ed. Gloria Hull, Schomburg Series (New York, Oxford University Press, 1988).

30. In her discussion of Alice Dunbar-Nelson, Gloria Hull elaborates on these similarities (*Color, Sex, and Poetry,* 51–52).

31. Her two novels are available in a single-volume edition: Nella Larsen, *Quicksand and Passing,* ed. Deborah McDowell (New Brunswick, N.J.: Rutgers University Press, 1986).

32. In an effort to discover what actually took place, the play, the story, and the relevant correspondence between Hughes and Hurston have recently been reprinted: see Langston Hughes and Zora Neale Hurston, *Mule Bone: A Comedy of Negro Life,* ed. George Houston Bass and Henry Louis Gates, Jr. (New York: HarperCollins, 1991).

33. The Schomburg Library of Nineteenth-Century Black Women Writers, ed. Henry Louis Gates, Jr. (New York: Oxford University Press, 1988). This series contains over forty volumes of works from the nineteenth century.

# THE SLEEPER WAKES

# The Sleeper Wakes

## JESSIE REDMON FAUSET

Amy recognized the incident as the beginning of one of her phases. Always from a child she had been able to tell when "something was going to happen." She had been standing in Marshall's store, her young, eager gaze intent on the lovely little sample dress which was not from Paris, but quite as dainty as anything that Paris could produce. It was not the lines or even the texture that fascinated Amy so much, it was the grouping of colors—of shades. She knew the combination was just right for her.

"Let me slip it on, Miss," said the saleswoman suddenly. She had nothing to do just then, and the girl was so evidently charmed and so pretty—it was a pleasure to wait on her.

"Oh, no," Amy had stammered. "I haven't time." She had already wasted two hours at the movies, and she knew at home they were waiting for her.

The saleswoman slipped the dress over the girl's pink blouse, and tucked the linen collar under so as to bring the edge of the dress next to her pretty neck. The dress was apricot-color shading into a shell pink and the shell pink shaded off again into the pearl and pink whiteness of Amy's skin. The saleswoman beamed as Amy, entranced, surveyed herself naively in the tall looking-glass.

Then it was that the incident befell. Two men walking idly through the dress-salon stopped and looked—she made an unbelievably pretty picture. One of them with a short, soft brown beard,—"fuzzy" Amy thought to herself as she caught his glance in the mirror—spoke to his companion.

"Jove, how I'd like to paint her!" But it was the look on the other man's face that caught her and thrilled her. "My God! Can't a girl be beautiful!" he said half to himself. The pair passed on.

Amy stepped out of the dress and thanked the saleswoman half absently. She wanted to get home and think, think to herself about that look. She had seen it before in men's eyes, it had been in the eyes of the men in the moving-picture which she had seen that afternoon. But she had not thought *she* could cause it. Shut up in her little room she pondered over it. Her beauty,—she was really good-looking then—she could stir people—men! A girl of seventeen has no psychology, she does not go beneath the surface, she accepts. But she knew she was entering on one of her phases.

She was always living in some sort of story. She had started it when as a child of five she had driven with the tall, proud, white woman to Mrs. Boldin's home. Mrs. Boldin was a bride of one year's standing then. She was slender and very, very comely, with her rich brown skin and her hair that crinkled thick and soft above a low forehead. The house was still redolent of new furniture; Mr. Boldin was spick and span—he, unlike the furniture, remained so for that matter. The white woman had told Amy that this henceforth was to be her home.

Amy was curious, fond of adventure; she did not cry. She did not, of course, realize that she was to stay here indefinitely, but if she had, even at that age she would hardly have shed tears, she was always too eager, too curious to know, to taste what was going to happen next. Still since she had had almost no dealings with colored people and she knew absolutely none of the class to which Mrs. Boldin belonged, she did venture one question.

"Am I going to be colored now?"

The tall white woman had flushed and paled. "You—" she began, but the words choked her. "Yes, you are going to be colored now," she ended finally. She was a proud woman, in a moment she had recovered her usual poise. Amy carried with her for many years the memory of that proud head. She never saw her again.

When she was sixteen she asked Mrs. Boldin the question which in the light of that memory had puzzled her always. "Mrs. Boldin, tell me—am I white or colored?"

And Mrs. Boldin had told her and told her truly that she did not know.

"A—a—mee!" Mrs. Boldin's voice mounted on the last syllable in a shrill crescendo. Amy rose and went downstairs.

Down the comfortable, but rather shabby dining-room which the Boldins used after meals to sit in, Mr. Boldin, a tall black man, with aristocratic features, sat practicing on a cornet, and Mrs. Boldin sat rocking. In all of their eyes was the manifestation of the light that Amy loved, but how truly she loved it, she was not to guess till years later.

"Amy," Mrs. Boldin paused in her rocking, "did you get the braid?" Of course she had not, though that was the thing she had gone to Marshall's for. Amy always forgot essentials. If she went on an errand, and she always went willingly, it was for the pure joy of going. Who knew what angels might meet one unawares? Not that Amy thought in biblical or in literary phrases. She was in the High School it is true, but she was simply passing through, "getting by" she would have said carelessly. The only reading that had ever made any impression on her had been fairy tales read to her in those long remote days when she had lived with the tall proud woman; and descriptions in novels or histories of beautiful, stately palaces tenanted by beautiful, stately women. She could pore over such pages for hours, her face flushed, her eyes eager.

At present she cast about for an excuse. She had so meant to get the braid. "There was a dress—" she began lamely, she was never deliberately dishonest.

Mr. Boldin cleared his throat and nervously fingered his paper. Cornelius ceased his awful playing and blinked at her short-sightedly through his thick glasses. Both of these, the man and the little boy, loved the beautiful, inconsequent creature with her airy, irresponsible ways. But Mrs. Boldin loved her too, and because she loved her she could not scold.

"Of course you forgot," she began chidingly. Then she smiled. "There was a dress that you looked at *perhaps*. But confess, didn't you go to the movies first?"

Yes, Amy confessed she had done just that. "And oh, Mrs. Boldin, it was the most wonderful picture—a girl—such a pretty one—and she was poor, awfully. And somehow she met the most wonderful people and they were so kind to her. And she married a man who was just tremendously rich and he gave her everything. I did so want Cornelius to see it."

"Huh!" said Cornelius who had been listening not because he was interested, but because he wanted to call Amy's attention to his playing as soon as possible. "Huh! I don't want to look at no pretty girl. Did they have anybody looping the loop in an airship?"

"You'd better stop seeing pretty girl pictures, Amy," said Mr. Boldin kindly. "They're not always true to life. Besides, I know where you can see all the pretty girls you want without bothering to pay twenty-five cents for it."

Amy smiled at the implied compliment and went on happily studying her lessons. They were all happy in their own way. Amy because she was sure of their love and admiration, Mr. and Mrs. Boldin because of her beauty and innocence and Cornelius because he knew he had in his foster-sister a listener whom his terrible practicing could never bore. He played brokenly a piece he had found in an old music-book. "*There's an aching void in every heart, brother.*"

"Where do you pick up those old things, Neely?" said his mother fretfully. But Amy could not have her favorite's feelings injured.

"I think it's lovely," she announced defensively. "Cornelius, I'll ask Sadie Murray to lend me her brother's book. He's learning the cornet, too, and you can get some new pieces. Oh, isn't it awful to have to go to bed? Good-night, everybody." She smiled her charming, ever ready smile, the mere reflex of youth and beauty and content.

"You do spoil her, Mattie," said Mr. Boldin after she had left the room. "She's only seventeen—here, Cornelius, you go to bed—but it seems to me she ought to be more dependable about errands. Though she is splendid about some things," he defended her. "Look how willingly she goes off to bed. She'll be asleep before she knows it when most girls of her age would want to be up in the street."

But upstairs Amy was far from asleep. She lit one gas-jet and pulled down the shades. Then she stuffed tissue paper in the keyhole and under the doors, and lit the remaining gas-jets. The light thus thrown on the mirror of the ugly oak dresser was perfect. She slipped off the pink blouse and found two scarfs, a soft yellow and a soft pink,—she had had them in a scarf-dance for a school entertainment. She wound them and draped them about her pretty shoulders and loosened her hair. In the mirror she apostrophized the beautiful, glowing vision of herself.

"There," she said, "I'm like the girl in the picture. She had nothing but her beautiful face—and she did so want to be happy." She sat down on the side of the rather lumpy bed and stretched out her arms. "I want to be happy, too." She intoned it earnestly, almost like an incantation. "I want wonderful clothes, and people around me, men adoring me, and the world before me. I want—everything! It will come, it will all come because I want it so." She sat frowning intently as she was apt to do when very much engrossed. "And we'd all be so happy. I'd give Mr. and Mrs.

Boldin money! And Cornelius—he'd go to college and learn all about his old airships. Oh, if I only knew how to begin!"

Smiling, she turned off the lights and crept to bed.

## II

Quite suddenly she knew she was going to run away. That was in October. By December she had accomplished her purpose. Not that she was the least bit unhappy but because she must get out in the world,—she felt caged, imprisoned. "Trenton is stifling me," she would have told you, in her unconsciously adopted "movie" diction. New York she knew was the place for her. She had her plans all made. She had sewed steadily after school for two months—as she frequently did when she wanted to buy her season's wardrobe, so besides her carfare she had $25. She went immediately to a white Y.W.C.A., stayed there two nights, found and answered an advertisement for clerk and waitress in a small confectionery and bakery-shop, was accepted and there she was launched.

Perhaps it was because of her early experience when as a tiny child she was taken from that so different home and left at Mrs. Boldin's, perhaps it was some fault in her own disposition, concentrated and egotistic as she was, but certainly she felt no pangs of separation, no fear of her future. She was cold too,—unfired though so to speak rather than icy,—and fastidious. This last quality kept her safe where morality or religion, of neither of which had she any conscious endowment, would have availed her nothing. Unbelievably then she lived two years in New York, unspoiled, untouched, going to work on the edge of Greenwich Village early and coming back late, knowing almost no one and yet altogether happy in the expectation of something wonderful, which she knew some day must happen.

It was at the end of the second year that she met Zora Harrison. Zora used to come into lunch with a group of habitués of the place—all of them artists and writers Amy gathered. Mrs. Harrison (for she was married as Amy later learned) appealed to the girl because she knew so well how to afford the contrast to her blonde, golden beauty. Purple, dark and regal, enveloped in velvets and heavy silks, and strange marine blues she wore, and thus made Amy absolutely happy. Singularly enough, the girl, intent as she was on her own life and experiences, had felt up to this time no yearning to know these strange, happy beings who surrounded her. She did miss Cornelius, but otherwise she was never lonely, or if she was she hardly knew it, for she had always lived an inner life to herself. But Mrs. Harrison magnetized her—she could not keep her eyes from her face, from her wonderful clothes. She made conjectures about her.

The wonderful lady came in late one afternoon—an unusual thing for her. She smiled at Amy invitingly, asked some banal questions and their first conversation began. The acquaintance once struck up progressed rapidly—after a few weeks Mrs. Harrison invited the girl to come to see her. Amy accepted quietly, unaware that anything extraordinary was happening. Zora noticed this and liked it. She had an apartment in 12th Street in a house inhabited only by artists—she was by no means one herself. Amy was fascinated by the new world into which she found herself ushered; Zora's surroundings were very beautiful and Zora herself was a study. She opened to the girl's amazed vision fields of thought and conjecture, phases of whose existence Amy, who was a builder of phases, had never dreamed. Zora had been a poor girl of good family. She had wanted to study art, she had deliberately married a rich man and as deliberately obtained in the course of four years a divorce, and she was now living in New York studying by means of her alimony and enjoying to its fullest the life she loved. She took Amy on a footing with herself—the girl's refinement, her beauty, her interest in colors (though this in Amy at that time was purely sporadic, never consciously encouraged), all this gave Zora a figure about which to plan and build a romance. Amy had told her the truth, but not all about her coming to New York. She had grown tired of Trenton—her people were all dead—the folks with whom she lived were kind and good but not "inspiring" (she had borrowed the term from Zora and it was true, the Boldins, when one came to think of it, were not "inspiring"), so she had run away.

Zora had gone into raptures. "What an adventure! My dear, the world is yours. Why, with your looks and your birth, for I suppose you really belong to the Kildares who used to live in Philadelphia, I think there was a son who ran off and married an actress or someone—they disowned him I remember,—you can reach any height. You must marry a wealthy man—perhaps someone who is interested in art and who will let you pursue your studies." She insisted always that Amy had run away in order to study art. "But luck like that comes to few," she sighed, remembering her own plight, for Mr. Harrison had been decidedly unwilling to let her pursue her studies, at least to the extent she wished. "Anyway you must marry wealth,—one can always get a divorce," she ended sagely.

Amy—she came to Zora's every night now—used to listen dazedly at first. She had accepted willingly enough Zora's conjecture about her birth, came to believe it in fact—but she drew back somewhat at such wholesale exploitation of people to suit one's own convenience, still she did not probe too far into this thought—nor did she grasp at all the infamy of exploitation of self. She ventured one or two objections however, but Zora brushed everything aside.

"Everybody is looking out for himself," she said fairly. "I am interested in you, for instance, not for philanthropy's sake, not because I am lonely, and you are charming and pretty and don't get tired of hearing me talk. You'd better come and live with me awhile, my dear, six months or a year. It doesn't cost any more for two than for one, and you can always leave when we get tired of each other. A girl like you can always get a job. If you are worried about being dependent you can pose for me and design my frocks, and oversee Julienne"—her maid-of-all-work—"I'm sure she's a stupendous robber."

Amy came, not at all overwhelmed by the good luck of it—good luck was around the corner more or less for everyone, she supposed. Moreover, she was beginning to absorb some of Zora's doctrine—she, too, must look out for herself. Zora *was* lonely, she *did* need companionship, Julienne *was* careless about change and old blouses and left-over dainties. Amy had her own sense of honor. She carried out faithfully her share of the bargain, cut down waste, renovated Zora's clothes, posed for her, listened to her endlessly and bore with her fitfulness. Zora was truly grateful for this last. She was temperamental but Amy had good nerves and her strong natural inclination to let people do as they wanted stood her in good stead. She was a little stolid, a little unfeeling under her lovely exterior. Her looks at this time belied her—her perfect ivory-pink face, her deep luminous eyes,—very brown they were with purple depths that made one think of pansies—her charming, rather wide mouth, her whole face set in a frame of very soft, very live, brown hair which grew in wisps and tendrils and curls and waves back from her smooth, young forehead. All this made one look for softness and ingenuousness. The ingenuousness was there, but not the softness—except of her fresh, vibrant loveliness.

On the whole then she progressed famously with Zora. Sometimes the latter's callousness shocked her, as when they would go strolling through the streets south of Washington Square. The children, the people all foreign, all dirty, often very artistic, always immensely human, disgusted Zora except for "local color"—she really could reproduce them wonderfully. But she almost hated them for being what they were.

"Br-r-r, dirty little brats!" she would say to Amy. "Don't let them touch me." She was frequently amazed at her protégée's utter indifference to their appearance, for Amy herself was the pink of daintiness. They were turning from MacDougall into Bleecker Street one day and Amy had patted a child—dirty, but lovely—on the head.

"They are all people just like anybody else, just like you and me, Zora," she said in answer to her friend's protest.

"You *are* the true democrat," Zora returned with a shrug. But Amy did not understand her.

Not the least of Amy's services was to come between Zora and the too pressing attention of the men who thronged about her.

"Oh, go and talk to Amy," Zora would say, standing slim and gorgeous in some wonderful evening gown. She was an extraordinarily attractive creature, very white and pink, with great ropes of dazzling gold hair, and that look of no-age which only American women possess. As a matter of fact she was thirty-nine, immensely sophisticated and selfish, even, Amy thought, a little cruel. Her present mode of living just suited her; she could not stand any condition that bound her, anything at all *exigeant*. It was useless for anyone to try to influence her. If she did not want to talk, she would not.

The men used to obey her orders and seek Amy sulkily at first, but afterwards with considerably more interest. She was so lovely to look at. But they really, as Zora knew, preferred to talk to the older woman, for while with Zora indifference was a role, second nature now but still a role—with Amy it was natural and she was also a trifle shallow. She had the admiration she craved, she was comfortable, she asked no more. Moreover she thought the men, with the exception of Stuart James Wynne, rather uninteresting—they were faddists for the most part, crazy not about art or music, but merely about some phase such as cubism or syncopation.

Wynne, who was much older than the other half-dozen men who weekly paid Zora homage—impressed her by his suggestion of power. He was a retired broker, immensely wealthy (Zora, who had known him since childhood, informed her), very set and purposeful and polished. He was perhaps fifty-five, widely traveled, of medium height, very white skin and clear, frosty blue eyes, with sharp, proud features. He liked Amy from the beginning, her childishness touched him. In particular he admired her pliability—not knowing it was really indifference. He had been married twice; one wife had divorced him, the other had died. Both marriages were unsuccessful owing to his dominant, rather unsympathetic nature. But he had softened considerably with years, though he still had decided views, was glad to see that Amy, in spite of

Zora's influence, neither smoked nor drank. He liked her shallowness—
she fascinated him.

Zora had told him much—just the kind of romantic story to appeal to
the rich, powerful man. Here was beauty forlorn, penniless, of splendid
birth,—for Zora once having connected Amy with the Philadelphia
Kildares never swerved from that belief. Amy seemed to Wynne everything a girl should be—she was so unspoiled, so untouched. He asked
her to marry him. If she had tried she could not have acted more
perfectly. She looked at him with her wonderful eyes.

"But I am poor, ignorant—a nobody," she stammered. "I'm afraid I
don't love you either," she went on in her pretty troubled voice, "though
I do like you very, very much."

He liked her honesty and her self-depreciation, even her coldness.
The fact that she was not flattered seemed to him an extra proof of her
native superiority. He, himself, was a representative of one of the
South's oldest families, though he had lived abroad lately.

"I have money and influence," he told her gravely, "but I count them
nothing without you." And as for love—he would teach her that, he
ended, his voice shaking a little. Underneath all his chilly, polished
exterior he really cared.

"It seems an unworthy thing to say," he told her wistfully, for she
seemed very young beside his experienced fifty-five years, "but anything
you wanted in this world could be yours. I could give it to you,—
clothes, houses and jewels."

"Don't be an idiot," Zora had said when Amy told her. "Of course,
marry him. He'll give you a beautiful home and position. He's probably
no harder to get along with than anybody else, and if he is, there is
always the divorce court."

It seemed to Amy somehow that she was driving a bargain—how
infamous a one she could not suspect. But Zora's teachings had sunk
deep. Wynne loved her, and he could secure for her what she wanted.
"And after all," she said to herself once, "it really is my dream coming
true."

She resolved to marry him. There were two weeks of delirious, bliss-
ful shopping. Zora was very generous. It seemed to Amy that the whole
world was contributing largely to her happiness. She was to have just
what she wanted and as her taste was perfect she afforded almost as
much pleasure to the people from whom she bought as to herself. In
particular she brought rapture to an exclusive modiste in Forty-second
Street who exclaimed at her "so perfect taste."

"Mademoiselle is of a marvelous, of an absolute correctness," she said.

Everything whirled by. After the shopping there was the small, impressive wedding. Amy stumbled somehow through the service, struck by its awful solemnity. Then later there was the journey and the big house waiting them in the small town, fifty miles south of Richmond. Wynne was originally from Georgia, but business and social interests had made it necessary for him to be nearer Washington and New York.

Amy was absolute mistress of himself and his home, he said, his voice losing its coldness. "Ah, my dear, you'll never realize what you mean to me—I don't envy any other man in this world. You are so beautiful, so sweet, so different!"

III

From the very beginning *he* was different from what she had supposed. To start with he was far, far wealthier, and he had, too, a tradition, a family-pride which to Amy was inexplicable. Still more inexplicably he had a race-pride. To his wife this was not only strange but foolish. She was as Zora had once suggested, the true democrat. Not that she preferred the company of her maids, though the reason for this did not lie *per se* in the fact that they were maids. There was simply no common ground. But she was uniformly kind, a trait which had she been older would have irritated her husband. As it was, he saw in it only an additional indication of her freshness, her lack of worldliness which seemed to him the attributes of an inherent refinement and goodness untouched by experience.

He, himself, was intolerant of all people of inferior birth or standing and looked with contempt on foreigners, except the French and English. All the rest were variously "guineys," "niggers," and "wops," and all of them he genuinely despised and hated, and talked of them with the huge intolerant carelessness characteristic of occidental civilization. Amy was never able to understand it. People were always first and last, just people to her. Growing up as the average colored American girl does grow up, surrounded by types of every hue, color and facial configuration she had had no absolute ideal. She was not even aware that there was one. Wynne, who in his grim way had a keen sense of humor, used to be vastly amused at the artlessness with which she let him know that she did not consider him to be good-looking. She never wanted him to wear anything but dark blue, or sombre mixtures always.

"They take away from that awful whiteness of your skin," she used to tell him, "and deepen the blue of your eyes."

In the main she made no attempt to understand him, as indeed she made no attempt to understand anything. The result, of course, was that such ideas as seeped into her mind stayed there, took growth and later bore fruit. But just at this period she was like a well-cared for, sleek, house-pet, delicately nurtured, velvety, content to let her days pass by. She thought almost nothing of her art just now except as her sensibilities were jarred by an occasional disharmony. Likewise, even to herself, she never criticized Wynne, except when some act or attitude of his stung. She could never understand why he, so fastidious, so versed in elegance of word and speech, so careful in his surroundings, even down to the last detail of glass and napery, should take such evident pleasure in literature of a certain pruhient type. He fairly revelled in the realistic novels which to her depicted sheer badness. He would get her to read to him, partly because he liked to be read to, mostly because he enjoyed the realism and in a slighter degree because he enjoyed seeing her shocked. Her point of view amused him.

"What funny people," she would say naively, "to do such things." She could not understand the liaisons and intrigues of women in the society novels, such infamy was stupid and silly. If one starved, it was conceivable that one might steal; if one were intentionally injured, one might hit back, even murder; but deliberate nastiness she could not envisage. The stories, after she had read them to him, passed out of her mind as completely as though they had never existed.

Picture the two of them spending three years together with practically no friction. To his dominance and intolerance she opposed a soft and unobtrusive indifference. What she wanted she had, ease, wealth, adoration, love, too, passionate and imperious, but she had never known any other kind. She was growing cleverer also, her knowledge of French was increasing, she was acquiring a knowledge of politics, of commerce and of the big social questions, for Wynne's interests were exhaustive and she did most of his reading for him. Another woman might have yearned for a more youthful companion, but her native coldness kept her content. She did not love him, she had never really loved anybody, but little Cornelius Boldin—he had been such an enchanting, such a darling baby, she remembered,—her heart contracted painfully when she thought as she did very often of his warm softness.

"He must be a big boy now," she would think almost maternally, wondering—once she had been so sure!—if she would ever see him again. But she was very fond of Wynne, and he was crazy over her just as Zora had predicted. He loaded her with gifts, dresses, flowers, jewels— she amused him because none but colored stones appealed to her.

"Diamonds are so hard, so cold, and pearls are dead," she told him. Nothing ever came between them, but his ugliness, his hatefulness to dependents. It hurt her so, for she was naturally kind in her careless, uncomprehending way. True, she had left Mrs. Boldin without a word, but she did not guess how completely Mrs. Boldin loved her. She would have been aghast had she realized how stricken her flight had left them. At twenty-two, Amy was still as good, as unspoiled, as pure as a child. Of course with all this she was too unquestioning, too selfish, too vain, but they were all faults of her lovely, lovely flesh. Wynne's intolerance finally got on her nerves. She used to blush for his unkindness. All the servants were colored, but she had long since ceased to think that perhaps she, too, was colored, except when he, by insult toward an employee, overt, always at least implied, made her realize his contemptuous dislike and disregard for a dark skin or Negro blood.

"Stuart, how can you say such things?" she would expostulate. "You can't expect a man to stand such language as that." And Wynne would sneer, "A man—you don't consider a nigger a man, do you? Oh, Amy, don't be such a fool. You've got to keep them in their places."

Some innate sense of the fitness of things kept her from condoling outspokenly with the servants, but they knew she was ashamed of her husband's ways. Of course, they left—it seemed to Amy that Peter, the butler, was always getting new "help,"—but most of the upper servants stayed, for Wynne paid handsomely and although his orders were meticulous and insistent the retinue of employees was so large that the individual's work was light.

Most of the servants who did stay on in spite of Wynne's occasional insults had a purpose in view. Callie, the cook, Amy found out, had two children at Howard University—of course she never came in contact with Wynne, the chauffeur had a crippled sister. Rose, Amy's maid and purveyor of much outside information, was the chief support of the family. About Peter, Amy knew nothing: he was a striking, taciturn man, very competent, who had left the Wynnes' service years before and had returned in Amy's third year. Wynne treated him with comparative respect. But Stephen, the new valet, met with entirely different treatment. Amy's heart yearned toward him, he was like Cornelius, with short-sighted, patient eyes, always willing, a little over-eager. Amy recognized him for what he was: a boy of respectable, ambitious parentage, striving for the means for an education; naturally far above his present calling, yet willing to pass through all this as a means to an end. She questioned Rosa about him.

"Oh, Stephen," Rosa told her, "yes'm, he's workin' for fair. He's got a brother at the Howard's and a sister at the Smith's. Yes'm, it do seem a little hard on him, but Stephen, he say, they're both goin' to turn roun' and help him when they get through. That blue silk has a rip in it, Miss Amy, if you was thinkin' of wearin' that. Yes'm, somehow I don't think Steve's very strong, kinda worries like. I guess he's sorta nervous."

Amy told Wynne. "He's such a nice boy, Stuart," she pleaded, "it hurts me to have you so cross with him. Anyway don't call him names." She was both surprised and frightened at the feeling in her that prompted her to interfere. She had held so aloof from other people's interests all these years.

"I *am* colored," she told herself that night. "I feel it inside of me. I must be or I couldn't care so about Stephen. Poor boy, I suppose Cornelius is just like him. I wish Stuart would let him alone. I wonder if all white people are like that. Zora was hard, too, on unfortunate people." She pondered over it a bit. "I wonder what Stuart would say if he knew I was colored?" She lay perfectly still, her smooth brow knitted, thinking hard. "But he loves me," she said to herself still silently. "He'll always love my looks," and she fell to thinking that all the wonderful happenings in her sheltered, pampered life had come to her through her beauty. She reached out an exquisite arm, switched on a light, and picking up a hand-mirror from a dressing-table, fell to studying her face. She was right. It was her chiefest asset. She forgot Stephen and fell asleep.

But in the morning her husband's voice issuing from his dressing-room across the hall, awakened her. She listened drowsily. Stephen, leaving the house the day before, had been met by a boy with a telegram. He had taken it, slipped it into his pocket, (he was just going to the mail-box) and had forgotten to deliver it until now, nearly twenty-four hours later. She could hear Stuart's storm of abuse—it was terrible, made up as it was of oaths and insults to the boy's ancestry. There was a moment's lull. Then she heard him again.

"If your brains are a fair sample of that black wench of a sister of yours—"

She sprang up then thrusting her arms as she ran into her pink dressing-gown. She got there just in time. Stephen, his face quivering, was standing looking straight into Wynne's smoldering eyes. In spite of herself, Amy was glad to see the boy's bearing. But he did not notice her.

"You devil!" he was saying. "You white-faced devil! I'll make you pay for that!" He raised his arm. Wynne did not blench.

With a scream she was between them. "Go, Stephen, go,—get out of the house. Where do you think you are? Don't you know you'll be hanged, lynched, tortured?" Her voice shrilled at him.

Wynne tried to thrust aside her arms that clung and twisted. But she held fast till the door slammed behind the fleeing boy.

"God, let me by, Amy!" As suddenly as she had clasped him she let him go, ran to the door, fastened it and threw the key out the window.

He took her by the arm and shook her. "Are you mad? Didn't you hear him threaten me, me,—a nigger threaten me?" His voice broke with nigger, "And you're letting him get away! Why, I'll get him. I'll set bloodhounds on him, I'll have every white man in this town after him! He'll be hanging so high by midnight—" he made for the other door, cursing, half-insane.

How, *how* could she keep him back! She hated her weak arms with their futile beauty! She sprang toward him. "Stuart, wait," she was breathless and sobbing. She said the first thing that came into her head. "Wait, Stuart, you cannot do this thing." She thought of Cornelius— suppose it had been he—"Stephen,—that boy,—he is my brother."

He turned on her. "What!" he said fiercely, then laughed a short laugh of disdain. "You are crazy," he said roughly, "My God, Amy! How can you even in jest associate yourself with these people? Don't you suppose I know a white girl when I see one? There's no use in telling a lie like that."

Well, there was no help for it. There was only one way. He had turned back for a moment, but she must keep him many moments—an hour. Stephen must get out of town.

She caught his arm again. "Yes," she told him, "I did lie. Stephen is not my brother, I never saw him before." The light of relief that crept into his eyes did not escape her, it only nerved her. "But I *am* colored," she ended.

Before he could stop her she had told him all about the tall white woman. "She took me to Mrs. Boldin's and gave me to her to keep. She would never have taken me to her if I had been white. If you lynch this boy, I'll let the world, your world, know that your wife is a colored woman."

He sat down like a man suddenly stricken old, his face ashen. "Tell me about it again," he commanded. And she obeyed, going mercilessly into every damning detail.

## IV

Amazingly her beauty availed her nothing. If she had been an older woman, if she had had Zora's age and experience, she would have been able to gauge exactly her influence over Wynne. Though even then in similar circumstances she would have taken the risk and acted in just the same manner. But she was a little bewildered at her utter miscalculation. She had thought he might not want his friends—his world by which he set such store—to know that she was colored, but she had not dreamed it could make any real difference to him. He had chosen her, poor and ignorant, but of a host of women, and had told her countless times of his love. To herself Amy Wynne was in comparison with Zora for instance, stupid and uninteresting. But his constant, unsolicited iterations had made her accept his idea.

She was just the same woman she told herself, she had not changed, she was still beautiful, still charming, still "different." Perhaps, that very difference had its being in the fact of her mixed blood. She had been his wife—there were memories—she could not see how he could give her up. The suddenness of the divorce carried her off her feet. Dazedly she left him—though almost without a pang for she had only liked him. She had been perfectly honest about this, and he, although consumed by the fierceness of his emotion toward her, had gradually forced himself to be content, for at least she had never made him jealous.

She was to live in a small house of his in New York, up town in the 80's. Peter was in charge and there was a new maid and a cook. The servants, of course, knew of the separation, but nobody guessed why. She was living on a much smaller basis than the one to which she had become so accustomed in the last three years. But she was very comfortable. She felt, at any rate she manifested, no qualms at receiving alimony from Wynne. That was the way things happened, she supposed when she thought of it at all. Moreover, it seemed to her perfectly in keeping with Wynne's former attitude toward her; she did not see how he could do less. She expected people to be consistent. That was why she was so amazed that he in spite of his oft iterated love, could let her go. If she had felt half the love for him which he had professed for her, she would not have sent him away if he had been a leper.

"Why I'd stay with him," she told herself, "if he were one, even as I feel now."

She was lonely in New York. Perhaps it was the first time in her life that she had felt so. Zora had gone to Paris the first year of her marriage and had not come back.

The days dragged on emptily. One thing helped her. She had gone one day to the modiste from whom she had bought her trousseau. The woman remembered her perfectly—"The lady with the exquisite taste for colors—ah, madame, but you have the rare gift." Amy was grateful to be taken out of her thoughts. She bought one or two daring but altogether lovely creations and let fall a few suggestions:

"That brown frock, Madame,—you say it has been on your hands a long time? Yes? But no wonder. See, instead of that dead white you should have a shade of ivory, that white cheapens it." Deftly she caught up a bit of ivory satin and worked out her idea. Madame was ravished.

"But yes, Madame Ween is correct,—as always. Oh, what a pity that the Madame is so wealthy. If she were only a poor girl—Mlle. Antoine with the best eye for color in the place has just left, gone back to France to nurse her brother—this World War is of such a horror! If someone like Madame, now, could be found, to take the little Antoine's place!"

Some obscure impulse drove Amy to accept the half proposal: "Oh! I don't know, I have nothing to do just now. My husband is abroad." Wynne had left her with that impression. "I could contribute the money to the Red Cross or to charity."

The work was the best thing in the world for her. It kept her from becoming too introspective, though even then she did more serious, connected thinking than she had done in all the years of her varied life.

She missed Wynne definitely, chiefly as a guiding influence for she had rarely planned even her own amusements. Her dependence on him had been absolute. She used to picture him to herself as he was before the trouble—and his changing expressions as he looked at her, of amusement, interest, pride, a certain little teasing quality that used to come into his eyes, which always made her adopt her "spoiled child air," as he used to call it. It was the way he liked her best. Then last, there was that look he had given her the morning she had told him she was colored—it had depicted so many emotions, various and yet distinct. There were dismay, disbelief, coldness, a final aloofness.

There was another expression, too, that she thought of sometimes— the look on the face of Mr. Packard, Wynne's lawyer. She, herself, had attempted no defense.

"For God's sake why did you tell him, Mrs. Wynne?" Packard asked her. His curiosity got the better of him. "You couldn't have been in love with that yellow rascal," he blurted out. "She's too cold really, to love anybody," he told himself. "If you didn't care about the boy why should you have told?"

She defended herself feebly. "He looked so like little Cornelius Boldin," she replied vaguely, "and he couldn't help being colored." A clerk came in then and Packard said no more. But into his eyes had crept a certain reluctant respect. She remembered the look, but could not define it.

She was so sorry about the trouble now, she wished it had never happened. Still if she had it to repeat she would act in the same way again. "There was nothing else for me to do," she used to tell herself.

But she missed Wynne unbelievably.

If it had not been for Peter, her life would have been almost that of a nun. But Peter, who read the papers and kept abreast of times, constantly called her attention, with all due respect, to the meetings, the plays, the sights which she ought to attend or see. She was truly grateful to him. She was very kind to all three of the servants. They had the easiest "places" in New York, the maids used to tell their friends. As she never entertained, and frequently dined out, they had a great deal of time off.

She had been separated from Wynne for ten months before she began to make any definite plans for her future. Of course, she could not go on like this always. It came to her suddenly that probably she would go to Paris and live there—why or how she did not know. Only Zora was there and lately she had begun to think that her life was to be like Zora's. They had been amazingly parallel up to this time. Of course she would have to wait until after the war.

She sat musing about it one day in the big sitting-room which she had had fitted over into a luxurious studio. There was a sewing-room off to the side from which Peter used to wheel into the room waxen figures of all colorings and contours so that she could drape the various fabrics about them to be sure of the best results. But today she was working out a scheme for one of Madame's customers, who was of her own color and size and she was her own lay-figure. She sat in front of the huge pier glass, a wonderful soft yellow silk draped about her radiant loveliness.

"I could do some serious work in Paris," she said half aloud to herself. "I suppose if I really wanted to, I could be very successful along this line."

Somewhere downstairs an electric bell buzzed, at first softly, then after a slight pause, louder, and more insistently.

"If Madame sends me that lace today," she was thinking, idly, "I could finish this and start on the pink. I wonder why Peter doesn't answer the bell."

She remembered then that Peter had gone to New Rochelle on business and she had sent Ellen to Altman's to find a certain rare velvet and had allowed Mary to go with her. She would dine out, she told them, so they need not hurry. Evidently she was alone in the house.

Well she could answer the bell. She had done it often enough in the old days at Mrs. Boldin's. Of course it was the lace. She smiled a bit as she went downstairs thinking how surprised the delivery-boy would be to see her arrayed thus early in the afternoon. She hoped he wouldn't go.

She could see him through the long, thick panels of glass in the vestibule and front door. He was just turning about as she opened the door.

This was no delivery-boy, this man whose gaze fell on her hungry and avid. This was Wynne. She stood for a second leaning against the door-jamb, a strange figure surely in the sharp November weather. Some leaves—brown, skeleton shapes—rose and swirled unnoticed about her head. A passing letter-carrier looked at them curiously.

"What are you doing answering the door?" Wynne asked her roughly. "Where is Peter? Go in, you'll catch cold."

She was glad to see him. She took him into the drawing room—a wonderful study in browns—and looked at him and looked at him.

"Well," he asked her, his voice eager in spite of the commonplace words, "are you glad to see me? Tell me what you do with yourself."

She could not talk fast enough, her eyes clinging to his face. Once it struck her that he had changed in some indefinable way. Was it a slight coarsening of that refined aristocratic aspect? Even in her sub-consciousness she denied it.

He had come back to her.

"So I design for Madame when I feel like it, and send the money to the Red Cross and wonder when you are coming back to me." For the first time in their acquaintanceship she was conscious deliberately of trying to attract, to hold him. She put on her spoiled child air which had once been so successful.

"It took you long enough to get here," she pouted. She was certain of him now. His mere presence assured her.

They sat silent a moment, the late November sun bathing her head in an austere glow of chilly gold. As she sat there in the big brown chair she was, in her yellow dress, like some mysterious emanation, some wraith-like aura developed from the tone of her surroundings.

He rose and came toward her, still silent. She grew nervous, and talked incessantly with sudden unusual gestures. "Oh, Stuart, let me give you tea. It's right there in the pantry off the dining-room. I can wheel the table in." She rose, a lovely creature in her yellow robe. He watched her intently.

"Wait," he bade her.

She paused almost on tiptoe, a dainty golden butterfly.

"You are coming back to live with me?" he asked her hoarsely.

For the first time in her life she loved him.

"Of course I am coming back," she told him softly. "Aren't you glad?

Haven't you missed me? I didn't see how you *could* stay away. Oh! Stuart, what a wonderful ring!"

For he had slipped on her finger a heavy dull gold band, with an immense sapphire in an oval setting—a beautiful thing of Italian workmanship.

"It is so like you to remember," she told him gratefully. "I love colored stones." She admired it, turning it around and around on her slender finger.

How silent he was, standing there watching her with his sombre yet eager gaze. It made her troubled, uneasy. She cast about for something to say.

"You can't think how I've improved since I saw you, Stuart. I've read all sorts of books—Oh! I'm learned," she smiled at him. "And Stuart," she went a little closer to him, twisting the button on his perfect coat, "I'm so sorry about it all,—about Stephen, that boy, you know. I just couldn't help interfering. But when we're married again, if you'll just remember how it hurts me to have you so cross—"

He interrupted her. "I wasn't aware that I spoke of our marrying again," he told her, his voice steady, his blue eyes cold.

She thought he was teasing. "Why you just asked me to. You said 'aren't you coming back to live with me—'"

Still she didn't comprehend. "But what do you mean?" she asked bewildered.

"What do you suppose a man means?" he returned deliberately, "when he asks a woman to live with him but not to marry him?"

She sat down heavily in the brown chair, all glowing ivory and yellow against its sombre depths.

"Like the women in those awful novels?" she whispered. "Not like those women!—Oh Stuart! you don't mean it!" Her very heart was numb.

"But you must care a little—" she was amazed at her own depth of feeling. "Why I care—there are all those memories back of us—you must want me really—"

"I do want you," he told her tensely. "I want you damnably. But—well—I might as well out with it—A white man like me simply doesn't marry a colored woman. After all what difference need it make to you? We'll live abroad—you'll travel, have all the things you love. Many a white woman would envy you." He stretched out an eager hand.

She evaded it, holding herself aloof as though his touch were contaminating. Her movement angered him.

"Oh, hell!" he snarled at her roughly. "Why don't you stop posing? What do you think you are anyway? Do you suppose I'd take you for my wife—what do you think can happen to you? What man of your own race could give you what you want? You don't suppose I am going to support you this way forever, do you? The court imposed no alimony. You've got to come to it sooner or later—you're bound to fall to some white man. What's the matter—I'm not rich enough?"

Her face flamed at that—"As though it were *that* that mattered!"

He gave her a deadly look. "Well, isn't it? Ah, my girl, you forget you told me you didn't love me when you married me. You sold yourself to me then. Haven't I reason to suppose you are waiting for a higher bidder?"

At these words something in her died forever, her youth, her illusions, her happy, happy blindness. She saw life leering mercilessly in her face. It seemed to her that she would give all her future to stamp out, to kill the contempt in his frosty insolent eyes. In a sudden rush of savagery she struck him, struck him across his hateful sneering mouth with the hand which wore his ring.

As *she* fell, reeling under the fearful impact of his brutal but involuntary blow, her mind caught at, registered two things. A little thin stream of blood was trickling across his chin. She had cut him with the ring, she realized with a certain savage satisfaction. And there was something else which she must remember, which she *would* remember if only she could fight her way out of this dreadful clinging blackness, which was bearing down upon her—closing her in.

When she came to she sat up holding her bruised, aching head in her palms, trying to recall what it was that had impressed her so.

Oh yes, her very mind ached with the realization. She lay back again on the floor, prone, anything to relieve that intolerable pain. But her memory, her thoughts went on.

"Nigger," he had called her as she fell, "nigger, nigger," and again, "nigger."

"He despised me absolutely," she said to herself wonderingly, "because I was colored. And yet he wanted me."

## V

Somehow she reached her room. Long after the servants had come in, she lay face downward across her bed, thinking. How she hated Wynne, how she hated herself! And for ten months she had been living off his money although in no way had she a claim on him. Her whole body burned with the shame of it.

In the morning she rang for Peter. She faced him, white and haggard, but if the man noticed her condition, he made no sign. He was, if possible, more imperturbable than ever.

"Peter," she told him, her eyes and voice very steady, "I am leaving this house today and shall never come back."

"Yes, Miss."

"And, Peter, I am very poor now and shall have no money besides what I can make for myself."

"Yes, Miss."

Would nothing surprise him, she wondered dully. She went on "I don't know whether you knew it or not, Peter, but I am colored, and hereafter I mean to live among my own people. Do you think you could find a little house or little cottage not too far from New York?"

He had a little place in New Rochelle, he told her, his manner altering not one whit, or better yet his sister had a four-room house in Orange, with a garden, if he remembered correctly. Yes, he was sure there was a garden. It would be just the thing for Mrs. Wynne.

She had four hundred dollars of her very own which she had earned by designing for Madame. She paid the maids a month in advance—they were to stay as long as Peter needed them. She, herself, went to a small hotel in Twenty-eighth Street, and here Peter came for her at the end of ten days, with the acknowledgement of the keys and receipts from Mr. Packard. Then he accompanied her to Orange and installed her in her new home.

"I wish I could afford to keep you, Peter," she said a little wistfully, "but I am very poor. I am heavily in debt and I must get that off my shoulders at once."

Mrs. Wynne was very kind, he was sure; he could think of no one with whom he would prefer to work. Furthermore, he often ran down from New Rochelle to see his sister; he would come in from time to time, and in the spring would plant the garden if she wished.

She hated to see him go, but she did not dwell long on that. Her only thought was to work and work and work and save until she could pay Wynne back. She had not lived very extravagantly during those ten months and Peter was a perfect manager—in spite of her remonstrances he had given her every month an account of his expenses. She had made arrangements with Madame to be her regular designer. The French woman guessing that more than whim was behind this move drove a very shrewd bargain, but even then the pay was excellent. With care, she told herself, she could be free within two years, three at most.

She lived a dull enough existence now, going to work steadily every morning and getting home late at night. Almost it was like those early days when she had first left Mrs. Boldin, except that now she had no high sense of adventure, no expectation of great things to come, which might buoy her up. She no longer thought of phases and the proper setting for her beauty. Once indeed catching sight of her face late one night in the mirror in her tiny work-room in Orange, she stopped and scanned herself, loathing what she saw there.

"You *thing!*" she said to the image in the glass, "if you hadn't been so vain, so shallow!" And she had struck herself violently again and again across the face until her head ached.

But such fits of passion were rare. She had a curious sense of freedom in these days, a feeling that at last her brain, her senses were liberated from some hateful clinging thralldom. Her thoughts were always busy. She used to go over that last scene with Wynne again and again trying to probe the inscrutable mystery which she felt was at the bottom of the affair. She groped her way toward a solution, but always something stopped her. Her impulse to strike, she realized, and his brutal rejoinder had been actuated by something more than mere sex antagonism, there was *race* antagonism there—two elements clashing. That much she could fathom. But that he despising her, hating her for not being white should yet desire her! It seemed to her that his attitude toward her— hate and yet desire, was the attitude in microcosm of the whole white world toward her own, toward that world to which those few possible strains of black blood so tenuously and yet so tenaciously linked her.

Once she got hold of a big thought. Perhaps there *was* some root, some racial distinction woven in with the stuff of which she was formed which made her persistently kind and unexacting. And perhaps in the same way this difference, helplessly, inevitably operated in making Wynne and his kind, cruel or at best indifferent. Her reading for Wynne reacted to her thought—she remembered the grating insolence of white exploiters in foreign lands, the wrecking of African villages, the destruction of homes in Tasmania. She couldn't imagine where Tasmania was, but wherever it was, it had been the realest thing in the world to its crude inhabitants.

Gradually she reached a decision. There were two divisions of people in the world—on the one hand insatiable desire for power; keenness, mentality; a vast and cruel pride. On the other there was ambition, it is true, but modified, a certain humble sweetness, too much inclination to trust, an unthinking, unswerving loyalty. All the advantages in the world accrued to the first division. But without bitterness she chose the second. She wanted to be colored, she hoped she was colored. She wished even that she did not have to take advantage of her appearance to earn a living. But that was to meet an end. After all she had contracted her debt with a white man, she would pay him with a white man's money.

The years slipped by—four of them. One day a letter came from Mr. Packard. Mrs. Wynne had sent him the last penny of the sum received from Mr. Wynne from February to November, 1914. Mr. Wynne had refused to touch the money, it was and would be indefinitely at Mrs. Wynne's disposal.

She never even answered the letter. Instead she dismissed the whole incident,—Wynne and all,—from her mind and began to plan for her future. She was free, free! She had paid back her sorry debt with labor, money and anguish. From now on she could do as she pleased. Almost she caught herself saying "something is going to happen." But she checked herself, she hated her old attitude.

But something *was* happening. Insensibly from the moment she knew of her deliverance, her thoughts turned back to a stifled hidden longing, which had lain, it seemed to her, an eternity in her heart. Those days with Mrs. Boldin! At night,—on her way to New York,—in the work-rooms,—her mind was busy with little intimate pictures of that happy, wholesome, unpretentious life. She could see Mrs. Boldin, clean and portly, in a lilac chambray dress, upbraiding her for some trifling, yet exasperating fault. And Mr. Boldin, immaculate and slender, with his noticeably polished air—how kind he had always been, she remembered. And lastly, Cornelius: Cornelius in a thousand attitudes and engaged in a thousand occupations, brown and near-sighted and sweet—devoted to his pretty sister, as he used to call her; Cornelius, who used to come to her as a baby as willingly as to his mother; Cornelius spelling out colored letters on his blocks, pointing to them stickily with a brown, perfect finger; Cornelius singing like an angel in his breathy, sexless voice and later murdering everything possible on his terrible cornet. How had she ever been able to leave them all and the dear shabbiness of that home! Nothing, she realized, in all these years had touched her inmost being, had penetrated to the core of her cold heart like the memories of those early, misty scenes.

One day she wrote a letter to Mrs. Boldin. She, the writer, Madame A. Wynne, had come across a young woman, Amy Kildare, who said that as a girl she had run away from home and now she would like to come back. But she was ashamed to write. Madame Wynne had questioned the girl closely and she was quite sure that this Miss Kildare had in no way incurred shame or disgrace. It had been some time since Madame

Wynne had seen the girl but if Mrs. Boldin wished, she would try to find her again—perhaps Mrs. Boldin would like to get in touch with her. The letter ended on a tentative note.

The answer came at once.

My dear Madame Wynne:

   My mother told me to write you this letter. She says even if Amy Kildare had done something terrible, she would want her to come home again. My father says so too. My mother says, please find her as soon as you can and tell her to come back. She still misses her. We all miss her. I was a little boy when she left, but though I am in the High School now and play in the school orchestra, I would rather see her than do anything I know. If you see her, be sure to tell her to come right away. My mother says thank you.

Yours respectfully,<br>CORNELIUS BOLDIN

The letter came to the modiste's establishment in New York. Amy read it and went with it to Madame. "I must go away immediately. I can't come back—you may have these last two weeks for nothing." Madame, who had surmised long since the separation, looked curiously at the girl's flushed cheeks, and decided that "Monsieur Ween" had returned. She gave her fatalistic shrug. All Americans were crazy.

"But, yes, Madame, if you must go, absolument."

When she reached the ferry, Amy looked about her searchingly. "I hope I'm seeing you for the last time. I'm going home, home!" Oh, the unbelievable kindness! She had left them without a word and they still wanted her back!

Eventually she got to Orange and to the little house. She sent a message to Peter's sister and set about her packing. But first she sat down in the little house and looked about her. She would go home, home— how she loved the word, she would stay there a while, but always there was life, still beckoning. It would beckon forever she realized to her adventurousness. Afterwards she would set up an establishment of her own,—she reviewed possibilities—in a rich suburb, where white women would pay for her expertness, caring nothing for realities, only for externals.

"As I myself used to care," she sighed. Her thoughts flashed on. "Then some day I'll work and help with colored people—the only ones who have really cared for and wanted me." Her eyes blurred.

She would never make any attempt to find out who or what she was. If she were white, there would always be people urging her to keep up the silliness of racial prestige. How she hated it all!

"Citizen of the world, that's what I'll be. And now I'll go home."

Peter's sister's little girl came over to be with the pretty lady whom she adored.

"You sit here, Angel, and watch me pack," Amy said, placing her in a little arm-chair. And the baby sat there in silent observation, one tiny leg crossed over the other, surely the quaintest, gravest bit of bronze, Amy thought, that ever lived.

"Miss Amy cried," the child told her mother afterwards.

Perhaps Amy did cry, but if so she was unaware. Certainly she laughed more happily, more spontaneously than she had done for years. Once she got down on her knees in front of the little arm-chair and buried her face in the baby's tiny bosom.

"Oh Angel, Angel," she whispered, "do you suppose Cornelius still plays on that cornet?"

FROM *THE CRISIS*, AUGUST–OCTOBER 1920

# Double Trouble

## JESSIE REDMON FAUSET

### I

Angélique came walking delicately down Cedarwood Street. You could see by the way she advanced, a way which fell just short of dancing that she was feeling to the utmost the pleasant combination of her youth, the weather and the season. Angélique was seventeen, the day was perfect and the year was at the spring.

Just before Cedarwood crosses Tenth, she stopped, her nice face crinkling with amusement and untied and retied the ribbon which fastened her trim oxford. Before she had finished this ritual Malory Fordham turned the corner and asked rather sternly if he might not perform the task. "Allow me to tie it for you," he had said with unrelieved formality.

"Sure I'll allow you." Angélique was never shy with those whom she liked. She replaced the subtler arts of the coquette with a forthrightness which might have proved her undoing with another boy. But not with Malory Fordham. Shy, pensive, and enveloped by the aura of malaise which so mysteriously and perpetually hung over his household he found Angélique's manner a source both of attraction and wonder. To him she was a radiant, generous storehouse of light and warmth which constantly renewed his chilled young soul.

"We're in luck this afternoon," said Angélique resuming her happy gait. "Sometimes I have to tie my shoes a dozen times. Once I took one shoe off and shook it and shook it, trying to get rid of make believe dust. I was glad you didn't turn up just then for I happened to look across the street and there was cousin Laurentine walking, you know that stiff poker-like way she goes—" Angélique bubbling with merriment imitated it—"I know she was disgusted seeing me like 'my son John, one shoe off and one shoe on.'"

"It's a wonder she didn't take you home," said Malory, admiring her.

"Oh, no! Cousin Laurentine wouldn't be seen walking up the street with me! She doesn't like me. Funny isn't it? But you know what's funnier still, Malory, not many folks around here do like me. Strange, don't you think, and living all my life almost in this little place? I never knew what it was to be really liked before you came except for Aunt Sal. I say to myself lots of times: 'Well, anyway, Malory likes me,' and then I'm completely happy."

"I'm glad of that," Malory told her, flushing. He was darker than Angélique for his father and mother had both been brown-skinned mulattoes, with a trace of Indian on his mother's side. Angélique's mother, whom she rarely saw, was a mulatto, too, but a very light one, quite yellow, and though she could not remember her father, she had in her mind's eye a concept of him which made him only the least shade darker than her mother. He had to be darker, for Angélique always associated masculinity with a dark complexion. She did not like to see men fairer than their wives.

Malory dwelt for several moments on Angélique's last remark. You could see him patiently turning the idea over and over. His high, rather narrow, forehead contracted, his almond, liquid eyes narrowed. His was a type which in any country but America would have commanded immediate and admiring attention. As it was even in Edendale he received many a spontaneous, if surreptitious, glance of approval.

He evolved an answer. "I don't know but you're right, Angélique. I think I must have been home six months before I met you, though I knew your name. I seem to have known your name a long time," he said musing slowly over some evasive idea. "But I never saw you, I guess, until that night when Evie Thompson's mother introduced us at Evie's party. I remember old Mrs. Rossiter seemed so queer. She said—"

"Yes, I know," Angélique interrupted, mimicking, "Oh, Miz Thompson, you didn't ever introduce them! That," concluded the girl with her usual forthrightness, "was because she wanted you to meet her Rosie—such a name Rosie Rossiter!—and have you dance attendance on her all evening!"

Fordham blushed again. "I don't know about that. Anyhow, what I was going to say was if I were you I wouldn't bother if the folks around here didn't like me. They don't like me either."

"No, I don't think they do very much. And yet it's different." Angélique explained puzzling out something. "They may not like you probably because you've lived away from home so long but they're willing to go with you. Now I think it's the other way around with me. They sort of like me, lots of the girls at times have liked me a great deal, new girls especially. But they shy away after a time. When Evie Thompson first came to this town she liked me better than she did any one else. I know she did. But after her mother gave that big party she acted different. She has never had me at a real party since and you know she entertains a lot—you're always there. Yet she's forever asking me over to her house when she hasn't company and then she's just as nice and her mother is always too sweet."

They were nearing the corner where they always parted. Cousin Laurentine did not allow Angélique to have beaux. "Perhaps they're jealous," Malory proposed as a last solution.

The girl's nice, round face clouded. She was not pretty but she bore about her an indefinable atmosphere of niceness, of freshness and innocence. "Jealous of the boys, you mean?" She bit her full red lip. "No, it's not that, none of the boys ever treats me very nicely, none of them ever has except you and Asshur Judson."

"Asshur Judson!" Malory echoed in some surprise. "You mean that tall, rough, farmer fellow? I'd have thought he'd be the last fellow in the world to know how to treat a nice girl like you."

"Mmh. He does, he did. You know the boys most of them" for the first time Fordham saw her shy, wistful—"when I say they're not nice I mean they are usually too nice. They try to kiss me, put their arms around me. Sometimes when I used to go skating I'd have horrid things happen. They'd tease the other girls, too, but with me they're different. They act as though it didn't matter how they treated me. Maybe it's because my father's dead."

"Perhaps," Malory acquiesced doubtfully, but he was completely bewildered. "And you say Asshur Judson was polite?"

"I'd forgotten Asshur. You didn't know him well, I think he came while you were in Philadelphia and he went away right after you came back. We'd been skating everyday. I wasn't with anyone, just down there in the crowd, and I struck off all alone. Bye and bye who should come racing after me but Asshur. I looked back and saw him and went on harder than ever. Of course he caught up to me, and when he did he took me right in his arms and held me tight. I struggled and fought so that I knew he understood I didn't like it, so he let me go. And then that hateful Harry Robbins came up and said: 'Don't you mind her, Jud, she's just pretending, she'll come around!'" Her voice shook with the shame of it.

"And then?" Malory prompted her fiercely.

"I heard Judson say just as mad, 'What the deuce you talking about Robbins?'"

Malory failed to see any extraordinary exhibition of politeness in that.

"Oh, but afterwards! You know my Cousin Laurentine doesn't allow me to have company. Of course he didn't know that, and that night he came to the house. Cousin Laurentine let him in and I heard her say: 'Yes, Angélique is in but she doesn't have callers.' And he answered: 'But I must see her, Miss Fletcher, I must explain something.' His voice sounded all funny and different. So I came running down stairs and asked him what he wanted.

"It was all so queer, Malory. He came over to me past Cousin Laurentine standing at the door like a dragon and he took both my hands, sort of frightened me. He said: 'You kid, you decent little kid! Treat 'em all like you treated me this afternoon, and try to forgive me. If you see me a thousand times you'll never have to complain of me again.' And he went."

"Funny," was Malory's comment. "Didn't he say anything more?"

"No, just went and I've got to go. Got to memorize a lot of old Shakespeare for tomorrow. Silly stuff from Macbeth. 'Double, double, toil and trouble.' Bye Malory."

"Good-bye," he echoed, turning in the direction of his home where his mother and his three plain older sisters awaited him. On his way he captured the idea which had earlier eluded him. He remembered speaking once before he had met her, of Angélique Murray to his old subdued household and of receiving a momentary impression of shock, of horror even, passing over his mother's face. He looked at his sisters and received the same impression. He looked at all four women again and saw nothing, just nothing, utter blankness, out of which came the voice of Gracie, his hostile middle sister. "Good heavens, Malory! Don't tell me that you know that Angélique Murray. I won't have you meeting her. She is ordinary, her whole family is the last thing in ordinariness. Now mind if you meet her, you let her alone."

At the time he had acquiesced, deeming this one of the thousand queer phases of his household with which he was striving so hard to become reacquainted. He had been a very little boy when he had been taken so hurriedly to live in Philadelphia, but his memory had painted them all so different.

In spite of his sister's warning Angélique's brightness when he met her, her frankness, her merriment proved too much for him. She was like an unfamiliar but perfectly recognizable part of himself. Pretty soon he was fathoms deep in love. But because he was a boy of practically no ingenuities but mechanical ones he could hit on nothing better than walking home from school with her. She was the one picture in the daily book of his life and having seen her he retired home each day like Browning's lovers to think up a scheme which would enable him sometime to tear it out for himself.

Angélique, hastening on flying feet, hoped that Cousin Laurentine would be out when she reached home. She could manage Laurentine's mother, Aunt Sal, even when she was as late as she was today. But before she entered the house she realized that for tonight at least she would be free from her cousin's hateful and scornful espionage. For peeping through the window which gave from the front room on to the porch she was able to make out against the soft inner gloom the cameo-like features of the Misses Courtney, the two young white women who came so often to see Aunt Sal and Laurentine. They were ladies of indubitable breeding and refinement, but for all their culture and elegance they could not eclipse Laurentine whose eyes shone as serene, whose forehead rose as smooth and classical as did their own. The only difference lay in their coloring. The Misses Courtney's skin shone as white as alabaster, their eyes lay, blue cornflowers, in that lake of dazzling purity. But Laurentine was crimson and gold like the flesh of the mango, her eyes were dark emeralds. Her proud head glowed like an amber carving rising from the green perfection of her dress. She was a replica of the Courtney sisters startlingly vivified. Angélique, on her way to the kitchen poising on noiseless feet in the outside hall, experienced anew her thrill at the shocking resemblance between the two white women and the colored one; a resemblance which missed completely the contribution of white Mrs. Courtney and black Aunt Sal, and took into account only the remarkable beauty of Ralph Courtney, the father of all three of these women.

Aunt Sal in the background of the picture was studying with her customary unwavering glance the three striking figures. The Misses Courtney had travelled in Europe, they spoke French fluently. But Laurentine had travelled in the West Indies and spoke Spanish. When the time came for the Misses Courtney to go, they would kiss Laurentine lightly on both cheeks, they would murmur: "Good-bye, Sister," and would trail off leaving behind them the unmistakable aura of their loyal, persistent, melancholic determination to atone for their father's ancient wrong. And Laurentine, beautiful, saffron creature, would rise and gaze after them, enveloped in a sombre evanescent triumph.

But afterwards!

Up in her room Angélique envisaged the reaction which inevitably befell her cousin after the departure of these visitors. For the next three weeks Laurentine would be more than ever hateful, proud, jealous, scornful, intractable. The older woman, the young girl shrewdly guessed, was jealous of her; jealous of her unblemished parentage, of her right to race pride, of her very youth, though her own age could not be more than twenty-eight. "Poor Cousin Laurentine," the child thought, "as though she could help her father's being white. Anything was liable to happen in those old slavery times. I must try to be nicer to her."

When later she opened the door to her cousin's tap her determination was put to a severe test, for Laurentine was in one of her nastiest moods. "Here is another one of those letters," she said bitingly, "from that young ruffian who pushed his way past me that night. If I had my way I'd burn up every one of them. I can't think how you manage to attract such associates. It will be the best thing in the world for all of us when your mother sends for you."

Angélique took Asshur's letter somewhat sullenly, though she knew the feeling which her cousin's outburst concealed. In that household of three women this young girl was the only one who could be said to receive mail. Even hers was, until very lately, almost negligible—a note or two from a proudly travelling schoolmate, some directions for making candy from Evie Thompson or from the girl who at that moment was espousing her inexplicable cause, a card or so from a boy and now this constant stream of letters from Asshur Judson. As she opened these last or sat down to answer them in the shaded green glow of the dining-room, she had seen Cousin Laurentine's face pale with envy under the saffron satin of her skin.

Laurentine received letters and cards from the Misses Courtney when they were abroad—a few bills—she made rather a practice of having charge accounts—and an occasional note from the white summer transient expressing the writer's pleasure with "that last dress you made me." Once the young divinity student who, while the pastor was on his vacation, took over the services of the African Methodist Episcopal Church, sent her a post card from Niagara Falls. Laurentine exhibited a strange negligence with regard to this card, it was always to be found in the litter of the sewing table. "Oh," she would say casually to the customer whom she was fitting, "that's a card from Mr. Deaver who substituted here last summer. Yes, he does seem to be a fine young man."

Angélique did not at once open Asshur's letter. She had too many lessons to get. Besides she knew what it would contain, his constant and unvarying injunction "to be good, to be decent" coupled with an account of his latest success in some branch of scientific agriculture; he was an enthusiastic farmer. She liked to hear from him, but she wished his interests were broader. Laying the letter aside unregretfully she fell to memorizing the witches' speech in Macbeth and then in her little English Handbook under the chapter on "The Drama—Greek Tragedy," she made a brief but interested foray among the peculiarities of the ancient stage. Reading of Greek masks, buskins and "unities" she forgot all about Asshur's letter until as usual Aunt Sal put her fine dark head in the door and told her in mild but unanswerable tones that it was "most nigh bedtime."

She jumped up then and began to undress. But first she read the letter. Just as she thought it began like all his former letters and would probably end the same. No, here was something different. Asshur had written:

"My father says I'm making great headway, and so does Mr. Ellis, the man on whose farm I'm experimenting. Next year I'll be twenty-one and father's going to let me work a small farm he owns right up here in northern New Jersey. But first I'm coming for you. Only you must keep good and straight like you were when I first met you. You darn spunky little kid. Mind, you be good, you be decent. I'm sure coming for you."

It was a queer love-letter. "So you'll come for me," said Angélique to her image in the glass. She shook out her short, black, rather wiry hair till it misted like a cloud about her childishly round face. "How do you know I'll go with you? I may find someone I like ten times better." Dimpling and smiling she imitated Malory's formality: "May I tie your shoe for you?"

All night she dreamed she was chasing Malory Fordham. Was it a game? If so why did he so doggedly elude her? Then when, laughing, she had overtaken him, why did he turn on her with round gaping mouth and horrid staring eyes that transformed him into a Greek tragic mask? Through open, livid lips came whistling strange words, terrible phrases whose import at first she could not grasp. When she did she threw her arm across her face with a fearful cry and fell back convulsed and shuddering into the arms of a dark, muffled figure whose features she fought vainly to discover.

## II

Edendale, like many another Jersey town, as well as all Gaul, was divided into three parts. In one section, the prettiest from a natural point of view, lived Italians, Polacks and Hungarians who had drifted in as laborers. In another section, elegant and cultivated, dwelt a wealthy and leisure class of white men of affairs, commuters, having big business interests in Philadelphia, Trenton, Newark and even New York. Occupying the traditional middle ground were Jews, small tradesmen, country lawyers and a large group of colored people ranging in profession from Phil Baltimore, successful ash-contractor to the equally successful physician, Dr. Thompson. This last group was rather closely connected with the wealthy white group, having in far preceding generations, dwelt with them as slaves or more recently as house servants. Sometimes as in the case of Aunt Sal Fletcher and the Courtneys, who following the Civil War had drifted into Jersey from Delaware, they had served in both capacities.

Malory and Angélique came to know the foreign quarters well. Here on the old Hopewell Road beginning nowhere and going nowhither they were surest of escaping the eye of a too viligant colored townsman as well as that of the occasional white customer for whom the girl's cousin sewed. Malory was in no danger from a possibility like this last for the Fordhams on the maternal side had been small but independent householders for nearly a century. Even now Mrs. Fordham lived on a small income which came partly from her father's legacy, partly from the sale of produce from a really good truck-farm. Her husband had showed a tendency to dissipate this income but he had died before he had crippled it too sorely. Malory was determined to have more money when he grew older, money which he would obtain by his own methods. He never meant to ask his family for anything. The thought of a possible controversy with the invincible Gracie turned him sick.

He would be an engineer, how or where he did not know. But there would be plenty of money for him and Angélique. Already all his dreams included Angélique. He had not told her but he loved her fervently with an ardor excelling ordinary passion, for his included gratitude, a rapt consciousness of the miracle which daily she wrought for him in the business of living. She was so vivid, so joyous, so generous, so much what he would wish to be that almost it was as though she were his very self. Every day he warmed his hands at that fire which she alone could create for him.

He it was who fought so keenly against the clandestine nature of their meetings. Not so Angélique. This child so soon, so tragically to be transformed into a woman, was still a romantic dreaming girl. Half the joy of this new experience lay in its secrecy. This was fun, great fun, to run counter to imperious, unhappy Laurentine, to know that while her cousin endured the condescending visit of the son of the ash-contractor in the hope that some day, somehow she m ght receive the son of the colored physician, she herself was the eagerly and respectfully chosen of the son of the first colored family in the county. This was nectar and ambrosia, their taste enhanced by secrecy.

But Malory hated it. He had not told his family about the girl because clearly for some fool reason they were prejudiced against her, and as for Angélique's family—no males allowed. Hence this impasse. But he wanted like many another fond lover to acquaint others with his treasure, to show off not only this unparalleled gem, but himself too. For in her presence he himself shone, he became witty, his shyness vanished. The Methodist Sunday School picnic was to be held the first week in June. His sisters never went; proud Laurentine would not think of attending. He told Angélique that he would take her.

"Wonderful!" she breathed. She had a white dress with red ribbons.

They met on that memorable day, rather late. Laurentine could not keep Angélique from attending the picnic, but she could make her late; she could make her feel the exquisite torture which envelops a young girl who has to enter alone and unattended the presence of a crowd of watchful acquaintances. Angélique, inwardly unperturbed,—she knew Malory would wait for her forever,—outwardly greatly chafing, enjoyed her cousin's barely concealed satisfaction at her pretended discomfiture. With a blithe indifference she went from task to task, from chore to chore. "Greek tragedy," she whispered gaily into the ear of Marcus, an adored black kitten.

Malory did not mind her lateness. Indeed he was glad of it. So much the more conspicuous their entrance to the grounds. As it chanced, practically the whole party was in or around the large pavilion grouped there to receive instructions from Mrs. Evie Thompson who had charge of the picnic. A great church worker, Mrs. Evie. When the two arrived the place was in an uproar, Mrs. Evie balanced perilously on a stool tried to out talk the noise. Presently she realized that her voice was unnecessarily loud, the sea of black, yellow, and of white faces had ebbed into quiet but not because of her. Malory just outside the wide entrance, in the act of helping Angélique up the rustic steps caught that same fleeting shadow of horror and dismay, that shadow which he had marked on the faces of his household, rippling like a wave over the faces of the crowd, touching for a second Mrs. Thompson's face and vanishing. Appalled, bewildered, he stood still.

Mrs. Thompson rushed to them. "You just happened to meet Angélique, Malory? You—you didn't bring her?" Her voice was low but anxious.

"Of course I brought her," he replied testily. What possessed these staring people? "Why shouldn't I bring her?"

"Why not indeed?" soothed Mrs. Thompson. She herself came from a "best family" in some nearby city. "It's such luck that's all. I was wishing for Angélique. She's such a help at a time like this, so skillful. I want her to help me cut sandwiches."

Malory, rather sulkily accepting this, allowed his guest to be spirited away to exercise this skill. The crowd drawing a vast, multi-throated breath dispersed. Mrs. Thompson was anything but skillful herself. In the course of the afternoon she cut her assistant's hand. "I don't anticipate any infection," she remarked, peering at the small wound with an oddly unrepentant air, but you'd better come home with me and let Doctor dress it. Sorry I can't invite you too, Malory, but there's hardly room in the buggy for four. Evie and I are both fat."

Malory passed a night of angry sleeplessness. "I don't know what to think of these people," he told Angélique when they met the next day. "Do you know what I want you to do? You come home with me now and meet my mother and sisters. When they get to know you, they'll like you too and I know they can make these others step around." It was the first time he had betrayed any consciousness of the Fordham social standing.

Angélique, nothing loth, agreed with him. She too had thought Mrs. Thompson extraordinary the day before, but she had not seen as Malory had the strange shadowy expression of horror. And in any case would have had no former memory to emphasize it.

The two moved joyously up the tree-lined street, Malory experiencing his usual happy reaction to Angélique's buoyancy. Nothing would ever completely destroy her gay equanimity he thought, feeling his troubled young spirit relax. There was no one like her he knew. His people, even Gracie, must love her. He was living at this time in the last years of the nineties and so was given to much reading of Tennyson. Angélique made him think of the Miller's daughter, who had "grown so dear, so dear." What of life and youth and cheerfulness would she not introduce into his drab household, musty with old memories, inexplicably tainted with the dessication of some ancient imperishable grief!

At the corner of the street he took her arm. They would march into the house bravely and he would say, "Mother, this is Angélique whom I love. I want you to love her too; you will when you know her." He perceived as he opened the gate that Angélique was nervous, frightened. Timidity was in her such an unusual thing that he felt a new wave of tenderness rising within him. On the porch just before he touched the knob of the screen door he laid his hand on hers.

"Don't be frightened," he murmured.

"Look," she returned faintly.

He spun about and saw pressed against the window-pane a face, the small, brown face of his sister Gracie. In the background above her shoulder hovered the head of the oldest girl Reba, her body so completely hidden behind Gracie's that for a second, it seemed to him fantastically, her head swung suspended in space. But only for a second did he think this, so immediately was his attention drawn, riveted to the look of horror, of hatred, of pity which was frozen, seared on the faces of his sisters.

"For God's sake, what is it?" he cried.

Gracie's hands made a slight outward movement toward Angélique, a warding off motion of faintness and disgust such as one might make involuntarily towards a snake.

"I'm going in; come Angélique," the boy said in exasperation. "Has the whole world gone crazy?"

Before he could open the door Reba appeared, that expression still on her face, like a fine veil blurring out her features. Would it remain there forever he wondered.

"You can't bring her in Malory, you musn't."

"Why musn't I? What are you talking about?" Strange oaths rose to his lips. "What's the matter with her?" He started to pull the door from his sister's grasp when Gracie came, pushed the door open and stepped out on the porch beside him.

"Oh Malory you must send her away! Come in and I'll tell you." She burst into tears.

Gracie his tyrant, his arch-enemy weeping! That startled him far more than that inexplicable look. The foundations of the world were tottering. He turned to his trembling companion. "Go home, Angel," he bade her tenderly. "Meet me tomorrow and we'll fix all this up." He watched her waver down the porch-steps then turned to his sisters:

"Now girls?"

Together they got him into the house and told him.

### III

Angélique said to herself, "I'll ask Aunt Sal,—Cousin Laurentine,—but what could they know about it? No I'll wait for Malory. Can I have the leprosy I wonder?" She went home, stripped and peered a long time in the mirror at her delicate, yellow body.

Next afternoon near the corner of Cedarwood and Tenth she untied and retied her shoes twenty times. Malory did not come. She shook out bushels of imaginary dust. He had not come, was never coming.

At the end of an hour she went to the corner and peered down Tenth Street. Yes— no—yes it was he coming slowly, slowly down the steps of the Boys' High School. Perhaps he was sick; when he saw her, he would be better. . . . He did not look in her direction; without so much as turning his head he came down the steps and started due west. Cedarwood Street lay east.

Without a second's hesitation she followed him. He was turning now out of Tenth north on Wheaton Avenue. After all you could go this way to the old Hopewell Road. Perhaps he had meant for her to meet him there. A block behind him, she saw him turn from Wheaton into the narrow footpath that later broadened into Hopewell Road. Yes, that was what he meant. She began to run then feeling something vaguely familiar about the act. On Hopewell Road she gained on him, called his name, "Malory, oh Malory." He turned around an instant shading his eyes from the golden June sunlight to make sure and spinning back began to run, almost leap away from her.

Bewildered, horrified, she plodded behind, leaving little clouds of white dust spiraling after her footsteps. As she ran she realized that he was fleeing from her in earnest; this was no game, no lover's playfulness.

He tripped over a tree root, fell, reeled to his feet and, breathless, found her upon him. She knew that this was her dream but even so she was unprepared for the face he turned upon her, a face with horrid staring eyes, with awful gaping lips, the face of a Greek tragic mask!

She came close to him. "Malory," she besought pitifully. Her hand moved out to touch his arm.

"Don't come near me!" His breath came whistling from his ghastly lips. "Don't touch me!" He broke into terrible weeping. "You're my sister—my sister!" He raised tragic arms to the careless sky. "Oh God how could you! I loved her, I wanted to marry her, and she's my sister!"

To proud Laurentine sitting in haughty dejection in the littered sewing-room, fingering a dog-eared postcard from Niagara Falls came the not unwelcome vision of her stricken cousin swaying, stumbling toward her.

"Laurentine, tell me! I saw Malory, Malory Fordham, he says, he says I'm his sister. How can that be? Oh Laurentine be kind to me, tell me it isn't true!" She would have thrown herself about the older woman's neck.

Inflexible arms held her off, pushed her down. "So you've found it out have you? You sailing about me with your pitying ways and your highty tighty manner. Sorry for Cousin Laurentine, weren't you? because her father was white and her mother wasn't married to him. But my mother couldn't help it. She had been a slave until she became a woman and she carried a slave's traditions into freedom.

"But her sister, your mother," the low hating voice went on, "whom my mother had shielded and guarded, to whom she held up herself and me—me—" she struck her proud breast—"as horrible examples,—your mother betrayed Mrs. Fordham, a woman of her own race who had been kind to her, and ran away with her husband." She spurned the grovelling girl with a disdainful foot. "Stop snivelling. Did you ever see me cry? No and you never will."

Angélique asked irrelevantly: "Why did you hate me so? I should think you'd pity me."

Her cousin fingered the postcard. "Look at me." She rose in her trailing red dress. "Young, beautiful, educated,—and nobody wants me, nobody who is anybody will have me. The ash-contractor's son offers,—not asks,—to marry me. Mr Deaver," she looked long at the postcard, "liked me, wrote me,—once—"

"Why did he stop?" Angélique asked in all innocence.

Laurentine flushed on her. "Because of you. You little fool, because of you! Must I say it again? Because my mother was the victim of slavery. People looked at me when I was a little girl; they used to say: 'Her mother couldn't help it, and she is beautiful.' They would have forgotten all about it. Oh why did your mother have to bring you home with us! Now they see you and they say: 'What! And her mother too! A colored man this time. Broke up a home. No excuse for that. Bad blood there. Best leave them alone.'"

She looked at Angélique with a furious mounting hatred. "Well you'll know all about it too. Wait a few years longer. You'll never be as beautiful as I, but you'll be pretty. And you'll sit and watch the years go by, and dread to look in your mirror for fear of what you'll find there. And at night you'll curse God,—but pshaw you won't,—" she broke off scornfully, "you'll only cry—"

Angélique crept up to her room to contemplate a future like Laurentine's.

Hours later Aunt Sal come in, her inscrutable dark face showing a blurred patch against the grey of the room. In her hand something gleamed whitely.

"Thought you might want yore letter," she said in her emotionless, husky voice.

Her letter, her letter from Asshur! Her letter that would reiterate: "Be a good kid and I'll come for you. . . ."

She seized it and fell half-fainting in the old woman's arms. "Oh Asshur I'll be good, I'll be good! Oh Aunt Sal, help me, keep me. . . . "

FROM *THE CRISIS*, AUGUST–SEPTEMBER 1923

# M*ary Elizabeth*

## JESSIE REDMON FAUSET

Mary Elizabeth was late that morning. As a direct result, Roger left for work without telling me goodbye, and I spent most of the day fighting the headache which always comes if I cry.

For I cannot get a breakfast. I can manage a dinner, one just puts the roast in the oven and takes it out again. And I really excel in getting lunch. There is a good delicatessen near us, and with dainty service and flowers. I get along very nicely. But breakfast! In the first place, it's a meal I neither like nor need. And I never, if I live a thousand years, shall learn to like coffee. I suppose that is why I cannot make it.

"Roger," I faltered, when the awful truth burst upon me and I began to realize that Mary Elizabeth wasn't coming. "Roger, couldn't you get breakfast downtown this morning? You know last time you weren't so satisfied with my coffee."

Roger was hostile. I think he had just cut himself shaving. Anyway, he was horrid.

"No, I can't get my breakfast downtown!" He actually snapped at me. "Really, Sally, I don't believe there's another woman in the world who would send her husband out on a morning like this on an empty stomach. I don't see how you can be so unfeeling."

Well, it wasn't "a morning like this," for it was just the beginning of November. And I had only proposed his doing what I knew he would have to do eventually.

I didn't say anything more, but started on that breakfast. I don't know why I thought I had to have hot cakes! The breakfast really was awful! The cakes were tough and gummy and got cold one second, exactly, after I took them off the stove. And the coffee boiled, or stewed, or scorched, or did whatever the particular thing is that coffee shouldn't do. Roger sawed at one cake, took one mouthful of the dreadful brew, and pushed away his cup.

"It seems to me you might learn to make a decent cup of coffee," he said icily. Then he picked up his hat and flung out of the house.

I think it is stupid of me, too, not to learn how to make coffee. But really, I'm no worse than Roger is about lots of things. Take "Five Hundred." Roger knows I love cards, and with the Cheltons right around the corner from us and as fond of it as I am, we could spend many a pleasant evening. But Roger will not learn. Only the night before, after I had gone through a whole hand with him, with hearts as trumps, I dealt the cards around again to imaginary opponents and we started playing. Clubs were trumps, and spades led. Roger, having no spades, played triumphantly a Jack of Hearts and proceeded to take the trick.

"But Roger," I protested, "you threw off."

"Well," he said, deeply injured, "didn't you say hearts were trumps when you were playing before?"

And when I tried to explain, he threw down the cards and wanted to know what difference it made; he'd rather play casino, anyway! I didn't go out and slam the door.

But I couldn't help from crying this particular morning. I not only value Roger's good opinion, but I hate to be considered stupid.

Mary Elizabeth came in about eleven o'clock. She is a small, weazened woman, very dark, somewhat wrinkled, and a model of self-possession. I wish I could make you see her, or that I could reproduce her accent, not that it is especially colored,—Roger's and mine are much more so—but her pronunciation, her way of drawing out her vowels, is so distinctively Mary Elizabethan!

I was ashamed of my red eyes and tried to cover up my embarrassment with sternness.

"Mary Elizabeth," said I, "you are late!" Just as though she didn't know it.

"Yas'm, Mis' Pierson," she said, composedly, taking off her coat. She didn't remove her hat,—she never does until she has been in the house some two or three hours. I can't imagine why. It is a small, black, dusty affair, trimmed with black ribbon, some dingy white roses and a sheaf of wheat. I give Mary Elizabeth a dress and hat now and then but, although I recognize the dress from time to time, I never see any change in the hat. I don't know what she does with my ex-millinery.

"Yas'm," she said again, and looked comprehensively at the untouched breakfast dishes and the awful viands, which were still where Roger had left them.

"Looks as though you'd had to git breakfast yourself," she observed brightly. And went out in the kitchen and ate all those cakes and drank that unspeakable coffee. Really she did and she didn't warm them up either.

I watched her miserably, unable to decide whether Roger was too finicky or Mary Elizabeth a natural born diplomat.

"Mr. Gales led me an awful chase last night," she explained. "When I got home yestiddy evenin', my cousin whut keeps house for me (!) tole me Mr. Gales went out in the mornin' en hadn't come back."

"Mr. Gales," let me explain is Mary Elizabeth's second husband, an octogenarian, and the most original person, I am convinced, in existence.

"Yas'm," she went on, eating a final cold hot cake, "en I went to look fer 'im, en had the whole perlice station out all night huntin' 'im. Look like they wusn't never goin' to find 'im. But I ses, 'Jes' let me look fer enough en long enough en I'll find 'im,' I ses, en I did. Way out Georgy Avenue, with the hat on ole Mis' give 'im. Sent it to 'im all the way fum Chicago. He's had it fifteen years, high silk beaver. I knowed he wusn't goin' too fer with that hat on.

"I went up to 'im, settin' by a fence all muddy, holdin' his hat on with both hands. En I ses, 'Look here, man, you come erlong home with me, en let me put you to bed.' En he come jest as meek! No o-me, I knowed he wusn't goin' fer with ole Mis' hat on."

"Who was old 'Mis,' Mary Elizabeth?" I asked her.

"Lady I used to work fer in Noo York," she informed me. "Me en Rosy, the cook, lived with her fer years. Ole Mis' was turrible fond of me, though her en Rosy used to querrel all the time. Jes' seemed like they couldn't git erlong. 'Member once Rosy run after her one Sunday with a knife, en I kep 'em apart. Reckon Rosy musta bin right put out with ole Mis' that day. By en by her en Rosy move to Chicaga, en when I married Mr. Gales, she sent 'im that hat. That old white woman shore did like me. It's so late, reckon I'd better put off sweepin' tel termorrer, ma'am."

I acquiesced, following her about from room to room. This was partly to get away from my own doleful thoughts. Roger really had hurt my feelings but just as much to hear her talk. At first I used not to believe all she said, but after I investigated once and found her truthful in one amazing statement, I capitulated.

She had been telling me some remarkable tale of her first husband and I was listening with the stupefied attention to which she always reduces me. Remember she was speaking of her first husband.

"En I ses to 'im, I ses, 'Mr. Gale,—' "

"Wait a moment, Mary Elizabeth," I interrupted, meanly delighted to have caught her for once. "You mean your first husband, don't you?"

"Yas'm," she replied. "En I ses to 'im, Mr. Gale, I ses—' "

"But Mary Elizabeth," I persisted, "that's your second husband, isn't it,—Mr. Gale?"

She gave me her long drawn "No-o-me! My first husband was Mr. Gale and my second husband is Mr. *Gales*. He spells his name with a Z, I reckon. I ain't never see it writ. Ez I wus sayin' I ses to Mr. Gale—' "

*And it was true!* Since then I have never doubted Mary Elizabeth.

She was loquacious that afternoon. She told me about her sister, "where's got a home in the country and where's got eight children." I used to read Lucy Pratt's stories about little Ephraim or Ezekiel, I forget his name, who always said "where's" instead of "who's," but I never believed it really till I heard Mary Elizabeth use it. For some reason or other she never mentions her sister without mentioning the home too. "My sister where's got a home in the country" is her unvarying phrase.

"Mary Elizabeth," I asked her once, "does your sister live in the country, or does she simply own a house there?"

"Yas'm," she told me.

She is fond of her sister. "If Mr. Gales wus to die," she told me complacently, "I'd go to live with her."

"If he should die," I asked her idly, "would you marry again?"

"Oh, no-o-me!" She was emphatic. "Though I don't know why I shouldn't, I'd come by it hones'. My father wus married four times."

That shocked me out of my headache. "Four times, Mary Elizabeth, and you had all those stepmothers!" My mind refused to take it in.

"Oh, no-o-me! I always lived with mamma. She was his first wife."

I hadn't thought of people in the state in which I had instinctively placed Mary Elizabeth's father and mother as indulging in divorce, but as Roger says slangily, "I wouldn't know."

Mary Elizabeth took off the dingy hat. "You see, papa and mamma—"

the ineffable pathos of hearing this woman of sixty-four, with a husband of eighty, use the old childish terms!

"Papa and mamma wus slaves, you know, Mis' Pierson, and so of course they wusn't exackly married. White folks wouldn't let 'em. But they wus awf'ly in love with each other. Heard mamma tell erbout it lots of times, and how papa wus the han'somest man! Reckon she wus long erbout sixteen or seventeen then. So they jumped over a broomstick, en they wus jes as happy! But not long after I come erlong, they sold papa down South, and mamma never see him no mo' fer years and years. Thought he was dead. So she married again."

"And he came back to her, Mary Elizabeth?" I was overwhelmed with the woefulness of it.

"Yas'm. After twenty-six years. Me and my sister where's got a home in the country—she's really my half-sister, see Mis' Pierson,—her en mamma en my step-father en me wus all down in Bumpus, Virginia, workin' fer some white folks, and we used to live in a little cabin, had a front stoop to it. En one day an ole cullud man come by, had a lot o' whiskers. I'd saw him lots of times there in Bumpus, lookin' and peerin' into every cullud woman's face. En jes' then my sister she call out, 'Come here, you Ma'y Elizabeth,' en that old man stopped, en he looked at me en he looked at me, en he ses to me, 'Chile, is yo' name Ma'y Elizabeth?'

"You know, Mis' Pierson, I thought he wus jes' bein' fresh, en I ain't paid no 'tention to 'im. I ain't sed nuthin' ontel he spoke to me three or four times, en then I ses to 'im, 'Go 'way fum here, man, you ain't got no call to be fresh with me. I'm a decent woman. You'd oughta be ashamed of yorself, an ole man like you!"

Mary Elizabeth stopped and looked hard at the back of her poor wrinkled hands.

"En he says to me, 'Daughter,' he ses jes' like that, 'daughter,' he ses, 'hones' I ain't bein' fresh. Is yo' name shore enough Ma'y Elizabeth?'

"En I tole him, 'Yas'r,'

"'Chile,' he ses, 'whar is yo' daddy?'

"'Ain't got no daddy.' I tole him peart-like. 'They done tuk 'im away fum me twenty-six years ago, I wusn't but a mite of a baby. Sol' 'im down the river. My mother often talks about it.' And oh, Mis' Pierson, you shoulda see the glory come into his face!

"'Yore mother!' he ses, kinda out of breath, 'yore mother! Ma'y Elizabeth, whar is your mother?'

"'Back thar on the stoop,' I tole 'im. 'Why, did you know my daddy?'

"But he didn't pay no 'tention to me, jes' turned and walked up the stoop whar mamma wus settin'! She wus feelin' sorta porely that day. En you oughta see me steppin' erlong after 'im.

"He walked right up to her and giv' her one look. 'Oh, Maggie,' he shout out, 'oh, Maggie! Ain't you know me? Maggie, ain't you know me?'

"Mamma look at 'im and riz up outa her cheer. 'Who're you?' she ses kinda trimbly, callin' me Maggie thata way? Who're you?'

"He went up real close to her, then, 'Maggie,' he ses jes' like that, kinda sad 'n tender, 'Maggie!' and hel' out his arms.

"She walked right into them. 'Oh! she ses, it's Cassius! It's Cassius! It's my husban' come back to me! It's Cassius!' They wus like two mad people.

"My sister Minnie and me, we jes' stood and gawped at 'em. There they wus, holding on to each other like two pitiful childrun, en he tuk her hands and kissed 'em.

"'Maggie,' he ses, 'you'll come away with me, won't you? You gona take me back, Maggie? We'll go away, you en Ma'y Elizabeth en me. Won't we Maggie?'

"Reckon my mother clean forgot about my step-father. 'Yes, Cassius,' she ses, 'we'll go away.' And then she sees Minnie, en it all comes back to her. 'Oh, Cassius,' she ses 'I cain't go with you, I'm married again, en this time fer real. This here gal's mine and three boys, too, another chile comin' in November!'"

"But she went with him, Mary Elizabeth," I pleaded. "Surely she went with him after all those years. He really was her husband."

I don't know whether Mary Elizabeth meant to be sarcastic or not. "Oh, no-o-me, mamma couldn't a done that. She wus a good woman. Her ole master, whut done sol' my father down river, brung her up too religious fer that, en anyways, papa was married again, too. Had his fourth wife there in Bumpus with 'im."

The unspeakable tragedy of it!

I left her and went up to my room, and hunted out my dark blue serge dress which I had meant to wear again that winter. But I had to give Mary Elizabeth something, so I took the dress down to her.

She was delighted with it. I could tell she was, because she used her rare and untranslatable expletive.

"Haytian!" she said. "My sister where's got a home in the country, got a dress look somethin' like this but it ain't as good. No-o-me. She got hers to wear at a friend's weddin',—gal she wus riz up with. Thet gal married well, too, lemme tell you; her husband's a Sunday School sup'rintender."

I told her she needn't wait for Mr. Pierson, I would put dinner on the table. So off she went in the gathering dusk, trudging bravely back to her Mr. Gales and his high silk hat.

I watched her from the window till she was out of sight. It had been such a long time since I had thought of slavery. I was born in Pennsylvania, and neither my parents nor grandparents had been slaves; otherwise I might have had the same tale to tell as Mary Elizabeth, or worse yet, Roger and I might have lived in those black days and loved and lost each other and futilely, damnably, met again like Cassius and Maggie.

Whereas it was now, and I had Roger and Roger had me.

How I loved him as I sat there in the hazy dark. I thought of his dear, bronze perfection, his habit of swearing softly in excitement, his blessed stupidity. Just the same I didn't meet him at the door as usual, but pretended to be busy. He came rushing to me with the *Saturday Evening Post*, which is more to me than rubies. I thanked him warmly, but aloofly, if you can get that combination.

We ate dinner almost in silence for my part. But he praised everything,—the cooking, the table, my appearance.

After dinner we went up to the little sitting-room. He hoped I wasn't tired,—couldn't he fix the pillows for me? So!

I opened the magazine and the first thing I saw was a picture of a woman gazing in stony despair at the figure of a man disappearing around the bend of the road. It was too much. Suppose that were Roger and I! I'm afraid I sniffled. He was at my side in a moment.

"Dear loveliest! Don't cry. It was all my fault. You aren't any worse about coffee than I am about cards! And anyway, I needn't have slammed the door! Forgive me, Sally. I always told you I was hard to get along with. I've had a horrible day,—don't stay cross with me, dearest."

I held him to me and sobbed outright on his shoulder. "It isn't you, Roger," I told him, "I'm crying about Mary Elizabeth."

I regret to say he let me go then, so great was his dismay. Roger will never be half the diplomat that Mary Elizabeth is.

"Holy smokes!" he groaned. "She isn't going to leave us for good, is she?"

So then I told him about Maggie and Cassius. "And oh, Roger," I ended futilely, "to think that they had to separate after all those years, when he had come back, old and with whiskers!" I didn't mean to be so banal, but I was crying too hard to be coherent.

Roger had got up and was walking the floor, but he stopped then aghast.

"Whiskers!" he moaned. "My hat! Isn't that just like a woman?" He had to clear his throat once or twice before he could go on, and I think he wiped his eyes.

"Wasn't it the—" I really can't say what Roger said here,—"wasn't it the darndest hard luck that when he did find her again, she should be married? She might have waited."

I stared at him astounded. "But, Roger," I reminded him, "he had married three other times, he didn't wait."

"Oh—!" said Roger, unquotable, "married three fiddlesticks! He only did that to try to forget her."

Then he came over and knelt beside me again. "Darling, I do think it is a sensible thing for a poor woman to learn how to cook, but I don't care as long as you love me and we are together. Dear loveliest, if I had been Cassius," he caught my hands so tight he hurt them,—"and I had married fifty times and had come back and found you married to someone else, I'd have killed you, killed you."

Well, he wasn't logical, but he was certainly convincing.

So thus, and not otherwise, Mary Elizabeth healed the breach.

From *The Crisis*, December 1919

# Wedding Day

## GWENDOLYN BENNETT

His name was Paul Watson and as he shambled down rue Pigalle he might have been any other Negro of enormous height and size. But as I have said, his name was Paul Watson. Passing him on the street, you might not have known or cared who he was, but any one of the residents about the great Montmartre district of Paris could have told you who he was as well as many interesting bits of his personal history.

He had come to Paris in the days before colored jazz bands were the style. Back home he had been a prize fighter. In the days when Joe Gans was in his glory Paul was following the ring, too. He didn't have that fine way about him that Gans had and for that reason luck seemed to go against him. When he was in the ring he was like a mad bull, especially if his opponent was a white man. In those days there wasn't any sympathy or nicety about the ring and so pretty soon all the ring masters got down on Paul and he found it pretty hard to get a bout with anyone. Then it was that he worked his way across the Atlantic Ocean on a big liner—in the days before colored jazz bands were the style in Paris.

Things flowed along smoothly for the first few years with Paul's working here and there in the unfrequented places of Paris. On the side he used to give boxing lessons to aspiring youths or gymnastic young women. At that time he was working so steadily that he had little chance to find out what was going on around Paris. Pretty soon, however, he grew to be known among the trainers and managers began to fix up bouts for him. After one or two successful bouts a little fame began to come into being for him. So it was that after one of the prize-fights, a colored fellow came to his dressing room to congratulate him on his success as well as invite him to go to Montmartre to meet "the boys."

Paul had a way about him and seemed to get on with the colored fellows who lived in Montmartre and when the first Negro jazz band played in a tiny Parisian cafe Paul was among them playing the banjo. Those first years were without event so far as Paul was concerned. The members of that first band often say now that they wonder how it was that nothing happened during those first seven years, for it was generally known how great was Paul's hatred for American white people. I suppose the tranquility in the light of what happened afterwards was due to the fact that the cafe in which they worked was one in which mostly French people drank and danced and then too, that was before there were so many Americans visiting Paris. However, everyone had heard Paul speak of his intense hatred of white folks. It only took two Benedictines to make him start talking about what he would do to the first "Yank" that called him "nigger." But the seven years came to an end and Paul Watson went to work in a larger cafe with a larger band, patronized almost solely by Americans.

I've heard almost every Negro in Montmartre tell about the night that a drunken Kentuckian came into the cafe where Paul was playing and said:

"Look heah, Bruther, what you all doin' ovah heah?"

"None ya bizness. And looka here, I ain't your brother, see?"

"Jack, do you heah that nigger talkin' lak that tah me?"

As he said this, he turned to speak to his companion. I have often wished that I had been there to have seen the thing myself. Every tale I have heard about it was different and yet there was something of truth in each of them. Perhaps the nearest one can come to the truth is by saying that Paul beat up about four full-sized white men that night besides doing a great deal of damage to the furniture about the cafe. I couldn't tell you just what did happen. Some of the fellows say that Paul seized the nearest table and mowed down men right and left, others say he took a bottle, then again the story runs that a chair was the instrument of his fury. At any rate, that started Paul Watson on his siege against the American white person who brings his native prejudices into the life of Paris.

It is a verity that Paul was the "black terror." The last syllable of the word, nigger, never passed the lips of a white man without the quick reflex action of Paul's arm and fist to the speaker's jaw. He paid for more glassware and cafe furnishings in the course of the next few years than is easily imaginable. And yet, there was something likable about Paul. Perhaps that's the reason that he stood in so well with the policemen of the neighborhood. Always some divine power seemed to intervene in his behalf and he was excused after the payment of a small fine with advice about his future conduct. Finally, there came the night when in a frenzy he shot the two American sailors.

They had not died from the wounds he had given them; hence his sentence had not been one of death but rather a long term of imprisonment. It was a pitiable sight to see Paul sitting in the corner of his cell with his great body hunched almost double. He seldom talked and when he did his words were interspersed with oaths about the lowness of "crackers." Then the World War came.

It seems strange that anything so horrible as that wholesale slaughter could bring about any good and yet there was something of a smoothing quality about even its baseness. There has never been such equality before or since such as that which the World War brought. Rich men fought by the side of paupers; poets swapped yarns with dry-goods salesmen, while Jews and Christians ate corned beef out of the same tin. Along with the general leveling influence came France's pardon of her prisoners in order that they might enter the army. Paul Watson became free and a French soldier. Because he was strong and had innate daring in his heart he was placed in the aerial squad and cited many times for bravery. The close of the war gave him his place in French society as a hero. With only a memory of the war and an ugly scar on his left cheek he took up his old life.

His firm resolutions about American white people still remained intact and many chance encounters that followed the war are told from lip to lip proving that the war and his previous imprisonment had changed him little. He was the same Paul Watson to Montmartre as he shambled up rue Pigalle.

Rue Pigalle in the early evening has a sombre beauty—gray as are most Paris streets and other-worldish. To those who know the district it is the Harlem of Paris and rue Pigalle is its dusky Seventh Avenue. Most of the colored musicians that furnish Parisians and their visitors with entertainment live somewhere in the neighborhood of rue Pigalle. Some time during every day each of these musicians makes a point of passing through rue Pigalle. Little wonder that almost any day will find Paul Watson going his shuffling way up the same street.

He reached the corner of rue de la Bruyere and with sure instinct his feet stopped. Without half thinking he turned into "the Pit." Its full name is The Flea Pit. If you should ask one of the musicians why it was so called, he would answer you to the effect that it was called "the pit" because all the "fleas" hang out there. If you did not get the full import of this explanation, he would go further and say that there were always "spades" in the pit and they were as thick as fleas. Unless you could understand this latter attempt at clarity you could not fully grasp what the Flea-Pit means to the Negro musicians in Montmartre. It is a tiny cafe of the genus that is called *bistro* in France. Here the fiddle players, saxophone blowers, drum-beaters and ivory ticklers gather at four in the afternoon for a porto or a game of billiards. Here the cabaret entertainers and supper musicians meet at one o'clock at night or thereafter for a whiskey and soda, or more billiards. Occasional sandwiches and a "quiet game" also play their parts in the popularity of the place. After a season or two it becomes a settled fact just what time you may catch so-and-so at the famous "Pit."

The musicians were very fond of Paul and took particular delight in teasing him. He was one of the chosen few that all of the musicians conceded as being "regular." It was the pet joke of the habitues of the cafe that Paul never bothered with girls. They always said that he could beat up ten men but was scared to death of one woman.

"Say fellow, when ya goin' a get hooked up?"

"Can't say, Bo. Ain't so much on skirts."

"Man alive, ya don't know what you're missin'—somebody little and cute telling ya sweet things in your ear. Paris is full of women folks."

"I ain't much on 'em all the same. Then too, they're all white."

"What's it to ya? This ain't America."

"Can't help that. Get this—I'm collud, see? I ain't got nothing for no white meat to do. If a woman eva called me nigger I'd have to kill her, that's all!"

"You for it, son. I can't give you a thing on this Mr. Jefferson Lawd way of lookin' at women."

"Oh, tain't that. I guess they're all right for those that wants 'em. Not me!"

"Oh you ain't so forty. You'll fall like all the other spades I've ever seen. Your kind falls hardest."

And so Paul went his way—alone. He smoked and drank with the fellows and sat for hours in the Montmartre cafes and never knew the companionship of a woman. Then one night after his work he was walking along the street in his queer shuffling way when a woman stepped up to his side.

"Voulez vous."

"Naw, gowan away from here."

"Oh, you speak English, don't you?"

"You an 'merican woman?"

"Used to be 'fore I went on the stage and got stranded over here."

"Well, get away from here. I don't like your kind!"

"Aw, Buddy, don't say that. I ain't prejudiced like some fool women."

"You don't know who I am, do you? I'm Paul Watson and I hate American white folks, see?"

He pushed her aside and went on walking alone. He hadn't gone far when she caught up to him and said with sobs in her voice:—

"Oh, Lordy, please don't hate me 'cause I was born white and an American. I ain't got a sou to my name and all the men pass me by cause I ain't spruced up. Now you come along and won't look at me 'cause I'm white."

Paul strode along with her clinging to his arm. He tried to shake her off several times but there was no use. She clung all the more desperately to him. He looked down at her frail body shaken with sobs, and something caught at his heart. Before he knew what he was doing he had said:—

"Naw, I ain't that mean. I'll get you some grub. Quit your cryin'. Don't like seein' women folks cry."

It was the talk of Montmartre. Paul Watson takes a woman to Gavarnni's every night for dinner. He comes to the Flea Pit less frequently, thus giving the other musicians plenty of opportunity to discuss him.

"How times do change. Paul, the woman-hater, has a Jane now."

"You ain't said nothing, fella. That ain't all. She's white and an 'merican too."

"That's the way with these spades. They beat up all the white men they can lay their hands on but as soon as a gang of golden hair with blue eyes rubs up close to them they forget all they ever said about hatin' white folks."

"Guess he thinks that skirt's gone on him. Dumb fool!"

"Don' be no chineeman. That old gag don' fit for Paul. He cain't understand it no more'n we can. Says he jess can't help himself, everytime she looks up into his eyes and asks him does he love her. They sure are happy together. Paul's goin' to marry her, too. At first she kept saying that she didn't want to get married cause she wasn't the marrying kind and all that talk. Paul jus' laid down the law to her and told her he never would live with no woman without being married to her. Then she began to tell him all about her past life. He told her he didn't care nothing about what she used to be jus' so long as they loved each other now. Guess they'll make it."

"Yeah, Paul told me the same tale last night. He's sure gone on her all right."

"They're gettin' tied up next Sunday. So glad it's not me. Don't trust these American dames. Me for the Frenchies."

"She ain't so worse for looks, Bud. Now that he's been furnishing the green for the rags."

"Yeah, but I don't see no reason for the wedding bells. She was right—she ain't the marrying kind."

. . . and so Montmartre talked. In every cafe where the Negro musicians congregated Paul Watson was the topic for conversation. He had suddenly fallen from his place as bronze God to almost less than the dust.

The morning sun made queer patterns on Paul's sleeping face. He grimaced several times in his slumber, then finally half-opened his eyes. After a succession of dream-laden blinks he gave a great yawn, and rubbing his eyes, looked at the open window through which the sun shone brightly. His first conscious thought was that this was the bride's day and that bright sunshine prophesied happiness for the bride throughout her married life. His first impulse was to settle back into the covers and think drowsily about Mary and the queer twists life brings about, as is the wont of most bridegrooms on their last morning of bachelorhood. He put this impulse aside in favor of dressing quickly and rushing downstairs to telephone to Mary to say "happy wedding day" to her.

One huge foot slipped into a worn bedroom slipper and then the other dragged painfully out of the warm bed were the courageous beginnings of his bridal toilette. With a look of triumph he put on his new gray suit that he had ordered from an English tailor. He carefully pulled a taffeta tie into place beneath his chin, noting as he looked at his face in the mirror that the scar he had received in the army was very ugly—funny, marrying an ugly man like him.

French telephones are such human faults. After trying for about fifteen minutes to get Central 32.01 he decided that he might as well walk around to Mary's hotel to give his greeting as to stand there in the lobby of his own, wasting his time. He debated this in his mind a great deal. They were to be married at four o'clock. It was eleven now and it did seem a shame not to let her have a minute or two by herself. As he went walking down the street towards her hotel he laughed to think of how one always cogitates over doing something and finally does the thing he wanted to in the beginning anyway.

Mud on his nice gray suit that the English tailor had made for him. Damn—gray suit—what did he have a gray suit on for, anyway. Folks with black faces shouldn't wear gray suits. Gawd, but it was funny that time when he beat up that cracker at the Periquet. Fool couldn't shut his mouth he was so surprised. Crackers—damn 'em—he was one nigger that wasn't 'fraid of 'em. Wouldn't he have a hell of a time if he went back to America where black was black. Wasn't white nowhere, black wasn't. What was that thought he was trying to get ahold of—bumping around in his head—something he started to think about but couldn't remember it somehow.

The shrill whistle that is typical of the French subway pierced its way into his thoughts. Subway—why was he in the subway—he didn't want to go any place. He heard doors slamming and saw the blue uniforms of the conductors swinging on the cars as the trains began to pull out of the station. With one or two strides he reached the last coach as it began to move up the platform. A bit out of breath he stood inside the train and looking down at what he had in his hand he saw that it was a tiny pink ticket. A first class ticket in a second class coach. The idea set him to laughing. Everyone in the car turned and eyed him, but that did not bother him. Wonder what stop he'd get off—funny how these French said descend when they meant get off—funny he couldn't pick up French—been here so long. First class ticket in a second class coach!— that was one on him. Wedding day today, and that damn letter from Mary. How'd she say it now, "just couldn't go through with it," white women just don't marry colored men, and she was a street woman, too. Why couldn't she have told him flat that she was just getting back on her feet at his expense. Funny that first class ticket he bought, wish he could see Mary—him a-going there to wish her "happy wedding day," too. Wonder what that French woman was looking at him so hard for? Guess it was the mud.

FROM *FIRE!!* NOVEMBER 1926

# F*ree*

## GEORGIA DOUGLAS JOHNSON

The funeral was over. The wife and the mistress sat facing each other in the old fashioned parlor of their common home, waiting for the will to be read. A September drizzle had set in and lent to the somber air of the house an added gloom. Stray bits of faded leaves and flowers from the many lovely floral wreathes were here and there upon the green plush carpet that covered the rectangular surface of the quiet room. Nashville had not seen such a long procession of carriages as had curled through her narrow streets at this noon hour in many a year. Dr. Ryan had been very popular. These two strangely linked women had just returned from the cemetery where all that remained of the tie that bound them, the late Paul Ryan—had been laid to rest. What would happen now that his portly, beaming, and genial personality had left them—poles apart together?

As Martha Ryan, hidden in the thick crepe of her black veil sat in church, her mind was darting here and there, picking at the tangled threads of her life. What would she do now? Always he had made decisions for her, now he lay there so still and cold in front of the altar as the preacher's voice threw sweet flattering words across his upturned face. Yes, always he had decided. Even when she had tried once to put her foot down on his bringing this young woman Rose Delaney to live

*55*

right in the house with them, twenty-five years ago . . . twenty-five long years! Had called her his new nurse, her lips curled in derision. For her, this baby-eyed woman, he had decided against her, his own wife. But the whole town knew the truth . . . you can't throw dust in people's eyes . . . nurse . . . nurse forsooth! And what could she do about it? Nothing, she was old and the girl was young!

Out of one corner of her eye she could see Rose's head bowed beside her. She was weeping, and well she might, for now, her protector was gone and she herself was boss. At last, boss in her own house, and out she'd go! Her friends had taunted her long enough, she'd show them how she'd handle the situation. Martha tightened her lips in determination. Tears, tears, let her cry, cry her eyes out. He'd stood between them and taken her part! Protected her against his own wife. Men were queer. Yet he had been good to her. She'd had nothing, nothing of which to complain but this, this one thing. Strange how numb and far-away like she had felt at the funeral, not like it was her own dead she was burying, but maybe the feeling would come later and then. . . . So now, here she was back home at last, waiting, waiting to hear his last commands!

The clock on the mantle struck two. Martha shivered. Lawyer Green had promised to follow them from the funeral. He should be here now. Said he just had to stop by his office and get the will. The will! What did it say? Would it leave her anything? Yes, she guessed it would. Something anyhow, so's she could go away—somewhere! Martha sighed, free, free from her at last!

Rose Delaney sitting across from Mrs. Ryan, her black hat a little awry, had noted the sigh and seen the shiver. She was keenly aware of her deep agitation. Something called to her from this woman's silence . . . she had always administered to her, served her . . . she needed her even now. Interestingly, she arose, casting a solicitous glance toward the brooding woman as she announced timidly that she was going to make a cup of hot tea. "You're chilly," she added, "it was awfully damp under foot at the cemetery."

A faint sound came from Mrs. Ryan's throat, whether of approval or not Rose couldn't make out, but she passed on out to the little kitchen where the soft tinkle of china was soon heard.

To make a cup of tea was an easy pleasure for Rose. She liked to serve, but somehow, today her hands seemed strangely awkward and she stumbled as she moved about the little kitchen. She was saying "Goodbye, Goodbye," to every little pot and pan that hung so shiny on the wall. She had loved to make them shine, for the woman with sad, sad questioning eyes liked them so. She had done her best. The day was over and now she must go—go away from this refuge that she had learned to love, this home, hers no longer.

As she placed the little silver tray before the tense woman with the steaming odor of the fragrant tea stealing upward she thought she detected a faint softening of her face, a small relaxation of the set jaw. She wasn't sure.

Sitting there with her hat still slantwise on her bowed head, Rose looked like a lonely traveler who sits in the station without a time table waiting for the next train with no fixed destination—just going!

A ring at the front door. Rose jumped, "It must be Lawyer Green," she murmured. She started for the door, then stopped suddenly and looked toward Mrs. Ryan; she was conscious of the new situation, its tenseness—was she expected to go—There was no movement, no sign from the still woman bent over her tea. Rose walked toward the door. As she moved away, Mrs. Ryan gradually raised her head and fixed her gaze upon Rose's retreating form. She had not been unmindful of Rose's hesitation about the door—aha! She had realized at once the change that had come about—she wasn't sure of herself anymore, not that she had been forward before, in fact, she had always deferred to her, served her well, had been kind and considerate, nursing her, but as her eyes followed the form moving bent and slow, another thought—another thought awoke like a thunder-clap in her mind! A new thought, so strangely new that she felt stunned . . . this woman who moved so slowly before her was not a young woman—she was old! old!!! Rose too was old. The years had passed and even Rose had lost her youth.

Mrs. Ryan was sitting in a kind of daze when Rose led Lawyer Green into the room. She paid no heed to his apologetic words, just sat gazing into space. Her mind had rushed back over the years to that day so long ago when Rose had first come into her home—a lovely young brown-eyed girl. Breaking away from her thoughts she fastened her eyes upon Rose as upon a stranger. This woman was new to her, new in her oldness. There was something sweet and comforting in the thought.

The tall solemn faced lawyer dropped awkwardly into a chair. He had a difficult duty to perform.

"I ask you two ladies to hear the will at once because—because . . . " He cleared his throat in embarrassment, then finished, "I thought it best for you both to have an understanding."

Placing his horn-rimmed glasses firmly on his nose, he looked at both women apprehensively and began reading: "I, Paul Ryan, being of sound mind—." He read on and on. There were several small bequests to former patients and to the hospital, and then—"The house and all my remaining property I bequeath and devise to my wife Martha Ryan, and my adopted daughter, Rose Delaney, equally share and share alike—"

The eyes of the two women met, hung together for a moment, and then Rose's glance fell.

The lawyer finished and again cleared his throat. "I'm sorry."

"I'm sorry," Rose whispered faintly. "I'll go away of course, Mrs. Ryan."

"Either of you can sell your share of the house to the other," the lawyer added. "You'd be willing to sell wouldn't you, Miss Delaney?"

"Oh certainly yes—anything Mrs. Ryan suggests will be all right with me. I'll cause no trouble at all. Now if you will excuse me I'll get a few things together and be leaving." She looked bewilderedly about her and stumbled from the room.

Lawyer Green looked at the set face of the widowed woman, arose and tried to offer some further advice. "Everything will be all right, I'm sure, Mrs. Ryan. Just consult me when you've come to a decision. The will is a little peculiar, but—ah—ah—the situation is a bit unusual."

She continued to hold the door ajar, her eyes following the lawyer's retreating form as it grew dimmer and dimmer and then vanished far down the street.

How quiet it was, both outside and in. Not a sound. Death-like in the street. She closed the door—still, how still inside. Her footfall was hushed in the red velvet carpet. Her world had come to an end—All things had come to an end.

Descending the stairs slowly came a bowed figure. She seemed to be feeling her way blindly, one hand slipping along the balustrade, the other holding a brown valise.

Martha stood near the door—waiting. She wondered why she waited. She didn't know. . . . Was it to say "Good-bye?" Did you stop to say "Good-bye" when you were asking, even demanding that some one should leave your house?

Rose knew that she was waiting for her to go—had waited for twenty-five years, waited for this moment for nearly a life-time!

Nearer and nearer crept the drooping form—she came alongside, set down the valise and slowly lifted her swimming eyes to Martha's face. Haltingly, how haltingly, she formed the words—her throat tightening like cords about them, they seemed squeezed from it.

"Well, well, I'll . . . be . . . go i n g. . . . " Martha's lips pressed more firmly together, her eyes following Rose's every move as she bent down to pick up the valise. A kind of stupor seemed to hold her speechless, she just watched and watched. Why didn't she say, "It's time you were going!" But no, she just stood still and watched wordless. Motionless.

How still the house was. Still and empty. It would be more still and empty. . . there would be no one to do little things for her . . . nurse her . . . comfort her . . . decide for her . . . no one to lean upon. . . . With a start she awoke to the moment. . . . Rose was going, her hand was turning the knob. . . . Martha watched with growing panic. . . . Rose paused a moment on the threshold, she looked back! and then Mrs. Ryan flung open her arms and cried brokenly, "Rose!"

UNKNOWN SOURCE, THE LIBRARY OF CONGRESS, HARMON FOUNDATION FILES, C. 1926–1930

# F*uneral*

## DOROTHY WEST

### I

Judy could not feel her mother. Nowhere in the wide expanse of bed was her large, warm body. And Judy dared not peer under the bed to see if some desperado had killed and concealed her. Tremors ran up and down her small body. Her hands grew hot and damp, and her feet quite cold and clammy. She wanted to scream for one of the aunts but could not.

Someone was creaking up the stairs. It was probably the desperado come back to finish off her. She shut her eyes tightly and tried to think of Jesus.

The blackness was suddenly thinned with silver. A drawer opened and shut. She heard her mother's unmistakable sniff and opened her eyes.

"You go back to sleep," said the mother.

But Judy sat up and stared solemnly. "You're crying."

"You go back to sleep," said the mother.

There was movement in the aunts' room. Judy could hear her father blowing his nose. A terrible fear wrenched her heart.

"Mums, mums, is my kitty dead?"

The mother laughed sharply and bitterly. "The hospital 'phoned. Poor Uncle Eben has passed away."

Judy lay back on her pillow. "Has he gone somewhere?" she asked doubtfully.

"He's gone home to God," said the mother with conviction.

Judy closed her eyes to shut out the comic image of an angelic Uncle Eben. When she opened them again it was day and time to get up for school.

She dressed leisurely. She had the realization that it did not matter whether she was late for school. She thought, "There is death in my family," and was proud.

She would go and say *good morning* to the aunts. The frail spinster sisters of her father adored her, and she liked to be petted. She always let a lock of hair hang over one eye, so that the favorite aunt might brush it away with a caressing hand and kiss her forehead.

The aunts sat silently by their coal fire. They were dressed in black. Their plain, dark faces were gaunt. Their hands were not steady in their laps.

Judy felt chilled and distressed. She went awkwardly to the favorite aunt and leaned against her knee. But the somber face was alien, and the unquiet hands did not flutter to her hair.

The elder aunt turned quietly to her sister. "Do you think the child has heard?"

"God spare her," said the favorite aunt, piously.

"Do you mean," Judy asked shrilly, "about Uncle Eben?"

The sharpness of it knifed their pathetic silence. Their mute mouths quivered. Their stricken eyes overflowed.

The image of Uncle Eben returned. But he was no longer amusing in robe and wings. Judy's breast burned. Her throat ached. She knew with intense agony that she was going to cry.

She turned and fled the room, gained her own, and flung herself prone on the bed. She burrowed her mouth in the pillow. She did not weep because Uncle Eben was dead. She wept out of a vast pity at the anguish of the living.

When she had quieted, she rose and bathed her heated face. She got together her little pile of books, set her cap on her tousled hair, slung her thick sweater over her arm, and went down the stairs.

The aunts had preceded her. They sat at the kitchen table drinking black coffee. The large and lovely yellow mother was eating heartily ham and eggs.

That strengthened Judy. She sat down and smiled.

"Don't you be late," said the mother.

The familiar greeting shut the door fast on Uncle Eben. The aunts were simply in dark clothes. This was the usual Tuesday morning.

"Can I have two pieces of cake in my lunch?" asked Judy.

Presently she was going down the long hill to the schoolhouse. She walked in the sun and lifted her face to the intermittent calls of wooing birds. Spring was just around the nearest corner, and Judy was glad.

She shot into her seat as the last bell rang.

Eulalie whispered to the back of her head: "I spent two hours on this beastly history."

Judy's mind raced back to the schoolroom. "I've not studied it!"

"Oh, Judy! First period, too!"

"I went and forgot! What on earth made me go and forget? I always do it first thing every morning." She thought sharply. "It was my uncle's dying! My Uncle Eben died, Eulalie."

"Oh!" said Eulalie, looking sorry.

Nora leaned out into the aisle. Her eyes were wide with sympathy. "Is there death in your family, Judy?"

A thrill of pride ran down Judy's spine. Her breath quickened. Her eyes were like stars.

"It's my Uncle Eben who lived in a Home on account of being blind."

"Did he die on account of being blind?" Eulalie ventured.

"I expect," quoted Judy glibly, "he had another stroke."

"But why did you come to school?" Nora wanted to know. "Death's very sad. My mummy puts away all our toys and pulls down the shades."

"I think," advised Eulalie, "you ought to tell teacher."

Judy was suddenly shy. She had not thought Uncle Eben's death quite warranted her telling Miss Doran. It was strange and thrilling to her, because she had never before known death in its immediacy. It would embarrass her acutely if Miss Doran stared coldly and questioningly. Still, Eulalie had spoken with some authority. And Judy liked to watch the transformation of people's faces.

She got up from her seat, flung up her small head, and went down the aisle. The class with one accord straightened and craned. Judy, under this undeviating concentration, felt that her head was waggling, and was conscious of her isolated darkness.

Miss Doran looked up, frowned, and laid down her pen. At a glance Judy saw that she had been preparing a history quiz. She grew panicky, and this nervousness sent quick tears to her eyes. Miss Doran's face smoothed and softened. The unexpected gentleness further confused her. She said miserably, with a catch in her voice, "My Uncle Eben's dead."

Her words rang out clearly in the quiet room. There was an audible gasp. Then Judy could hear the triumphant whispering of Eulalie and Nora.

Miss Doran's arms went about her. "Judy, dear child, I'm sorry. Shall you want to return home, darling, or did your mother think it best to get you away from it all this morning?"

Judy was ashamed. She did not know how to tell Miss Doran that the momentous Thing was not lying importantly in her mother's parlor, but was somewhere in a vast hospital whose name she could not remember. She dreaded Miss Doran's jerking away from her in scorn. After all, families were huge affairs. Perhaps, to an experienced woman like Miss Doran, only death in the house really mattered.

Judy could not lie. "No'm," she said unhappily.

Miss Doran did not understand. "Then, of course, I excuse you, Judy. I cannot expect you to have your mind on your studies. Stay out in the open as much as you can. You need not return until after the funeral."

With a gentle pat she sent the child out. The class stared after her as one might stare after a favorite heroine.

Judy went racing down the corridor, her mind caught away to adventure. She knew that tomorrow her mother would pack her off to school again. But today was hers. And she had a quarter in her pocket. For the first time in her ten years, she was out on her own. She would poke her nose down various streets and browse in the library. She would eat her lunch on a park bench and buy a bag of candy. She would ride to the end of the car line and back. If she dared, she would even venture into an inexpensive movie. Death in the family was a holiday.

II

The exciting morning passed.

Father continually flipped out an enormous black-bordered handkerchief. He had on a black tie and an uncomfortable collar. He also had on Uncle Eben's shoes and hat and overcoat. Mother had said that with Uncle Eben's closetful of good black clothes simply hanging in the Home, it was foolish of father to buy a funeral outfit. Father had called a cab. Judy had begged the ride. They had come back fairly sitting on top of Uncle Eben's belongings.

The aunts were shrouded in long black veils. Only the whites of their eyes glimmered, and their sparse teeth when they talked.

The lovely, flushed mother had flung back her becoming short veil. Judy thought her mother was beautiful. They smiled at each other.

Judy had on the dark dress that she wore on rainy days. The favorite aunt had bought her a pair of black silk stockings. When she passed the hall mirror, she slyly admired them.

Somebody rang the bell. The father said meaningly: "It's the autymobile, I guess." The mother, with an apologetic look, pulled down her veil.

Judy did not want to get out of the car. She wished that she were a baby and could kick and scream, or that she were nearer the mother and could wheedle. But then she remembered that she meant to be a great writer and must welcome every experience. She got out bravely.

A light-skinned lady in a crumpled frock led them into a parlor. She made little noises in her throat and told them she was sorry. Judy caught the terrifying word body, and went and cowered against the window. The father and the mother and the aunts disappeared.

But in a moment the favorite aunt was back and beckoning her.

"You must come and look at him, Judy. He's beautiful."

Judy prayed, "God, don't let his teeth click," and crossed the threshold.

A dozen familiar and unfamiliar people sat in a small room on insecure chairs. A pretty woman peered into an open box and made the sign of the cross. About the box were unattractive bunches of fresh and wilted flowers. Judy knew suddenly that this was a coffin and that Uncle Eben was in it. She trailed after the favorite aunt like a young lamb to the slaughter.

"Smile down at him, Judy."

A curious Thing made in the image of an unhappy man lay in a satin-lined casket. If Judy dared touch the smooth, dark cheek, she would find it a brown clay in her hand. She wished she could ask her mother, who alone might understand, whether Uncle Eben was somewhere else and this was a plaster cast.

"Go sit by your mother," whispered the favorite aunt.

Judy tiptoed to the uncertain seat in the front row and sat quietly, her hands folded in her lap and her ankles crossed.

Slowly she became aware that the dim blob protruding above the rim of the casket was the tip of a nose. She was bewitched and held and gradually horrified.

But her horror was caught away by the violent sound of the father's sobs. She jerked up her head and stared at him.

In all of her life she had never seen a man cry. To her tears were the weakness of children and women, who had not the courage of men. She was fascinated and appalled. The father's head wobbled weakly. He made strangled snorts in his throat. Tears streamed down his cheeks and ran into the corners of his mouth. His nose dripped.

She was ashamed. Her own eyes filled with tears. Her body burned. She thought in extremist torture, "My father is weak, and I am the child of my father. . . . "

The mother bent to her. "Judy, comfort your father."

She swayed as if she had been struck.

"He musn't cry like that, Judy."

She raised her sick eyes to her mother's face. "Mummy, what do I do?"

"Just slip your hand into his. He loves you, Judy."

That did not move her. A stranger wept beside her. She felt her stomach collapse. With a great effort she kept herself steady. Had the father's life depended upon it, she could not have stretched out a soothing hand.

"Mummy," she cried, "I can't!" and burrowed against her.

An oily yellow man in a tight frock coat leaned down to the mother. "Are you pleased with the body?"

"He's beautiful," said the mother.

"For much or little I turn 'em out the same. I'd appreciate your coming to me whenever—God forbid!—you have to."

He swung out a heavy watch and said humorously, "Our kind of people!"

"Yes. Service was set for three," said the mother primly.

"Our kind of people," he repeated. "That cullud preacher is probably somewheres chewing the rag with Sister Fullbosom."

The mother and the undertaker laughed softly.

There was a small stir in the back of the room. Somebody importantly rushed down the length of it. The undertaker bustled to the newcomer's side nd led him to the small pulpit. With a careless glance at the body, the young preacher shifted out of his coat, glanced at his watch, cleared his throat, and plunged into a wailing spiritual that grew in volume and poignancy as the rest of the mourners joined in.

The aunts, too, swayed and moaned in unison. Presently, the father lifted his head and keened. But Judy did not want the mother to sing. She did not want to feel the swell of song from stomach to bosom and throat. She held her head tight against the mother to stem the rise of it.

The song hushed at the last stanza. The chorus whimpered out in a muted medley of unmusical voices. The preacher fumbled in his pocket, took out several soiled bits of paper, extracted and unfolded a rumpled sheet, and clamped on his glasses.

He stared at the illegible name of the deceased and slurred over it. He read automatically: "Born March 2, 1868, in Charleston, South Carolina. Died April 3, 1919, in this city. He rounded fifty-one years. Professed religion at the age of eighteen. Married wife, Mary, who died in childbirth in 1894. Came North, entered Pullman service, and was faithful servitor for twenty years. Was retired and pensioned, after total blindness, in 1914. He was never known to touch liquor or cards. He lived humble, and served his God, and died in the arms of Jesus at two a. m. Tuesday morning. He leaves a sorrowing brother and his wife, and two sorrowing sisters, and a sorrowing niece to mourn their loss."

Judy pulled at her mother. "Mums, why did he read that? What did he say it for? What did he mean about our sorrowing?"

The mother shrugged impatiently, thought a bit, and yielded kindly: "It's an obituary, Judy, and God knows we are sorry."

Suddenly to Judy this word that she had never heard before became a monstrous symbol, not of life but of one's living. She drew away from her mother. Her mind strained toward the understanding of this new discovery. She must think it through like a woman.

She thought with shame: I have not really cried for Uncle Eben. I am not really a sorrowing niece . . . . She shut her eyes against the unreality of the casket. And then she was a little girl again, just five, and had on Uncle Eben's glasses, and was bouncing on his knee. But she found herself sliding to the floor. The ludicrous glasses fell from her nose and shattered. She pricked her finger, blood spurted, and she screamed. Above her scream rose Uncle Eben's tortured wail: "God in heaven, I'm blind!" Then the blood did not matter. She tried to piece together Uncle Eben's glasses, in panic that she would be blamed for his blindness.

Later there was the strange Uncle Eben with bandages over his eyes, and pain on his mouth, and hot, trembling hands that went ceaselessly over her face. And there was the sightless Uncle Eben, very old and shrivelled and shaky, going uncertainly on a cane that tapped and tapped and tapped. Then there was the mother with a pursed mouth, and the father gesturing angrily, and the mother's unforgettable words: "I married you, not your whole helpless family." Then Uncle Eben went off to a Home on a cane that tapped and tapped.

Judy cried now, unchildishly and terribly, in regret that Uncle Eben had ever lived. She had the sharp thought: Uncle Eben's life and Uncle Eben's death do not really matter. . . . She was no longer a small child reasoning. Even her word images were mature. She was seeing deeply the tragedy of commonplace existence.

Her attention was acute now. She was keenly aware of her own absorption. The egotism that at all times swayed her was compelling her to store up impressions. She knew with bitterness that when she was older and abler, the events of this day would crowd into her mind with the utmost clearness and find release through her own particular medium of words. Only as it might serve her as a plot for a story—and the horror of this overwhelmed her—had the poor life and death of Uncle Eben any meaning.

He had left no child, nor book, nor even ennobling longings to thread into eternity the wisp of his spirit.

III

A big black man was shyly speaking. He called Uncle Eben a brother worker. He said that he was glad to be here to represent the Pullman company, and pointed out their unlovely flowers. He made a large gesture of introducing his wife, and sat down relievedly.

She advanced toward the casket. She was brown and buxom and soiled. Her voice was not beautiful.

"I never knew our dear brother personally, but I feel very close to all Pullman porters on account of my husband's being one of the head ones. I tries to come to their funerals as often as I can. I am proud to say that last year I didn't miss one.

"I'm not much on pome writing, but most people seems to like these little verses which I composed for Pullman Brother Jessey's death in 1916. I generally reads it at funerals. With your kind indulgence, I'll read it at this one."

She ducked her head as a child might, and recited in an unmusical tremolo:

" '*My tears overflow as I look down upon our dear brother.*
*The eyes that could open are shut.*
*The tongue that could speak is mute.*
*The feet that traversed o'er the earth are still by our Maker's will.*
*We weep beside this casket, we the wife, we the children, we the sorrowing*
 *friends.*
*We cannot realize that this is but the shell.*
*Already in spirit our dear brother stands before his Maker.*
*And God sits on His golden throne passing judgment.*
*We who knew this dear man know with confidence that the gates have been*
 *opened to him.*
*He lived clean and died humble, and that counts.*

*Do not take it too much to heart, dear relatives and friends.*
*We all got a time to go, and some go soon, and some go late.*
*Just lay your burden on the Lord, and he will gladly lighten your load.*
*The Devil is a toad!'"*

She went and sat down.

Judy could hear little sputters of praise. The aunts were pressing the soiled lady's hands. Over her head the father bent to the mother and said earnestly: "Real sad and appropriate."

The young preacher went to stand above the body. He was suddenly so wild-eyed that Judy thought he must be drunk.

He said heatedly: "This man ain't happy. This poor brother died in despair. No undertaker's art could smooth out all his suffering. He was worried to death, that's what. Why ain't he having a big funeral in some dicty church 'stead of you asking somebody you never seen before to come round here? 'Cause none of you thought he was worth a high falutin' funeral. I feels for this man."

Judy simply held her breath. She dared not stare up at her parents, but she was aware of her mother's nervous twitching.

The preacher went on: "I didn't come here to preach this funeral in hopes of getting five or ten dollars. I don't want no money. Get this straight. I wouldn't take it. I ain't doing a bit more for this dead brother than I want somebody, out of the kindness of his heart, to do some day for me."

Judy thought that rather admirable.

"You all been bragging 'bout him being a Pullman porter. That's first cousin to being a slave. Why ain't you put it right? For twenty years our dead brother's been an 'umble cog in a wheel.

"The trouble with our kind of people is we don't stick together. The white man does, and the white man rules the world. We got to organize! Us that is on top has got to help us that is at the bottom. But what uppity Negro will? But don't you all get me started. I never know when to stop. Jesus, guide this soul over Jordan. Amen."

He practically leaped into his coat and came to shake hands with the mother.

"Thank you, sister," Judy heard, as he patted her hat and passed on to the father.

Judy tugged at her mother. "Mums, why did he thank you? Oughtn't you to have thanked him?"

"Ssh! For the money, child. Stop asking questions."

"What money, mums? Did you give him money?"

"Judy, I'm warning you! For the funeral, child. You got to give them a little something."

Judy was simply struck. "But, mummy, he said he wouldn't take it!"

The mother whispered wearily: "They got to say something, child."

Two efficient men came to close the casket. The father was led by the light-skinned lady to take a last look. He came back considerably stricken and leaned against Judy. She slipped her arm around him. Through her small body wave upon wave of maternal passion surged. She was no longer contemptuous. Her heart swelled with compassion.

The efficient men trundled the box out on castors. The father and the mother followed. Judy went between the aunts into the sunny street.

The casket went neatly into a wooden box in the hearse. The flowers were piled around it. The door would not shut, and the undertaker fiddled and frowned.

Judy thought in alarm: I couldn't bear it if Uncle Eben spilled in the street. . . .

But presently the door banged shut. Judy followed the family into the first car.

The mother immediately flung back her veil. Her lovely face was flushed and excited. The father squirmed in his shoes. The aunts tried hard to go on with their weeping, but could not.

The undertaker poked in his head. "We're ready to start. Mister and Missus Tilly, and Missus Mamie Wicks, and Miss Eva Jenkins are following in the second car. It'll be quite a ride, so you all settle comfortable." He made a gesture. "That little thing there is an ash tray. Ashes to ashes." He laughed kindly and shut them in.

The hearse started off. In a moment their motor was rolling smoothly. Judy settled back, liking it very much, and wishing she could look out the window.

"No mind that preacher was right," said the father, loosing his laces.

"He wasn't nobody's fool," said the elder aunt.

The contrary mother said smartly: "I didn't like his talking like that at a funeral."

"We got to organize," the father remembered. "There ain't no set time to preach that."

"Funerals should be sad," said the mother.

"God knows!" sighed the favorite aunt.

"Still," agreed the father, "I didn't like him flinging up to us about Eben."

The mother voiced coldly: "Sounded to me like he was posted."

The favorite aunt drew up her delicate body. "Then it must be your conscience. God is my witness that until that man stood in the pulpit, I couldn't have told you he was white or black."

"Eben died careworn and weary," said the elder aunt. "That young man didn't need his glasses to tell him that."

The mother's voice shook. "I got as much pity as anybody, but, more than that, I got a child. And that child comes close to me as God, Himself! Now that Eben's gone to glory, I can praise his virtues as loud as anyone. But Eben had his faults, and I won't shut my eyes to them. He let himself go in his blindness. He wasn't careful. He wasn't always— clean. I mean to bring up my child like a white child. There ain't nothing going to sicken her little stomach. There ain't nothing going to soil her little mind."

Judy rhymed under her breath: "Funerals should be sad and mums had got a mad." But she was ashamed and thought tenderly: How much my mummy loves me, as much as God, and that's a sin, and she knows it. She isn't afraid. Does she love me because I'm me, or does she love me because I mean to be a great writer? I have talent. But there are geniuses. Am I a genius? What is a genius? If I have a child, I shan't want her to be a genius. I should be jealous. It's wicked to be jealous. I don't care. Nobody knows it because I'm so sweet, but I like to be first in every- thing. I don't want a baby, anyway. They hurt, and the way they come isn't nice. But, of course, I don't really believe it. I'd die if I thought my mummy and daddy could do a thing like that. I wish everything could be beautiful. People, and the things they say, and the things they do. Daddy has a flat nose. My mummy is beautiful. I like light people. Why is it wicked to like light people? I'm glad Uncle Eben's dead. Once I saw Uncle Eben being nasty. If I had a little boy baby, I'd be ashamed to touch him. I'm very wicked. I'm afraid of dead people. I'm afraid, afraid! At night they fly about in white shrouds. I don't want to be sent up to bed without mummy.

She made a little cradle of her hands.

"You all didn't hear Eva Jenkins moaning and groaning," said the elder aunt.

The mother seemed to increase. "Carrying on like a fool!"

The father added: "I reckon she realized Eben's bit of money won't never come to her now."

The favorite aunt said gently: "I think she really loved him."

The elder aunt made a coarse joke. "Yeh, him and his money."

"Eva Jenkins ain't young," said the favorite aunt. "It wasn't love she wanted—"

"You struck it right," the father cut in unkindly. "It was ease in her old age, and a blind old shoe what couldn't keep track of her comings and goings."

The mother said with definiteness: "Ever since that trouble in lodge meeting eight years ago, Eva Jenkins had it in for me. It's my opinion she wanted poor Eben just on account of spite, so's to take his little lump of money away from me and mine."

"I fixed her good," the father triumphed, "when I got my brother Eben to sign every penny over to me."

"And you broke her heart," said the favorite aunt. "She knew that, alone, she could never give Eben the comforts his nature demanded." She went on broodingly: "I guess she wonders now did we. People has got to lie flat on their backs before they find out what's false and what's true."

Judy thought with pride: My aunty is good. I want to be good like my aunty. But I love my mummy best, even though my mummy tells lies. My mummy and daddy care about money. I never, never want to. . . .

The elder aunt snapped up the back curtain. "Still at it," she reported grimly.

"Jerk in down in her face," the father commanded, "to show her how much she's wanted at my brother Eben's funeral. You got to be common with some folks before they understand."

The aunt did so with such vengeance that one of the side shades flew up, and Judy caught a little pool of sun in her cradle, and folded her hands to shut the glare out of her baby's eyes.

"I could eat a horse and wagon," said the mother.

"I don't know why 'tis," said the father, "but funerals make me hungry."

"I set a nice dinner back on the stove. I'll suttinly be glad to pitch into it. There's nothing I like more than I like chicken and rice and thick brown gravy."

The father reminisced sentimentally: "There's nothing I like more than I like the black-eyed peas and ham and cabbage my mammy used to give us."

The favorite aunt contributed frigidly: "I don't see how you two can put your minds on food. All I want is a strong cup of tea and maybe a sliver of toast."

"The dead are dead," said the father. "The living has needs of the body."

"The mother weeps for her child. Outside of that, I guess there ain't much honest sorrow wasted."

"Them as trusts God and believes in the resurrection has no need to weep. I shall meet my brother Eben in the promised land."

Judy thought sharply how awful it must be to be old! To know that your sun may set tomorrow! She would guard her growing. She would end each day with some delight. She would do good deeds! When she had reached Uncle Eben's age, she must not die unhonored. But then she had the image of the baker's wife shrieking in the back of the shop: "My baby's dead! My little baby's dead!" The young could die, too. Death was not the weak surrender of the old. Death was God in his heaven counting out souls.

But how could God let a little baby die? Why did he let it be born? If God is good, how can he bear to see its mother cry? People should be glad. To be glad is to be beautiful. When I am sad, my lip droops. When I am glad, I'm like my mummy. Everything should be beautiful. Why does a God let things be ugly? How can a *God* let things be ugly? There is not really a Santa Claus. Can I be me if there is not a God? I wish I could ask my mummy. But my mummy tells lies. It's wicked to lie to your little girl. When I tell lies, my throat burns, and I tremble. I'll never, never lie to my little girl. But I'll never, never have one. She might die. And then I should hate God. And if I could not say, "God! God!" I should want to die, too. . . .

The car had stopped. Judy peered ahead and saw the undertaker dash up a pebbled path. After a bit a bell tolled once, then again, and again. The hearse wound up a narrow road. The white slabs stood out sharply in the gathering dusk. A few fresh flowers reared their lovely heads. Green grass sprouted.

The hearse halted. Irish workingmen came ambling. The undertaker again poked in his head, and said that he had got a nice plot, and that their brother was to be laid under six feet only. Judy didn't know just why that mattered. But the father thanked him and bent to tie his laces.

They got out of the car. The undertaker shepherded them in order. The casket went perilously. Presently they stood above the open earth. The undertaker began giving crisp commands.

The mother said sharply: "Judy, go stand on that board. It's an old saying, 'The cold you catch at a funeral lasts until your own.'"

Judy went to stand on the board, teetering a little.

She heard Mrs. Tilly whispering: "I hope there ain't no long rigmarole. We got that other funeral."

Eva Jenkins came to stand beside her. "You're growing, Judy. I'm sorry your Uncle Eben couldn't live to be proud of you."

Judy stared up at the gentle-voiced woman. "I'm going to be a great writer."

"You are going to be something that's beautiful. And God knows there is need of beauty in this world."

"To be beautiful is to be glad. I hate funerals!"

"To be really beautiful, Judy, is to come through pain and sorrow and parting without bitterness."

Judy looked hard at Eva Jenkins and thought that she was beautiful.

The casket was lowered. The undertaker got a shovelful of earth and came first to the father. "Assist us in the burial of our dead," he suggested. The father took a handful and weakly scattered it. Shortly the workingmen were at it in earnest.

The undertaker fussily arranged the flowers. He detached a wilted carnation and offered it to the mother. Judy thought innocently: I guess they have favors at funerals just like at parties. . . . But when she was passed a flower she clasped her hands behind her back and looked very stubborn. She had heard the father say, "I'll keep mine forever," and had not believed him, and had been distressed.

The undertaker began to shake hands all around. They turned toward the cars.

Mr. Tilly said softly to the father: "The company pays for the funeral, brother."

The father exclaimed in gratitude: "God bless them! I'll write them a letter of thanks in the morning. All this talk 'bout organization! Sometimes I think the Pullman porter is biting the hands what feeds him."

## IV

The hearse had started. Judy watched it careen down the road in a wild dash to Mrs. Tilly's other funeral. Mrs. Tilly, in the second car, madly followed. Their car, too, went swiftly and the driver whistled snatches of popular songs.

Two blocks away from their street, a motor swung around the corner into their fender. Their driver, who had to make Mrs. Tilly's other funeral, too, cursed softly, halted his car, and went to make investigations.

The father, who loved excitement, followed him into the thick of it.

"Folks lon't have no respect for funerals nor nothing nowadays," said the elder aunt.

The favorite aunt argued: "With the blinds up and the shofer singing, how was they to tell this was a funeral?"

The mother neatly concluded: "If we was standing on our heads, he hadn't no right to run into us."

They impatiently fidgeted. But they did not think it proper to get out and walk home from a funeral.

The father and the chauffeur returned in triumph. The father gave the chauffeur his card and urged him to summon him for a witness. When he was settled again, he said easily, "Looks like I lost my posy."

Judy was glad to be home. She did not want any supper. But the aunts and the mother in fresh aprons ignored her.

The steaming supper was set on the table. They gathered round. The father said, "Do you remember how Eben loved chicken?" and tore into it. Judy, remembering, could not swallow.

The mother said impatiently: "Quit that fiddlin' and eat your supper."

"I'm not hungry," Judy said faintly.

"Of course you are," the elder aunt protested contentedly.

The father added facetiously: "All cullud children like chicken."

For the overwrought child the day culminated in this. She snatched up her plate and flung it on the floor. Her speech was almost indistinguishably thick. She was never to know where she got the words.

"I won't eat funeral-baked meats! I won't! Nobody can make me!"

It was almost as if she saw the hot food turn to straw in their open mouths.

"You march yourself out of here and go to bed," shrilled the mother, "and God give me strength to spank you in the morning."

Judy went, with her head high and her spirit quaking.

She went up the unlighted stairs with her eyes shut tight against the apparition of Uncle Eben. But the darkness so terrified her that she made a lattice of her fingers, and slowly opened her eyes on the lesser horror.

She gained her room, and snapped on the light, and leaned against the door. She was so weak that for a long moment there was no sound nor movement save her strangled breathing and the beating of her heart. She dared not go into the closet for her nightgown, nor did she dare stand long on the treacherous floor. She got to the bed and huddled in its center.

With one terrified motion she ripped off her dress. Her shoes followed, then her stockings. In her bloomers and waist she got under the covering and frantically hid her face under the sheet.

She could not uncover it. Surely, if she did, a grinning ghost would swoop down upon her. She lay and shivered and tortured herself with the floating image of Uncle Eben. In sheer terror she began to sob, and went on sobbing, and could not stop.

By and by she slept.

FROM THE *SATURDAY EVENING QUILL*, APRIL 1928

# The Typewriter

DOROTHY WEST

It occurred to him, as he eased past the bulging knees of an Irish wash lady and forced an apologetic passage down the aisle of the crowded car, that more than anything in all the world he wanted not to go home. He began to wish passionately that he had never been born, that he had never been married, that he had never been the means of life's coming into the world. He knew quite suddenly that he hated his flat and his family and his friends. And most of all the incessant thing that would "clatter clatter" until every nerve screamed aloud, and the words of the evening paper danced crazily before him, and the insane desire to crush and kill set his fingers twitching.

He shuffled down the street, an abject little man of fifty-odd years, in an ageless overcoat that flapped in the wind. He was cold, and he hated the North, and particularly Boston, and saw suddenly a barefoot pickaninny sitting on a fence in the hot, Southern sun with a piece of steaming corn bread and a piece of fried salt pork in either grimy hand.

He was tired, and he wanted his supper, but he didn't want the beans, and frankfurters, and light bread that Net would undoubtedly have. That Net had had every Monday night since that regrettable moment fifteen years before when he had told her—innocently—that such a supper tasted "right nice. Kinda change from what we always has."

He mounted the four brick steps leading to his door and pulled at the bell, but there was no answering ring. It was broken again, and in a mental flash he saw himself with a multitude of tools and a box of matches shivering in the vestibule after supper. He began to pound lustily on the door and wondered vaguely if his hand would bleed if he smashed the glass. He hated the sight of blood. It sickened him.

Some one was running down the stairs. Daisy probably. Millie would be at that infernal thing, pounding, pounding. . . . He entered. The chill of the house swept him. His child was wrapped in a coat. She whispered solemnly, "Poppa, Miz Hicks an' Miz Berry's orful mad. They gointa move if they can't get more heat. The furnace's birnt out all day. Mama couldn't fix it." He said hurriedly, "I'll go right down. I'll go right down." He hoped Mrs. Hicks wouldn't pull open her door and glare at him. She was large and domineering, and her husband was a bully. If her husband ever struck him it would kill him. He hated life, but he didn't want to die. He was afraid of God, and in his wildest flights of fancy couldn't imagine himself an angel. He went softly down the stairs.

He began to shake the furnace fiercely. And he shook into it every wrong, mumbling softly under his breath. He began to think back over his uneventful years, and it came to him as rather a shock that he had never sworn in all his life. He wondered uneasily if he dared say "damn." It was taken for granted that a man swore when he tended a stubborn furnace. And his strongest interjection was "Great balls of fire!"

The cellar began to warm, and he took off his inadequate overcoat that was streaked with dirt. Well, Net would have to clean that. He'd be damned—! It frightened him and thrilled him. He wanted suddenly to rush upstairs and tell Mrs. Hicks if she didn't like the way he was running things, she could get out. But he heaped another shovelful of coal on the fire and sighed. He would never be able to get away from himself and the routine of years.

He thought of that eager Negro lad of seventeen who had come North to seek his fortune. He had walked jauntily down Boylston Street, and even his own kind had laughed at the incongruity of him. But he had thrown up his head and promised himself: "You'll have an office here some day. With plate-glass windows and a real mahogany desk." But, though he didn't know it then, he was not the progressive type. And he became successively, in the years, bell boy, porter, waiter, cook, and finally janitor in a down town office building.

He had married Net when he was thirty-three and a waiter. He had married her partly because—though he might not have admitted it— there was no one to eat the expensive delicacies the generous cook gave him every night to bring home. And partly because he dared hope there might be a son to fulfill his dreams. But Millie had come, and after her twin girls who had died within two weeks, then Daisy, and it was tacitly understood that Net was done with child-bearing.

Life, though flowing monotonously, had flowed peacefully enough until that sucker of sanity became a sitting-room fixture. Intuitively at the very first he had felt its undesirability. He had suggested hesitatingly that they couldn't afford it. Three dollars: food and fuel. Times were hard, and the twenty dollars apiece the respective husbands of Miz Hicks and Miz Berry irregularly paid was only five dollars more than the thirty-five a month he paid his own Hebraic landlord. And the Lord knew his salary was little enough. At which point Net spoke her piece, her voice rising shrill. "God knows I never complain 'bout nothin'. Ain't no other woman got less than me. I bin wearin' this same dress here five years an' I'll wear it another five. But I don't want nothin'. I ain't never wanted nothin'. An' when I does as', it's only for my children. You're a poor sort of father if you can't give that child jes' three dollars a month to rent that typewriter. Ain't 'nother girl in school ain't got one. An' mos' of 'ems bought an' paid for. You know yourself how Millie is. She wouldn't as' me for it till she had to. An' I ain't going to disappoint her. She's goin' to get that typewriter Saturday, mark my words."

On a Monday then it had been installed. And in the months that followed, night after night he listened to the murderous "tack, tack, tack" that was like a vampire slowly drinking his blood. If only he could escape. Bar a door against the sound of it. But tied hand and foot by the economic fact that "Lord knows we can't afford to have fires burnin' an' lights lit all over the flat. You'all gotta set in one room. An' when y'get tired settin' y' c'n go to bed. Gas bill was somep'n scandalous last month."

He heaped a final shovelful of coal on the fire and watched the first blue flames. Then, his overcoat under his arm, he mounted the cellar stairs. Mrs. Hicks was standing in her kitchen door, arms akimbo. "It's warmin'," she volunteered.

"Yeh," he was conscious of his grime-streaked face and hands, "it's warmin'. I'm sorry 'bout all day."

She folded her arms across her ample bosom. "Tending a furnace ain't a woman's work. I don't blame your wife none 'tall."

Unsuspecting he was grateful. "Yeh, it's pretty hard for a woman. I always look after it 'fore I goes to work, but some days it jes' ac's up."

"Y'oughta have a janitor, that's what y'ought," she flung at him. "The same cullud man that tends them apartments would be willin'. Mr.

Taylor has him. It takes a man to run a furnace, and when the man's away all day—"

"I know," he interrupted, embarrassed and hurt, "I know. Tha's right, Miz Hicks tha's right. But I ain't in a position to make no improvements. Times is hard."

She surveyed him critically. "Your wife called down 'bout three times while you was in the cellar. I reckon she wants you for supper."

"Thanks," he mumbled and escaped up the back stairs.

He hung up his overcoat in the closet, telling himself, a little lamely, that it wouldn't take him more'n a minute to clean it up himself after supper. After all Net was tired and prob'bly worried what with Miz Hicks and all. And he hated men who made slaves of their women folk. Good old Net.

He tidied up in the bathroom, washing his face and hands carefully and cleanly so as to leave no—or very little—stain on the roller towel. It was hard enough for Net, God knew.

He entered the kitchen. The last spirals of steam were rising from his supper. One thing about Net she served a full plate. He smiled appreciatively at her unresponsive back, bent over the kitchen sink. There was no one could bake beans just like Net's. And no one who could find a market with frankfurters quite so fat.

He sank down at his place. "Evenin', hon."

He saw her back stiffen. "If your supper's cold, 'tain't my fault. I called and called."

He said hastily, "It's fine, Net, fine. Piping."

She was the usual tired housewife. "Y'oughta et your supper 'fore you fooled with that furnace. I ain't bothered 'bout them niggers. I got all my dishes washed 'cept yours. An' I hate to mess up my kitchen after I once get it straightened up."

He was humble. "I'll give that old furnace an extra lookin' after in the mornin'. It'll las' all day to-morrow, hon."

"An' on top of that," she continued, unheeding him and giving a final wrench to her dish towel, "that confounded bell don't ring. An'—"

"I'll fix it after supper," he interposed hastily.

She hung up her dish towel and came to stand before him looming large and yellow. "An' that old Miz Berry, she claim she was expectin' comp'ny. An' she knows they must 'a' come an' gone while she was in her kitchen an' couldn't be at her winder to watch for 'em. Old liar," she brushed back a lock of naturally straight hair. "She wasn't expectin' nobody."

"Well, you know how some folks are—"

"Fools! Half the world," was her vehement answer. "I'm goin' in the front room an' set down a spell. I bin on my feet all day. Leave them dishes on the table. God knows I'm tired, but I'll come back an' wash 'em." But they both knew, of course, that he, very clumsily, would.

At precisely quarter past nine when he, strained at last to the breaking point, uttering an inhuman, strangled cry, flung down his paper, clutched at his throat and sprang to his feet, Millie's surprised young voice, shocking him to normalcy, heralded the first of that series of great moments that every humble little middle-class man eventually experiences.

"What's the matter, poppa? You sick? I wanted you to help me."

He drew out his handkerchief and wiped his hot hands. "I declare I must 'a' fallen asleep an' had a nightmare. No, I ain't sick. What you want, hon?"

"Dictate me a letter, poppa. I c'n do sixty words a minute.—You know, like a business letter. You know, like those men in your building dictate to their stenographers. Don't you hear 'em sometimes?"

"Oh, sure, I know, hon. Poppa'll help you. Sure. I hear that Mr. Browning—Sure."

Net rose. "Guess I'll put this child to bed. Come on now, Daisy, without no fuss.—Then I'll run up to pa's. He ain't bin well all week."

When the door closed behind them, he crossed to his daughter, conjured the image of Mr. Browning in the process of dictating, so arranged himself, and coughed importantly.

"Well, Millie—"

"Oh, poppa, is that what you'd call your stenographer?" she teased. "And anyway pretend I'm really one—and you're really my boss, and this letter's real important."

A light crept into his dull eyes. Vigor through his thin blood. In a brief moment the weight of years fell from him like a cloak. Tired, bent, little old man that he was, he smiled, straightened, tapped impressively against his teeth with a toil-stained finger, and became that enviable emblem of American life: a business man.

"You be Miz Hicks, huh, honey? Course we can't both use the same name. I'll be J. Lucius Jones. J. Lucius. All them real big doin' men use their middle names. Jus' kinda looks big doin', doncha think, hon? Looks like money, huh? J. Lucius." He uttered a sound that was like the proud cluck of a strutting hen. "J. Lucius." It rolled like oil from his tongue.

His daughter twisted impatiently. "Now, poppa—I mean Mr. Jones, sir—please begin. I am ready for dictation, sir."

He was in that office on Boylston Street, looking with visioning eyes through its plate-glass windows, tapping with impatient fingers on its real mahogany desk.

"Ah—Beaker Brothers, Park Square Building, Boston, Mass. Ah—Gentlemen: In reply to yours at the seventh instant I would state—"

Every night thereafter in the weeks that followed, with Daisy packed off to bed, and Net "gone up to pa's" or nodding inobtrusively in her corner there was the chamelion change of a Court Street janitor to J. Lucius Jones, dealer in stocks and bonds. He would stand, posturing importantly, flicking imaginary dust from his coat lapel, or, his hands locked behind his back, he would stride up and down, earnestly and seriously debating the advisability of buying copper with the market in such a fluctuating state. Once a week, too, he stopped in at Jerry's, and after a preliminary purchase of cheap cigars, bought the latest trade papers, mumbling an embarrassed explanation: "I got a little money. Think I'll invest it in reliable stock."

The letters Millie typed and subsequently discarded, he rummaged for later, and under cover of writing to his brother in the South, laboriously with a great many fancy flourishes, signed each neatly typed sheet with the exalted J. Lucius Jones.

Later, when he mustered the courage he suggested tentatively to Millie that it might be fun—just fun, of course!—to answer his letters. One might—he laughed a good deal louder and longer than necessary—he'd be J. Lucius Jones, and the next night—here he swallowed hard and looked a little frightened—Rockefeller or Vanderbilt or Morgan—just for fun, y'understand! To which Millie gave consent. It mattered little to her one way or the other. It was practice, and that was what she needed. Very soon now she'd be in the hundred class. Then maybe she could get a job!

He was growing very careful of his English. Occasionally—and it must be admitted, ashamedly—he made surreptitious ventures into the dictionary. He had to, of course. J. Lucius Jones would never say "Y'got to" when he meant "It is expedient." And, old brain though he was, he learned quickly and easily, juggling words with amazing facility.

Eventually he bought stamps and envelopes—long, important-looking envelopes—and stammered apologetically to Millie, "Honey, poppa thought it'd help you if you learned to type envelopes, too. Reckon you'll have to do that, too, when y'get a job. Poor old man," he swallowed painfully, "came round selling these envelopes. You know how 'tis. So I had to buy 'em." Which was satisfactory to Millie. If she saw through her father, she gave no sign. After all, it was practice, and Mr. Hennessey had said that—though not in just those words.

He had got in the habit of carrying those self-addressed envelopes in his inner pocket where they bulged impressively. And occasionally he would take them out—on the car usually—and smile upon them. This one might be from J. P. Morgan. This one from Henry Ford. And a million-dollar deal involved in each. That narrow, little spinster, who, upon his sitting down, had drawn herself away from his contact, was shunning J. Lucius Jones!

Once, led by some sudden, strange impulse, as an outgoing car rumbled up out of the subway, he got out a letter, darted a quick, shamed glance about him, dropped it in an adjacent box, and swung aboard the car, feeling, dazedly, as if he had committed a crime. And the next night he sat in the sitting-room quite on edge until Net said suddenly, "Look here, a real important letter come to-day for you, pa. Here 'tis. What you s'pose it says," and he reached out a hand that trembled. He made brief explanation. "Advertisement, hon. Thassal."

They came quite frequently after that, and despite the fact that he knew them by heart, he read them slowly and carefully, rustling the sheet, and making inaudible, intelligent comments. He was, in these moments, pathetically earnest.

Monday, as he went about his janitor's duties, he composed in his mind the final letter from J. P. Morgan that would consummate a big business deal. For days now letters had passed between them. J. P. had been at first quite frankly uninterested. He had written tersely and briefly. He wrote glowingly of the advantages of a pact between them. Daringly he argued in terms of billions. And at last J. P. had written his next letter would be decisive. Which next letter, this Monday, as he trailed about the office building, was writing itself on his brain.

That night Millie opened the door for him. Her plain face was transformed. "Poppa—poppa, I got a job! Twelve dollars a week to start with! Isn't that *swell*!"

He was genuinely pleased. "Honey, I'm glad. Right glad," and went up the stairs, unsuspecting.

He ate his supper hastily, went down into the cellar to see about his fire, returned and carefully tidied up, informing his reflection in the bathroom mirror, "Well, J. Lucius, you c'n expect that final letter any day now."

He entered the sitting-room. The phonograph was playing. Daisy was singing lustily. Strange. Net was talking animatedly to—Millie, busy with needle and thread over a neat, little frock. His wild glance darted to the table. The pretty, little centerpiece, the bowl and wax flowers all neatly arranged: the typewriter gone from its accustomed place. It seemed an hour before he could speak. He felt himself trembling. Went hot and cold.

"Millie—your typewriter's—gone!"

She made a deft little in and out movement with her needle. "It's the eighth, you know. When the man came to-day for the money, I sent it back. I won't need it no more—now!—The money's on the mantlepiece, poppa."

"Yeh," he muttered. "All right."

He sank down in his chair, fumbled for the paper, found it.

Net said, "Your poppa wants to read. Stop your noise, Daisy."

She obediently stopped both her noise and the phonograph, took up her book, and became absorbed. Millie went on with her sewing in placid anticipation of the morrow. Net immediately began to nod, gave a curious snort, slept.

Silence. That crowded in on him, engulfed him. That blurred his vision, dulled his brain. Vast, white, impenetrable. . . . His ears strained for the old, familiar sound. And silence beat upon them. . . . The words of the evening paper jumbled together. He read: J. P. Morgan goes—

It burst upon him. Blinded him. His hands groped for the bulge beneath his coat. Why this—this was the end! The end of those great moments—the end of everything! Bewildering pain tore through him. He clutched at his heart and felt, almost, the jagged edges drive into his hand. A lethargy swept down upon him. He could not move, nor utter sound. He could not pray, nor curse.

Against the wall of that silence J. Lucius Jones crashed and died.

FROM *OPPORTUNITY,* JULY 1926

# Prologue to a Life

## DOROTHY WEST

In 1896 Luke Kane had met and married Lily Bemis. He had been very much in love with her. And she had literally fallen at his feet, stumbling over his bicycle, lying flat before the back door, and sprawling before him, her full skirts billowing about her, and quite all of the calves of her legs showing.

Luke, in an instant, was out of the kitchen, and had gathered the hired girl in his arms, and was cursing his bicycle and soothing her in the same breath.

She was small and soft. Though her face was hidden against his breast, he saw that her arms were golden, and her dark hair wavy and long.

"Is that your old bicycle?" Lily asked tearfully. "You're fixin' to kill somebody."

"Ain't I the biggest fool!" he agreed.

She got herself out of his arms and, sitting down on the steps, she tried to do things with her clothes and hair.

"What anybody'd put an old bicycle right in the doorway for—"

But he was staring into her eyes.

"How long you been working for Miz Trainor?"

"I've seen you before," she told him. "Lots."

"Yeh? Don't you speak to nobody?"

"Gentlemen to whom I been introduced. Oh, yes."

"I'm somebody round these parts," he boasted. "Ever heard of Manda Kane?"

"Sure. We get our fancy cakes from her when we're having parties and things."

"I'm her son," he informed her, proudly. "I been up here delivering. My name's Luke."

"Yeh?" Her eyes were bright with interest. "Mine's Lily Bemis."

"Come from the South?"

"Born there. Yes. But I came up with the Mitchells when they came. That's been five years. But then old Miz Mitchell died, and the two girls got married. I never cared much for old Mister Mitchell, so I came on to Springfield. 'Cause Mamie Cole went on to Boston and said I could take her place here. I knew Miz Trainor was good and all, and didn't have no small children. So I sorta thought I'd try it. Gee, I'm young and everything. If I don't like it here, I can travel on."

He plumped down beside her.

"Listen," he said softly, "I hope you'll like it here."

Her eyes were two slits and dangerous.

"Why—Luke?"

"'Cause, then," he said huskily, "you'll stay. And I can be likin' you."

She bent to him suddenly. "You're the funniest coon. Your eyes are blue as blue."

"Yeh. It's funny, black as I am," he said modestly.

She put two slim yellow fingers against his cheek. "You're not black at all. You're just dark brown. I think you're a beautiful color."

His eyes that were like a deep sea glowed with gratitude. "I sorta like yours the best."

"Oh, me, I'm not much!" she said carelessly. "What makes you think I'm pretty?"

"I dunno. You're so little and soft and sweet. And you ain't so shy."

She was instantly on her feet. "If you think I'm bold, sitting out here with you, when we never been introduced—"

"Looka here!" He was on his feet, too. "Women's the funniest things. I'm liking you 'cause you're not like everyone else, and you're bristling! I can have any girl in this little old town of Springfield I want. But I'm not making up to any 'cause I ain't found none that suited me. My mother's orful particular. We got a name in this town. You're the first girl I'm liking, and you're cutting up!"

But she was inside of the screen door now, and he saw her hook it. She came very close to it, but she was careful not to press her nose against it.

"Listen, Mr. Kane, I like you, too. I want to meet you proper. What would folks say if they knew we met like this? Me with two buttons off my shirtwaist and my hair net torn? But tomorrow's prayer meeting night, and I'm going. I'm an A.M.E. If that's your church, too, you come on over. I'll get Miz Hill to get Reverend Hill to introduce us proper."

He gulped. "Can I bring you home after?"

She considered it. "Maybe I'll let you be keeping my company," she promised.

There followed a whirlwind month of courtship. Lily had a hundred moods. They were a hundred magnets drawing Luke. She did not love him. Deep within her was an abiding ambition to see her race perpetuated. Though she felt that her talents were of a high order, she knew she would escape greatness through her lack of early training. And she had the mother instinct. Thus she would rather bear a clever child. In her supreme egoism she believed the male seed would only generate it. She would not conceive of its becoming blood of her child's blood, and flesh of her child's flesh. Men were chiefly important as providers. She would have married any healthy man with prospects. . . .


Late in the summer Lily and Luke were married. Lily didn't want a church wedding. They were married in Reverend Hill's front parlor. Miz Hill and Manda Kane stood up with them. Ma Manda was tearful. She was losing her only son to a low-voiced yellow woman. She knew the inescapable bond of soft skin and hair.

Lily, standing quietly by Luke's side, felt a vast contentment. She respected the man she was marrying. She faced the future calmly. She only wanted their passion to be strong enough to yield a smart and sturdy son.

Later that day they were on a train that was bound, by the back door route, for Boston. They sat in the coach with their little belongings piled all about them. Luke made sheep's eyes at Lily and felt very proud. He was wondering whether it was obvious that they had just been married. He rather wanted the phlegmatic passengers to admire his golden bride.

He drew her round dark head on to his shoulder, and caught his hand in the tendrils of her hair.

"Guess I'm the happiest man in the world, and the proudest."

"Ho, you're not proud of me!"

"You are the moon and the stars, Lily, and the bright sun."

She twisted her head and looked deep into his kind eyes.

"Luke, do you love me as much as that?"

"You watch me," he told her. "I'll bring you the world on a silver platter. Lily, I'll make you a queen."

She rubbed her little hand up and down his arm.

"How much money we got now, Luke?"

"Enough," he boasted, "to live like millionaires for maybe a week in Boston."

"Luke," she said earnestly, "we're not going back. Ever."

He was pleased. "Our honeymoon will last wherever we are."

She was almost impatient. "It ain't that!"

He drew away from her and stared down at her hard.

"What in the name of God—"

"Let's eat," she said, and dug about for Ma Manda's hamper.

She put the linen napkin on her lap and laid out the sandwiches, licking her fingers when the mayonnaise or jam or butter had oozed through.

"Chicken," she announced, "and ham, and I reckon this is po'k, Luke!"

He balanced the coffee on his knee. "There's cups somewheres, Lily."

Presently they were hungrily eating, Luke almost wolfishly.

"We've caught our train," said Lily, with a little nervous laugh. He was making her rather ill.

He took a great gulp of coffee.

"Always was a fast eater. Father before me was."

Her hand tightened over his. "You could die," she said with real concern, "of indigestion."

He ducked his head suddenly and kissed her wrist.

"But I'll make you your million before I do."

Thus she let him go back to his eating, and she gave him an almost indulgent smile.

Once in the vast South Station they stood for a moment, bewildered. They both felt newly married and foolishly young. Lily had a sudden sense of panic. Suppose Ma Manda never forgave them. Suppose Luke died or deserted her. Suppose she was never able to bear a child.

And then she saw Mamie Cole coming toward them. She flew into her arms.

"The blushing bride and groom!" cried Mamie, and offered her cheek to Luke.

"Well, it's nice to see you," said Luke, rather shyly after kissing her.

"I'm only off for an hour," she explained, "so we better get up to the
flat. I got you three real nice rooms, Lily, in front."

"Three—?" echoed Luke. His voice fell in disappointment. "I kinda
thought—a hotel—"

"Luke!" Lily caught his arm fast. Her brown eyes were dark with
pleading. "Luke, it's not a hotel room I want. It's a home."

He asked in bewilderment: "Here—in Boston?"

"Listen, we're not going back. We're laying our corner-stone here.
There's far and away more business in Boston than in Springfield. Just
you see. I want my husband. Luke, I want my home. I want my—son.
Back home we'd have to live with your mother. She's got that big house.
And, Luke, I can't get along with no women. I almost hate women.
They're not honest. They're weaklings. They care about cheap things.
God knows you're going to find it hard to live with me—and *you* love
me. I don't want nothing but my man and my son. That's me, Luke."

He had the most terrible longing to take her in his arms.

"Your man and your son? Lily, my girl, you've got your man. By God,
you'll have your son. . . . "


In 1898 Lily gave birth to twins.

They were boys, with Lily's soft yellow skin and fine brown eyes, and
all about them the look of her, somehow. Jamie and John. They were
completely sons of Lily. To her they were gods.

Luke had been getting on in a fair sort of way before the twins were
born. He had opened a tiny lunch stand in the South End. Lily had been
helping with the cooking. After a barely perceptible start, business had
picked up nicely. Luke could cook almost as well as his mother. And Lily,
growing prettier and plumper every day, and rapidly learning badinage,
was an obvious attraction.

She worked until the week before the twins were born. Then Ma
Manda, in panicky self-reproach, hurried on to Boston, saw to it that a
proper girl was hired, packed Lily off to the New England Hospital, and
looked about at houses. She decided on a red-brick one on a quiet street
in Brookline, and bought it through a profiteering agent. She ordered
atrocious furniture on the credit plan (Lily returned it piece by piece
later), and awaited the birth of her grandchild in grim satisfaction.

To the triumphant Lily the world existed for two golden babies.
These were her lives to shape and guide. These were her souls to
expand. She, with her constant faith, must quicken their geniuses.

So the years passed. Jamie and John were three and able to read. Then

John at four could bang out a harmony on the new upright piano. Jamie at six was doing third grade lessons. . . .

They were nine. And Lily's pride, and joy, and love, and life. They had not cried in their cradle. They had never been jealous of each other. They had given her and Luke wholeheartedly their love. They wrote regularly and beautifully to their grandmother. Their teachers adored them. Despite their talents, they were manly, and popular with children. They had never been ill. They were growing like weeds. John, at the Boston Conservatory, had been singled out as an extraordinary pupil. His little sensitive face had stared out of many daily papers. Jamie, in the seventh grade, leading his class, was the marvel of his school. He could solve the mathematical problems of high school students. He could also discuss his future with calm assurance. . . .

Lily was thirty-two now. And a housewife. Occasionally she swept into the shop which had been yearly enlarged until it comprised three wide windows and twenty-two tables. The doctors and lawyers who frequented the place would rise and eagerly greet her. She was completely complacent. She was fat, but her skin was firm and soft to Luke's touch. Her eyes were clear and content. There were always tender anecdotes about her boys. Jamie and John. The realization of her dreams, the growing fulfillment of her hopes, the latent genius quickening.

She walked in peace. She knew ten years of utter harmony. She was therefore totally unprepared for any swift disruption.

In 1908 the twins were ten. Though they were young men now with certain futures, they were still very charming, and went swimming or skating with the boys on their block whenever they were called for. . . .

It was on the last day of March, going all too meekly like a lamb, that Lily, in her kitchen, making the raisin-stuffed bread pudding the twins adored, sat down suddenly with her hand to her throat, and her heart in a lump against it. She was alone, but she knew she was not ill. She made no attempt to cry out to a neighbor. She could see, as clearly as though she stood at the pond's edge, the twins, their arms tight about each other, crashing through the treacherous ice, making no outcry, their eyes wide with despair, dragged swiftly down, brought up again to break her heart forever, and Jamie's red scarf, that Ma Manda had knitted for him, floating. . . .

Within twenty minutes three frightened children brought her the news. Two days later their bodies were found. Lily identified them in a dim dank morgue.

The twins lay together in a satin-lined casket in the flower-filled parlor. They were very lovely in their last sleep. The undertaker's art had restored them and enhanced them. There was about their mouths that too exquisite beauty that death brings to the mouths of children who die in pain. Dead, they were more similar than living. And it was James who looked like John. . . .

James and John were Lily. James and John were dead. Only the fact that she had watched her heart and soul flung into the earth with her sons kept Lily's body alive. She was spiritually a dead woman walking in the patient hope of physical release. There was no youth in her any more. Her body was no longer firm, but flabby. Her eyes were lusterless. Her lips that had always been a little too thin were a line now that went sharply down at each corner. And the voice that had bantered richly with her boys, that had thrilled like a girl's at the intimate bass of a man, was quavering, and querulous, and, all too often, still. . . .

Ma Manda stayed on. Lily wanted it. They were held by their mutual bereavement. The twins, dead, were more potent than ever they could have been, living. Now Lily and Ma Manda knew there was nothing these boys could not have done, no world they would not have conquered, had they lived.

Ma Manda one week-end returned to Springfield, sold her house and the two fine mares, and her business and her lease to a prosperous German. Her only sentimentalities were two ribboned packets of letters.

Luke was sorry that the twins were dead, but his heart was not broken. Lily was his world. While she lived there was hope, and love, and life. He had no real conception of the genius of the twins. He had always thought of them as smart little boys. Now death had shattered their spell for him. He even wondered vaguely why it did not occur to Lily she might have another child.

One night, after a silent meal that Luke had cooked himself to tempt the too light appetite of his women, Lily rose abruptly from the supper table, and with the knuckles of her clenched fists showing white, said in a voice that she tried to keep steady: "Luke, I'm sleeping in the twins' room tonight. I—I guess I'll go on up now. G'night, Ma Manda. 'Night, Luke."

An hour later, when he softly tried the door, it was locked.

A year passed. Lily, a little mad in her constant communion with her dead, had grown somehow hauntingly lovely, with her loosened hair always tangled, her face thin and pale and exquisite, and her eyes large and brightly knowing. Now she was voluble with Ma Manda, though there were no notes in her voice. She kept up a continual stream of pathetic reminiscences. And she went about her house with her hands outstretched briefly to caress some memorial to her boys.

Ma Manda indulged her. To her there was only beauty in Lily's crazy devotion. She had loved Luke's golden sons more than she had ever loved Luke. As with Lily, throughout their growing, they had become her sole reality. With the ancient's idea of duty, she kept their memory fresh, her sorrow keen. She went regularly to a Baptist church and wailed when the preacher harangued the dead.

And always for Luke, in his starved normal passion, surprisingly not the brute, Lily's light body was a golden mesh.

Lily had sat by an open window, staring up at the stars, her bare feet on a chilled floor, her nightgown fluting in the wind. Presently she had begun to sneeze. Soon her eyes and her nose were running. When she got into Jamie's white bed, she felt a great wave engulf her. In the morning she was very ill.

Lily felt that she was dying. And she was afraid to die. She hated pain. She had given no thought to death before the death of her twins. After that she had thought of her going as only a dreamless sleeping and a waking with her sons. Now there was something in her chest that was making her last hours torture. And a cough that tore her from the hot pillows and started that jerk and pull in her heart. Sometimes her breath was a shudder that shook her body.

In the first hours of the third night, she clutched at Ma Manda and stared up at her with eyes so full of piteous appeal that Ma Manda said sharply and involuntarily: "Lily, my child, you best let Luke in. He's a great one for healing. There's the power of the Almighty in his hands."

Lily made a little gesture of acquiescence. Ma Manda went softly, fumbling in her tears.

Luke bent over Lily. His blue eyes burned. They were dark and deep and glowing. She felt her own eyes caught in them. Felt her senses drowning. He flung one hand up to the sky, the fingers apart and un-bending. The other he pressed against her chest till his flesh and her flesh were one.

He was exalted and inspired. The muscles leaped in his arm. He was trembling and black and mysterious.

"Lily, my girl, God's going to help you. God in His heaven's got to hear my prayer! Just put your faith in me, my darling. I got my faith in

Him. I got a gift from the heavenly Father. Praise His name! Lily, my Lily, I got the power to heal!"

Strength surged out of him—went swinging down through the arm upraised, flashed through his straining body, then shot down and tingled in his fingers which had melted into her breast. They were like rays, destroying. Five streams of life, pouring into her sick veins, fierce, tumultuous, until the poison and the pain burst into rivulets of sweat that ran swift and long down her quivering body, and presently left her washed clean and quiet and very, very tired.

Then Luke's words came in a rush, in the voice of one who had fought a hard fight, or run a long race, yet deep and tremblingly beautiful.

"God, be praised! God, the Maker, we humbly thank Thee! Thou heard! Thou heard!! Thou gave me strength to heal! O God, this poor child—my Lily—she's well! She can rise and take up her bed and walk! O God, Thou art the Father of all living! Thou art life! Thou art love! Thou art love!! Thou art love!!!"

He slumped down on his knees and burst into wild tears. His head went bumping against Lily's breast.

In her relief and gratitude and wonderment, she felt her first compassion for her husband. In his weakness she was strong. She was a mother.

He clung to her. He was a man sick with passion.

Presently she said: "Lie with me, Luke," and drew him up into her arms.

For Lily, and for Luke, and for Ma Manda, after a week or two, that night, crowded out of their consciousness, might have never been. Lily went back to her inner life; Ma Manda to the spiritual needs of her daughter-in-law and the physical needs of her son; Luke to the old apathetic content in Lily's apparent contentment.

But one Sunday morning as he lay staring at a bright patch of sunlight on the wall and hearing faintly the bells of the Mission Church without emotion, the door creaked sharply.

Lily came in and stood at the foot of his bed.

He sat up in real surprise and made a vague gesture toward his bathrobe.

Her eyes were level into his and full of scorn. Her face was pale and proud. Her lips were a thin twist of contempt.

She was so lovely and so terrible in her fury that he caught his breath.

He scuttled down to the foot of the bed and gripped her wrist tight. "Lily, you sick? For God's sake, what ails you?"

She flung her arm free. "I'm going to have a child. Another child! Well, it's yours. I've borne my babies. And I've buried them. This is your little black brat, d'you hear? You can keep it or kill it. If it wasn't for my babies in heaven, I'd get rid of it with the deadliest poison. But I can't damn my soul to hell for a wretched child that may be born dead. And if it lives"—her voice was a wail—"I curse it to my despair!"

For the first time since his childhood, Luke flung himself down full length on the bed and cried. . . .

In the months that followed, Ma Manda and Luke, in their terrific watchfulness, had a nine months' travail, too.

Lily's child was born on a spring morning in a labor so fierce that both of them, after hours of struggle, lay utterly spent; the child in the big white crib that had been the twins', the mother, for the last time, on her own great mahogany bed.

Lily was conscious, and calm. She was dying as she had wanted to die, painlessly. She felt no curiosity about her baby. She had heard a sharp whisper, "It's a girl," which she had half expected, and had turned her face from the sound of it to summon all of her strength for a bitter chuckle.

Presently Luke came to stare down at her. His eyes were filled with great desperation. He, too, had forgotten the new baby. Lily was dying.

"Lily"—his voice was deep and tender—"just put your faith in God. My Father has never failed me. He'll pull you through."

She was quietly exalted. "I have come through."

"Lily, I love you. Don't act that way. Put your hand in mine. Let me help you, my darling."

His hand went out to her. She saw the fingers stiffen, straighten, and the muscles pulling in his arm.

But she made no move.

"Are you too weak? Let me raise your hand. The power of God is in me. It leaps like a young ram. Only touch me, Lily!"

Ma Manda, kneeling at the foot of the bed, wrung her hands and wailed, "Only touch him, Lily!"

Her eyes were wide and seeking. Her mouth was tremulous and beautiful. With a tremendous effort she raised herself up from her pillow. Her braids went lopping over her breasts.

Her hands went out, slowly, gropingly. Luke waited, quivering, his heart in his mouth.

But then she sighed sharply. Her hands clasped tightly. Her eyes were passionate. Her face was glorious.

It was Ma Manda who scrambled to her feet and laid her back on the pillow, and knew that she was dead, and gently brushed the lids over her eyes. In the instant when her soul leaped to the sun, the new baby whimpered, once, then again, and was still. Luke turned toward it with a furious oath. He bent over the crib and looked down at the tiny dark bundle that was scarcely anything at all, with its quiet hands and shut eyes.

In the sudden hope that it had died, he put his hand over its heart.

The baby opened its eyes. They were blue—as deeply blue as his own, but enormous and infinitely sad. It was their utter despairing that moved him. He felt for this child a possessive tenderness such as the twins had never inspired. It was a woman-child. He understood her frailty.

So he knelt and slapped her face hard, and breathed into her mouth, and cried out *Lily! Lily!* naming her. He urged the strength in his spatulate fingers to quicken the beat of her heart. He prayed, "God, be merciful!" again and again.

She broke into a lusty wail and fell into a normal sleep, with the tears still wet on her cheeks.

Lily was dead, and Lily was not dead. A mother is the creator of life. And God cannot die.

FROM THE *SATURDAY EVENING QUILL*, APRIL 1929

# One Boy's Story

## MARITA BONNER

I'm glad they got me shut up in here. Gee, I'm glad! I used to be afraid to walk in the dark and to stay by myself.

That was when I was ten years old. Now I am eleven.

My mother and I used to live up in the hills right outside of Somerset. Somerset, you know is way up State and there aren't many people there. Just a few rich people in big houses and that's all.

Our house had a nice big yard behind it, beside it and in front of it. I used to play it was my fortress and that the hills beside us were full of Indians. Some days I'd go on scouting parties up and down the hills and fight.

That was in the summer and fall. In the winter and when the spring was rainy, I used to stay in the house and read.

I love to read. I love to lie on the floor and put my elbows down and read and read myself right out of Somerset and of America—out of the world, if I want to.

There was just my mother and I. No brothers—no sisters—no father. My mother was awful pretty. She had a roundish plump, brown face and was all plump and round herself. She had black hair all curled up on the end like a nice autumn leaf.

She used to stay in the house all the time and sew a lot for different ladies who came up from the big houses in Somerset. She used to sew and I would pull the bastings out for her. I did not mind it much. I liked to look at the dresses and talk about the people who were to wear them.

Most people, you see, wear the same kind of dress all the time. Mrs. Ragland always wore stiff silk that sounded like icicles on the window. Her husband kept the tea and coffee store in Somerset and everybody said he was a coming man.

I used to wonder where he was coming to.

Mrs. Gregg always had the kind of silk that you had to work carefully for it would ravel into threads. She kept the boarding house down on Forsythe Street. I used to like to go to that house. When you looked at it on the outside and saw all the windows and borders running up against it you thought you were going in a palace. But when you got inside you saw all the little holes in the carpet and the mended spots in the curtains and the faded streaks in the places where the draperies were folded.

The pale soft silk that always made me feel like burying my face in it belonged to Mrs. Swyburne. She was rich—awful rich. Her husband used to be some kind of doctor and he found out something that nobody else had found out, so people used to give him plenty of money just to let him tell them about it. They called him a specialist.

He was a great big man. Nice and tall and he looked like he must have lived on milk and beef-juice and oranges and tomato juice and all the stuff Ma makes me eat to grow. His teeth were white and strong so I guess he chewed his crusts too.

Anyhow, he was big but his wife was all skinny and pale. Even her eyes were almost skinny and pale. They were sad like and she never talked much. My mother used to say that those who did not have any children did not have to talk much anyhow.

She said that to Mrs. Swyburne one time. Mrs. Swyburne had been sitting quiet like she used to, looking at me. She always looked at me anyhow, but that day she looked harder than ever.

Every time I raised up my head and breathed the bastings out of my face, I would see her looking at me.

I always hated to have her look at me. Her eyes were so sad they made me feel as if she wanted something I had.

Not that I had anything to give her because she had all the money and cars and everything and I only had my mother and Cato, my dog, and some toys and books.

But she always looked that way at me and that day she kept looking so long that pretty soon I sat up and looked at her hard.

She sort of smiled then and said, "Do you know, Donald. I was wishing I had a little boy just like you to pull out bastings for me, too."

"You couldn't have one just like me," I said right off quick. Then I quit talking because Ma commenced to frown even though she did not look up at me.

I quit because I was going to say, "Cause I'm colored and you aren't," when Ma frowned.

Mrs. Swyburne still sort of smiled; then she turned her lips away from her teeth the way I do when Ma gives me senna and manna tea.

"No," she said, "I couldn't have a little boy like you, I guess."

Ma spoke right up, "I guess you do not want one like him! You have to talk to him so much."

I knew she meant I talked so much and acted so bad sometimes.

Mrs. Swyburne looked at Ma then. She looked at her hair and face and right down to her feet. Pretty soon she said: "You cannot mind that surely. You seem to have all the things I haven't anyway." Her lips were still held in that lifted, twisted way.

Ma turned around to the machine then and turned the wheel and caught the thread and it broke and the scissors fell and stuck up in the floor. I heard her say "Jesus," to herself like she was praying.

I didn't say anything. I ripped out the bastings. Ma stitched. Mrs. Swyburne sat there. I sort of peeped up at her and I saw a big fat tear sliding down her cheek.

I kind of wiggled over near her and laid my hand on her arm. Then Ma yelled: "Donald, go and get a pound of rice! Go now, I said."

I got scared. She had not said it before and she had a lot of rice in a jar in the closet. But I didn't dare say so. I went out.

I couldn't help but think of Mrs. Swyburne. She ought not to cry so easy. She might not have had a little boy and Ma might have—but she should have been happy. She had a great big house on the swellest street in Somerset and a car all her own and some one to drive it for her. Ma only had me and our house which wasn't so swell, but it was all right.

Then Mrs. Swyburne had her husband and he had such a nice voice. You didn't mind leaning on his knee and talking to him as soon as you saw him. He had eyes that looked so smiling and happy and when you touched his hands they were soft and gentle as Ma's even if they were bigger.

I knew him real well. He and I were friends. He used to come to our house a lot of time and bring me books and talk to Ma while I read.

He knew us real well. He called Ma Louise and me Don. Sometimes he'd stay and eat supper with us and then sit down and talk. I never could see why he'd come way out there to talk to us when he had a whole lot of rich friends down in Somerset and a wife that looked like the only doll I ever had.

A lady gave me that doll once and I thought she was really pretty—all pale and blonde and rosy. I thought she was real pretty at first but by and by she seemed so dumb. She never did anything but look pink and pale and rosy and pretty. She never went out and ran with me like Cato did. So I just took a rock and gave her a rap up beside her head and threw her in the bushes.

Maybe Mrs. Swyburne was pale and pink and dumb like the doll and her husband couldn't rap her with a rock and throw her away.

I don't know.

Anyhow, he used to come and talk to us and he'd talk to Ma a long time after I was in bed. Sometimes I'd wake up and hear them talking. He used to bring me toys until he found out that I could make my own toys and that I liked books.

After that he brought me books. All kinds of books about fairies and Indians and folks in other countries.

Sometimes he and I would talk about the books—especially those I liked. The one I liked most was called "Ten Tales to Inspire Youth."

That sounds kind of funny but the book was great. It had stories in it all about men. All men. I read all of the stories but I liked the one about the fellow named Orestes who went home from the Trojan War and found his mother had married his father's brother so he killed them. I was always sorry for the women with the whips of flame like forked tongues who used to worry him afterwards. I don't see why the furies pursued him. They knew he did it because he loved his father so much.

Another story I liked was about Oedipus—a Greek too—who put out his eyes to hurt himself because he killed his father and married his mother by mistake.

But after I read "David and Goliath," I just had to pretend that I was David.

I swiped a half a yard of elastic from Ma and hunted a long time until I found a good forked piece of wood. Then I made a swell slingshot.

The story said that David asked Jehovah (which was God) to let his slingshot shoot good. "Do thou lend thy strength to my arm, Jehovah," he prayed.

I used to say that too just to be like him.

I told Dr. Swyburne I liked these stories.

"Why do you like them?" he asked me.

"Because they are about men," I said.

"Because they are about men! Is that the only reason?"

Then I told him no; that I liked them because the men in the stories were brave and had courage and stuck until they got what they wanted, even if they hurt themselves getting it.

And he laughed and said, to Ma: "Louise, he has the blood, all right!"

And Ma said: "Yes! He is a true Gage. They're brave enough and put their eyes out too. That takes courage all right!"

Ma and I are named Gage, so I stuck out my chest and said: "Ma, which one of us Gages put his eyes out?"

"Me," she said—and she was standing there looking right at me!

I thought she was making fun. So I felt funny.

Dr. Swyburne turned red and said: "I meant the other blood of course. All the Swyburnes are heroes."

I didn't know what he meant. My name is Gage and so is Ma's so he didn't mean me.

Ma threw her head up and looked at him and says: "Oh, are they heroes?" Then she says real quick: "Donald go to bed right now!"

I didn't want to go but I went. I took a long time to take off my clothes and I heard Ma and Dr. Swyburne talking fast like they were fussing.

I couldn't hear exactly what they said but I kept hearing Ma say: "I'm through!"

And I heard Dr. Swyburne say: "You can't be!"

I kind of dozed to sleep. By and by I heard Ma say again: "Well, I'm through!"

And Dr. Swyburne said: "I won't let you be!"

Then I rolled over to think a minute and then go downstairs maybe.

But when I rolled over again, the sun was shining and I had to get up.

Ma never said anything about what happened so I didn't either. She just walked around doing her work fast, holding her head up high like she always does when I make her mad.

So I never said a thing that day.

One day I came home from school. I came in the back way and when I was in the kitchen I could hear a man in the front of the room talking to Ma. I stood still a minute to see if it was Dr. Swyburne though I knew he never comes in the afternoon.

The voice didn't sound like his so I walked in the hall and passed the door. The man had his back to me so I just looked at him a minute and didn't say anything. He had on leather leggins and sort of uniform like soldiers wear. He was stooping over the machine talking to Ma and I couldn't see his face.

Just then I stumbled over the little rug in the hall and he stood up and looked at me.

He was a colored man! Colored just like Ma and me. You see, there aren't any other people in Somerset colored like we are, so I was sort of surprised to see him.

"This is my son, Mr. Frazier," Ma said.

I said pleased to meet you and stepped on Ma's feet. But not on purpose. You know I kind of thought he was going to be named Gage and be some relation to us and stay at our house awhile.

I never saw many colored people—no colored men—and I wanted to see some. When Ma called him Frazier it made my feet slippery so I stubbed my toe.

"Hello, son!" he said nice and quiet.

He didn't talk like Ma and me. He talked slower and softer. I liked him straight off so I grinned and said: "Hello yourself."

"How's the books?" he said then.

I didn't know what he meant at first but I guessed he meant school. So I said: "Books aren't good as the fishin'."

He laughed out loud and said I was all right and said he and I were going to be friends and that while he was in Somerset he was going to come to our house often and see us.

Then he went out. Ma told me he was driving some lady's car. She was visiting Somerset from New York and he would be there a little while.

Gee, I was so glad! I made a fishing rod for him that very afternoon out of a piece of willow I had been saving for a long time.

And one day, he and I went down to the lake and fished. We sat still on top a log that went across a little bay like. I felt kind of excited and couldn't say a word. I just kept looking at him every once in a while and smiled. I did not grin. Ma said I grinned too much.

Pretty soon he said: "What are you going to be when you grow up, son?"

"A colored man," I said. I meant to say some more, but he hollered and laughed so loud that Cato had to run up to see what was doing.

"Sure you'll be a colored man! No way to get out of that! But I mean this: What kind of work are you going to do?"

I had to think a minute. I had to think of all the kinds of work men did. Some of the men in Somerset were farmers. Some kept stores. Some swept the streets. Some were rich and did not do anything at home but they went to the city and had their cars driven to the shop and to meet them at the train.

All the conductors and porters make a lot of scramble to get those men on and off the train, even if they looked as if they could take care of themselves.

So I said to Mr. Frazier: "I want to have an office."

"An office?"

"Yes. In the city so's I can go in to it and have my car meet me when I come to Somerset."

"Fat chance a colored man has!" he said.

"I can too have an office!" I said. He made me sore. "I can have one if I want to! I want to have an office and be a specialist like Dr. Swyburne."

Mr. Frazier dropped his pole and had to swear something awful when he reached for it though it wasn't very far from him.

"Why'd you pick him?" he said and looked at me kind of mad like and before I could think of what to say he said: "Say son, does that guy come up to see your mother?"

"Sure he comes to see us both!" I said.

Mr. Frazier laughed again but not out loud. It made me sore all over. I started to hit him with my pole but I thought about something I'd read once that said even a savage will treat you right in his house—so I didn't hit him. Of course, he wasn't in my house exactly but he was sitting on my own log over my fishing places and that's like being in your own house.

Mr. Frazier laughed to himself again and then all of a sudden he took the pole I had made him out of the piece of willow I had been saving for myself and laid it across his knees and broke it in two. Then he said out loud: "Nigger women," and then threw the pole in the water.

I grabbed my pole right out of the water and slammed it across his face. I never thought of the hook until I hit him, but it did not stick in him. It caught in a tree and I broke the string yanking it out.

He looked at me like he was going to knock me in the water and even though I was scared, I was thinking how I'd let myself fall if he did knock me off—so that I could swim out without getting tangled in the roots under the bank.

But he didn't do it. He looked at me a minute and said: "Sorry, son! Sorry! Not your fault."

Then he put his hand on my hair and brushed it back and sort of lifted it up and said: "Like the rest."

I got up and said I was going home and he came too. I was afraid he would come in but when he got to my gate he said: "So long," and walked right on.

I went on in. Ma was sewing. She jumped up when I came in. "Where is Mr. Frazier?" she asked me. She didn't even say hello to me!

"I hit him," I said.

"You hit him!" she hollered. "You *hit* him! What did you do that for? Are you crazy?"

I told her no. "He said 'nigger women' when I told him that Dr. Swyburne was a friend of ours and came to see us."

Oh Ma looked terrible then. I can't tell you how she did look. Her face sort of slipped around and twisted like the geography says the earth does when the fire inside of it gets too hot.

She never said a word at first. She just sat there. Then she asked me to tell her all about every bit that happened.

I told her. She kept wriggling from side to side like the fire was getting hotter. When I finished, she said: "Poor baby! My baby boy! Not your fault! Not your fault!"

That made me think of Mr. Frazier so I pushed out of her arms and said: "Ma your breast pin hurts my face when you do that!"

She leaned over on the arms of her chair and cried and cried until I cried too.

All that week I'd think of the fire inside of the earth when I looked at Ma. She looked so funny and she kept talking to herself.

On Saturday night we were sitting at the table when I heard a car drive up the road.

"Here's Dr. Swyburne!" I said and I felt so glad I stopped eating.

"He isn't coming here!" Ma said and then she jumped up.

"Sure he's coming," I said. "I know his motor." And I started to get up too.

"You stay where you are!" Ma hollered and she went out and closed the door behind her.

I took another piece of cake and began eating the frosting. I heard Dr. Swyburne come up on the porch.

"Hello, Louise," he said. I could tell he was smiling by his voice.

I couldn't hear what Ma said at first but pretty soon I heard her say: "You can't come here any more!"

That hurt my feelings. I liked Dr. Swyburne. I liked him better than anybody I knew besides Ma.

Ma stayed out a long time and by and by she came in alone and I heard Dr. Swyburne drive away.

She didn't look at me at all. She just leaned back against the door and said: "Dear Jesus! With your help I'll free myself."

I wanted to ask her from what did she want to free herself. It sounded like she was in jail or an animal in a trap in the woods.

I thought about it all during supper but I didn't dare say much. I thought about it and pretended that she was shut up in a prison and I was a time fighter who beat all the keepers and got her out.

Then it came to me that I better get ready to fight to get her out of whatever she was in. I never said anything to her. I carried my air-rifle on my back and my slingshot in my pocket. I wanted to ask her where her enemy was, but she never talked to me about it; so I had to keep quiet too. You know Ma always got mad if I talked about things first. She likes to talk, then I can talk afterwards.

One Sunday she told me she was going for a walk.

"Can I go?" I asked her.

"No," she said. "You play around the yard."

Then she put her hat on and stood looking in the mirror at herself for a minute. All of a sudden I heard her say to herself: "All I need is strength to fight out of it."

"Ma'am?" I thought she was talking to me at first.

She stopped and hugged my head—like I wish she wouldn't sometimes and then went out.

I stayed still until she got out of the yard. Then I ran and got my rifle and slingshot and followed her.

I crept behind her in the bushes beside the road. I cut across the fields and came out behind the willow patch the way I always do when I am tracking Indians and wild animals.

By and by she came out in the clearing that is behind Dr. Somerset's. They call it Somerset's Grove and it's named for his folks who used to live there—just as the town was.

She sat down so I lay down in the bushes. A sharp rock was sticking in my knee but I was afraid to move for fear she'd hear me and send me home.

By and by I heard someone walking on the grass and I saw Dr. Swyburne coming up. He started talking before he got to her.

"Louise," he said. "Louise! I am not going to give anything up to a nigger."

"Not even a nigger woman whom you took from a nigger?" She lifted her mouth in the senna and manna way.

"Don't say that!" he said. "Don't say that! I wanted a son. I couldn't have taken a woman in my own world—that would have ruined my practice. Elaine couldn't have a child!"

"Yes," Ma said. "It would have ruined you and your profession. What did it do for me? What did it do for Donald?"

"I have told you I will give him the best the world can offer. He is a Swyburne!"

"He is *my* child," Ma hollered. "It isn't his fault he is yours!"

"But I give him everything a father could give his son!"

"He has no name!" Ma said.

"I have too!" I hollered inside of me. "Donald Gage!"

"He has no name," Ma said again, "and neither have I!" And she began to cry.

"He has blood!" said Dr. Swyburne.

"But how did he get it? Oh, I'm through. Stay away from my house and I'll marry one of my men so Donald can be somebody."

"A nigger's son?"

"Don't say that again," Ma hollered and jumped up.

"Do you think I'll give up a woman of mine to a nigger?"

Ma hollered again and hit him right in his face.

He grabbed her wrists and turned the right one, I guess because she fell away from him on that side.

I couldn't stand any more. I snatched out my slingshot and pulled the stone up that was sticking in my knee.

I started to shoot. Then I remembered what David said first, so I shut my eyes and said it: "Do thou, Jehovah (which is God today), lend strength to my arm."

When I opened my eyes Ma had broken away and was running toward the road. Dr. Swyburne was standing still by the tree looking after her like he was going to catch her. His face was turned sideways to me. I looked at his head where his hair was brushed back from the side of his face.

I took aim and let the stone go. I heard him say: "Oh, my God!" I saw blood on his face and I saw him stagger and fall against the tree.

Then I ran too.

When I got home Ma was sitting in her chair with her hat thrown on the floor beside her and her head was lying back.

I walked up to her: "Ma," I said real loud.

She reached out and grabbed me and hugged my head down to her neck like she always does.

The big breast-pin scratched my mouth. I opened my mouth to speak and something hot and sharp ran into my tongue.

"Ma! Ma!" I tried to holler. "The pin is sticking in my tongue!"

I don't know what I said though. When I tried to talk again, Ma and Dr. Somerset were looking down at me and I was lying in bed. I tried to say something but I could not say anything. My mouth felt like it was full of hot bread and I could not talk around it.

Dr. Somerset poured something in my mouth and it felt like it was on fire.

"They found Shev Swyburne in my thistle grove this afternoon," he said to Ma.

Ma look up quick. "*Found* him! What do you mean?"

"I mean he was lying on the ground—either fell or was struck and fell. He was dead from a blow on the temple."

I tried to holler but my tongue was too thick.

Ma took hold of each side of her face and held to it, then she just stared at Dr. Somerset. He put a lot of things back in his bag.

Then he sat up and looked at Ma. "Louise," he said, "why is all that thistle down on your skirt?"

Ma looked down. So did I. There was thistle down all over the hem of her dress.

"You don't think I killed him, do you?" she cried, "you don't think I did it?" Then she cried something awful.

I tried to get up but I was too dizzy. I crawled across the bed on my stomach and reached out to the chair that had my pants on it. It was hard to do—but I dragged my slingshot out of my pocket, crawled back across the bed and laid it in Dr. Somerset's knees. He looked at me for a minute.

"Are you trying to tell me that you did it, son?" he asked me.

I said yes with my head.

"My God! My God!! His own child!!!"

Dr. Somerset said to Ma: "God isn't dead yet."

Then he patted her on the arm and told her not to tell anybody nothing and they sat down and picked all the thistle down out of the skirt. He took the slingshot and broke it all up and put it all in a paper and carried it downstairs and put it in the stove.

I tried to talk. I wanted to tell him to leave it so I could show my grandchildren what I had used to free Ma like the men do in the books.

I couldn't talk though. My tongue was too thick for my mouth. The next day it burnt worse and things began to float around my eyes and head like pieces of wood in the water.

Sometimes I could see clearly though and once I saw Dr. Somerset talking to another man. Dr. Somerset was saying: "We'll have to operate to save his life. His tongue is poisoned. I am afraid it will take his speech from him."

Ma hollered then: "Thank God! He will not talk! Never! He can't talk! Thank God! Oh God! I thank Thee!" And then she cried like she always does and that time it sounded like she was laughing too.

The other man looked funny and said: "Some of them have no natural feeling of parent for child!"

Dr. Somerset looked at him and said: "You may be fine as a doctor but otherwise you are an awful fool."

Then he told the other man to go out and he began talking to Ma.
"I understand! I understand," he said. "I know all about it. He took
you away from somebody and some of these days he might have taken
Donald from you. He took Elaine from me once and I told him then
God would strip him for it. Now it is all over. Never tell anyone and I
will not. The boy knows how to read and write and will be able to live."

So I got a black stump in my mouth. It's shaped like a forked whip.

Some days I pretend I am Orestes with the Furies' whips in my mouth
for killing a man.

Some days I pretend I am Oedipus and that I cut it out for killing my
own father.

That's what makes me sick all over sometimes.

I killed my own father. But I didn't know it was my father. I was
freeing Ma.

Still—I shall never write that on my paper to Ma and Dr. Somerset
the way I have to talk to them and tell them when things hurt me.

My father said I was a Swyburne and that was why I liked people to be
brave and courageous.

Ma says I am a Gage and that is why I am brave and courageous.

But I am both, so I am a whole lot brave, a whole lot courageous. And I
am bearing my Furies and my clipped tongue like a Swyburne and a
Gage—'cause I am both of them.

FROM *THE CRISIS*, NOVEMBER 1927

# Drab Rambles

## MARITA BONNER

I am hurt. There is blood on me. You do not care. You do not know me. You do not know me. You do not care. There is blood on me. Sometimes it gets on you. You do not care I am hurt. Sometimes it gets on your hands—on your soul even. You do not care. You do not know me.

You do not care to know me, you say, because we are different. We are different you say.

You are white, you say. And I am black.

You do not know me.

I am all men tinged in brown. I am all men with a touch of black. I am you and I am myself.

You do not know me. You do not care, you say.

I am an inflow of God, tossing about in the bodies of all men: all men tinged and touched with black.

I am not pure Africa of five thousand years ago. I am you—all men tinged and touched. Not old Africa into somnolence by a jungle that blots out all traces of its antiquity.

I am all men. I am tinged and touched. I am colored. All men tinged and touched; colored in a brown body.

Close all men in a small space, tinge and touch the Space with one blood—you get a check-mated Hell.

A check-mated Hell, seething in a brown body, I am.

I am colored. A check-mated Hell seething in a brown body. You do not know me.

You do not care—you say.

But still, I am you—and all men.

I am colored. A check-mated Hell seething in a brown body.

Sometimes I wander up and down and look. Look at the tinged-in-black, the touched-in-brown. I wander and see how it is with them and wonder how long—how long Hell can seethe before it boils over.

How long can Hell be check-mated?

Or if check-mated can solidify, if this is all it is?

If this is all it is.

THE FIRST PORTRAIT

He was sitting in the corridor of the Out-Patients Department. He was sitting in the far corner well out of the way. When the doors opened at nine o'clock, he had been the first one in. His heart was beating fast. His heart beat faster than it should. No heart should beat so fast that you choke at the throat when you try to breathe. You should not feel it knocking—knocking—knocking—now against your ribs, now against something deep within you. Knocking against something deep, so deep that you cannot fall asleep without feeling a cutting, pressing weight laid against your throat, over your chest. A cutting, pressing weight that makes you struggle to spring from the midst of your sleep. Spring up.

It had beat like that now for months. At first he had tried to work it off. Swung the pick in his daily ditch digging—faster—harder. But that had not helped it at all. It had beaten harder and faster for the swinging. He had tried castor oil to run it off of his system. Someone told him he ate too much meat and smoked too much. So he had given up his beloved ham and beef and chicken and tried to swing the pick on lighter things.

It would be better soon.

His breath had begun to get short then. He had to stop oftener to rest between swings. The foreman, Mike Leary, had cursed at first and then moved him back to the last line of diggers. It hurt him to think he was not so strong as he had been.—But it would be better soon.

He would not tell his wife how badly his heart knocked. It would be better soon. He could not afford to lay off from work. He had to dig. Nobody is able to lay off work when there is a woman and children to feed and cover.

The castor oil had not helped. The meat had been given up, even his little pleasure in smoking. Still the heart beat too fast. Still the heart beat so he felt it up in the chords on each side of his neck below his ears.—But it would be better soon.

It would be better. He had asked to be let off half a day so he could be at the hospital at ten o'clock. Mike had growled his usual curses when he asked to get off.

"What the hell is wrong wit' you? All you need is a good dose of whiskey!"

He had gone off. When the doors of the Out-Patients Department opened, he was there. It took him a long time to get up the stairs. The knocking was in his throat so. Beads of perspiration stood grey on his black-brown forehead. He closed his eyes a moment and leaned his head back.

A sound of crying made him open them. On the seat beside him a woman held a baby in her arms. The baby was screaming itself red in the face, wriggling and twisting to get out of its mother's arms on the side where the man sat. The mother shifted the child from one side to the other and told him with her eyes, "You ought not to be here!"

He had tried to smile over the knocking at the baby. Now he rolled his hat over in his hands and looked down.

When he looked up, he turned his eyes away from the baby with its mother. The knocking pounded. Why should a little thing like that make his heart pound. He must be badly off to breathe so fast over nothing. The thought made his heart skip and pound the harder.

But he would be better soon.

Other patients began to file in. Soon the nurse at the desk began to read names aloud. He had put his card in first but she did not call him first. As she called each name, a patient stood up and went through some swinging doors.

Green lights—men in white coats—nurses in white caps and dresses filled the room it would seem, from the glimpses caught through the door. It seemed quiet and still, too, as if everyone were listening to hear something.

Once the door swung open wildly and an Italian came dashing madly through—a doctor close behind him. The man threw himself on the bench: "Oh God! Oh God! I ain't that sick, I ain't so sick I gotta die! No! You don't really know. I ain't so sick!"

The doctor leaned over him and said something quietly. The nurse brought something cloudy in a glass. The man drank it. By and by he was led out—hiccuping but quieter.

Back in his corner, his heart beat smotheringly. Suppose that had been he? Sick enough to die! Was the dago crazy, trying to run away? Run as he would, the sickness would be always with him. For himself, he would be better soon.

"Peter Jackson! Peter Jackson. Peter Jackson. Five, Sawyer Avenue!" The nurse had to say it twice before he heard through his thoughts.

Thump. The beat of his heart knocked him to his feet. He had to stand still before he could move.

"Here! This way." The nurse said it so loudly—so harshly—that the entire room turned around to look at him.

She need not be so hateful. He only felt a little dizzy. Slowly he felt along the floor with his feet. Around the corner of the bench. Across the space beside the desk. The nurse pushed open the door and pressed it back. "Dr. Sibley?" she called.

The door swung shut behind him. Along each side of the room were desks. Behind each, sat a doctor. When the nurse called "Dr. Sibley," no one answered, so Jackson stood at the door. His heart rubbed his ribs unnecessarily.

"Say! Over here!"

The words and the voice made his heart race again.—But he would be better now. He turned toward the direction of the voice, met a cool pair of blue eyes boring through tortoise-rimmed glasses. He sat down.

The doctor took a sheet of paper. "What's your name?"

His heart had been going so that when he said "Peter Jackson," he could make no sound the first time.

"Peter Jackson."

"How old are you?"

"Fifty-four."

"Occupation? Where do you work?"

"Day laborer for the city."

"Can you afford to pay a doctor?"

Surprise took the rest of his breath away for a second. The question had to be repeated.

"I guess so. I never been sick."

"Well, if you can afford to pay a doctor, you ought not to come here. This clinic is for foreigners and people who cannot pay a doctor. Your people have some of your own doctors in this city."

The doctor wrote for such a long time on the paper then that he thought he was through with him and he started to get up.

"Sit down." The words caught him before he was on his feet. "I haven't told you to go anywhere."

"I thought—," Jackson hung on his words uncertain.

"You needn't! Don't think! Open your shirt." And the doctor fitted a pair of tubes in his ears and shut out his thoughts.

He fitted the tubes in his ears and laid a sieve-like piece of rubber against his patient's chest. Laid it up. Laid it down. Finally he said: "What have you been doing to this heart of yours? All to pieces. All gone."

Gone. His heart was all gone. He tried to say something but the doctor snatched the tube away and turned around to the desk and wrote again.

Again he turned around: "Push up your sleeve," he said this time.

The sleeve went up. A piece of rubber went around his arm above the elbow. Something began to squeeze—knot—drag on his arm.

"Pressure almost two hundred," the doctor shot at him this time. "You can't stand this much longer."

He turned around. He wrote again. He wrote and pushed the paper away. "Well," said the doctor, "you will have to stop working and lie down. You must keep your feet on a level with your body."

Jackson wanted to yell with laughter. Lie down. If he had had breath enough, he would have blown all the papers off the desk, he would have laughed so. He looked into the blue eyes. "I can't stop work," he said.

The doctor shrugged: "Then," he said, and said no more.

Then! Then what?

Neither one of them spoke.

Then what?

Jackson wet his lips: "You mean—you mean I got to stop work to get well?"

"I mean you have to stop if you want to stay here."

"You mean even if I stop you may not cure me?"

The blue eyes did go down toward the desk then. The answer was a question.

"You don't think I can make a new heart, do you? You only get one heart. You are born with that. You ought not to live so hard."

Live hard? Did this man think he had been a sport? Live hard. Liquor, wild sleepless nights—sleep-drugged, rag-worn, half-shoddy days? That instead of what it had been. Ditches and picks. Births and funerals. Stretching a dollar the length of ten. A job, no job; three children and a wife to feed; bread thirteen cents a loaf. For pleasure, church—where he

was too tired to go sometimes. Tobacco that he had to consider twice
before he bought.

"I ain't lived hard! I ain't lived hard!" he said suddenly. "I have worked
harder than I should, that's all."

"Why didn't you get another job?" the doctor snapped. "Didn't need
to dig ditches all your life."

Jackson drew himself up; "I had to dig ditches because I am an ignorant black man. If I was an ignorant white man, I could get easier jobs. I
could even have worked in this hospital."

Color flooded the doctor's face. Whistles blew and shrieked suddenly
outside.

He started for the door. Carefully. He must not waste his strength.
Rent, food, clothes. He could not afford to lay off.

He had almost reached the door when a hand shook him suddenly. It
was the doctor close behind him. He held out a white sheet of paper.
"Your prescription," he explained, and seemed to hesitate. "Digitalis. It
will help some. I am sorry."

Sorry for what? Jackson found the side-walk and lit his pipe to steady
himself. He had almost reached the ditches when he remembered the
paper. He could not find it. He went on.

THE SECOND PORTRAIT

By twelve o'clock, noon, the washroom of Kale's Fine Family Laundry
held enough steam to take the shell off a turtle's back. Fill tubs with
steaming water at six o'clock, set thirty colored women to rubbing and
shouting and singing at the tubs and by twelve o'clock noon the room is
over full of steam. The steam is thick—warm—and it settles on your
flesh like a damp fur rug. Every pore sits agape in your body; agape—
dripping.

Kale's Fine Family Laundry did a good business. Mr. Kale believed in
this running on oiled cogs. Cogs that slip easily—oiled from the lowest
to the highest.

Now the cogs lowest in his smooth machinery were these thirty tubs
and the thirty women at the tubs. I put the tubs first, because they were
always there. The women came and went. Sometimes they merely went.
Most all of them were dark brown and were that soft bulgy fat that no
amount of hard work can rub off of some colored women. All day long
they rubbed and scrubbed and sang or shouted and cursed or were silent
according to their natures.

Madie Frye never sang or shouted or cursed aloud. Madie was silent. She sang and shouted and cursed within. She sang the first day she came there to work. Sang songs of thanksgiving within her. She had needed that job. She had not worked for ten months until she came there. She had washed dishes in a boarding house before that. That was when she first came from Georgia. She had liked things then. Liked the job, liked the church she joined, liked Tom Nolan, the man for whom she washed dishes.

One day his wife asked Madie if she had a husband. She told her no. She was paid off. Madie, the second, was born soon after. Madie named her unquestioningly Madie Frye. It never occurred to her to name her Nolan, which would have been proper.

Madie bore her pain in silence, bore her baby in a charity ward, thanked God for the kindness of a North and thanked God that she was not back in Culvert when Madie was born, for she would have been turned out of church.

Madie stopped singing aloud then. She tried to get jobs—dishwashing—cleaning—washing clothes—but you cannot keep a job washing someone's clothes or cleaning their home and nurse a baby and keep it from yelling the lady of the house into yelling tantrums.

Madie, second, lost for her mother exactly two dozen jobs between her advent and her tenth month in her mother's arms.

Madie had not had time to feel sorry for herself at first. She was too busy wondering how long she could hold each job. Could she keep Madie quiet until she paid her room rent? Could she keep Mrs. Jones from knowing that Madie was down under the cellar stairs in a basket every day while she was upstairs cleaning, until she got a pair of shoes?

By the time she went to work in Kale's Hand Laundry, she had found the baby a too great handicap to take to work. She began to leave Madie with her next door neighbor, Mrs. Sundell, who went to church three times every Sunday and once in the week. She must be good enough to keep Madie while her mother worked. She was. She kept Madie for two dollars a week and Madie kept quiet for her and slept all night long when she reached home with her mother. Her mother marvelled and asked Mrs. Sundell how she did it.

"Every time she cries, I give her paregoric. Good for her stomach."

So the baby grew calmer and calmer each day. Calmer and quieter. Her mother worked and steamed silently down in Kale's tub room. Worked, shouting songs of thanksgiving within her for steady money and peaceful nights.

June set in, and with it, scorching days. Days that made the thick steam full of lye and washing-powder eat the lining out of your lungs. There was a set of rules tacked up inside the big door that led into the checking-room that plainly said: "This door is never to be opened between the hours of six in the morning and twelve noon. Nor between the hours of one and six p.m."

That was to keep the steam from the checkers. They were all white and could read and write so they were checkers.

One day Madie put too much lye in some boiling water. It choked her. When she drew her next breath, she was holding her head in the clean cool air of the checking-room. She drew in a deep breath and coughed. A man spun across the floor and a white hand shot to the door. "Why the hell don't you obey the rules?" He slammed the door and Madie stumbled back down the stairs.

A girl at the end tub looked around. "Was that Mr. Payne?" she asked. Madie was still dazed; "Mr. Payne?" she asked.

"Yah. The man what closed the door."

"I don't know who he was."

The other laughed and drew closer to her. "Better know who he is," she said.

Madie blinked up at her. "Why?"

The girl cocked an eye: "Good to know him. You can stay off sometimes—if he likes you." That was all that day.

Another day Madie was going home. Her blank brown face was freshly powdered and she went quietly across the checking-room. The room was empty it seemed at first. All the girls were gone. When Madie was half across the room she saw a man sitting in the corner behind a desk. He looked at her as soon as she looked at him. It was the man who had yanked the door out of her hand, she thought. Fear took hold of her. She began to rush.

Someone called. It was the man at the desk. "Hey, what's your rush?" The voice was not loud and bloody this time. It was soft—soft—soft—like a cat's foot. Madie stood still afraid to go forward—afraid to turn around.

"What, are you afraid of me?" Soft like a cat's foot. "Come here."

—Good to know him—

Madie made the space to the outer door in one stride. The door opened in. She pushed against it.

"Aw, what's the matter with you?" Foot-steps brought the voice nearer. A white hand fitted over the doorknob as she slid hers quickly away.

Madie could not breathe. Neither could she lift her eyes. The door opened slowly. She had to move backward to give it space. Another white hand brushed the softness of her body.

She stumbled out into the alley. Cold sweat stood out on her.

Madie second had cost her jobs and jobs. She came by Madie keeping that first job.

Madie was black brown. The baby was yellow. Was she now going to go job hunting or have a sister or brother to keep with Madie second?

Cold perspiration sent her shivering in the alley.

And Madie cursed aloud.


Not in my day or your tomorrow—perhaps—but somewhere in God's day of meeting—somewhere in God's day of measuring full measures overflowing—the blood will flow back to you—and you will care.

FROM *THE CRISIS*, DECEMBER 1927

# Nothing New

## MARITA BONNER

There was, once high on a hillside, a muddy brook. A brook full of yellow muddy water that foamed and churned over a rock bed.

Halfway down the hillside the water pooled in the clearest pool. All the people wondered how the muddy water cleared at that place. They did not know. They did not understand. They only went to the pool and drank. Sometimes they stooped over and looked into the water and saw themselves.

If they had looked deeper they might have seen God.

People seldom look that deep, though. They do not always understand how to do things.

They are not God. He alone understands.


You have been down on Frye Street. You know how it runs from Grand Avenue and the L to a river; from freckled-faced tow heads to yellow Orientals; from broad Italy to broad Georgia, from hooked nose to square black noses. How it lisps in French, how it babbles in Italian, how it gurgles in German, how it drawls and crawls through Black Belt dialects. Frye Street flows nicely together. It is like muddy water. Like muddy water in a brook.

Reuben Jackson and his wife Bessie—late of Georgia—made a home of three rooms at number thirteen Frye Street.

"Bad luck number," said the neighbors.

"Good luck number," said Reuben and Bessie.

Reuben did not know much. He knew only God, work, church, work and God. The only things Bessie knew were God, work, Denny, prayer, Reuben, prayer, Denny, work, work, work, God.

Denny was one thing they both knew beside God and work. Denny was their little son. He knew lots of things. He knew that when the sun shone across the room a cobwebby shaft appeared that you could not walk up. And when the water dripped on pans in the sink it sang a tune: "Hear the time! Feel the time! Beat with me! Tap-ty tap! T-ta-tap! Ta-ty-tap!" The water sang a tune that made your feet move.

"Stop that jigging, you Denny," Bessie always cried. "God! Don't let him be no dancing man." She would pray afterwards. "Don't let him be no toy-tin fool man!"

Reuben watched him once sitting in his sun shaft. Watched him drape his slender little body along the floor and lift his eyes toward the sunlight. Even then they were eyes that drew deep and told deeper. With his oval clear brown face and his crinkled shining hair, Denny looked too—well as Reuben thought no boy should look. He spoke:

"Why don't you run and wrestle and race with the other boys? You must be a girl. Boys play rough and fight!"

Denny rolled over and looked up at his father. "I ain't a girl!" he declared deliberately.

He started around the room for something to fight to prove his assertion. The cat lay peacefully sleeping by the stove. Denny snatched hold of the cat's tail to awaken it. The cat came up with all claws combing Denny.

"My God, ain't he cruel," screamed his mother. She slapped Denny and the cat apart.

Denny lay down under the iron board and considered the odd red patterns that the claws had made on his arms. . . . A red house and a red hill. Red trees around it; a red path running up the hill . . .

"Make my child do what's right," prayed Bessie ironing above him.

People are not God. He alone understands.

Denny was running full tilt down a hillside. Whooping, yelling, shouting. Flying after nothing. Young Frye Street, mixed as usual, raced with him.

There was no school out here. There were no street cars, no houses, no ash-cans and basement stairs to interfere with a run. Out here you could run straight, swift, in one direction with nothing to stop you but your own lack of foot power and breath. A picnic "out of town" pitched your spirits high and Young Frye Street could soar through all twelve heavens of enjoyment.

The racers reached the foot of the hill. Denny swerved to one side. A tiny colored girl was stooping over in the grass.

"Hey, Denny!" she called. Denny stopped to let the others sweep by.

"Hey, Margaret!" he answered. "What you doing?"

Margaret held up a handful of flowers. "I want that one." She pointed to a clump of dusky purple milkweeds bending behind a bush.

Denny hopped toward it.

He had almost reached it when the bush parted and a boy stepped out: "Don't come over here," he ordered. "This is the white kids' side!"

Denny looked at him. He was not of Frye Street. Other strange children appeared behind him. "This is a white picnic over here! Stay away from our side."

Denny continued toward his flower. Margaret squatted contentedly in the grass. She was going to get her flower.

"I said not to come over here," yelled the boy behind the bush.

Denny hopped around the bush.

"What you want over here?" the other bristled.

"That flower!" Denny pointed.

The other curved his body out in exaggerated childish sarcasm. "Sissy! Picking flowers." He turned to the boys behind him. "Sissy nigger! Picking flowers!"

Denny punched at the boy and snatched at the flower. The other stuck out his foot and Denny dragged him down as he fell. Young Frye Street rushed back up the hill at the primeval howl that set in.

Down on the ground, Denny and the white boy squirmed and kicked. They dug and pounded each other.

"You stay off the white kids' side, nigger!"

"I'm going to get that flower, I am!" Denny dragged his enemy along with him as he lunged toward the bush.

The flower beckoned and bent its stalk. On the white kids' side. Lovely, dusky, purple. Bending toward him. The milky perfume almost reached him. On the white kids' side. He wanted it. He would get it. Something ripped.

Denny left the collar of his blouse in the boy's hand and wrenched loose. He grabbed at the stem. On the white kids' side. Bending to him—slender, bending to him. On the white kids' side. He wanted it. He was going to have it—

The boy caught up to him as he had almost reached the flower. They fell again.—He was going to get that flower. He was going to. Tear the white kid off. Tear the white hands off his throat. Tear the white kid off his arms. Tear the white kid's weight off his chest. He'd move him—

Denny made a twist and slid low to the ground, the other boy beneath him, face downward. He pinned the boy's shoulders to the ground and clutching a handful of blonde hair in either hand, beat his head against the ground.

Young Frye Street sang the song of triumph. Sang it long and loud. Sang it loud enough for Mrs. Bessie Jackson—resting under a clump of trees with other mothers—to hear.

"I know them children is fighting!" she declared and started off in the direction of the yelling.

Halfway she met Margaret, a long milkweed flower dragging in one hand: "Denny," she explained, holding it up.

"I knew it," cried his mother and ran the rest of the way. "Stop killing that child," she screamed as soon as she had neared the mob. She dragged Denny off the boy. Dragged him through the crowd under the tree. Then she began:

"Look at them clothes. Where is your collar at? All I do is try to fix you up and now look at you! Look at you! Even your shirt torn!"

"Just as well him tear that for what he said," Denny offered.

This approximated "sauce" or the last straw or the point of overflow. His mother was staggered. Was there nothing she could do? Unconsciously she looked up to Heaven, then down to earth. A convenient bush flaunted nearby. She pulled it up—by the roots.

—On the white kids' side. The flower he wanted.—

God understands, doesn't He?


It had been a hard struggle. Reuben was still bitter and stubborn:

"What reason Denny got to go to some art school? What he going to learn there?"

"Art! Painting!" Bessie defended. "The teachers at the high school say he know how to paint special like. He'd ought to go, they said."

"Yes, they said, but they ain't going to pay for him. He ought to go somewhere and do some real man's work. Ain't nothin' but women paddlin' up and down, worryin' about paintin'."

"He's going all the same. Them teachers said he was better—!"

"Oh, all right. Let him go."

And Denny went to the Littler Art School. Carried his joyous six-foot, slender, brown self up on Grand Avenue, across, under, the elevated towers—up town. Up town to school.

"Bessie Jackson better put him on a truck like Annie Turner done her Jake," declared colored Frye Street. "Ain't no man got no business spendin' his life learnin' to paint."

"He should earn money! Money!" protested one portion of Frye Street through its hooked noses.

"Let him marry a wife," chuckled the Italians.

"He's going to learn art," said Denny's mother.

Denny went. The Littler School was filled with students of both sexes and of all races and degrees of life. Most of them were sufficiently gifted to be there. Days there when they showed promise. Days there when they doubted their own reasons for coming.

Denny did as well and as badly as the rest. Sometimes he even did things that attracted attention.

He himself always drew attention, for he was tall, straight and had features that were meant to go with the blondest hair and the bluest eyes. He was not blond though. He was clean shaven and curly haired and brown as any Polynesian. His eyes were still deep drawing—deep telling. Eyes like a sea-going liner that could drift far without getting lost; that could draw deep without sinking.

Some women scrambled to make an impression on him. If they had looked at his mouth they would have withheld their efforts.

Anne Forest was one of the scramblers. She did not know she was scrambling, though. If anyone had told her that she was, she would have exploded, "Why! He is a nigger!"

Anne, you see, was white. She was the kind of girl who made you feel that she thrived on thirty-nine cent chocolates, fifteen-dollar silk dress sales, twenty-five cent love stories and much guilty smootchy kissing. If that does not make you sense her water-waved bob, her too carefully rouged face, her too perfumed person, I cannot bring her any nearer to you.

Anne scrambled unconsciously. Denny was an attractive man. Denny knew she was scrambling—so he went further within himself.

Went so far within himself that he did not notice Pauline Hammond who sat next to him.

One day he was mixing paint in a little white dish. Somehow the dish capsized and the paint flowed over the desk and spattered.

"Oh, my heavens!" said a girl's voice.

Denny stood up: "I beg your pardon." He looked across the desk.

Purple paint was splashed along the girl's smock and was even on her shoes.

"Oh, that's all right! No harm done at all," she said pleasantly.

Nice voice. Not jagged or dangling. Denny looked at her again. He dipped his handkerchief into the water and wiped off the shoes.

That done, they sat back and talked to each other. Talked to each other that day and the next day. Several days they talked.

Denny began to notice Pauline carefully. She did not talk to people as if they were strange hard shells she had to crack open to get inside. She talked as if she were already in the shell. In their very shell.

—Not many people can talk that soul-satisfying way. Why? I do not know. I am not God. I do not always understand—.

They talked about work; their life outside of school. Life. Life out in the world. With an artist's eye Denny noted her as she talked. Slender, more figure than heavy form, molded. Poised. Head erect on neck, neck uplifted on shoulders, body held neither too stiff nor too slack. Poised and slenderly molded as an aristocrat.

They thought together and worked together. Saw things through each other's eyes. They loved each other.

One day they went to a Sargent exhibit—and saw Anne Forest. She gushed and mumbled and declared war on Pauline. She did not know she had declared war, though.

"Pauline Hammond goes out with that nigger Denny Jackson!" she informed all the girls in class the next day.

"With a nigger!" The news seeped through the school. Seeped from the President's office on the third floor to the janitor down below the stairs.

Anne Forest only told one man the news. He was Allen Carter. He had taken Pauline to three dances and Anne to one. Maybe Anne was trying to even the ratio when she told him: "Pauline Hammond is rushing a nigger now."

Allen truly reeled. "Pauline! A nigger?"

Anne nodded. "Denny Jackson—or whatever his name is," she hastened to correct herself.

Allen cursed aloud. "Pauline! She's got too much sense for that! It's that nigger rushing after her! Poor little kid! I'll kill him!"

He tore off his smock with a cursing accompaniment. He cursed before Anne. She did not matter. She should have known that before.

Allen tore off the smock and tore along the hall. Tore into a group gathered in a corner bent over a glass case. Denny and Pauline were in the crowd, side by side. Allen walked up to Denny.

"Here you," he pushed his way in between the two. "Let this white girl alone." He struck Denny full in the face.

Denny struck back. All the women—except Pauline—fled to the far end of the room.

The two men fought. Two jungle beasts would have been kinder to each other. These two tore at each other with more than themselves behind every blow.

"Let that white woman alone, nigger! Stay on your own side!" Allen shouted once.—On your own side. On the white kids' side. That old fight—the flower, bending toward him. He'd move the white kid! Move him and get the flower! Move him and get what was his! He seized a white throat in his hands and moved his hands close together!


He did move the white kid. Moved him so completely that doctors and doctors and running and wailing could not cause his body to stir again. Moved him so far that Denny was moved to the County Jail.

Everything moved then. The judge moved the jury with pleas to see justice done for a man who had sacrificed his life for the beautiful and the true. The jury moved that the old law held: one life taken, take another.

Denny—they took Denny.

Up at the school the trustees moved. "Be it enacted this day—no Negro student shall enter within these doors—."

The newspapers moved their readers. Sent columns of description of the "hypnotized frail flower under the spell of Black Art." So completely under the spell she had to be taken from the stand for merely screaming in the judge's face: "I loved him! I loved him! I loved him!" until the court ran over with the cries.

Frye Street agreed on one thing only. Bessie and Reuben had tried to raise Denny right.

After that point, Frye Street unmixed itself. Flowed apart.

Frye Street—black—was loud in its utterances. "Served Denny right for loving a white woman! Many white niggers as there is! Either Bessie or Reuben must have loved white themselves and was 'shamed to go out open with them. Shame to have that all come out in that child! Now he rottenin' in a murderer's grave!"

White Frye Street held it was the school that had ruined Denny. Had not Frye Street—black and white—played together, worked together, shot crap together, fought together without killing? When a nigger got in school he got crazy.

Up on the hillside the clear water pooled. Up on the hillside people come to drink at the pool. If they looked over, they saw themselves. If they had looked deeper—deeper than themselves—they might have seen God.

But they did not.

People do not do that—do tey?

They do not always understand. Do they?

God alone—He understands.

FROM *THE CRISIS*, NOVEMBER 1926

# The Closing Door

## ANGELINA WELD GRIMKÉ

I was fifteen at the time, diffident and old far beyond my years from much knocking about from pillar to post, a yellow, scrawny, unbeautiful girl, when the big heart of Agnes Milton took pity upon me, loved me and brought me home to live with her in her tiny, sun-filled flat. We were only distantly related, very distantly, in fact, on my dead father's side. You can see, then, there was no binding blood-tie between us, that she was under absolutely no obligation to do what she did. I have wondered time and again how many women would have opened their hearts and their homes, as Agnes Milton did, to a forlorn, unattractive, homeless girl-woman. That one, fine, free, generous act of hers alone shows the wonder-quality of her soul.

Just one little word to explain me. After my father had taken one last cup too many and they had carried him, for the last time, out of the house into which he had been carried so often, my mother, being compelled to work again, returned to the rich family with whom she had been a maid before her marriage. She regarded me as seriously, I suppose, as she did anything in this world; but it was impossible to have me with her. I was passed along from one of her relatives to another. When one tired of me, on I went to the next. Well, I can say this for each and all of them, they certainly believed in teaching me how to work! Judging by the number of homes in which I lived until I was fifteen, my mother was rich indeed in one possession—an abundance of relatives.

And then came Agnes Milton.

Have you ever, I wonder, known a happy person? I mean a really happy one? He is as rare as a white blackbird in this sombre-faced world of ours. I have known two and only two. They were Agnes Milton and her husband Jim. And their happiness did not last. Jim was a brown, good-natured giant with a slow, most attractive smile and gleaming teeth. He spoke always in a deep sad drawl, and you would have thought him the most unhappy person imaginable until you glimpsed his black eyes fairly twinkling under their half-closed lids. He made money— what is called "easy money"—by playing ragtime for dances. He was one of a troupe that are called "social entertainers." As far as Jim was concerned, it would have slipped away in just as easy a manner, if it hadn't been for Agnes. For she, in spite of all her seeming carefree joyousness was a thrifty soul. As long as Jim could have good food and plenty of it, now and then the theatre, a concert or a dance, and his gold-tipped cigarettes, he didn't care what became of his money.

"Oh, Ag!"

If I close my eyes I can hear his slow sad voice as clearly as though these ten long years had not passed by. I can hear the click of the patent lock as he closed the flat door. I can hear the bang of his hat as he hung it on the rack. I can get the whiff of his cigarette.

"Oh, Ag!"

"That you, Jim?" I can see Agnes' happy eyes and hear her eager, soft voice.

And then after a pause, that sad voice:

"No, Ag!"

I can hear her delighted little chuckle. She very seldom laughed outright.

"Where are you, anyway?" It was the plaintive voice again.

"Here!"

And then he'd make believe he couldn't find her and go hunting her all over that tiny flat, searching for her in every room he knew she was not. And he'd stumble over things in pretended excitement and haste and grunt and swear all in that inimitable slow way of his. And she'd stand there, her eyes shining and every once in a while giving that dear little chuckle of hers.

Finally he'd appear in the door panting and disheveled and would look at her in pretended intense surprise for a second and then he'd say in an aggrieved voice:

"'S not fair, Agnes! 'S not fair!"

She wouldn't say a word, just stand there smiling at him. After a little, slowly, he'd begin to smile too.

That smile of theirs was one of the most beautiful things I have ever seen and each meeting it was the same. Their joy and love seemed to gush up and bubble over through their lips and eyes.

Presently he'd say:

"Catch!"

She'd hold up her little white apron by the corners and he'd put his hand in his pocket and bring out sometimes a big, sometimes a little, wad of greenbacks and toss it to her and she'd catch it, too, I can tell you. And her eyes would beam and dance at him over it. Oh! she didn't love the money for itself but him for trusting her with it.

For fear you may not understand I must tell you no more generous soul ever lived than Agnes Milton. Look at what she did for me. And she was always giving a nickel or a dime to some child, flowers or fruit to a sick woman, money to tide over a friend. No beggar was ever turned away empty, from her flat. But she managed, somehow, to increase her little hoard in the bank against that possible rainy day.

Well, to return. At this juncture, Jim would say oh! so sadly his eyes fairly twinkling:

"Please, m'a'm, do I get paid today too?"

And then she'd screw up her mouth and twist her head to the side and look at him and say in a most judicial manner:

"Well, now, I really can't say as to that. It strikes me you'll have to find that out for yourself."

Oh! they didn't mind me. He would reach her, it seemed, in one stride and would pick her up bodily, apron, money and all. After a space, she'd disentangle herself and say sternly, shaking the while her little fore-finger before his delighted eyes:

"Jim Milton, you've overdrawn your wages again."

And then he'd look oh! so contrite and so upset and so shocked at being caught in such a gigantic piece of attempted fraud.

"No?" he'd say. If you only could have heard the mournful drawl of him.

"No? Now, is that so? I'm really at heart an honest, hardworking man. I'll have to pay it back."

He did. I can vouch for it.

Sometimes after this, he'd swing her up onto his shoulder and they'd go dashing and prancing and shrieking and laughing all over the little flat. Once after I had seen scared faces appearing at various windows, at times like these, I used to rush around and shut the windows down tight. Two happy children, that's what they were then—younger even than I.

There was just the merest suspicion of a cloud over their happiness, these days; they had been married five years and had no children.

It was the mother heart of Agnes that had yearned over me, had pity upon me, loved me and brought me to live in the only home I have ever known. I have cared for people. I care for Jim; but Agnes Milton is the only person I have ever really loved. I love her still. And before it was too late, I used to pray that in some way I might change places with her and go into that darkness where though, still living, one forgets sun and moon and stars and flowers and winds—and love itself, and existence means dark, foul-smelling cages, hollow clanging doors, hollow monotonous days. But a month ago when Jim and I went to see her, she had changed—she had receded even from us. She seemed—how can I express it?—blank, empty, a grey automaton, a mere shell. No soul looked out at us through her vacant eyes.

We did not utter a word during our long journey homeward. Jim had unlocked the door before I spoke.

"Jim," I said, "they may still have the poor husk of her cooped up there but her soul, thank God, at least for that, is free at last!"

And Jim, I cannot tell of his face, said never a word but turned away and went heavily down the stairs. And I, I went into Agnes Milton's flat and closed the door. You would never have dreamed it was the same place. For a long time I stood amid all the brightness and mockery of her sun-drenched rooms. And I prayed. Night and day I have prayed since, the same prayer—that God, if he knows any pity at all may soon, soon release the poor spent body of hers.

I wish I might show you Agnes Milton of those far off happy days. She wasn't tall and she wasn't short; she wasn't stout and she wasn't thin. Her back was straight and her head high. She was rather graceful, I thought. In coloring she was Spanish or Italian. Her hair was not very long but it was soft and silky and black. Her features were not too sharp, her eyes clear and dark, a warm leaf brown in fact. Her mouth was really beautiful. This doesn't give her I find. It was the shining beauty and gayety of her soul that lighted up her whole body and somehow made her her. And she was generally smiling or chuckling. Her eyes almost closed when she did so and there were the most delightful crinkles all about them. Under her left eye there was a small scar, a reminder of some childhood escapade, that became, when she smiled, the most adorable of dimples.

One day, I remember, we were standing at the window in the bright sunlight. Some excitement in the street below had drawn us. I turned to her—the reason has gone from me now—and called out suddenly:

"Agnes Milton!"

"Heavens! What is it?"

"Why, you're wrinkling!"

"Wrinkling! Where?" And she began inspecting the smooth freshness of her housedress.

"No, your face," I exclaimed. "Honest! Stand still there in that light. Now! Just look at them all around your eyes."

She chuckled.

"How you ever expect me to see them I don't know, without a glass or anything!"

And her face crinkled up into a smile.

"There! That's it!—That's how you get them."

"How?"

"Smiling too much."

"Oh no! Lucy, child, that's impossible."

"How do you mean impossible? You didn't get them that way? Just wait till I get a glass."

"No, don't," and she stopped me with a detaining hand. "I'm not doubting you. What I mean is—it's absolutely impossible to smile too much."

I felt my eyes stretching with surprise.

"You mean," I said, "you don't mind being wrinkled? You, a woman?"

She shook her head at me many times, smiling and chuckling softly the while.

"Not the very littlest, tiniest bit—not this much," and she showed me just the barest tip of her pink tongue between her white teeth. She smiled, then, and there was the dimple.

"And you only twenty-five?" I exclaimed.

She didn't answer for a moment and when she did she spoke quietly:

"Lucy, child, we've all got to wrinkle sometime, somehow, if we live long enough. I'd much rather know mine were smile ones than frown ones." She waited a second and then looked at me with her beautiful clear eyes and added, "Wouldn't you?"

For reply I leaned forward and kissed them. I loved them from that time on.

Here is another memory of her—perhaps the loveliest of them all and yet, as you will see, tinged with the first sadness. It came near the end of our happy days. It was a May dusk. I had been sewing all the afternoon and was as close to the window as I could get to catch the last of the failing light. I was trying to thread a needle—had been trying for several minutes, in fact, and was just in the very act of succeeding when two soft hands were clapped over my eyes.

"Oh, Agnes!" I said none too pleasantly. It was provoking. "There! You've made me lose my needle."

"Bother your old needle, cross patch!" she said close to my ear. She still held her hands over my eyes.

I waited a moment or so.

"Well," I said, "what's the idea?"

"Please don't be cross," came the soft voice still close to my ear.

"I'm not."

At that she chuckled.

"Well!" I said.

"I'm trying to tell you something. Sh! not so loud."

"Well, go ahead then; and why must I sh!"

"Because you must."

I waited.

"Well!" I said a third time, but in a whisper to humor her. We were alone in the flat, there was no reason I could see for this tremendous secrecy.

"I'm waiting for you to be sweet to me."

"I am. But why I should have to lose my needle and my temper and be blinded and sweet just to hear something—is beyond me."

"Because I don't wish you to see me while I say it."

Her soft lips were kissing my ear.

"Well, I'm very sweet now. What is it?"

There was another little pause and during it her fingers over my eyes trembled a little. She was breathing quicker too.

"Agnes Milton, what *is* it?"

"Wait, I'm just trying to think *how* to tell you. Are you sure you're very sweet?"

"Sure."

I loved the feel of her hands and sat very still.

"Lucy!"

"Yes."

"What do you think would be the loveliest, loveliest thing for you to know was—was—there—close—just under your heart?"

But I waited for no more. I took her hands from my eyes and turned to look at her. The beauty of her face made me catch my breath.

At last I said:

"You mean—" I didn't need to finish.

"Yes! Yes! And I'm so happy, happy, happy! And so is Jim."

"Agnes, Oh my dear, and so am I!" And I kissed her two dear eyes. "But why mustn't I whoop? I've simply got to," I added.

"No! No! No! Oh, sh!" And for the very first time I saw fear in her eyes.

"Agnes," I said, "what is it?"

"I'm—I'm just a little afraid, I believe."

"Afraid!" I had cried out in surprise.

"Sh! Lucy!—Yes."

"But of what?" I spoke in a half whisper too. "You mean you're afraid you may die?"

"Oh, no, not that."

"What, then?"

"Lucy," her answer came slowly a little abstractedly, "there's—such—a thing—as being—*too* happy,—*too* happy."

"Nonsense," I answered.

But she only shook her head at me slowly many times and her great wistful eyes came to mine and seemed to cling to them. It made my heart fairly ache and I turned my head away so that she couldn't see her fears were affecting me. And then quite suddenly I felt a disagreeable little chill run up and down my back.

"Lucy," she said after a little.

"Yes," I was looking out of the window and not at her.

"Do you remember Kipling's 'Without Benefit of Clergy?'"

I did and I said so. Agnes had Kipling bound in ten beautiful volumes. She loved him. At first that had been enough for me, and then I had come to love him for himself. I had read all of those ten volumes through from cover to cover, poetry and all.

"You haven't forgotten Ameera, then?"

"No."

"Poor Ameera!" She was thoughtful a moment and then went on: "She knew what it was to be too happy. Do you remember what she said once to Holden?"

Again I felt that queer little shiver.

"She said many things, as I remember, Agnes. Which?"

"This was after Tota's death."

"Well!"

"They were on the roof—she and Holden—under the night."

Her eyes suddenly widened and darkened and then she went on:

"She turned to Holden and said: 'We must make no protestations of delight but go softly underneath the stars, lest God find us out.'" She paused. "Do you remember?"

"Yes," I answered, but I couldn't look at her.

"Well," she spoke slowly and quietly, "I have a feeling here, Lucy," and she placed her left hand against her heart, "here, that Jim and you and I must go softly—very softly—underneath the stars."

Again I felt that unpleasant chill up and down my back.

She stood just where she was for a little space, her hand still against her heart and her eyes wide, dark and unseeing, fixed straight ahead of her. Then suddenly and without a sound she turned and went towards the door and opened it.

I started to follow her, but she put up her hand.

"No, Lucy, please—I wish to be alone—for a little."

And with that she went and shut the door very slowly, quite noiselessly behind her. The closing was so slow, so silent, that I could not tell just when it shut. I found myself trembling violently. A sudden and inexplicable terror filled me as that door closed behind her.

We were to become accustomed to it, Jim and I, as much as it was possible to do so, in those terrible days that were to follow. We were to become used to entering a room in search of Agnes, only to find it empty and the door opposite closing, closing, almost imperceptibly, noiselessly—and, yes, at last irrevocably—between us. And each time it happened the terror was as fresh upon me as at the very first.

The days that immediately followed I cannot say were really unhappy ones. More to humor Agnes at first than anything else "we went softly." But as time passed even we became infected. Literally and figuratively we began to go "softly under the stars." We came to feel that each of us moved ever with a finger to his lips. There came to be also a sort of expectancy upon us, a listening, a waiting. Even the neighbors noticed the difference. Jim still played his ragtime and sang, but softly; we laughed and joked, but quietly. We got so we even washed the dishes and pots and pans quietly. Sometimes Jim and I forgot, but as certainly as we did there was Agnes in the door, dark-eyed, a little pale and her, "Oh, Jim!—Oh, Lucy! Sh!"

I haven't spoken of this before because it wasn't necessary. Agnes had a brother called Bob. He was her favorite of all her brothers and sisters. He was younger than she, five years, I think, a handsome, harum-scarum, happy-go-lucky, restless, reckless daredevil, but sweet-tempered and good hearted and lovable withal. I don't believe he knew what fear was. His home was in Mississippi, a small town there. It was the family home, in fact. Agnes had lived there herself until she was seventeen or eighteen. He had visited us two or three times and you can imagine the pandemonium that reigned at such times, for he had come during our happy days. Well, he was very fond of Agnes and, as irresponsible as he seemed, one thing he never failed to do was to write her a letter every single week. Each Tuesday morning, just like clock-work, the very first mail there was his letter. Other mornings Agnes was not so particular, but Tuesday mornings she always went herself to the mailbox in the hall.

It was a Tuesday morning about four months, maybe, after my first experience with the closing door. The bell rang three times, the postman's signal when he had left a letter, Agnes came to her feet, her eyes sparkling:

"My letter from Bob," she said and made for the door.

She came back slowly, I noticed, and her face was a little pale and worried. She had an opened and an unopened letter in her hand.

"Well, what does Bob say?" I asked.

"This—this isn't from Bob," she said slowly. "It's only a bill."

"Well, go ahead and open his letter," I said.

"There—there wasn't any, Lucy."

"What!" I exclaimed. I was surprised.

"No. I don't know what it means."

"It will come probably in the second mail," I said. "It has sometimes."

"Yes," she said, I thought rather listlessly.

It didn't come in the second mail nor in the third.

"Agnes," I said. "There's some good explanation. It's not like Bob to fail you."

"No."

"He's busy or got a girl maybe."

She was a little jealous of him and I hoped this last would rouse her, but it didn't.

"Yes, maybe that's it," she said without any life.

"Well, I hope you're not going to let this interfere with your walk," I said.

"I had thought—" she began, but I cut her off.

"You promised Jim you'd go out every single day," I reminded her.

"All right, Agnes Milton's conscience," she said smiling a little. "I'll go then."

She hadn't been gone fifteen minutes when the electric bell began shrilling continuously throughout the flat.

Somehow I knew it meant trouble. My mind immediately flew to Agnes. It took me a second or so to get myself together and then I went to the tube.

"Well," I called. My voice sounded strange and high.

A boy's voice answered:

"Lady here named Mrs. James Milton?"

"Yes." I managed to say.

"Telegram fo' you'se."

It wasn't Agnes, after all. I drew a deep breath. Nothing else seemed to matter for a minute.

"Say!" the voice called up from below. "Wot's de mattah wid you'se up dere?"

"Bring it up." I said at last. "Third floor, front."

I opened the door and waited.

The boy was taking his time and whistling as he came. "Here!" I called out as he reached our floor.

It was inside his cap and he had to take it off to give it to me.

I saw him eyeing me rather curiously.

"You Mrs. Milton?" he asked.

"No, but this is her flat. I'll sign for it. She's out. Where do I sign? There? Have you a pencil?"

With the door shut behind me again, I began to think out what I had better do. Jim was not to be home until late that night. Within five minutes I had decided. I tore open the yellow envelope and read the message.

It ran: "Bob died suddenly. Under no circumstances come. Father."

The rest of that day was a nightmare to me. I concealed the telegram in my waist. Agnes came home finally and was so alarmed at my appearance, I pleaded a frightful sick headache and went to bed. When Jim came home late that night Agnes was asleep. I caught him in the hall and gave him the telegram. She had to be told, we decided, because a letter from Mississippi might come at any time. He broke it to her the next morning. We were all hard hit, but Agnes from that time on was a changed woman.

Day after day dragged by and the letter of explanation did not come. It was strange, to say the least.

The Sunday afternoon following, we were all sitting, after dinner, in the little parlor. None of us had been saying much.

Suddenly Agnes said:

"Jim!"

"Yes!"

"Wasn't it strange that father never said how or when Bob died?"

"Would have made the telegram too long and expensive, perhaps," Jim replied.

We were all thinking, in the pause that followed, the same thing, I dare say. Agnes' father was not poor and it did seem he might have done that much.

"And why, do you suppose I was not to come under any circumstances? And why don't they write?"

Just then the bell rang and there was no chance for a reply.

Jim got up in his leisurely way and went to the tube.

Agnes and I both listened—a little tensely, I remember.

"Yes!" we heard Jim say, and then with spaces in between:

"Joe?—Joe who?—I think you must have made a mistake. No, I can't say that I do know anyone called Joe. What? Milton? Yes, that's my name! What? Oh! Brooks. Joe Brooks?—"

But Agnes waited for no more. She rushed by me into the hall.

"Jim! Jim! It's my brother Joe."

"Look here! Are you Agnes' brother, Joe?" Jim called quickly for him. "Great Jehoshaphat! Man! Come up! What a mess I've made of this."

For the first time I saw Jim move quickly. Within a second he was out of the flat and running down the stairs. Agnes followed to the stairhead and waited there. I went back into the little parlor, for I had followed her into the hall, and sat down and waited.

They all came in presently. Joe was older than Agnes but looked very much like her. He was thin, his face really haggard and his hair quite grey. I found out afterward that he was in his early thirties but he appeared much older. He was smiling, but the smile did not reach his eyes. They were strange aloof eyes. They rested on you and yet seemed to see something beyond. You felt as though they had looked upon something that could never be forgotten. When he was not smiling his face was grim, the chin firm and set. He was a man of very few words, I found.

Agnes and Jim were both talking at once and he answered them now and then in monosyllables. Agnes introduced us. He shook hands, I thought in rather a perfunctory way, without saying anything, and we all sat down.

We steered clear quite deliberately from the thoughts uppermost in our minds. We spoke of his journey, when he left Mississippi, the length of time it had taken him to come up and the weather. Suddenly Agnes jumped up:

"Joe, aren't you famished?"

"Well, I wouldn't mind a little something, Agnes," he answered, and then he added: "I'm not as starved as I was traveling in the South, but I have kind of a hollow feeling."

"What do you mean?" she asked.

"Jim-Crow cars," he answered laconically.

"I'd forgotten," she said. "I've been away so long."

He made no reply.

"Aren't conditions any better at all?" she asked after a little.

"No, I can't say as they are."

None of us said anything. She stood there a minute or so, pulling away at the frill on her apron. She stopped suddenly, drew a long breath, and said:

"I wish you all could move away, Joe, and come North."

For one second before he lowered his eyes I saw a strange gleam in them. He seemed to be examining his shoes carefully from all angles. His jaw looked grimmer than ever and I saw a flickering of the muscles in his cheeks.

"That would be nice," he said at last and then added, "but we can't, Agnes. I like my coffee strong, please."

"Joe," she said, going to the door. "I'm sorry, I was forgetting."

I rose at that.

"Agnes, let me go. You stay here."

She hesitated, but Joe spoke up:

"No, Agnes, you go. I know your cooking."

You could have heard a pin drop for a minute. Jim looked queer and so did Agnes for a second and then she tried to laugh it off.

"Don't mind Joe. He doesn't mean anything. He always was like that."

And then she left us.

Well, I was hurt. Joe made no attempt to apologize or anything. He even seemed to have forgotten me. Jim looked at me and smiled, his nice smile, but I was really hurt. I came to understand, however, later. Presently Joe said:

"About Agnes! We hadn't been told anything!"

"Didn't she write about it?"

"No."

"Wanted to surprise you, I guess."

"How long?" Joe asked after a little.

"Before?"

"Yes."

"Four months, I should say."

"That complicates matters some."

I got up to leave. I was so evidently in the way.

Joe looked up quietly and said:

"Oh! don't go! It isn't necessary."

I sat down again.

"No, Lucy, stay." Jim added. "What do you mean 'complicates?'"

Joe examined his shoes for several moments and then looked up suddenly.

"Just where is Agnes?"

"In the kitchen, I guess." Jim looked a trifle surprised.

"Where is that?"

"The other end of the flat near the door."

"She can't possibly hear anything, then?"

"No."

"Well, then, listen Jim, and you, what's your name? Lucy? Well, Lucy, then. Listen carefully, you two, to every single word I am going to say." He frowned a few moments at his shoes and then went on: "Bob went out fishing in the woods near his shack, spent the night there, slept in wet clothes, it had been raining all day, came home, contracted double pneumonia and died in two days time. Have you that?"

We both nodded. "That's the story we are to tell Agnes."

Jim had his mouth open to ask something, when Agnes came in. She had very evidently not heard anything, however, for there was a little color in her face and it was just a little happy again.

"I've been thinking about you, Joe," she said. "What on earth are you getting so grey for?"

"Grey!" he exclaimed. "Am I grey?" There was no doubt about it, his surprise was genuine.

"Didn't you know it?" She chuckled a little. It was the first time in days.

"No, I didn't."

She made him get up, at that, and drew him to the oval glass over the mantel.

"Don't you ever look at yourself, Joe?"

"Not much, that's the truth." I could see his face in the mirror from where I sat. His eyes widened a trifle, I saw, and then he turned away abruptly and sat down again. He made no comment. Agnes broke the rather little silence that followed.

"Joe!"

"Yes!"

"You haven't been sick or anything, have you?"

"No, why?"

"You seem so much thinner. When I last saw you you were almost stout."

"That's some years ago, Agnes."

"Yes, but one ought to get stouter not thinner with age."

Again I caught that strange gleam in his eyes before he lowered them. For a moment he sat perfectly still without answering.

"You can put it down to hard work, if you like, Agnes. Isn't that my coffee I smell boiling over?"

"Yes, I believe it is. I just ran in to tell you I'll be ready for you in about ten minutes."

She went out hastily but took time to pull the portière across the door. I thought it strange at the time and looked at Jim. He didn't seem to notice it, however, but waited, I saw, until he had heard Agnes' heel taps going into the kitchen.

"Now," he said, "what do you mean when you say that is the story we are to tell Agnes?"

"Just that."

"You mean—" he paused "that it isn't true?"

"No, it isn't true."

"Bob didn't die that way?"

"No."

I felt myself stiffening in my chair and my two hands gripping the two arms of my chair tightly. I looked at Jim. I sensed the same tensioning in him. There was a long pause. Joe was examining his shoes again. The flickering in his cheeks I saw was more noticeable.

Finally Jim brought out just one word:

"How?"

"There was a little trouble," he began and then paused so long Jim said:

"You mean he was—injured in some way?"

Joe looked up suddenly at Jim, at that, and then down again. But his expression even in that fleeting glance set me to trembling all over. Jim, I saw, had been affected too. He sat stiffly bent forward. He had been in the act of raising his cigarette to his lips and his arm seemed as though frozen in mid-air.

"Yes," he said, "injured." But the way in which he said "injured" made me tremble all the more.

Again there was a pause and again Jim broke it with his one word: "How?"

"You don't read the papers, I see," Joe said.

"Yes, I read them."

"It was in all the papers."

"I missed it, then."

"Yes."

It was quiet again for a little.

"Have you ever lived in the South?" Joe asked.

"No."

"Nice civilized place, the South," Joe said.

And again I found myself trembling violently. I had to fight with might and main to keep my teeth from chattering. And yet it was not what he had said but his tone again.

"I hadn't so heard it described," Jim said after a little.

"No?—You didn't know, I suppose, that there is an unwritten law in the South that when a colored and a white person meet on the sidewalk, the colored person must get off into the street until the white one passes?"

"No, I hadn't heard of it."

"Well, it's so. That was the little trouble."

"You mean—"

"Bob refused to get off the sidewalk."

"Well?"

"The white man pushed him off. Bob knocked him down. The white man attempted to teach the 'damned nigger' a lesson." Again he paused.

"Well?"

"The lesson didn't end properly. Bob all but killed him."

It was so still in that room that although Jim was sitting across the room I could hear his watch ticking distinctly in his vest pocket. I had been holding my breath when I was forced to expel it, the sound was so loud they both turned quickly towards me, startled for a second.

"That would have been Bob." It was Jim speaking.

"Yes."

"I suppose it didn't end there?"

"No."

"Go on, Joe." Even Jim's voice sounded strained and strange.

And Joe went on. He never raised his voice, never lowered it. Throughout, his tone was entirely colorless. And yet as though it had been seared into my very soul I remember word for word, everything he said.

"An orderly mob, in an orderly manner, on a Sunday morning—I am quoting the newspapers—broke into the jail, took him out, slung him up to the limb of a tree, riddled his body with bullets, saturated it with coal oil, lighted a fire underneath him, gouged out his eyes with red hot irons, burnt him to a crisp and then sold souvenirs of him, ears, fingers, toes. His teeth brought five dollars each." He ceased for a moment.

"He is still hanging on that tree.—We are not allowed to have even what is left."

There was a roaring in my ears. I seemed to be a long way off. I was sinking into a horrible black vortex that seemed to be sucking me down. I opened my eyes and saw Jim dimly. His nostrils seemed to be two black wide holes. His face was taut, every line set. I saw him draw a great deep breath. The blackness sucked me down still deeper. And then suddenly I found myself on my feet struggling against that hideous darkness and I heard my own voice as from a great distance calling out over and over again, "Oh, my God! Oh, my God! Oh, my God!"

They both came running to me, but I should have fainted for the first and only time in my life but that I heard suddenly above those strange noises in my ears a little choking, strangling sound. It revived me instantly. I broke from them and tried to get to the door.

"Agnes! Agnes!" I called out.

But they were before me. Jim tore the portière aside. They caught her just as she was falling.

She lay unconscious for hours. When she did come to, she found all three of us about her bed. Her bewildered eyes went from Jim's face to mine and then to Joe's. They paused there, she frowned a little. And then we saw the whole thing slowly come back to her. She groaned and closed her eyes. Joe started to leave the room but she opened her eyes quickly and indicated that he was not to go. He came back. Again she closed her eyes.

And then she began to grow restless.

"Agnes!" I asked, "is there anything you want?"

She quieted a little under my voice.

"No," she said, "No."

Presently she opened her eyes again. They were very bright. She looked at each of us in turn a second time.

Then she said:

"I've had to live all this time to find out."

"Find out what, Agnes?" It was Jim's voice.

"Why I'm here—why I'm here."

"Yes, of course." Jim spoke oh! so gently, humoring her. His hand was smoothing away the damp little curls about her forehead.

"It's no use your making believe you understand, you don't." It was the first time I had ever heard her speak irritably to Jim. She moved her head away from his hand.

His eyes were a little hurt and he took his hand away.

"No." His voice was as gentle as ever. "I don't understand, then."

There was a pause and then she said abruptly:

"I'm an instrument."

No one answered her.

"That's all—an instrument."

We merely watched her.

"One of the many."

And then Jim in his kindly blundering way made his second mistake. "Yes, Agnes," he said, "Yes."

But at that, she took even me by surprise. She sat up in bed suddenly, her eyes wild and staring and before we could stop her, began beating her breast.

"Agnes," I said, "Don't! Don't!"

"I shall," she said in a strange high voice.

Well, we let her alone. It would have meant a struggle.

And then amid little sobbing breaths, beating her breast the while, she began to cry out: "Yes!—Yes!—I!—I!—An instrument of reproduction!—another of the many!—a colored woman— doomed!—cursed!—put here!—willing or unwilling! For what?—to bring children here—men children—for the sport—the lust—of possible orderly mobs—who go about things—in an orderly manner—on Sunday mornings!"

"Agnes," I cried out. "Agnes! Your child will be born in the North. He need never go South."

She had listened to me at any rate.

"Yes," she said, "in the North. In the North.—And have there been no lynchings in the North?"

I was silenced.

"The North permits it too," she cried. "The North is silent as well as the South."

And then as she sat there her eyes became less wild but more terrible. They became the eyes of a seeress. When she spoke again she spoke loudly, clearly, slowly:

"There is a time coming—and soon—when no colored man—no

colored woman—no colored child, born or unborn—will be safe—in this country."

"Oh Agnes," I cried again, "Sh! sh!"

She turned her terrible eyes upon me.

"There is no more need for silence—in this house. God has found us out."

"Oh Agnes," the tears were frankly running down my cheeks. "We must believe that God is very pitiful. We must. He will find a way."

She waited a moment and said simply:

"Will He?"

"Yes, Agnes! Yes!"

"I will believe you, then. I will give Him one more chance. Then, if He is not pitiful, then if He is not pitiful—" But she did not finish. She fell back upon her pillows. She had fainted again.

Agnes did not die, nor did her child. She had kept her body clean and healthy. She was up and around again, but an Agnes that never smiled, never chuckled any more. She was a grey pathetic shadow of herself. She who had loved joy so much, cared more, it seemed, for solitude than anything else in the world. That was why, when Jim or I went looking for her we found so often only the empty room and that imperceptibly closing, slowly closing, opposite door.

Joe went back to Mississippi and not one of us, ever again, mentioned Bob's name.

And Jim, poor Jim! I wish I could tell you of how beautiful he was those days. How he never complained, never was irritable, but was always so gentle, so full of understanding, that at times, I had to go out of the room for fear he might see my tears.

Only once I saw him when he thought himself alone. I had not known he was in his little den and entered it suddenly. I had made no sound, luckily, and he had not heard me. He was sitting leaning far forward, his head between his hands. I stood there five minutes at least, but not once did I see him stir. I silently stole out and left him.

It was a fortunate thing that Agnes had already done most of her sewing for the little expected stranger, for after Joe's visit, she never touched a thing.

"Agnes!" I said one day, not without fear and trepidation it is true. "Isn't there something I can do?"

"Do?" she repeated rather vaguely.

"Yes. Some sewing?"

"Oh! sewing," she said. "No, I think not, Lucy."

"You've—you've finished?" I persisted.

"No."

"Then—" I began.

"I hardly think we shall need any of them." And then she added, "I hope not."

"Agnes!" I cried out.

But she seemed to have forgotten me.

Well, time passed, it always does. And on a Sunday morning early Agnes' child was born. He was a beautiful, very grave baby with her great dark eyes.

As soon as they would let me, I went to her.

She was lying very still and straight, in the quiet, darkened room, her head turned on the pillow towards the wall. Her eyes were closed.

"Agnes!" I said in the barest whisper. "Are you asleep?"

"No," she said. And turned her head towards me and opened her eyes. I looked into her ravaged face. Agnes Milton had been down into Hell and back again.

Neither of us spoke for some time and then she said:

"Is he dead?"

"Your child?"

"Yes."

"I should say not, he's a perfect darling and so good."

No smile came into her face. It remained as expressionless as before. She paled a trifle more, I thought, if such a thing was possible.

"I'm sorry," she said finally.

"Agnes!" I spoke sharply. I couldn't help it.

But she closed her eyes and made no response.

I sat a long time looking at her. She must have felt my gaze for she slowly lifted her lids and looked at me.

"Well," she said, "what is it, Lucy?"

"Haven't you seen your child, Agnes?"

"No."

"Don't you wish to see it?"

"No."

Again it was wrung out of me:

"Agnes, Agnes, don't tell me you don't love it."

For the first and only time a spasm of pain went over her poor pinched face.

"Ah!" she said, "That's it." And she closed her eyes and her face was as expressionless as ever.

I felt as though my heart were breaking.

Again she opened her eyes.

"Tell me, Lucy," she began.

"What, Agnes?"

"Is he—healthy?"

"Yes."

"Quite strong?"

"Yes."

"You think he will live, then?"

"Yes, Agnes."

She closed her eyes once more. It was very still within the room.

Again she opened her eyes. There was a strange expression in them now.

"Lucy!"

"Yes."

"You were wrong."

"Wrong, Agnes?"

"Yes."

"How?"

"You thought your God was pitiful."

"Agnes, but I do believe it."

After a long silence she said very slowly:

"He—is—not."

This time, when she closed her eyes, she turned her head slowly upon the pillow to the wall. I was dismissed.


And again Agnes did not die. Time passed and again she was up and about the flat. There was a strange, stony stillness upon her, now, I did not like, though. If we only could have understood, Jim and I, what it meant. Her love for solitude, now, had become a passion. And Jim and I knew more and more that empty room and that silently, slowly closing door.

She would have very little to do with her child. For some reason, I saw, she was afraid of it. I was its mother. I did for it, cared for it, loved it.

Twice only during these days I saw that stony stillness of hers broken.

The first time was one night. The baby was fast asleep, and she had stolen in to look at him, when she thought no one would know. I never wish to see such a tortured, hungry face again.

I was in the kitchen, the second time, when I heard strange sounds coming from my room. I rushed to it and there was Agnes, kneeling at the foot of the little crib, her head upon the spread. Great, terrible racking sobs were tearing her. The baby was lying there, all eyes, and beginning to whimper a little.

"Agnes! Oh, my dear! What is it?" The tears were streaming down my cheeks.

"Take him away! Take him away!" she gasped. "He's been cooing, and smiling and holding out his little arms to me. I can't stand it! I can't stand it."

I took him away. That was the only time I ever saw Agnes Milton weep.


The baby slept in my room, Agnes would not have him in hers. He was a restless little sleeper and I had to get up several times during the night to see that he was properly covered.

He was a noisy little sleeper as well. Many a night I have lain awake listening to the sound of his breathing. It is a lovely sound, a beautiful one—the breathing of a little baby in the dark.

This night, I remember, I had been up once and covered him over and had fallen off to sleep for the second time, when, for I had heard absolutely no sound, I awoke suddenly. There was upon me an overwhelming utterly paralyzing feeling not of fear but of horror. I thought, at first, I must have been having a nightmare, but strangely instead of diminishing, the longer I lay awake, the more it seemed to increase.

It was a moonlight night and the light came in through the open window in a broad, white, steady stream.

A coldness seemed to settle all about my heart. What was the matter with me? I made a tremendous effort and sat up. Everything seemed peaceful and quiet enough.

The moonlight cut the room in two. It was dark where I was and dark beyond where the baby was.

One brass knob at the foot of my bed shone brilliantly, I remember, in that bright stream and the door that led into the hall stood out fully revealed. I looked at that door and then my heart suddenly seemed to stop beating! I grew deathly cold. The door was closing slowly, imperceptibly, silently. Things were whirling around. I shut my eyes. When I opened them again the door was no longer moving; it had closed.

*What had Agnes Milton wanted in my room?* And the more I asked myself that question the deeper grew the horror.

And then slowly, by degrees, I began to realize there was something wrong within that room, something terribly wrong. But what was it?

I tried to get out of bed, but I seemed unable to move. I strained my eyes, but I could see nothing—only that bright knob, that stream of light, that closed white door.

I listened. It was quiet, very quiet, too quiet. But why too quiet? And then as though there had been a blinding flash of lightening I knew— the breathing wasn't there.

Agnes Milton had taken a pillow off of my bed and smothered her child.

One last word. Jim received word this morning. The door has finished closing for the last time—Agnes Milton is no more. God, I think, may be pitiful, after all.

From the *Birth Control Review*, September–October 1919

# Bathesda of
# Sinners Run

## MAUDE IRWIN OWENS

It was like reading the Books of Chronicles, to read in the Thornton family history of the attending succession of slave women that formed the single line of Bathesda's ancestry. The Thorntons had always boasted of their seven generations of slave housekeepers who had directly descended from the housekeeper of the first American Thornton. They would proudly point out the precious, faded entries, so faithfully recorded in the old genealogy. The paternal side of the issue was always politely ignored in strict accordance with the manners and customs of the South.

The scapegrace of the younger son of an English baron, Richard Thornton, was founder of the family. When gambling debts and foul dueling forced him to flee his native land, he decided upon the colony of George II under Governor Oglethorpe. His first slave purchase was written in two sentences which seemed to wink and laugh up at the reader with its tan ink and old fashioned lettering. It read:

"On this day did I barter my gold hilted sword, some lace and several shillings to that villain from the Virginia colony whom I do sorely despise—for a black wench to cook my porridge, brew my tea and wash my linen. She is comely withal and methinks, the temper of a noble blooded colt; so I have named the vixen, Jezebel."

From this Jezebel on the issue became mulatto and less mulatto: for it was written that Jezebel foaled a likely mustard-colored filly whose father and master, with malicious humor, named for his King and the colony.

So Jezebel became the mother of Georgie; who begat Abigail; whose brat was Callie; whose offspring was Ruth; whose child was Viney; whose daughter was Anne; and twenty years after slavery, came Bathesda.

To the utter amazement and chagrin of her erstwhile master and mistress, when the bell of freedom tolled for those in bondage, Anne betook herself from under the Thornton roof, in spite of all the inducements and cajoleries the Thorntons offered.

She married Enoch Creek, a fusion of Creek Indian, Negro and white and who chose to select his surname from the Indian blood which dominated his being. He was a bitter man, having no faith or belief in mankind or the institutions and principles of mankind; a religion of hatred that banned all but Anne and much later, little Bathesda.

They founded a tiny home at Sinners Run, the Negro suburb of Thorntonville, Georgia, that had been called after a famous camp-meeting revival sermon preached there, years back. Their cabin was a little apart and elevated from other huts and shacks of the Sinners Run people, so that they could look down upon the road which was alternatingly red clay or yellow mud and note the comings and goings of those who lived upon it.

Anne attended the Sinners Run Baptist Church regularly and prayed that her husband find salvation. Enoch traded at the store because it was necessary—but after that, all socializing with their neighbors ceased; unless in the case of illness, when Anne was a ministering angel and healer of the small community. Within her lean yellow hands was the strange, soothing power to allay pain, and from her husband, she learned much of the Indian mysteries of roots and herbs for medicinal use.

They were thrifty and got along. For twenty years they worked, saved, improved their little two room home, and the acre upon which it stood. Anne was an expert needlewoman as Viney, Ruth and Callie had been before her; and she was in great demand in all the big houses down in Thorntonville. Enoch hired himself out as a plantation farmer, and in spite of his scowling silence, was known as a good hand.

Then, at the age of forty—when all hope of bearing the traditional girl-child had flown from the heart of Anne, it happened; and Bathesda made her advent into the life of Sinners Run.

Enoch smiled for the first time—his squinting Indian eyes snapping with delight at the yellow gypsy-like Anne in the role of Madonna, with the robust little papoose that was his. Of course the Thorntons got wind of it, investigated and greedily annexed one more generation to old Jezebel's descendants, although the essence of reflected glory had lost its flavor since the inconvenient Emancipation. The distinction of being the first of her line born out of slavery, was the most disgraceful thing that could have been written about Bathesda, into the sacred Annals, according to Thornton opinion.

Two weeks later, Enoch stepped on a rusty spike. Blood-poisoning set in and, in spite of their combined knowledge of medicine and healing— his time had come to leave Anne and Bathesda, before Anne had convinced him there was a God.

Anne turned from the unmarked grave, and faced the world alone with her baby, unflinchingly—with that calm independence that asked no pity. She went about her sewing at the houses of her patrons, for a while, carrying her infant with her.

But as Bathesda began to toddle about, Anne realized her child should have home life, and be allowed to play in the vegetable patch and flower garden which Enoch had so painstakingly planted. So Anne took only work such as she could do at home, and her little daughter grew to be the marvel of the country side—a healthy, lovely child.

She attended the broken down school-house to be taught by a wizened old maid from Connecticut a few months a year, and she sat at her mother's knee during the school period . . . both struggling eagerly to master a clear fluent English. Anne, being ardently religious, insisted that the little girl read her Bible and attend church regularly, in which she was reluctantly obeyed.

Thus Bathesda grew up to womanhood. Beautiful—of deep-rooted intelligence handicapped by inadequate schooling, a pagan love for the gorgeous wonders of Nature and a passion for all things artistic. She became adept at the fine French seams and hemming; learned to feather-stitch the picturesque quilts on the huge frame, to weave highly imaginative Indian designs out of the bright silken rags into rugs and mats, to make the difficult Yankee hook rug, the knowledge of which had been introduced South by a Yankee Thornton bride; and best of all, she became an expert copier of the old antebellum samplers. Anne's sampler embroidering frame looked worm-eaten—it was so old; and Bathesda considered it with great reverence.

They made a picture to be remembered, sitting together at their artistic labors—the older woman and her daughter. Anne invariably talked religion to Bathesda having sensed a silent indifference which bespoke much of Enoch's atheism. When at the stuffy little church, the sermon had become highly exhortive, and the worshiper's down-trodden souls burst forth in howling primitive devotion to a God they desperately believed in—even when great tears spilled down her quiet mother's cheeks, Bathesda's sole reaction was a disdainfully cold squinting of her pretty black eyes.

"It's Enoch! It's Enoch!" mourned old Anne, as she watched the child of her old age flower into radiant womanhood with no change of heart.

"But Mother," Bathesda would say, "you take on so 'bout nothin'. Ain't we happy? We have always been different from them in our way of livin' and doin' things and so how can you expect me to be like them in their church doin's? You are not like them when you feel the spirit, Mother. You cry a little bit, but I have never seen you rear and tear and stomp and scream 'halleluliah' like someone crazy . . . I hate it! My church is the purple mist stealin' ahead of the red dawn—the chirpin' wood-chucks; wild wood blossoms! If I ever 'get religion' Mother 'twill be in that kind of church, and not among the sweaty, hysterical hypocrites of your church. Why! I believe to my soul, Mother, you are the only real Christian among them, and do the least testifyin'!"

"Child—you don't understand. It is as real with them as life itself! It is given to each to work out his own destiny in the Lord, in his own way. It is the feelin' that they are weak and sinful that overpowers them so—in their strivin' to follow the Good Book."

"I don't care 'bout them anyways, Mother. We are better colored folks . . . that's all. It just ain't in them to be better. Look at their homes. Bare plank floors that all their scrubbin' and scourin' don't improve; walls plastered with newspapers full of pictures that they think are pretty; gunny-sacks tacked up to the windows . . . ugh! Give them their winter supply of potatoes, rice and hog meat . . . let them go to church and give chitterlin' suppers . . . plenty of shoutin' and back-bitin' and they are happy all winter long, Mother. But—look at our home!"

She waved her pale brown hand proudly around the room in which they sat. The walls were whitewashed. The floor was covered with a huge rag rug rich with colorful stripes and the single square window was draped with deep rose curtains that fluttered happily in the breeze. They had been made from flour bags soaked in kerosene to remove the printing, and dyed with berry juice. There were two fine old pieces of colonial mahogany in this outer room—a gigantic highboy and a marble-topped medicine chest. The other articles of furniture were three rush-bottomed chairs and a table that Enoch had made, and carved all over with the weirdly grotesque totem-pole gargoyles. Upon the mantel over the fireplace were a brilliant basket and two odd potteries also relics of the Creek strain in the father of Bathesda. Small painted tubs and cans were in interesting groups about the room, filled with plants of various sorts.

"I don't suppose I should say I hate them, Mother dear," Bathesda continued, "but I can get along without them. I shall do as you have always done . . . when they're sick, I'll make them well if they call upon me—but I don't . . . I can't be one of them in religion or otherwise."

"Ah, my child," sadly smiled Anne, "you may have inherited the sense of medicine from Enoch, your father, but the Divine gift of healing can never descend upon a disbeliever . . . and you are the first of us women who has not been born with the gift since Mother Jezebel. She, even in her early day, was a Christian convert."

At this, Bathesda would shake her head impatiently as if flinging aside the admonitions of her mother, and the two long black braids would flare about her arms and shoulders. Then, bowing earnestly over her work, she would concentrate upon the exact copying of probably old Viney's intricately designed sampler with the words—"Little flakes make the biggest snow," ordered by an antique dealer from Savannah.

Bathesda's mother died in her sixtieth year, and never had there been such a funeral in the history of Sinners Run. Unlike her husband who had only a faithful wife and new born babe to follow him to his grave— the entire countryside turned out to do honor to Anne Creek. All of the present generation of Thorntons came from their town house in Savannah, in full force, much to the awe of the Sinners Run folk. They even hinted about how appropriate and fitting it would be if Anne were buried beside Viney, in Thorntonville; but Bathesda was obdurate.

"Thank you, Mr. and Mrs. Thornton, but my mother's place is beside her husband. My father has been alone out there, long enough."

So the Thorntons had a second lesson in Negro independence.

"Promise me, my daughter, that you will seek Jesus!" gasped Anne in her last consciousness. "Go to the church—seek Him until you find Him . . . and He will give you your birthright like he has given it to all the rest of us. Promise your poor old Mammy, Bathesda . . . baby!"

And so she had promised to seek religion and the power to heal the sick.

Bathesda lived on, as the years rolled by, much as when Anne lived. She made beautiful things with her graceful slender hands, and more money than she needed in her simple mode of living. She lived alone with the spirit presences of her parents, except for the loyal protection of a watch dog. She cared for the gay little flower garden tenderly and kept her graves freshly decorated in flower season. She grew her vegetables, also the roots and herbs with which she concocted her famous medicinal recipes. She attended the Sinners Run Baptist Church and contributed to its support; but the Indian in her worshiped only the wonders of Nature and she put no other gods before the beauty of the earth.

The colored people of Sinners Run envied and hated her, yet maintained a deceitful courtesy that permitted them to call upon her when in need of intervention with white people, money or in sickness. Her ability to always smooth the way for them, in any form of distress, was known with a certainty that was uncanny to their superstitious minds. She could do all except smooth out actual pain like her mother had done. However, she did her all, in the name of Anne . . . she herself caring little for these crude mean-hearted and petty people, who grinned in her face for favors, and hissed "half white bastard" behind her back. This last amused her, however, since her intelligence allowed her to see no difference between the black and yellow progeny of the illicit unions of slavery.

"What queer religion these folks have," laughed the woman, "it breaks forth in a certain place, and at a certain fixed time, then they lose it 'til the next time."

The women were especially incensed against her, because—if they married at all, they invariably marritd men who Bathesda had rejected. She allowed each suitor in his time, to visit her, sit as long as he pleased admiring her at the embroidering rack, while she, with serene indifference, hoped he would make his departure in time for her to take her dog and go to the crest for the sunset, or some such solitary jaunt. She could say "no" with a cool pleasantness that retained their goodwill; but the wives to whom she gave the men up, hated her venomously for so doing. Hated her for wrapping her long glossy braids around and around her head in a coronet which made her a queen among them. Hated her for appearing so youthful despite her forty-seven years. Hated her for not shouting at church, and for failing to testify or profess. Hated her for having the prettiest house and garden in the community—for making the medicine that cured them. Hated her for weaving and embroidering while they took in washing, or labored beside their men in the cotton and corn fields. Hated her for her chaste aloofness of man, while they bore large families in the morass of poverty and misery. Hated her for showing contempt for the edicts of fashions and mail order houses up North or the cheap stores in Thorntonville and Savannah and for wearing the simply made, richly embroidered garments which none could duplicate. For all these reasons, the women of Sinners Run despised Bathesda.

Among them, she had one sincere friend in the person of young Becky Johnson. The dark-skinned girl had sought Bathesda in a frenzy one stormy midnight. Bathesda had donned her cape and accompanied the wild young mother to the bedside of her baby who was strangling with dyptheria. It was a simple deed; the swabbing of the little throat with boiled vinegar and salt, with a few directions, but the brown girl had hugged Bathesda's knees and kissed her comfortably shod feet in feverish adoration. The father, too, had looked dumb gratitude with brimming eyes. After this incident, Becky took Li'l Jim up to see Bathesda regularly, and Bathesda became greatly attached to the small family, such devotion from Becky having awakened within her cold nature, something akin to affection.

Becky's sister, mother and grandmother, strongly disapproved of this friendship. The sister, whose name was Cisseretta, was somewhat of a belle, and when rigged up in the cast-off clothes of the white people for whom she worked, was, for Sinners Run, quite elegant. She was light brown, with hazel eyes that were sly and coquettish. Her hair was of that yellowish cotton-batten sort, known as riney. She meant to marry better than had her older sister, and scorned the field hands as prospective husbands, although she was not averse to keeping them from dancing attendance on the less discriminating girls of her set.

The mother, Eliza Lambert, was about Bathesda's age and a malicious "yes" woman to gossip and trouble making, although too stupid herself to even instigate a healthy lie.

The grandmother, Granny Lou, was an ancient crone, black as pitch, who had lost track of her age, but knew everything pertaining to a scandalous nature concerning the families of both races for miles around. She sat in one corner year in and year out, wrapped in filthy shawls and hoods summer and winter, smoking her foul clay pipe, and spitting snuff into the maw of the tumble-down stove, or gumming her vicious old tales. She was reputed to be the oldest woman in that section of Georgia, and to have borne more children than she herself knew; Eliza, being her youngest, to whom she had hitched herself. Just as most of the trouble making and under-current of evilness in the neighborhood could usually be traced to the chair of Granny Lou and Lambert household, so was she guilty of inciting most of the fierce antipathy among the women, against Bathesda.

One particular early autumn morning, she pursed and screwed her shrunken lips around to settle the snuff and saliva making a "Mpwhumn-mpwhumn" noise, and began lisping to Eliza who was washing:

"Heh, heh! Ah sees whar dat-ar new ministah done gine sottin' up to Thesdy's already—heh, heh! 'Pears lak to me dat you 'omans ain't slaves no moah an' oughten't go fer to put up wid sich cayin' on. Lize . . . Yo' Cissy tryin' to sot huh cap foah him, but 'pears lak to me, effen she gits him, won't be twell dat Thesdy's chawed 'im up an' spat him back at huh! Heh, heh!" and as if to suit the word with the action, she spat into the pink wood ashes which were falling out of the stove pit.

"Tain't nothin' to them Jezebel 'omans, noways. De white folks make me sick cayin' on so high 'bout dem. Day all sold dere souls to de debbil. Don't dey fool 'round wid roots 'n things? . . . mind how dey nebber show dere natchul age lak we'uns does?"

The silence that followed was broken by the sudsy slapping of wet clothes with home made lye soap. Eliza was too busy to bother about her old mother's chatter this morning, but Granny Lou was nothing loath to amusing herself.

"Becky, lak a li'l fool . . . she run up dere case day yaller 'oman do foah dat brat ahern, jis what any of ussen coulda did. Ah knows, chal! Yo Granny Lou knowed dem f'om way back to Callie!"

"Kyah, kyah, kyah! Granny Lou—hush yo mouf," laughingly yelled Eliza above the suds, steam and slop, with perspiration dripping from her corn-rowed head into the tub.

Cisseretta, who had entered the room unnoticed, flared up angrily at the old hag's challenge—

"I wants Brother Parson Brown, and I's shore goin' to git him. 'Tain't goin' to be after Thesdy done chawed him, either, Granny!" So saying, she jammed her hands down upon her hips with her legs astride and frowned belligerently from her mother to her grinning grandmother.

The pine door swung open admitting Becky, resplendent in a soft white dress carrying Li'l Jim who was sportive in a blue smock and cap. The three women were aghast at the sudden picture. Poor Becky who was content to drudge in a one room cabin with her baby, for a husband who scarcely could pay for his fat back and meal down at the store,— what right had she to look nicer than Cisseretta, the acknowledged social leader of Sinners Run!

"Whar'd je git dem cloes?" darkly inquired Eliza of her daughter.

"Oh Mammy! Ain't dey jist swell? Miss Thesdy done made dis up special foh me out o' brand new goods case Ah told huh 'twas my second year married, today! See Li'l Jim? Ain't he grand? I has a big suppah foh

Big Jim when he gits home and thought I would run in an' let you folks see us."

"Humph! 'Miss' Thesdy! Since whin did we start 'Missin" yaller niggers? Was Parson Brown anywhere bouts up there?" this from Cisseretta.

"Seems to me dat dose clo'es would scorch yo' skin, chal. Dat Thesdy is a woman wid no religion whatsomever," exasperatingly sighed Eliza.

"Jes' gib yo' all dose cloes fuh to git yo' wrapped up in huh, fudder—dan she gine conjuh yo' . . . heah me, now, heah me!" snapped old Granny Lou with a portentious shaking of her beshawled head.

Poor Becky! All her joyous happiness so quickly transformed to bitter antagonism.

"How come yo'all hates that pore woman so? What she done done aginst you? All I seed she done was good! She's up dere in huh own pretty li'l house, amindin' huh business, and you folks down heah hatin' huh! Cisseretta? You won't make no hit wid Parson Brown . . . hatin' Miss Thesdy, 'case he thinks she is jest grand! As for me and Big Jim, she saved our boy's life which is moah dan you what's his own kin-folks done, and we loves huh, even ef she ain't done professed 'ligion. From what I seed of huh and knowed of younes, she's a heap sight nigh to God dan you folks who eat out yo' hearts wid hatin' huh!"

She gathered the bewildered Li'l Jim up and left the scene of unsympathetic relatives, muttering to herself—"Gawd! Effen I stayed widdem any longer I would lose my own 'ligion. They's my own folks, but dey simply breed evilness, and I doesn't blame sweet Miss Thesdy from not minglin' wid 'em 'ceptin' when she has to."

In the Lambert cabin, Granny Lou was grunting—"See dat? She done got dat chal tu'ned agin huh own folks already . . . an' de preachuh eatin' out ob huh hand,"—with a cunning glance at Cisseretta.

"For two cents, Granny—" whined Cisseretta, petulantly, "I'd git the women together and go up to her ol' house and beat her up!"

"Kyah kyah! Lawsy me! Hush yo' mouf, chal!" elaborately guffawed her mother.

"Go hade, den . . . go hade! Do moah—an' talk less, honey!" huskily whimpered the old woman to her infuriated grandchild.

The day had been a busy one for Bathesda. She had contracted to make reproductions of the old samplers for an important Jewish antique dealer of Atlanta. Little Alice Thornton, quite grown up, and home from college, had motored out to see her, bringing with her her fiancé from Boston, an artist. He had begged for the privilege of painting Bathesda in all the glory of her little cottage and embroidering frames.

To please Alice, she consented, on condition that it wouldn't interfere with her work.

"Like one of Millet's peasant women," he had said—"and that interior! Worthy of the old Dutch masters."

The young minister had sat awhile, explaining his well meant plan of progress for his congregation, which she knew would never be accepted by the deluded Sinners Run folks, the present pastor being their first seminary man. They understood only the old fashioned untrained "called-but-not-sent" type of ministering.

Becky and Li'l Jim dropped in with the new things she had made for them and the sight of the mother and child transformed by her handiwork, thrilled her deeply.

She bent her queenly head over the crimson, green and purple threads she was interweaving so intricately into the words—"Heart within, God without" on the square of yellow, and smiled the smile of the middle-aged who had all they wanted in life—peace, pleasant labor, and contentment. Why should she be sad because of a God who withheld Himself, or the doubtful power of healing a people who despised her?

She decided to pick a fresh cabbage for her supper, and going to the door, was surprised to see Cisseretta Lambert approaching. With shifting eyes, and lowered brow, she informed Bathesda they had come to fetch her for a friend. At the little picket gate stood an old rickety homemade cart with ill matched wheels, drawn by a sorry nag whose hips punctured his skin in miss-meal significance. Eliza was driving and perched beside her for all the world like a bundled up mummy, sat Granny Lou.

"We kin fotch you there and back in no time, Thesdy. New folks jest come to Sinners Run, and powerful sick."

Bathesda hurriedly threw a light shawl around her shoulders with a strong sense of foreboding which she forcibly thrust out of her mind and joined the trio at the cart.

She and Cisseretta rode backwards with their feet swinging, and nothing was said by the four women as the half dead animal faltered along the lonely road pulling the unbalanced, lurching, wabbling vehicle behind them.

Then Eliza . . .

"Kyah kyah! Heah we all is, folksies! Kyah kyah! Lawdy, Lawdy, Lawd!"

Bathesda turned from the back end of the wagon and saw glaring malevolently at her, the dark faces of ten or twelve women. They were as a pack of hungry hounds eager to be off on the chase. Cisseretta leaped from her seat on the wagon and rudely grabbed Bathesda, causing her to stumble to the ground on her knees. As if waiting for the initiative action from their leader, they pounced upon her, dragging her by the arms up the sloping hill side. The decrepit conveyance with the beswaddled old woman, was left standing on the road.

The maddened women yelled violent invectives—brandished whips, twigs and sticks aloft, dragging her roughly uphill, not allowing her to regain her foothold or the freedom of her arms.

"Thought you'd git yo' claws on Revern Bro Brown, didn't you? We see 'bout dat, won't we? Cain't feed him none o' yo' hoodoo vittles . . . nuh-uh!"

"Yes indeedy. We is gwine to see 'bout all dis heah monkey business yo' been cayin' on all dese yeahs wid de men folks. . . . "

"Think you better dan ussens, doesn't you? Humph! Old half white niggers make me sick . . . cain't be white an' cain't be black!"

"Naw! We niggers don't want you and de white folks won't hab you!"

"Lawdy, Lawdy, Lawd today! Yeowh!"

"Pull huh ol' plaits down! Make me tiahd wid huh ol' dawg har! Wouldn't have straight har, mahself—Revelations say as plain as day— 'har lak lambs wool' like ussen got. . . . "

"Sis Grenn? Dis is shoah a holy deed Cisseretta done called on us to do . . . to protect ouah poah pastor from de wiles ob dis sinner woman. . . . "

"Kyah kyah! Lawd today!"

They reached the summit of the hill which was capped with a small patch of woods. A few of the trees had recently been chopped down, judging by the fresh stumps. The several women in whose clutches Bathesda had fallen, suddenly released their hold on her and jumped back out of her reach. But Bathesda merely stomped the caked dirt from her shoes and torn skirt, threw a quiet searching glance around the semi-circle of women, and made to swing her loosened braids around her head.

This action galled Cisseretta, who saw in it a self assurance, a composure that was shaking the courage of her vigilance committee. She sprang at Bathesda heavily with an angry snarl, pushing her back into a tree which instantaneously crashed to the earth, sideways, sending Cisseretta and all the women scrambling and yelping down the hill.

"Conjuh woman! conjuh . . . Lawd Ah's feared!"

"Hoodoo stuff! Told yo'all we oughten to bother wid huh!"

"Lawd! Jist 'low me to git home once moah . . . please!"

"Cisseretta done got ussen into dis mess . . . !"

From the opposite direction came two white men, hurrying toward Bathesda who stood arranging her hair beside the fallen tree.

"Anybody hurt, Auntie? We are clearing these here woods for Ben Lovett who has bought the strip, and my buddy here—he sprained his joint while chopping down that 'un a few minutes ago. We went up to my shack after some liniment and we didn't 'reckon anyone would come along before we got back. The tree was nearly cut thru and I 'spec a slight jostle knocked her over."

"No one was hurt. It fell to the side," murmured the yellow woman absently—eyes searching into the distance.

A delicate tenderness played over her face, and kindly wrinkles appeared about her mouth and forehead. Like Haggard's "She," Bathesda unexpectedly looked her age, all at once. She had dropped the cloak of a hardened, held-over youth, and taken on the ethereal robe of an inner beauty—a soul transformation had taken place.

She, for the first time, turned directly to the lumberjacks, and asked of the one with the bandaged arm—

"Is it bad?"

"Hurts mightily and swellin' every second."

She unwrapped the crude bandage wiped away the stench of liniment, cupped her two hands about the swollen arm and gazed upward—her thin lips moving almost imperceptibly while the men stood transfixed.

She finally withdrew her hands, clenched them into tight fists and then shook them open and away from her, as if throwing off the contamination of alien flesh.

"Now . . . it is well!"

"Bill! Honest to John! She's right! The dad burned misery had gone completely, and look! The swellin' is goin' down right before my very eyes!"

"Good God! It is a miracle we've just witnessed! The woman's a saint." And he hastily crossed himself while the other man tested his healed arm by swinging an ax.

Bathesda went down the hill with wide masculine strides—the light winds causing her snagged skirt and white apron to billow and flurry. Her eyes were two muddy pools of tears. She was testifying.

"Up Calvary's rugged brow did I go, this day with Thee, dear Lord . . . To the very foot of the Cross . . . and I saw the bloody nails in Thy precious feet . . . the cruel thorns . . . and the bitter cup was spared me

. . . me, a worthless worm . . . but Thou didst drink it to the dregs!"

And she went home with a new power—with understanding, tolerance and forgiveness; to be one of her people; to take care of Becky with her Li'l Jim and Big Jim; and the fragrant drops of rain pelted her in gentle benediction.

FROM *THE CRISIS*, MARCH–APRIL 1928

# The Foolish and the Wise

## Sallie Runner Is Introduced to Socrates

### LEILA AMOS PENDLETON

Mrs. Maxwell Thoro (born Audrey Lembre) tiptoed down the spacious hall toward the kitchen of her dwelling whence issued sounds, not exactly of revelry but—perhaps jubilation would be a better fit. For in a high soprano voice her colored maid-of-all-work, Sallie Runner, for the past half-hour had been informing to the accompaniment of energetic thumps of a flatiron, whomsoever it might concern that she had a robe, a crown, a harp and wings.

Mrs. Thoro moved quietly for, enjoyable as was Sallie's repertoire, one could never tell when she would do some even more enjoyable improvising, and her employer knew from long experience that Sallie's flights were much freer and more artistic when she was unaware of an audience.

Just as Mrs. Thoro reached the kitchen door the soloist started off on the verse, "I gotta shoes," so she stood quietly listening until the verse ended:

> "I gotta shoes, yo' gotta shoes,
> All a Gawd's chillun gotta shoes;
> Wen I getto hebben goin' to put on my shoes
> An' skip all ober Gawd's hebben.
> Hebben, Hebben! Ever'buddy hollerin' 'bout hebben.

159

*Ain't goin' dere.*
*Hebben, hebben, goin' to skip all ober Gawd's hebben."*

As the singer ceased she whirled around upon her employer with a loud laugh. "Ha, ha, Miss Oddry!" cried she. "I knowed yo' was dere. I sho is glad yo' done come, 'cause I'se mighty lonesome an' powerful tired. Jes' was thinkin' to myseff dat I'se goin' to try to swade Brother Runner to move away from Starton. Nobuddy don't do nothin' here but git bornd, git married an' git daid, an' wurk, wurk, wurk! Miss Oddry, I'se goin' to tell yo' a secret."

"What is it, Sallie?" inquired Mrs. Thoro.

"I don't lak to wurk. Nuvver did."

"Why, Sallie! That is a surprise," replied her employer. "I should never have guessed it, for there is not a more capable maid in town than you are."

"Yasum, I guess dat's right. I wurks wid my might an' I does whut my hands finds to do, but tain't my nature doe. Muss be my Ma's trainin' an' mazin-grace-how-sweet-de-sound mixed togedder, I reckon. Miss Oddry, does yo' know whut I'd ruther do dan anything? I'd ruther know how to read an' write dan anything in de whole, wide world, an' den I'd nuvver do nothin' else but jes' dem two."

"Well, Sallie, I'm sure you would get very tired of reading and writing all the time; but you're not too old to learn."

"Nome, not too ole, mebbe, but too dumb an' too soft in de haid, I reckun. Miss Oddry, couldn't yo' read to me or talk to me on ironin' days 'bout sumpin' outside uv Starton? Cose I wouldn't want yo' round under my feet on wash-days, but ironin' days is fine fur lissening."

"Why yes, Sallie, I'd love to do that. Why didn't you ask me before? Mr. Thoro and I are re-reading an old school course, just for the fun of it, and I'll share it with you. I'm sure you would enjoy hearing about some of earth's greatest characters. How would you like to have me tell you about Socrates?"

"Sockertees? Huh! Funny name! Sockertees whut?"

"Well, in his time men seldom had more than one name, Sallie. He was the son of Sophroniscus and Phaenarete. He was a sculptor and a philosopher."

"Gosh!" cried Sallie. "A sculpture an' a lossipede! Wusser an' mo' uv it! But go on, Miss Oddry, tell me mo' 'bout him."

"Socrates was born about 469 years before our Lord, and died at the age of seventy. He is said to have had thick lips, a flat nose, protruding eyes, bald head, a squat figure, and a shambling gait."

"Why!" exclaimed Sallie. "He was a cullud gentmun, warn't he? Musta looked jes' lak Brudder Runner, 'cordin' to dat."

"Oh no, Sallie, he wasn't colored."

"Wal, ef he been daid all dat long time, Miss Oddry, how kin yo' tell his color?"

"Why he was an Athenian, Sallie. He lived in Greece."

"Dar now! Dat settles it! Ever'buddy knows dat my cullud folks sho do lak grease."

"Oh Sallie! 'Greece' was the name of his country, just as 'America' is the name of ours." Sallie grunted.

"Socrates," continued Mrs. Thoro, "was a very wise, just, and good man, and he loved his country and his countrymen very much. He used to delight in wandering through the streets of Athens, convArsing with those whom he met, giving them the benefit of the truths he had discovered and seeking to obtain from each more truth or new light. He spent the whole day in public, in the walks, the workshops, the gymnasiums, the porticoes, the schools and the market place at the hour it was most crowded, talking with everyone without distinction of age, sex, rank or condition. It was said that 'as he talked the hearts of all who heard him leaped up and their tears gushed out.'"

"Hole, on Miss Oddry," interrupted Sallie, "Jes' wanta ax yo' one queshun. While ole Sockertees was runnin' round the streets, shootin' off his lip an' makin' peepul cry, who was takin' keer uv his fambly? Sounds mo' an' mo' lak Brudder Runner to me."

"Well, Sallie, he had a very capable wife who bore him three sons and whose name was Xanthippe. No doubt she managed the household. The only fault Socrates found with her was that she had a violent temper."

Sallie slammed the flatiron down and braced herself against the board, arms akimbo, eyes flashing with indignation.

"Vilent temper?" cried she. "Vilent temper? Whut 'oman wouldn't had a vilent temper in a fix lak dat? I sho do symperthize wid Zantipsy an' I doesn't blame her fur gittin' tipsy needer, pore thing. I betcha she was es sweet es a angel befo' she got mahred, 'cause whut it takes to change yo' disposition, a man lak dat sho is got. It's jes' es much es a 'oman kin do to take keer uv her house right an' raise her chillun right wen her husband is doin' all he kin to hepp her, less mo' wen he ain't doin' nothin' but goin' round runnin' he mouf. Dis ain't de fust time I'se met a gentmun who loves he kentry mo' dan he do he home folks. Go on, Miss Oddry, dear, tell me some mo' 'bout Reveral Eyesire Runner's twin brudder."

"Of course, Sallie," said Mrs. Thoro laughing, "Socrates was human and had his faults, but all in all he was a noble character."

"I hopes so Miss Oddry, but I'll have to hear mo' fo' I 'cide."

"Socrates," resumed Mrs. Thoro, "believed in signs and omens and in following warnings received in his dreams; he also claimed that there was an inner voice which had guided him from childhood."

"Miss Oddry," expostulated Sallie, "yo' keep on tellin' me Sockertees warn't cullud, but yo' keep on tellin' me cullud things 'bout him. Wen we all b'lieve in signs an' dreams yo' all allus says, 'It's jes' darky super-stishun an' ignunce.' How yo' splain dat?"

"Well, Sallie, in those days the most learned people were very super-stitious. Of course we know better now."

"How yo' know yo' knows better, Miss Oddry? How yo' know yo' don't know wusser? Dere's one thing I done found fur sho, an' dat is dat de mo' folks knows de less dey knows. I b'lieves in dreams an' wen I follers dem I goes right. Cose I ain't nuvver heerd no cujjus voice, but ef ole Sockertees say he heard it I b'lieve he heerd it. Nobuddy can't prove he didn't."

"Very true, Sallie, but,—"

"Jes' one minute, Miss Oddry, please. Dere's sumpin' I been thinkin' a long time, an' now I knows it. An' dat is dat wen yo' come right down to de fack-trufe uv de inside feelin's, peepul is all alak; black ones is lak white ones an' dem ole anciente ones lak Sockertees is jes' lak dese here ones right now."

"I believe there is some truth in that, Sallie, but shall I go on about Socrates?"

"Oh, yassum, Miss Oddry, I do love to hear 'bout him."

"He tried most earnestly to make people think, to reason out what was right and what was wrong in their treatment of each other. He constantly repeated, 'Virtue is knowledge; Vice is ignorance,' while to the young his advice was always, 'Know thyself.'"

"Humph!" interrupted Sallie. "Mighty good advice, Miss Oddry, but it's some job, b'lieve me. I'se es ole es Methusalum's billy goat now an' I ain't nuvver found myseff out yit. Dere's some new kink comin' out ev'ry day. How 'bout you, Miss Oddry?"

"I think you are right, Sallie. But don't you think we are better off if we study ourselves than if we just blunder along blindly?"

"Oh, yasum, I guess so. But how did ole Sockertees come out wid all his runnin' round an' talkin'?"

"Very sadly, I am sorry to say. Very sadly. Most of the Athenians entirely misunderstood him."

"Bound to," said Sallie.

"He made a great many unscrupulous enemies."

"Bound to," said Sallie.

"They accused him of being the very opposite of what he was."

"Bound to," said Sallie.

"And finally they tried him and condemned him to death."

Sallie set down the flatiron and folded her arms, while her eyes flew wide open in astonishment. "What?" she exclaimed. "Jes' fur talkin'? Wal I-will-be-swijjled!"

"Yes," continued Mrs. Thoro. "They imprisoned him and sent him a cup of hemlock, which is a deadly poison, to drink."

"But he had mo' gumption dan to drink it, I hope?"

"It was the law of his country, Sallie, and Socrates was always a law-abiding citizen."

"Wal, fur gosh sake!" cried Sallie. "Whut in de world was de use uv him havin' all dat tongue ef he couldn't use it to show dem peepul wherein? He mouts well been es dumb es a doodlebug!"

"But," explained Mrs. Thoro, "he had spent his whole life in trying to make the Athenians love and honor and obey their laws and he was willing to die for the same cause. He had many friends who loved him truly and they tried to persuade him to escape, but by unanswerable arguments he proved to them how wrong they were."

"Humph!" grunted Sallie. "Tonguey to de last! An' in de wrong way to de wrong ones."

"Plato, who was a friend as well as a pupil," continued Mrs. Thoro, "tells how beautifully Socrates died. He took the cup of hemlock quite calmly and cheerfully and drained it to the dregs. When his friends could not restrain their sorrow for the loss they were about to sustain, he reproved them and urged them to remember what they were about to bury, not Socrates, but the shell which had contained him, for he, himself, was about to enter the joys of the blessed. He tried to the last to make them see that unless they honored and obeyed all laws, their country could not long survive, because lawlessness was the same as suicide."

"Miss Oddry," said Sallie, solemnly, "don't yo' wisht we had one million of dem Sockertees down here in ower sunny Soufland?"

FROM *THE CRISIS*, MARCH 1921

# The Foolish and the Wise

## Sanctum 777 N.S.D.C.O.U. Meets Cleopatra

### LEILA AMOS PENDLETON

The hour for opening had passed but, strange to say, Sister Sallie Runner, the All Highest Mogul of Sanctum 777, "Notable Sons and Daughters of Come On Up," had not yet arrived. The members stood around in groups and wondered what had happened, for Sis Runner was never late. True the Vice-All Highest, Sister Susan Haslum, was present and technically it was her duty to open the meeting; but the members of the Sanctum had a very poor opinion of her ability. Sallie had once voiced the general feeling when she said to her:

"Sis Haslum, seems lak to me dat yo' knowlidge box is allus onjinted an' de mentals of yo' mind clean upsot. How yo' 'spect to rule dis Sanctum wen yo' time come I cain't tell. Pears lak to me de bes' thing we kin do will be to 'lect yo' Grand Past All Highest an' give yo' de grand claps now an' be done wid it. Den we won't have to worry wid yo' settin' in dis cheer an' trying to zide."

The suggestion was not acted upon, but as the members waited tonight they wished very earnestly it had been; for then Sister Tulip Brawler would have been in line to preside (as she was Most Mightiest), and no one doubted her ability. When the thoughts of the members had reached this uncertain state, Notable Brother Brown spoke up:

"High Notables, Sons and Daughters, Brothers and Sisters, Officers and Members," he said, "I moves dat we close dis here Sanctum tonight befo' we opens it an' journey 'round to Sis Runner's house to see what all's de matter wid her."

"Sho! Sho! To be certingly," responded the Sanctum unanimously, but just as they were putting on their wraps, in bustled Sallie, breathless but smiling.

"I knowd it," said she, as soon as she could catch her breath, "I jes knowd you all would git tired a waitin'. I tole Reveral Runner so. But dat man is some sick an' whut part ain't sick is scared to death; an' no wonder, as much debilmunt as he's allus up to. Jes as I were puttin' on my hat to come here he dragged in de doe, lookin' lak a ghost. 'Brudder Runner,' says I, 'Is dat yo' or yo' apparatus?' He diden make no answer but jes pinted to his chist. Wal, yo' orter seen me hop 'round. Yo' know he already done had newmonny twict. I had some creso an' dats good for de longs; den I chopped up some Turmooda onyuns an' bound him up in dat an' salt. When he mence to feel better I turned him over to Obellina. She's jes as gooda nuss as me an' she are wrapped up in her pa 'cause she ain't on to his curbs. Come on, chilluns, less open de lodge. We'll leave off de gowns an' crowns an' mit de regular openin' 'cause it's so late, but I gotta fine ole ancienty story to tel yo' an' dis time it's 'bout a cullud lady."

At this the Sanctum was all excitement and officers and members hurriedly took their stations. Sallie gave the altar in front of her five raps, then said she, "High Notibuls, yo' kin pas to de secertary's desk one by one an' pay yo' dues. Sis Dolum an' Sis Spots tend to passin' de cookies. Does yo' all think you kin do all dem things an' lissen to me too?"

"Oh yas, All Highest," came a number of voices. "We's jes crazy to hear yo'."

"Wal," proceeded Sallie, in her stateliest manner, "dis here lady I'se goin' to tell 'bout tonight were bornd right spang in Egupt an' dats in Afriky. She were a sho nuff queen too, wid lords an' ladies an' sojers an' servunts. Her name were Clea Patrick."

"All Highest," cautiously inquired Sister Ann Tunkett, Vice-Most Mightiest, "is yo' rale sho she were cullud?"

"I is," responded Sallie. "Cose, Mis Oddry beat me down she warn't, but I knows better 'cause I were lookin' right at her. She were one a dese here high browns wid wavy hair an' rosy cheeks, lookin' jes lak dat Donarine Elett whut were runnin' arter Reveral Runner dat time. Least he 'cuse her of runnin' arter him wen dey got cot up wid, but I knows who were doin' de most runnin'."

"Is Mis Oddry got Clea Patrick's picter, All Highest?" inquired Sis Tunkett.

"Yas, an' de nex' time yo' come 'round I'll show it to yo'. Clea Patrick were one of dese here long-haided, long-nosed, long-eyed, slim gals dat jes nachel come into de world to make trubble. An' she sho made it. Fust off her King pa died wen she were only eighteen years ole an' lef his kentry fur her an' her lil brudder Tallmy to rule togedder. But whut should Tallmy's gardeens do but grab de whole bisness an' leave Clea wid nuffin."

"Now ain't dat jes lak some men!" exclaimed Sis Bawler. "Seem lak de vurry idear of Wimmin rulin' anything but de cook kitching sets um wild."

"It's de fack—trufe," replied Sallie. "Yo all knows dat as long as I were settin' on dis floor Brudder Runner were a jim-dandy member of de 'Come On Ups.' Soon as I mence to move 'round de cheers, he mence to git restless. Den wen yo' all 'lect me All Highest he jes nachel coulden stan' it. So he goes off an' jines dat 'Everlastin' Order of Hezzakites' an' he ain't been back here sence."

"Dats right, All Highest. Dats jes whut he done, but I nuvver seen through it befo'." said Vice-Most Mightiest Tunkett.

"Wal I seen through him. He's jes de same as a winda-pane to me. But ef I'da knowd whut I knows now or ef I'da lissened to my ma he'd nuvver got me in his clinches. Longs as I diden do nuthin' but work fur him an' be a skillyun he were as pleased as punch, but jes as soon as peepul act lak dey thot I could do sumpin else sides dat he got sore. An' dat was de vurry way dem men acted wid Clea Patrick. But dey diden know her yit! Ha! Ha! Dey haden foamed her quaintence. She skipped 'round an' got herself a big army an' de way she fout um were sumpin' pretty, 'cause evry one of dem sojers was in love wid her. Den right in de middle of all dat here come dat Julyus Siezer."

"Who were he, All Highest?" inquired Sis Haslum.

"Why he were dat great Roaming gineral sumpin' lak Elleckzandry, only he were borned a long time afterward. Wal as soon as he got in gunshot of her, Clea Patrick mence rollin' dem long eyes at him. She done a right cute thing doe—she wind herself all up in a big bufull rug an' make her servunts carry it to Siezer an' say, 'Here's a present Queen Clea Patrick sont you.' Den wen dey onroll it, out she jump an' dat ole jack went crazy over her. Now he were ole nuff to be her grandpa an' he had a wife at home, sides bein' bald-haided, an' dey warn't no scuse fur de way he carried on."

"Wal, All Highest," drawled Most Mightiest Brawler, "Yo' know whut dey say 'bout a ole fool."

"Yas," returned Sallie, "an' I ain't nuvver seen dat sayin' fail yit. Dis here Siezer were a good zample of it, too. Why he took Clea Patrick back to Roam wid him an' put her in a fine palace an' was gittin' ready to go fum extreemity to extromity. But dem Roamings say, 'Looka here, we's tired a dis foolishness. Nuff's good as a feast. We all cain't die togedder—somebuddy is got to die fust an' it might's well be yo'.' So dey jump on Siezer in de State House one day an' fill him fulla daggers."

"Oh! Oh! My! My!" cried the Sanctum.

"Yas indeedy," replied Sallie nonchalantly. "Cose when I fust got quainted wid dem ole ancienties, dat murdarin' an' momockin' way dey had worried me a lot. But I'se usedta it now. Yo' know you kin git usedta anybuddy dyin' but yosef. Wal wen dis here Siezer died, Clea Patrick lit out fur home an' took dey lil son Siezeron wid her. An' its a good thing dey got away so slick 'cause dem Roamings woulda finished um bofe. But it do seem lak peepul nuvver knows whut dey raiely wants. When Siezer were daid evry'buddy got sorry an' when his will were read an' dey found out dat he had left a whole lotta money to de vurry ones dat had kilt him, why dem Roamings rose up an' made dose killers fly an' burnt up all dey homes an' done um up so bad dey wisht dey nuvver hada seen dat Siezer, less mo' kilt him."

"Wal," Most Mightiest Bawler interposed, "doesn't yo' think dat were fair an' square, All Highest?"

"Oh, I guess so," the All Highest replied, "but dem ole ancienties done so many quare things yo' nuvver coud tell whedder dey was comin' or goin'. Wal, arter Siezer were daid his main frend name Mark an Tony took up de battle. Arter fightin' in evry derection he wint sailin' down to Egupt. When Clea Patrick heerd he were comin' she diden git into no carpet dis time. No indeedy! She puts on her gladdes' rags an' jewls an' fumes an' gits in her fines' boat all kivvered wid gold an' silver, an' has her servunts all decked in dey grandes' clothes holdin' parasols over her an' wavin' fans at her an' way she sail to meet Mark an Tony. She already knowd him wen she were in Roam wid dat Siezer an' mebbe dey lak one another den, yo' can't tell. Anyhow dey sho lak each udder arter at meetin'. Sho did!"

"Ef she look anything lak Donarina an' was all fixed up lak you says, I knows she were one uvvermo hartbreaker," put in Sis Haslum.

Sallie transfixed her with a look and went on. "Mark an Tony furgot all erbout Roam an' home an' wife an' everything but Clea Patrick. He warnt no ole man lak Siezer so dey was mo' on a quality. Dey played games togedder an' went a huntin' an' a fishin' togedder lak lil boy an' gurl. Sides, Clea would sing to Mark an' play fur him an' talk to him in seben langwitches."

"It's a wunder Mark's wife haden got onto um," commented Sis Tunkett.

"She did. She were one of dem strong-arm wimmin an' she starts up a great war, hopin' dat Mark will come on home an' git into it; but he were too busy. He an' Clea useter dress up in masks an' servunt's clothes at nights an' run up an' down de streets an' play Holler Ween pranks on peepul when it warnt no Holler Ween. Den agin dey would put on dey grandes' robes an' crowns an' give de bigges' kinda ceptions to dey frends an' eat an' drink tel dey coulden see. An' den in the middle of dem doins Mark's wife upped an' died."

"Ah, de pore soul!" sighed Sis Haslum, "Dat Clea Patrick orta be shamed a hersef."

"Wal," resumed the All Highest, "Mark went on to meet the yuther great Roaming gineral name Tavius an' what should he do but make a match 'tween his sister an' Mark."

"Good gosh!" exclaimed Bawler, "an' Clea Patrick yit livin'? Now don't you know dere's trubble comin' in lobs an' gobs? Diden dat Tavius had gumption nuff to know dat a man whut won't be true to one wife, won't be true to two?"

"Wal," Sallie replied, "pears lak of he uvver knowd it he furgot it or else he were hopin' fur de bes'. Anyhow, fur a while Mark kep' rale straight. But arter while he hadta leave home to go to de wars agin an' when he got not so fur fum Clea Patrick—uh! uh!—he sont fur her an' give her not rings an' bracelits an' things lak dat, but rivers an' moutings an' cities an' countries."

"Jes whut I knowd!" triumphed Sis Bawler. "Dese here madeup matches allus scares me. Land knows deres times wen its harda nuff to stand a match yo done made yosef, less mo 'one dats made fur yo'."

"Mark an Tony found dat out aright. He done a lil mo' fightin' 'round erbout den he hikes hissef spang down to Egupt an' dar he stays wid Clea Patrick."

"Ah ha!" Sis Bawler cried. "Tole yo' so! Tole yo' so!"

"But," Sallie went on, "dem Roamings feel dersef much more degraced by Mark an Tony's doin's, an' dey is tired a Clea Patrick hoodoodlin' dey bes' ginerals so dey clar war agin her."

"Serve her jes right!" Sis Tunkett cried indignantly. "Don't care ef she were a cullud queen. I don't hole wid no sich capers. She orta lef dem wimmin's husbands lone."

"Dats right! Dats right!" chorused the Sanctum.

"Yas," Sallie agreed. "My ole mudder allus said dat 'Right wrongs no one.' Wal, Mark an Tony an' Clea Patrick gethered all dey sojers an' sailurs an' off dey go to fight de Roamings. Wen de battle got hot, Clea got scared an' back home she went ascootin'. Stidda Mark an Tony stayin' dere an' fightin' lak a rale sojer, whut muss he do but take a fast boat an' lite out arter Clea Patrick. Cose wen de leaders lef, the sojers stop fightin' an' de inimy captured dem all an' den hiked out arter Clea an' Mark."

"Wal warn't dat sumpin!" exclaimed Sis Haslum.

"Dem two," continued Sallie, "knowd evry'thing were over den, so dey et an' drunk an' carried on wusser dan uvver, tel dem Roamings come clean into de city. Den Clea Patrick hide hersef wid her maids in a big monimint an' made her servunts tell Mark she were daid. I cain't imagine why she done dat 'cause dat news on top a all de res' of his trubbles jes nachel broke his heart an' he run his own swoad clean fru his body. Den when dey come back an' say Clea Patrick warnt daid he made dem carry him to her. I reckon dey love one another much as dem kinda peepul kin, 'cause when she saw him dyin' at her feet, she 'cides she diden wanta live widout him. So she put a pizenous wiper in her breast to sting her an' in a lil while she were dead."

"Poe thing," Sis Haslum sighed. "Poe thing. Mebbe ef her ma hada lived she woulda been a better gurl."

"Mebbe so," answered Sallie, "mebbe so. High Notabuls, de hour is late. We will close by singin' 'Dy soul be on dy gard.'"

FROM *THE CRISIS*, MAY 1922

# Cross Crossings Cautiously

## ANITA SCOTT COLEMAN

Sam Timons rarely thought in the abstract. His thoughts as were his affections were marshalled concretely. His affections were rolled into a compact and unbreakable ball which encircled his wife Lettie and his young son Sammy. His thoughts—he did not think much—but such as his thoughts were, they involved this, if he did a good turn for somebody, somebody else would quite naturally do him or his a good turn also.

Usually Sam was a cheerful creature. Work and love; love and work, that, boiled down to brass tacks, is the gist of all life, and Sam possessed both. Even though at present, he was out of a job.

He walked along the sandy road stirring up miniature dust clouds with every step for his heavy feet shuffled wearily with the burden of his dejected body.

He felt down and out. He was at the end of his rope. One dollar in his pocket. He gripped it in his fingers. All he had. But he could not give up. The ball of his affection, as it were, trundled along before him luring him on. He was "hoofing it" to another town to try again.

"Saw wood . . . clean house, paint barns, chop weeds . . . plow, anything, suh. . . . Just so it's work so's I can earn somethin'. I'm a welder by trade, but they don't hire cullud."

Behind him stretched the long, dusty way he had come. Before him a railroad zigzagged his path. As his feet lifted to the incline, he raised his eyes, and met advice from a railroad crossing sign:

CROSS CROSSINGS CAUTIOUSLY

He paused to spell out the words, repeating them painstakingly. Then he went on. A little beyond and across the tracks another huge sign caught his attention.

Soon, he had halted beside this one, letting his eyes sidle up and down and over the gaily painted board. Now he was staring open-mouthed at the glaring yellow lion who crouched to spring, now, at the flashy blond lady pirouetting on a snow white mount. He stood quite still thinking. Wouldn't Lettie and little Sam be wild to see such a show.


"'Lo Mister."

Sam swung around like a heavy plummet loosed from its mooring. "Gee . . . Mister, you 'fraid of me?"

A little girl hardly more than a baby addressed him. She was regarding him with the straight unabashed gaze of the very innocent and of the very wise.

"I want you to carry me to the circus," she announced, when their mutual survey of one another seemed to her enough.

Sam's eyes were fixed on the web-fine, golden hair escaping from two torn places in the child's hat. Already he had seen that the eyes searching his were blue. . . . He fidgeted. He made a move to go.

"Oh, don't, don't go," beseeched the child. "Mother has to 'tend a meeting, and father is always busy. There is no one else. Mother said I might if only somebody'd take me. See." She thrust out a little smudgy fist—and opening it, revealed a shiny new fifty-cent piece. "This is mine," she said plaintively, "Can't we go?"


Mrs. Maximus McMarr was a busy woman. She managed to attend fourteen clubs each week, but that excluded any time to manage Claudia, her five-year-old daughter. Claudia's father considered children woman's responsibility. One advantage or disadvantage this sort of bringing up gave Claudia, she always got what she wanted.

Something about her made Sam do her bidding now.

They were half way between the McMarr place and the circus grounds before he thought about what he was doing. He clutched at the dollar in his pocket. He wanted to laugh, guessed he was nervous. Suddenly, he stopped abruptly—there was another of those signs where the train's right-of-way intersected another dusty country road.

## CROSS CROSSINGS CAUTIOUSLY

"Oh do come on," urged the child jerking his hand in an ecstasy of delight and impatience.

Further on a half-grown lad passed them, but stopped and turned to watch them down the road. As the man and the little girl drew out of sight, he faced about and pelted up the road.

The noise of the circus leapt up to meet and welcome Sam and Claudia. The music of the band was sweet to their ears. Sam reveled in it and Claudia's little feet danced over the road. Even the bellowing and roars of the wild animals left them undismayed. It was circus day.

Mrs. McMarr had alighted from a friend's car and remained standing beside it, to talk. Both women observed the runner at the same time. Mrs. McMarr felt her heart skid upward into her throat. Claudia had not appeared. She divined that the messenger tended evil for no other than her precious baby. She made up her mind to swoon even before she received the tidings.

The friend went in search of McMarr who for once allowed himself an interruption. Close-lipped, he tumbled off his harvester and rushed pell-mell across his field.

All afternoon, Claudia had been surfeited with care. One after another had tendered and petted and caressed her. Even her father had been solicitous. She curled up, drowsy and very tired, in the big arm chair.

The rain that had threatened to fall all day suddenly commenced like the tat-a-rat-tat of far-off drums. Claudia was wide awake. She sat up. Remembering. The circus band! The monkeys in their little red coats! Her circus man! Something had happened. What?

The impulse to know surmounted the fear she harbored of her father. She slipped over to his chair. He had been very kind today. Perhaps . . . he wouldn't mind telling her . . . Where her circus man was?

FROM *OPPORTUNITY,* JUNE 1930

# Three Dogs and a Rabbit

## ANITA SCOTT COLEMAN

"This, that I'm about to relate," said Timothy Phipps, "isn't much of a story, though, you might upon hearing it weave it into a ripping good yarn. I'm not much of a talker or writer. Now maybe when I'm in my cups or in the last stages of a delirious fever—I might attempt to— write." He tilted his head, with its fringe of rough grey hair, a bit backwards and sidewise and laughed. His laughter seeming to echo— write, write, write.

Tinkling with fine spirits and good humor, he ceased laughing to inquire roguishly: "What, say, are the ingredients of a story? A plot? Ah, yes, a plot. Ho! ho! ho! The only plot in this rigmarole, my dear fellow, is running, hard to catch, a sure enough running plot. Characters. To be sure we must have characters: A pretty girl, a brave hero, a villain and love. A setting. Of course there must be a setting, an atmosphere, a coloring. We'll say moonlight and a rippling brook and a night bird singing nocturnal hymns in a forest of love. Love pirouetting in the silvery moonlight, love splashing and singing in a rippling brook. Love trilling and fluting in a bird's song—Love and a pretty girl—Love and a brave hero—Love and a villain made penitent and contrite; because of love. Bye the bye, there is no living person who could not fancy the beginning, imagine the entanglements, conceive the climax, unfold the

*173*

developments, reveal the solution and picture the finale, having such material at hand. But," laughed Timothy, "none such—none such in what I'm a-telling."

Shedding his joviality for a more serious mien, he queried—

"Have you ever thought how very few really lovely women one meets in a life time? Our pretty young debutantes are far too sophisticated; while our age-mellowed matrons affect *naiveté*, and our bustling house-wives are too preoccupied with directing the destinies of nations to be attractive in the least.

"Men? Bother the men. We are but animals at best. Alert and crafty, lazy and jovial; just as chance decrees, and monotonously alike in our dependence upon woman. All of us are made or marred by our contacts with women. Whenever chance draws her draperies aside to allow a lovely woman to cross our path, it leaves an ineffaceable mark upon our countenance and traces indelible patterns of refinement upon our character.

"Unfortunately, I am of a critical turn of mind together with a pernicious inclination to believe with the ancient Greeks that an ugly body houses an ugly soul and that loveliness dwells only in beautiful temples.

"Certainly, certainly this inclination has led me into more than one blind alley. Ah, if I could only wield the pen as skillfully as I can this—" He flourished a carving knife, for we were at a table and he was occupied at the moment in carving the *pièce de résistance*. "I would tell the world how untrue my premise is. And what a cruel fallacy outer loveliness ofttimes proves itself to be.

"Despite this, my contrary nature clings like a leech to the belief that beautiful temples are invariably beautiful within.

"And it chanced, I say chanced, since there is the probability that someone not half so lovely might have done the same deed, and had such been the case my belief would have suffered a terrible set-back. It chanced that the loveliest woman I ever saw was the most [inwardly] beautiful.

"I saw her first under amazing circumstances. Circumstances so extraordinary they seem unreal to this day, but I won't linger upon them, because they make another story. My second sight of her was in a crowded court-room and it was then while she sat very primly upon the culprit's bench that I had my first opportunity really to see her.

"She was a little woman. Feel as you like towards all other types, but a little woman has appeal. Especially, a little old woman with silvery hair, and an unnameable air about her, that is like fingers forever playing upon the chords of sweetest memories. All this, and a prettiness beside, a trifle faded of course, but dainty and fragile and lovely—rare, you might say, as a bit of old, old lace. And kindliness overlaying this, to lend a charm to her beauty that jewel or raiment could not render. Her silvery hair crinkled almost to the point of that natural curliness which Negro blood imparts. The kind of curl that no artificial aid so far invented can duplicate. Her eyes were extremely heavy-lidded, which is, as you know, a purely Negro attribute, and her mouth had a fullness, a ripeness, exceedingly—*African.*

"That she was anything other than a white American was improbable, improbable indeed. She, the widow of old Colonel Ritton, deceased, of Westview. As dauntless and intrepid a figure as ever lived to make history for his country. His career as an Indian fighter, pioneer and brave, open opposer of the lawlessness which held sway over the far West in the late sixties is a thing that is pointed to with pride and made much of, by Americans. Three notable sons, high standing in their respective vocations, paid her the homage due the mother of such stalwart, upright men as themselves. Two daughters, fêted continuously because of their beauty, were married into families, whose family-tree flourished like the proverbial mustard-seed, unblighted before the world.

"There had to be some reason why a lady of her standing was forced to appear in court. The truth is, it was not because of the greatness of her offense; but because of the unusualness of her misconduct which had raised such a hue and cry; until drastic methods had to be resorted to.

"The charge against her was one of several counts, the plaintiffs being three very stout gentlemen, florid-faced, heavy-jowled, wide-paunched to a man. Each of them diffused a pomposity; which while being imposing managed somehow to be amusing. Their very manner bespoke their grim determination to punish the defendant. Their portly bodies fairly bristled with the strength of this intention. The muscles in their heavy faces worked as though the currents of their thoughts were supplied by volts of wonderment, shocking and bewildering. They charged, first: That the defendant willfully hampered them in the fulfillment of their authorized duty. Second: That the defendant had knowingly aided a criminal to evade the hands of the law, by sheltering the said criminal in or about her premises. Third: That the defendant had spoken untruthfully with intent to deceive by denying all knowledge of said criminal's whereabouts. Fourth: That the concealment of said criminal constituted a tort; the criminal being of so dangerous a character, his being at liberty was a menace to the commonwealth."

Timothy Phipps paused, as he busied himself, serving generous slices of baked ham to his guests. In the act of laying a copious helping upon his own plate, he commenced again, to unreel his yarn.

"There is no joy in life so satisfying, so joyous, as that of having our belief strengthened—to watch iridescent bubbles—our castles in the air—settle, unbroken upon firm old earth. To hear our doubts go singing through the chimneys of oblivion. Ah, that's joy indeed. And it is what I experienced that never-to-be forgotten day in the dinkiest little court-room in the world.

"A rainy spell was holding sway and a penetrating drizzle oozed from the sky as though the clouds were one big jelly-bag hung to drip, drip, drip. I was sogged with depression; what with the weather and the fact that I was marooned in a very hostile section of my native land, it was little wonder that my nerves were jumpy and a soddenness saturated my spirits, even though I knew that the fugitive was free and making a rough guess at it, was to remain so. But an emotion more impelling than curiosity forced me to linger to witness the outcome of old Mrs. Ritton's legal skirmish.

"From a maze of judicial meanderings, these facts were made known.

"The old Ritton house was a big rambling structure built at some period so long ago, the time was forgotten. It was not a place of quick escapes, for no such thing as fleeing fugitives had been thought of, in its planning. Unexpected steps up and steps down made hasty flight hazardous. Unlooked for corners and unaccountable turns called for leisurely progress and long halls with closed doors at their furthest end, opening into other chambers, were hindrances no stranger could shun. All told, the house as it stood was a potent witness against the defendant, each of its numerous narrow-paned windows screeched the fact that none but the initiated could play at hide-and-seek within its walls.

"Many pros and cons were bandied about as to why the run-away Negro had entered Ritton's house. That he had done an unwonted thing went without saying—since hunted things flee to the outposts of Nature, shunning human habitation as one does a pestilence: to the long, long road girt by a clear horizon, where dipping sky meets lifting earth, on, on to the boundless space, away to the forest where wild things hover, or a dash to the mountains to seek out sheltering cave and cavern.

"At first, it was thought that entering the Ritton house was a 'dodge' but subsequent happenings had proven the supposition false. It was quite clear that he had gone in for protection and had found it.

"The claimants carefully explained to the court, how they had chased the Negro down Anthony, up Clements and into Marvin, the street which ran north and south beneath the Ritton-house windows. They were not but a few lengths behind the fugitive—not close enough, you understand, to lay hold upon him; nor so near that they could swear that someone signalled from an open window in the Ritton house. How-be-it, they saw the Negro swerve from the street, dart through the Ritton's gate, dash down the walk, and enter the Ritton house. Less than five minutes afterwards they, themselves, pursued the Negro step by step into the building; to find upon entering it a room so spacious that the several pieces of fine old furniture arranged within it did not dispel an effect of emptiness, while the brilliant light of early afternoon showered upon everything, sparklingly, as if to say, 'No place to hide in here' and over beside an open window old lady Ritton sat very calmly, knitting. And upon being questioned she had strenuously denied that a black man had preceded them into her chamber.

"Finally the point was reached, when the defendant took the stand. And the Lord knows, so much depended, that is, as far as I was concerned, upon what she would or would not say—well, what she said makes my story.

"'Gentlemen, the thing you desire me to tell you, I cannot. Though, I think if I could make you understand a little of my feelings, you will cease—all of you being gentlemen—endeavoring to force me to divulge my secret.

"'You, all of you, have been born so unfettered that you have responded to your every impulse; perhaps it will be hard to realize the gamut of my restraint, when I swear to you, gentlemen, that in all my life, I have experienced no great passion and responded to the urge of only two impulses—two—but two—and these, gentlemen, have become for me a sacred trust.

"'It was years ago when I felt the first impulse and answered it. It has no apparent connection with the present occurrence. Yet, possibly, for no other reason than an old lady's imagining, the memory of that first occasion has leaped across the years to interlace itself with this.

"'Wait, gentlemen. I will tell you all about it. This turbulence has awakened old dreams and old longings and opened the doors of yester-years in the midst of an old lady's musing; but it is worth all the worry. Yes, 'tis worth it.

"'It is strange what mighty chains are forged by impulses and none of us know the strength that is required to break them. My first impulse wrought me much of happiness—very much happiness, gentlemen. Bear with an old lady's rambling—your Honor, and I shall relate just how it happened.

"'I was ten years old, when my master—

"'Pardon? Yes? Yes, Sirs—My master.

"'I was ten years old; when my master gave up his small holdings in the South and came West with his family, his wife,—my mistress—a daughter and two sons and myself. We traveled what was then the tortuous trail that begins east of the Mississippi and ended in the rolling plains beside the Rio Grande. Our trip lasted a fortnight longer than we expected or had planned for. Once along the way, we were robbed. Again, we were forced to break camp and flee because a warring band of Indians was drawing near. Afterwards, we found to our dismay, that a box of provisions had been forgotten or had been lost. Misfortune kept very close to us throughout our journey, our food was all but gone. There was wild game for the killing, but ammunition was too precious to be squandered in such manner. Master had already given the command that we were to hold in our stomachs and draw in our belts until we reached some point where we could restock our fast dwindling supplies.

"'One day, an hour before sun-down, we struck camp in a very lovely spot—a sloping hill-side covered with dwarf cedars and scrub oaks, a hill-side that undulated and sloped until it merged into a sandy-golden bottomed ravine. We pitched our camp in a sheltered nook in this ravine. The golden sand still warm from the day's sunshine made a luxurious resting place for our weary bodies. Below us, a spring trickled up through the earth and spread like lengths of sheerest silk over the bed of sand.

"'In a little while our camp-fire was sending up curling smoke-wreaths, smoke-blue into the balmy air and a pot of boiling coffee—our very last—added its fragrance to the spice of cedars and the pungency of oaks. Sundown came on, and a great beauty settled over everything. Nature was flaunting that side of herself which she reveals to the wanderer in solitary places: the shy kisses she bestows upon the Mountain's brow and, passion-warmed, glows in flagrant colors of the sunset; the tender embrace with which she wraps the plains and the glistening peace shines again in sparkling stars. Beauty that is serene and beauty that brings peace and calm and happiness and is never found in towns or crowded cities.

"'Our three hounds—faithful brutes that had trailed beside us all the weary miles—sat on their haunches and lifted their heads to send up long and doleful cries into the stillness.

"'Here—here—" cried Master. "Quit that!—Come, come, we'll take a walk and maybe scare up something to fill the pot tomorrow." He ended by whistling up to the prancing dogs and they were off. Up the hillside they went, the dogs, noses to earth, skulking at Master's heels or plunging into the under-brush on a make-believe scent.

"'I sat in the warm sand, a lonely slave-child, watching Master and the dogs until they reached the hill-top. Almost on the instant, the dogs scared up a rabbit. What a din they made yelping, yip, yap, yap and Master halooing and urging them to the race. The frightened rabbit ran like the wind, a living atom with the speed of a flying arrow. Straight as a shooting star, it sped: until turning suddenly it began bounding back along the way it had come. The ruse worked. The dogs sped past, hot on his trail of the dodging rabbit, many paces forward before they were able to stop short and pick up the scent once more. And the rabbit ran, oh, how he ran tumbling, darting, swirling down the hillside, terror-mad, fright-blind, on he came, the dogs on his trail once more, bounding length over length behind him. One last frantic dash, one desperate leap and the rabbit plunged into my lap. I covered the tiny trembling creature with my hands, just in time, before the great hounds sprang towards me. With great effort I kept them off and managed to conceal my captive in the large old-fashioned pocket of my wide skirt.

"'Master, disgruntled at his dogs and quite ireful—it is no little thing for a hungry man to see a tempting morsel escape him—came up to question me. "That rabbit—that rabbit—which way did it go?"

"'When I replied "Don't know," he became quite angry and beat me. Gentlemen, the scars of that long ago flogging I shall carry to my grave. Our food was nearly gone and it was I, the slave-girl, who knew the lack most sorely. But I did not give the rabbit over to my master.'

"She paused a little while and in all my life I never before knew such quiet; you could actually feel the silence.

"'It is strange, strange how far reaching the consequences of an impulse may be. Howard, my master's son, witnessed everything. He had always teased me. His favorite pastime had been to annoy the slave-girl with his pranks, but he changed from that day. That day, when he saw his father beat me. And it was he, Gentlemen, who taught me to forget the scars of serfdom and taught me the joys of freedom. In all truth, Sirs, I am the widow of Colonel Howard Monroe Ritton of Westview.'

"There is no use tying to tell you about that," declared Timothy. "It's an experience as indescribable as it is unforgettable. That little old white-haired woman standing alone in the midst of all those hostile people, tearing apart with such simple words the whole fabric of her life. I think it was her loveliness that held them spell-bound; the power of her beauty, that kept them straining their ears to catch every word she said. As if suddenly awakened to her surroundings, she cleared her throat nervously, and hurriedly concluded her story.

" 'The necessity of my being here, Gentlemen, is the outcome of my second impulse, an impulse, Gentlemen, nothing more. Each afternoon I sit in my west chamber beside my sunny windows, there is a whole beautiful row of them, as one can see by passing along the street . . . I like the sunshine which pours through them of an afternoon, and I like to knit. And I like to watch the passersby. And, I think, Gentlemen, whenever I sit there I can recall more easily the things that are passed, the old friends, the old places, the old loves and the old hurts which, somehow, have no longer the power to bring pain.

" 'So I was peering—my eyes are not so good—into the street and I saw a cloud of dust, all of a sudden. I thrust my head a little ways through the window, then, I saw a man running; on looking closer, I saw that he was black.

" 'Then a queer thing happened, Gentlemen; the first time in years on years, I remembered the days of my bondage. And curiously, yes, curiously I recalled. Wait. No, I did not recall it. I swear to you, Gentlemen, a picture formed before me; a hilly slope overgrown with trees of scrub oak and dwarf cedars—a golden sand-bottomed ravine and twilight falling upon miles on miles of wind-swept prairie, and peace, sweet and warm and kind, brushing my soul and turning my thoughts towards God. And I heard it, the strident yelps of three strong dogs. I saw it—a tiny furry rabbit running for its life. I tell you—it was real, Gentlemen. And while I looked, it faded—changed—glowed into another picture— the one that was being enacted out in the street. It glimmered back to fancy and flashed again to fact, so swiftly, I could not distinguish which. Then, Sirs, they merged and both were one . . . The black man who was running so wildly was only a little terror-mad rabbit. The three stout gentlemen there,' (she pointed, quite like a child toward the fat policemen, while a ripple of laughter floated across the room), 'and the crowd which followed after, very strangely, Gentlemen, every person in it had the visage of my master. I think I cried out at that, Sirs. Yes. Certainly I cried—at that.

" 'Then the black man was in my presence, inside my sunny west-chamber, and I was forced to act—act quickly—.

" 'The picture had to be finished, Gentlemen. The rabbit, no, the man—had to be protected. Thank you, Sirs. That is all.'

"Yes," said Timothy Phipps, pensively. "I was the running black gentlemen in the story—" He tilted his head a bit backwards and sideways and laughed. His laughter echoing—joy—joy—joy!

FROM *THE CRISIS*, JANUARY 1926

# B*lue A*loes

## OTTIE BEATRICE GRAHAM

Who can account for an impulse? Surely not a youth of twenty. Who would account on a day whose skies were blue and whose streams were clearest silver? Oh, not a youth of twenty.

Then Joseph was answering the call that only the young can know when he threw off shoes and top clothes and leaped into the silver of deep, smooth Little River. It flowed in front of Aloe House. Threw off shoes and stockings, and leaping, called to Melrose, living in Aloe House.

"Melrose!" he called, flashing through space and flipping into the water. Across to the opposite bank he swam, speeding like an islander. And climbing up to land by roots and hanging bushes, forth he stepped—youth on a sunny morning! Blessed son of the gods, singing impromptus to a maiden. "Melrose!" And the morning breeze carried the music over the water. Soon the boy followed. He had seen the slender form come out from the little house. But though he swam swiftly and straight, the girl was not there to greet him. He was disappointed but not surprised. Granna had interfered. He knew. Since she could not swim with him, at least they could walk together. So he threw himself flat upon the grass along the bank, stretching out full length to dry.

Little time passed before he heard a dragging footstep. For a moment he thought he was dreaming a dream that was bad. He was supposed to move away upon the approach of the dragging footstep, but he would not move today. He would remain and sing to Melrose if the old woman cursed him doubly. He would—ah, he could not move now if he wanted to. She stood over him.

"Lazy young dog!" she started, and there came such a torrent of maledictions as Joseph had never before heard. At first he had laughed at her. It amused him to hear an old hag going into fury because his young limbs, uncovered, breathed the sun; because he persisted in his love for the girl; because she loved him in return. At first it was funny but soon it ceased to amuse, and he joined in her tirade. Finally Granna dragged away, and she scowled and fussed. Fussed like something from the lower regions. Joseph hurried into his clothes and followed behind her, sullen and determined. Ach! she turned upon him.

"I tell you, ef I puts a sho nuf curse on yu, yu won't forget it soon. Runnin' aroun' heah half naked, an' callin' all ovah the place fo that gal, an' she ready ah' fixin' to come out in the river with yu lak a young fool. Jus' come on an' take her out ef yu think yu kin. I'll fix yu!"

And the boy put in his part. "Oh, you think I'm afraid of your black magic, you old witch! But I'm not, and I'll teach Melrose not to be. And she'll stop making your aloes cures and the people will stop coming to bring you money for nothing. You old witch, you old witch! You old wi-hitch! Here's what I think of your aloes and your house full of aloes branches. *Now* conjure me!" And his laugh was so wild and shrill with anger it dulled the clanging of the falling tubs he had kicked over in his rage. They held the drippings of aloes.

With the dying away of the furor came a soft crying, then a young, tremulous voice. "Jo!" It wailed softly. "Jo! You don't know what you have done. Jo!" Around the corner of the little house crept the girl, Melrose, frightened and ready to flee. The old woman had disappeared into the house. Soon, however, she returned. Even before the girl could reach her boy.

"Come on, Melrose, come on," called Joseph. The girl had started back. "Come on, she won't hurt you." Granna stopped and glared upon them while the boy talked that she might hear.

"She hates you because you're more beautiful than she would have you; because you are younger than she would have you. She hates you because you love me and her aloes can't stop you!" And he laughed long and lustily. Granna looked on.

Melrose had reached his side. "Hush, Jo, you've done enough. That was the last of the drippings from the blue leaves, and they came from far away. Someone brought them to her on a boat from an island. Listen!"

The woman, already bent from age, was bending farther over, and mumbling, mumbling, mumbling. The violet blue substance, part liquid, part resin, flowed past her in a slow stream. A slow stream from its tumbled tubs. And she, running with it, then running back, mumbled, mumbled, mumbled. The girl and her boy stood looking, the girl, frankly distressed, the boy alarmed in spite of himself.

"It's the curse!" Melrose trembled. Joseph held her hand. They were two children.

"How can it hurt? The stuff is no more than a medicine."

"Oh, but,—"

"It's her foolishness. I'll take you away from the South and its superstitions. Look at her now, the old witch." Granna was on her knees now, splashing handfuls of the substance.

Melrose turned where she stood. "I'll have to go away now, Jo. I can't go back. No! You can't go back either." Joseph had not turned where he stood. Instead, he moved toward the woman. The blue stuff flowed between them.

"Don't cross it, Jo. You can never get rid of the curse if you cross her stream!" And this served only to make him dare. He strode to the stream and jumped across.

"I'm going to take Melrose away!" he yelled. He was quite close upon Granna, but he hollered as though she had been deaf. Perhaps he did not know it. He trembled. "Melrose living under the same roof with you. Lord, what a crime! I'll take her from you, old Ashface, out here in the woods. I'll take her from the South and superstition!"

Granna had been kneeling. Now she stood. But she did not measure to the height of the stripling before her. She squinted and blinked up at him, and her wrinkled black face *was* ashen with the heat of temper. She was wont to sing hymns as she brewed aloes, but she seldom talked. This late mad outburst had taken her strength, therefore, and she quivered as she stood. An aloe string hung about her neck. The Negroes of Africa's west coast wore such cords, but that gave no clue to Granna. None knew of her origin. They only knew of the pretty child she had raised. She looked up at Joseph, and he down at her. From a short distance came the soft crying of the young and tremulous voice.

"Takin' my gal, is yu? Well, tell uh don' come back when yu turn to anothuh. Ungrateful yaller devil!" A fresh thunder clap. They gyrated and all but spat in each other's faces. Youth is wild, and sometimes old age too.

"Oh, you say that again, old woman! You judge me by yourself, no doubt. I'll rid you of your hateful self!"

"Hi! You dar to tuch me." She was witch now, if ever. Her withered old hand touched the cord about her neck, and she snatched it off and dashed it in the face of Joseph. "Yu know what hit yu? Blue aloes!" And she screamed out a grating haw-haw.

Melrose ran to Joseph. For a moment he thought he was blinded. He went, by her hand, to the river, and together they bathed the bruised eyes. Then they started off to the future, empty handed, looking not behind them. Aloe House was still. And the silence deafened, so that neither heard the other catching little breaths at the outset of their journey. Neither heard. The sun now was too hot, the day was now too dry. Melrose coughed. Joseph spoke.

"Her medicines don't cure your cough."

"I got the cough from her."

"Huh!"

"All medicines can't cure a cough." They turned from the road and sat under a tree. Town was still far off.

"What of magic, can it cure a cough?" They looked at each other.

"There isn't any magic, Jo. I'm not afraid of magic."

"You were afraid back there."

"But I've come away for good. Not afraid now." They resumed their walking—new pilgrims on the search for happiness.

"I'll take you away from the South," said the youth. Brave youth.

"Can't take me from the South, Jo. I have to stay in the South with this cough. It will go, but I'll have to stay here. Jo, where are we going?"

"Up on the hill to my father's house. It is all that I have, my father's house. When I came back last year I closed it. I paddled down Little River and found you. Now I shall open it again. We'll stay there until the cough goes."

"That will be a long time."

They neared the town. Silence had flown, but a town does not exist without its noises. This was called a pretty town, but the girl thought it drab and choky. The country behind was sweet. They entered the town. People stared or nodded, or smiled or shook their heads. In a very short time the whole town knew that Joseph was opening the old home for the girl from Aloe House. One street led up a hill overlooking its section of the town. Up the hill they went, Melrose and Joseph, looking back not once.

The house stood silent like the country along the road; the grounds were silent like the house. The girl felt thankful. They would be away from the town. The afternoon was waning. In its soft, drowsy heat Joseph went down the hill again. Melrose waited under a tree. The trees up here were gracious; their shade was cooling. How could men live in towns—narrow, stuffy places? Where had Jo lived down there? He had lived with the parson. The parson—the parson—oh! There was another thing about towns. They required parsons with love. Well, that would not matter, only it had not occurred to her before this. Love—parsons—what places were towns! Towns—country—country—Granna! But there was no magic. Aloes—just a medicine—no magic. "Till he turned to another—turned to another." But he was coming back already, and someone else was with him. The parson. She knew the parson. He had visited her when she first got the cough. Granna had been very rude. There were others coming too. Was the town moving up to kill the quiet of the hill? She sat still, rising not until Joseph spoke.

"You know who this is, Melrose. We let the others come. They can take back good news now. They'll take back one kind or another, you know." So they were married up on the hill. The crowd, curious, around them. The house, yet unopened. The "guests" carried their news back to the town.

At the parson's house they were feasted, Melrose and Joseph. The parson was kind; so was his wife. The house on the hill was opened and left to the night, that the stale air and the moths might drain out. At the parson's house they were feasted and taught to look brightly on the future. Youth must never fear the future. These were merely words of advice; there was no fear here. With morning came work for Joseph and gifts from neighbors for the girl. Southerners are good-hearted.

Time brought only happiness. Joseph taught his young wife all he had learned North in schools. He would take her there some day, to the North. Then the girl would cough and he knew she could not go. But it was happiness, this living on the hill where the town was out of sight, and the trees whispered, and the yellow-brown creature moved about singing with the low, tremulous voice. Children from the town came up. He taught her and she taught them. Children from the town—all kinds. Little pale things with scraggly locks, little pale things with heavy locks. Brown little things with silken curls, brown little things with kinky curls. They and Melrose. Melrose and they.

Time landed one day a strange cargo. Happiness a bit discolored, came with the bringing of a plant. With a plant. A gardener, an old man working about the town, brought it. A beautiful thing, and rare. Melrose thanked the man with slight strain in her voice. As soon as he had gone she dashed it on the ground, stamping it again and again, until it was bruised and broken. Bruised and broken beyond recovery. She knew most of the species of the aloe. This was akin to the blue. That Joseph might not know of it, she buried the fragments under a great flower jar. But fear and sadness descended upon her. She had brushed aside this silliness long, long ago, and now it had seized her again. Joseph said the mind could be better controlled. This she told herself many times, saying, "It is absurd to fear nothing. It is absurd!" But her cough grew worse and she trembled about her duties. She walked down the hill to meet Joseph.

"Jo, could you ever love anyone else?" They were coming to the house.

"Could anyone else be you, honey?" And he kissed her lightly as they passed the great flower jar. She shook just a little and coughed a lot. That night she sobbed aloud in her sleep.

Melrose grew paler. She felt that the cough was worse. On warm evenings Joseph paddled a canoe. Went drifting down Little River. Joseph was not afraid of things, yet he never took the left branch of the river. The left branch of Little River flowed past Aloe House. It had been several years now since he took Melrose away, and neither of them mentioned it. Whether it still was there he did not know, nor did he go to see. So the right branch of the river was his, and he nosed round the bend automatically. On warm evenings Melrose went with him. Now she stayed home on the hill. She felt that her cough was worse. Now Joseph paddled alone.

On the water he hummed little melodies. He wished Melrose could play the piano better. Then he wished she were here on the water. Here singing with him on the water. No voice sang like hers. In the morning he would send for another doctor. She must not be pale. He splashed the water and drifted. The night. Melrose would love the night out here. They had never come this far.

There came on the still air music. When had he heard such music! Music from a piano. He paddled to come nearer to it. Looking around, he saw a huge mansion on a hill. From this mansion came the music. Came the tones of silver. Light streamed from a topmost window. To a landing he guided the tiny boat and listened. The music stopped and directly the light went out. Surprised, Joseph started back, paddling hard all the way. Melrose stood at the window when he reached the house. He told her of the night. Told her of the music. Told her how he had missed her.

Next night he went again. Went in the little boat down Little River. Down the right branch, drifting and paddling till he heard the silver melody. Music in the night from the mansion on a hill. Melrose would like it so. If she would come but once. Come but once to hear. He listened at the landing. The music ceased and the light went out. Immediately Joseph moved the canoe. At home on his hill Melrose waited. Patiently stood at the window. Again he told her of the night. Of the music.

Melrose next day was weary. She longed for the night to come. She would go this night in the canoe. Please Joseph and go on the river. But the day burned by. It was hot. When evening came she was tired. At the meal she smied, but the smile was a dismal effort. Joseph set out earlier. Melrose was weary, the air was sultry. He must get out in the boat.

On the river it was cooler. He drifted all the way. And even at the mansion night had not yet come. No music sounded except the whirring of the wind through the trees. At the landing Joseph looked up. At the window, away up high, there stood a woman. The house below her was closed. Joseph started and stared. A paddle slipped from his hand into the river, and he uttered a short cry. "Melrose!" The house was near the river. He could see clearly, but he could not believe.

The woman stepped upon a little balcony outside her window and pitched something to him. It fell by chance into the boat—a beautifully grained paddle, its arm set with a gem of blue. She raised a finger to her lips and motioned him to go. The music came as he paddled away. As he pulled away in a daze. Night had fallen when he reached his hill. Melrose stood by the window. He told her of part of the trip. Of the music and of finding a paddle, but not of a woman who was her second self.

"Let me see the paddle, Jo," she asked. He brought it to her.

"The stone is lapis-lazuli." She was calm like mist on the bog. "The wood is aloe. It is very old; the fragrance is faint." She handed it back to Joseph. He looked at the paddle and then at his wife.

"Shall I throw it away?" She nodded. "I will." Late in the night Joseph awakened talking in his sleep. "I wish I could take her away," he was saying, "take her from the South."

Then he slept again and dreamed of her—of Melrose. But the dream became muddled, and he saw one time his Melrose—saw next time this woman. She came on the balcony and turned to his wife. Melrose came and turned to the woman. Then they came together and submerged into one. He was glad to awake. Glad to find Melrose whom he knew. At sundown he would go once more that he might see this person who was like her.

He went. At sundown he went that he might see. She stood at the window and waved to him. Again she was garbed in blue. Soft, sighing blue. She had worn blue on yesterday. Her window seemed a haze of blue. Joseph seemed rather to sense this than to see it. He gazed at her face. "Melrose!" It was not her skin alone. There were hundreds in the South like that. Brown-yellow and yellow-brown. Nor was it alone her hair. Black—deep black like crows. Nor yet her gently pursued, red lips. But her sway when she stepped to the balcony. Her eyes like dark, melted pansies. Her waving—her languorous waving. Melrose was in her being.

Joseph returned the next evening, and the next, and the next. Many days he came at dusk, staring bewildered. He spoke no more of his trips. Melrose asked naught about them. One time a rain came suddenly. All day the heat had stifled, but there had been little sun. Joseph was on the river. He would have turned and hurried back, but the music, more silver than the rain, came through the cooling air. He went to the landing and listened. Soon the woman, beautiful in her blue, appeared at the window. It rained too hard for her to step out, but she beckoned for him to come in. She dropped a big key, an old, rusty thing. A key seldom used, no doubt. Doing her gestured bidding, he opened a large side door. Steps, walled off from the rest of the place, wound straight up from the doorway to the top of the house. The lady, lovely person, met him. From a little anteroom she led him to where she had stood at the window. As he entered this larger room he was struck by the odor of aloes. Pleasant as the perfume was, it sickened him. For a second his head swam and he heard the low crying of Melrose's voice. He wanted to run away. Run like a little boy.

The rain on the roof was cheery but this scented, strange room was sad. It was blue. Blue from floor to ceiling, with rugs and low chairs of velvet and pillows and hangings of silk. A huge, blue opalescent dome hung low from the center ceiling. A piano, a handsome thing, stately in lacquered blue, stood beneath the dome. The walls were like a paneled, morning sky. Joseph gazed at the ceiling—at the floor—all about him. The woman stood at the window. "Like Melrose," Joseph whispered. She had forgotten him, no doubt. She was so still; he continued gazing. Now the dome. The woman turned, and while he gazed at pearl blue opalescence, she rested her eyes on him. He felt her looking and turned. And though he suspected the focusing of her eye, he flinched when their glances met. She came close to him and stood. At this range her face was older than his wife's. Even so, it was rather young, and almost as beautiful.

"The rain will cease," she said. Her voice was that of Melrose grown older. She wore a string of aloes about her throat. Joseph noticed them and gulped.

"I thank you, Madame, for your kind favor. The rain has stopped already. You were good to take me in. Now I must leave." She held his arm lightly to detain him.

"It is almost dark," said she, "and the sky is clearing. The sky from my window is wonderful at night." She returned to her window without asking him to stay. Joseph went with her. Pale stars twinkled through sailing fleece. The sky darkened as it cleared.

"Why have you come in your little boat to watch at my window every evening?"

"Your playing, Madame, and you." Then she played for him. Played on the blue piano and brought forth silver notes. He listened long to her playing before he arose to go. He thanked her once more and started but she held him again.

"You have not seen my treasures," she said, "I have treasures. Rare things from Sokotra." She turned to a curtained corner and opened a chest of deep drawers. Proudly she drew forth trinkets. Trinkets of many descriptions. Metal necklaces and anklets of aloes. Aloe bracelets and anklets of metal. Rings and head-dresses and luckstones and bangles. Powdered perfumes of aloes and myrrh. Wood of aloes set with jewels. Aloes and cassia for scenting garments. Joseph was in a stupor.

"Rare things from Sokotra—Rare things from Sokotra." The words hummed in his brain. His brain seemed tight and bursting.

"I must go now, Madame. I must go." He heard himself saying this.

"Yes, you must go now, hurry. Hurry or they'll find you here!" The surprise of this statement destroyed the stupor. Joseph fled from the room.

The woman came close behind him. At the top of the stairs they stopped. He would have taken her hand to say goodbye, but she clung to him until he kissed her. Kissed her many times. Half way down the stairs he heard her voice calling—calling to him, "Hurry!"

Outside the night was quiet. The stars, once pale, were glowing. This air was not laden with aloes. He paddled home in a listless fear. A fear that was dull and thumping. Melrose was sleeping—and the room was blue. Oh, this was delusion. He would sleep it away. Sleep it away forever. But the morning came and the room was blue. Melrose dressed in blue. She had draped their room in blue. This was pretty he told her. This change from rose to blue. But he wondered why she made it—why she made it.

Every evening he went on the river. Went before the darkness came. The woman stepped onto the balcony and threw her kisses to him. Each time he looked to see her beckon. But she did not call him, and he wondered who else was there with her. He dared not go unless she beckoned. Beckoned and dropped the key. He listened when she played, and watched her light go out. She made the room dark that the night might come in. The night with its flickering stars. He listened when she played, then paddled home.

At home one night he found aloes. Found his garden set with aloes. Straightway he sought Melrose. She waited at the window.

"Why do you have about you this thing which you fear?" he asked.

"But I do not fear it any longer. You taught me not to fear."

"They are beautiful. You did not find them here?"

"Imported. A species of the Blue from Sokotra."

"Where?"

"Sokotra."

Joseph hushed. Something rang in his mind. "Rare things from Sokotra. Rare things from Sokotra." He looked with unstill eyes at Melrose. She looked quite steadily at him.

"Did you ever have kin in Sokotra?" he queried.

"No one knows but Granna. I know nothing of myself."

"Where is Sokotra, Melrose?"

"Some place on an island." Melrose talked little recently; she moved about more, however. She felt that she was better. That the cough was growing faint.

On the night that Joseph brought the paddle Melrose had felt a quaking. Her heart had sunk within her. Within her something whispered, "When he turns to another. When he turns to another." Why she had felt this she did not know, but the quaking was there in her heart. Somehow she had known that the paddle had not been found. Someone had given it to him. The nights had passed slowly from that time. From that time the day had changed. There was something she must discover. Something was taking Joseph. She had followed him the next night. Down the river he had paddled his tiny craft and she had run behind along the bank. The trees and shrubbery had hidden her. She had followed to the mansion. Had seen the lovely creature; compared her with herself. She had returned the morning after while Joseph was away, but the house had been silent, and the woman's window closed. Again she had gone at evening, after Joseph rode ahead. With him she had seen the greetings and with him heard the music.

Once when rain showered he had entered the house. The woman had
tossed him a key. Melrose had come out of hiding and run to go in
behind him. The door had locked behind Joseph, and she had dropped
to the ground. On her knees she had sobbed aloud. Had called out to her
husband. She had not known that her voice reached him, riding on the
night like a broken spirit. By the door she had remained until he passed
her. Passed her without seeing, and in haste. The odor of aloes had
passed with him and she had laughed in pity at herself. At home she had
reached the bed just before he came. For some time their room had been
blue (she had seen that the woman wore it). But Joseph had first noticed
this this night.

Now Melrose felt sorrow in her heart. Sorrow mingled with disdain.
Adorned in blue, she had moved about the hill, silent, but stronger and
fearless. When the children came up from the town she laughed and
told them stories. Stories of Granna, a shrivelled old woman who believed in witchery. Of an island where aloes grow—an island on the way
to India. There people dwelt in rubble-built huts, and lived on dates and
milk; and aloes kept them well and in health, and scented all their
garments. Granna had lived there long ago, chasing goats and wild asses
over the hills. Once Joseph listened to the tales, and he searched his
wife's face for understanding. He did not know she ever talked of Granna. And Melrose felt sorrow in her heart. Sorrow and disdain. Her
husband was bewitched and she was losing fear. She seldom coughed.

At dusk she ran behind the canoe, trailing him down the river. The
woman came on the balcony. She kissed him her hand and he stretched
out his arms, pantomiming love. One night she dropped down an aloe
leaf. Melrose found it later. At once she filled her home with aloes, rare
specimens from the island. Joseph asked about them and found her
unperturbed.

Soon one evening, Melrose went ahead of Joseph. Ran swiftly along
the river to the mansion on the hill. At the window stood the woman.
Waiting already for Joseph. She did not see the figure darting quickly
behind trees, stooping under bushes, slipping to her stairway door. But
soon she heard a knocking. A knocking, knocking, knocking and she
came very softly down the steps. Without asking from the inside what
was wanted, she opened wide the door.

They stood like stone, these women. Stone images reflected in a
mirror. Melrose had not seen her close before. She had not seen
Melrose ever. But now a look of knowing flitted across her face, then a
look of awful fear, and she backed to the steps and turned and ran.
Leaped like a frightened deer. Midway she wheeled again. Melrose had

not moved. Back down the stairs the woman came, the look of killing in her eyes. She muttered.

"They'll not know," came the words thick and bitten, and away she flew repeating, "They'll not know."

Melrose started after her, but she knew that Joseph would come. She expected the woman back also, and she must hold her ground. She ascended the stairs trembling. Trembling from what had passed, and what was yet to come. At the top was an antechamber. No one was within. In the large room she had a notion that she walked into the sky. Into a sky perfumed with aloes. At the window she waited. Looked out on the river. Little River. She listened for the woman, but the woman did not return.

The canoe came gliding. Joseph's brown face was handsome. She would beckon as the woman had once done. Beckon and please him. He would come through the open door and she would kill him. Kill him in this room of blue. Yield to the curse. He looked up smiling and she tried to smile. Joseph frowned and looked harder. He would say goodbye to this woman; she was uncanny. No one should be like Melrose. He did not want this woman's smiles. He would say goodbye. Say goodbye and go. His boat nosed cross-wise. He was turning.

"Jo!" came his name from the window. "Jo!" short and quick. "Jo!" the long wail Melrose!

She did not call again. She leaned against the window, convulsed with tears and sobbing. Sobbing and shaking. Moaning. Joseph ran to the door and found it open. Found no one upstairs but Melrose. He gathered her up and took her down like a baby in his arms. He could understand nothing, but he did not ask. It was not time to ask. Home he took her in the boat. Through the town they strolled, two lovers. Lovers reconciled.

Little groups of people stood about the streets. At the hill a crowd was jabbering. Eyes centered on Melrose and Joseph. Jabbering started afresh. Faces peered. Faces black and white and yellow, brown and tan and red and black. On the hill policemen guarded. Kept the crowd away. In a porch swing rested the body. The woman was dead. The woman from the mansion. She had tried to kill a white man on the street, and then she had run in the way of a horse. She had been insane. Now she was dead. They were awaiting the ambulance. Awaiting the coming of aid. The woman had been near the hill. People said she belonged there. Joseph chilled through. Melrose burned. They both said it was a mistake. The people had made an error. The ambulance came and took her away.

In the town the people whispered. Some said this woman was the mother of Melrose. Said Granna took Melrose when she was born. Was born of a father not black. Said the woman came from an island. Was brought by a southern family. In the town the secrets spread. "The woman, frightened, had lost her mind. She would not leave the house. The family moved and provided for her there. They left someone to keep her. No one had ever seen the person." Joseph heard the whisperings. "Whoever came, she thought to be her lover. Whoever came, she wooed in careful secrecy. Melrose was her child. Melrose her child." The whispers came to Melrose.

Joseph and Melrose went to find Granna. Back in the country down Little River—down the left branch to Aloe House. After a southern secret. They knocked at the door. Granna was not there. Nothing was there.

From *The Crisis*, August 1924

# To *a Wild Rose*

## OTTIE BEATRICE GRAHAM

"Ol' man, ol' man, why you looking at me so?" Tha's what you sayin',
son. Tha's what you sayin'. Then you start a-singin' that song agin, an' I
reckon I'm starin' agin. I'm just a wonderin', son. I'm just a-wonderin'.
How is it you can sing them words to a tune an' still be wantin' for
material for a tale? "Georgia Rose." An' you jus' sing the words an' they
don't say nothin' to you? Well listen to me, young un, an' write what you
hear if you want to. Don't laugh none at all if I hum while I tell it, 'cause
maybe I'll forget all about you; but write what you hear if you want to.

Thar's just me in my family, an' I never did know the rest. On one o'
them slave plantations 'way down in the South I was a boy. Wasn't no
slave very long, but know all about it jus' same. 'Cause I was proud,
they all pestered me with names. The white uns called me red nigger
boy an' the black uns called me red pore white. I never 'membered no
mother—just the mammies 'round the place, so I fought when I had to
and kep' my head high without tryin' to explain what I didn't understan'.

Thar was a little girl 'round the house, a ladies' maid. Never was thar
angel more heavenly. Flo they called her, an' they said she was a young
demon. An' they called her witch, an' said she was too proud. Said she
was lak her mother. They said her mother come down from Oroonoka
an' Oroonoka was the prince captured out o' Africa. England took the

*195*

prince in the early days o' slavery, but I reckon we got some o' his kin. That mean we got some o' his pride, young un, that mean we got some o' his pride. Beautiful as was that creature, Flo, she could 'ford bein' proud. She was lak a tree—lak a tall, young tree, an' her skin was lak bronze, an' her hair lak coal. If you look in her eyes they was dreamin', an' if you look another time they was spaklin' lak black diamonds. Just made it occur to you how wonderful it is when somethin' can be so wild an' still so-fine lak. "My blood is royal! My blood is African!" Tha's how she used to say. Tha's how her mother taught her. Oroonoka! African pride! Wild blood and fine.

Thar was a fight one day, one day when things was goin' peaceful. They sent down from the big house a great tray of bones from the chicken dinner. Bones for me! Bones for an extra treat! An' the men an' the women an' the girls an' the boys all come round in a ring to get the treat. The Butler stood in the center, grinnin' an' makin' pretty speeches about the dinner an' the guests up at the big house. An' I started wigglin' through the legs in the crowd till I got up to the center. Then I stood up tall as I could and I hissed at the man, an' the words wouldn't stay down my throat, an' I hollered right out, "Fool—black fool!" An' 'fore he could do anything a-tall, I kicked over his tray of gravy an' bones. Bones for me! Bones for an extra treat!

The old fellah caught me an' started awackin', but I was young an' tough an' strong, an' I give him the beatin' of his life. Pretty soon come Flo to me "Come here, Red-boy," she say, an' she soun' like the mistress talkin', only her voice had more music an' was softer. "Come here, Red-boy," she say, "we have to run away. *I* would not carry the tray out to the quarters, an' *you* kicked it over. We're big enough for floggin' now, an' they been talkin' about it at the big house. They scared to whip me, 'cause they know I'll kill the one that orders it done first chance I get. But they mean to do somethin', and they mean to get you good, first thing."

We made little bundles and stole off at supper time when everybody was busy, an' we hid way down in the woods. 'Bout midnight they came almost on us. We knew they would come a-huntin'. The hounds gave 'em 'way with all their barkin', and the horses gave 'em 'way steppin' on shrubbery. The river was near an' we just stepped in; an' when we see we couldn't move much farther 'less they spot us, we walked waist deep to the falls. Thar we sat hidin' on the rocks, Flo an' me, with the little falls a-tumblin' all over us, an' the search party walkin' up an' down the bank, cussin' an' swearin' that Flo was a witch. Thar we sat under the falls lak two water babies, me a-shiverin', an' that girl a-laughin'. Yes, such laughin'! Right then the song rose in my heart tha's been thar ever since. It's a song I could never sing, but tha's been thar all a same. Son, you never seen nothin' lak that. A wild thing lak a flower—lak a spirit— sittin' in the night on a rock, laughin' through the falls, with a laugh that trickled lak the water. Laughin' through the falls at the hunters.

After while they went away an' the night was still. We got back to the bank to dry, but how we gonna dry when we couldn't make a fire? Then my heart start a-singin' that song again as the light o' the moon come down in splashes on Flo. She begin to dance. Yes suh, dance. An' son, you never seen nothin' lak that. A wild thing lak a flower the wind was a-chasin'—lak a spirit a-chasin' the wind. Dancin' in the woods in the light o' the moon.

"Come Red-boy, you gotta get dry." And we join hands an' whirled round together till we almost drop. Then we eat the food in our little wet bundles—wet bread an' wet meat an' fruit. An' we followed the river all night long, till we come to a little wharf about day break. A Negro overseer hid us away on a small boat. We sailed for two days, an' he kep' us fed in hidin'. When that boat stopped we got on a ferry, an' he give us to a man an' a woman. Free Negroes, he told us, an' left us right quick.

I ain't tellin' you, young un, where it all happen 'cause that ain't so particular for your material. We didn't have to hide on the ferry-boat, an' everybody looked at us hard. The lady took Flo an' the man took me, an' we all sat on deck lak human bein's. When we left the ferry we rode in a carriage, an' finally we stopped travellin' for good. Paradise never could a' been sweeter than our new home was for me. They said it was in Pennsylvania. A pretty white house with wild flowers everywhere. An' they went out an' brought back Flo to set 'em off. An' when I'd see her movin' round among 'em, 'an I'd ask her if she wasn't happy, she'd throw back that throat o' bronze, an' smile lak all o' Glory. "I knew I'd be free, Red-boy. Tha's what my mother said I'd have to be. My blood is African! My blood is royal!" Then the song come a-singin' itself again in my heart, an' I hush up tight. Wild thing waterin' wild things—wild thing in a garden.

Thar come many things with the years; the passin' o' slavery an' the growin' up o' Flo. Thar wasn't nothin' else much that made any difference. I went to the city to work but I went to visit Flo an' the people most every fortnight. One time I told her about my love; told her I wanted her to be my wife. An' she threw back her curly head, but she didn't smile her bright smile. She closed her black eyes lak as though she was in pain, an' lak as though the pain come from pity. An' I hurried up an' said I knew I should a-gone to school when they tried to make me, but I could take care o' her all a same. But she said it wasn't that—wasn't that.

"Red-boy," she said, "I couldn't be your wife, 'cause you—you don't know what you are. It wouldn't matter, but *I* am *African* and my blood is *royal!*"

She fell on my shoulder a-weepin', an' I understood. Her mother stamped it in her. Oroonoka! Wild blood and fine.

I went away as far as I could get. I went back to the South, an' I went around the world two years, a-workin' on a ship, an' I saw fine ladies everywhere. I saw fine ladies, son, but I ain't seen none no finer than her. An' the same little song kep' a-singin' itself in my heart. I went to Africa, an' I saw a prince. Pride! Wild blood an' fine.

Thar was somethin' that made me go back where she was. Well, I went an' she was married, an' lived in the city. They told me her husband come from Morocco an' made translations for the gover'ment.

"Morocco," I thought to myself. "That's a man knows what he is. She's keepin' her faith with her mother."

I rented me a cottage. I wanted to wait till she come to visit. They said she'd come. I settled down to wait. Every night I listen to the March wind a-howlin' while I smoked my pipe by the fire. One night I caught sound o' somethin' that wasn't the wind. I went to my door an' I listen, an' I heard a voice 'way off, kind a-moanin' an' kind a-chantin'. I grabbed up my coat an' hat an' a lantern. Thar was a slow, drizzlin' rain, an' I couldn't see so well even with the lantern. I walked through the woods towards where I last heard the voice a-comin'. I walked for a good long time without hearin' anything a-tall. Then thar come all at once, straight ahead o' me, the catchin' o' breath an' sobs, an' I knew it was a woman. I raised my lantern high an' thar was Flo. Her head was back, an' she open an' shut her eyes, an' opened an' shut her eyes, an' sobbed an' caught her breath.

An', spite o' my wonderin' an' bein' almost scaired, that little song started up in me harder than ever. Son, you never seen nothin' lak that. A wild, helpless thing lak a thistle blowed to pieces—a wild, helpless thing lak a spirit chained to earth. Trampin' along in the woods in the night, with the March wind a-blowin' her along. Trampin' along, a-sobbin' out her grief to the night.

Thar wasn't no words for me to say; I just carried her in my arms to the fire in my house. I took off her coat an' her shoes an' put her by the fire, an' I wipe the rain out o' her hair. She was a-clutchin' somethin' in her hand, but I ain't said nothin' yet. I knew she'd tell me. After while she give the thing to me. It was a piece o' silk, very old an' crumpled. A piece of paper was tacked on it. Flo told me to read it. That time when we run away from the plantation she took a little jacket all braided with silk in her bundle. 'Twas the finest jacket her mother used to wear. This dreary night, when Flo come to visit, she start a-ransackin' her old trunk. She come across the jacket and ripped it up; an' she found the paper sewed to the linin'. An' when I read what was on the paper, I knew right off why I found her in the woods, a-running lak mad in the March night wind.

Her mother had a secret, an' she put it down on paper 'cause she couldn't tell it, an' she had to get it out—had to get it out. Thar was tears in every word an' they made tears in my eyes. The blood o' Oroonoka was tainted—tainted by the blood of his captor. The father o' her little girl was not Negro, an' the pride in her bein' was wounded. She was a slave woman, an' she was a beauty, an' she couldn't 'scape her fate. Thar was tears, tears, tears in every word.

I looked at Flo; her head was back. I never did see a time when her head wasn't back. It couldn't droop. She threw it back to laugh, an' she threw it back to sigh. Now she was a-starin' at the fire, an' the fire was a-flarin' at her. Wild thing lak a spirit—lak a scaired bird ready to fly. Oroonoka! Blood o' Oroonoka tainted.

"Red-boy," she said to me, an' she never look away from the fire. "Red-boy, I'm lookin' for a baby. I'm lookin' for a baby in the winter. How am I gonna welcome my baby? Anything else wouldn't matter so much—anything else but white. *That* blood in me—in my baby! Oh, Red-boy, I ain't royal no more!" I couldn't say much, but I took her hand an' I smoothed her hair, an' I led her back to the white house down the way.

Thar in the country she stayed on an' on, an' I stayed on too. Her husband come to see her every week, an' he look proud. He look proud an' happy, an' she look proud an' sad. She wandered in the woods an' she sang a low song. An' she stood at the gate an' she fed the birds. An' she sat on the grass an' she gazed at the sky. Wild thing, still an' proud— wild thing, still an' sad.

An' she stayed on an' on till the winter come. An' the baby come with the winter. She lie in the bed with the baby in her arm. Son, you never see nothin' lak that. A wild thing lak a flowerin' rose—lak a tired spirit. Flower goin', goin'; bud takin' its place. She said somethin' 'fore she died. She look at me an' said it.

"Red-boy, my blood is royal, but it's paled. Don't tell her,—yes tell her. Tell her about the usurpers o' Oroonoka's blood."

But I never did tell her, I went away again an' I stay twenty years. I just find out not long ago where her father went to live. I went to see 'em an' I make myself known. I didn't do so much talkin', so the miss entertain me. She played on the piano and forgot that she was a-playin'. Right then she was her mother. Yes suh, thar sat Flo. Wild thing! Royal blood! Paled, no doubt, but royal all a same.

Then she turned around, an' she wasn't Flo no longer. The brown skin was thar, an' the black, wild eyes, an' the curly dark hair. She spoke soft an' low, but she never did say, "*My* blood is royal! I am *African.*" An' she never did say "Red-boy." Her father had never told her about Oroonoka—that was it. An' I come back too late to tell her.

Well it don't matter no how, I thought, so long as she can hold her head lak that, an' long as she can look so beautiful, an' long as she make her mark in the world with that music. But the little song started a-singin' itself in my heart, an' I could see the flower agin.

Tha's your material boy. 'Member how I told it to you, a-fishin' on the river edge. 'Member how you was a-singin' "Georgia Rose." Thar's your material. Georgia Rose. Oroonoka. A wild, young thing, an' a little song in an old man's heart.

FROM *THE CRISIS*, JUNE 1923

# H*is Great Career*

## ALICE DUNBAR-NELSON

The travel-scarred motorcar came to a pause in the driveway of the great mountain mansion. "The Squire," as he was lovingly called for miles around, greeted the owner of the car as he rather stiffly set foot on the ground.

"It's good of you to come up here to see us in our mountain fastness," he said warmly.

"Didn't know you lived here until we broke down somewhere in your peaks and crags, and Martin inquired of the nearest civilized house."

The Squire talked cheerfully as he carried the bags of the great criminal lawyer up the broad walk.

"We're having a big house party here," he explained the group of guests on the veranda. "My wife's birthday, and when we give a party up here, it means a weekend stay, for we have to go so far for our festivities, it would be a pity to go right home."

The great lawyer was introduced to the fluttering and flattered group of maidens and wives, and to the hearty men who hovered on the edges. He bent his great grizzled fame over small eager hands, while his host stood by, enjoying his embarrassment in the pause before he went to his room.

"And so you're married?" asked the lawyer, as they went up the broad stairs.

"Fifteen years. You remember when my health broke eighteen years ago? I found *her* here in a sanitarium, wrecked too, and 'sick of that disease called life.' Between us, we mended our lives, and then she didn't care for the east and all that it means any more than I did—so we stayed, and here we are."

The great lawyer revelled in the scene, a marvelous panorama spreading out from the window.

"Prominent citizen, leader of the community, and the rest?" he asked smilingly.

The Squire was modest. "Well, we've helped build the community, and all that sort of thing. You can't live in a place without being part of it. And you, old Hard-head, you've become one of the most famous lawyers in the country!"

The lawyer waved a deprecating hand. "I'm motoring in out of the way places now to forget it awhile."

The veranda was not in a mood to allow him to forget. Famous celebrities did not drop into their lives often enough for them to be blasé. The lawyer put down the excellent cocktail that his host brought him in lieu of tea, and inquired for the mistress of the house. She had ridden to town for a last bit of foolery for tonight's costume party, explained the Squire.

The almond-eyed widow was subtly intent on opening up a flood of reminiscences. She fluttered slender hands and widened black eyes suggestively. Even the great lawyer's habitual taciturnity relaxed under the enveloping warmth of remembering the night she had sworn to be avenged on the slim, pale woman, who had taken him, her legitimate prey. A wife and a widow since, but the almond eyes still avid for vengeance.

"You must have had some interesting experiences, have you not? Oh, do tell us about some of your early struggles."

The great lawyer expanded under the enveloping perfume of her incense.

"Well," he began, his great voice booming softly in the mountain sunlight, "I shall never forget my first case. I was a briefless barrister, and hungry, or I would not have taken it. Everyone concerned in the affair is dead now, so I can smile at it. My first client was a murderer, a woman. She confessed the truth to me, and expected me to clear her."

"And did you?" chorused an octave of soprano voices.

"Yes. It was the beginning of my career."

A soft intake of breath from the window, and a flattering flutter from the rest of the veranda left the great lawyer to turn to his host.

But the Squire was oblivious, for coming up the walk was the mistress of the mansion. His soul was in his eyes as he watched her. Her eyes glowed, and her face was wind-whipped from riding; she had taken off her hat and her packages dangled from her arm. The lawyer stood in intent stillness. The same lithe form. The same aureole of auburn hair, as yet untinged by gray. The same still, quiet little face with deep pools of eyes. The same questioning droop of head. She came quickly up the walk and onto the veranda with incredible lightness.

"My dear," said the Squire, his voice a protecting caress, "this is—"

But she extended her hand smilingly to the great lawyer, grasping his with welcoming warmth.

"I did not die, you see," she said in her deep, vibrant voice, "The west gave me health and happiness," and still holding his hand with proprietary grasp, she turned to the group on the veranda.

"Mr. Booth is an old friend of mine, too. You see, I was his very first client, and I flatter myself that I started him on his great career."

CA. 1928–1932, UNPUBLISHED

# Summer Session

## ALICE DUNBAR-NELSON

"You were flirting with him!"

"I was not. I don't know how to flirt."

"So you say, but you can put up a pretty good imitation."

"You're mistaken."

"I am not. And a man you never saw before in your life. And a common taxi driver."

"He's not a common taxi driver."

"How do you know?"

"I just know."

"Strange exchange of intimacies for the first meeting."

"I tell you—"

"Shut up!"

"I won't shut up, and don't you dare tell me that again!"

There was a warning note in her usually gentle voice; an ominous tightening of her soft lips; a steely glint in her violet eyes. Logan heeded the warning and sat in grim silence, while Elise ground gears and otherwise mishandled her little car through the snarled traffic of Amsterdam Avenue.

"You told me 114th Street, and I waited for you there for a half hour, and I got jammed in the traffic and things went wrong, and this young man got out of his taxi, and straightened me out. And while I waited for you he just stayed and talked."

"To your delight."

"What was I to do? Push him away from the running board? I was standing still, and I couldn't drive away since I was waiting for you."

"I told you 115th Street, and there I stood on the corner in the broiling sun for a half hour, while you were carrying on a flirtation with a taxi driver, until I walked back, thinking you might have had an accident."

"Don't you say flirtation to me again. You said 114th Street. You never speak plain over the telephone anyhow."

"Anything else wrong with me since you've met your new friend— The Taxi Adonis?"

Elise brought the car to a grinding, screeching pause in front of the movie house which was their objective. They sat through the two hours of feature and news and cartoons and comedy and prevues in stony silence. They ate a grim meal together in the usual cafeteria, and she set him down at the men's dormitory of the university in the same polite and frigid silence. Logan glanced at her now and then just a trifle apprehensively. He had never seen just this trace of hardness in her, like the glint of unexpected steel beneath soft chiffon. But his manly dignity would not permit him to unbend. He answered her cold good-night with one as cold, and for the first time in that summer session, during which they had grown to know and like one another, they parted without making a future date.

He waited for her next day at luncheon hour, as she came from her class with a half dozen other chattering summer-school teacher-students. His manner was graciously condescending.

"Shall we have luncheon together?" Lordly and superior as usual.

She flashed her usual violet-eyed smile of delight, but he felt, rather than saw, that the smile did not quite reach the eyes; that the violets were touched as by premature frost.

"What I can't quite understand," he pursued, after he had brought her tray, deftly removed the salad, tea, and crackers, and placed the tray behind the next chair, "is, if you are skillful enough to drive from Portland, Maine, to New York alone and without disaster, how you can get mixed up in a mere traffic jam on Amsterdam Avenue, and have to have a taxi driver get you out."

Elise's brows went up at the awkward English, so at variance with his usual meticulous and precise phrasing, and a haunting query clouded her eyes. Logan quenched an embarrassed "Hem" in iced tea.

"I did not drive from Portland," was her final response. "I came from my own town, twenty-seven miles beyond Portland."

There was no particular reason for Elise's driving down Amsterdam Avenue after classes that afternoon, but she did and a friendly red light brought her to a halt at 114th Street. Adonis—Logan's sneering cognomen stuck in her mind, and she realized with a guilty start how ruggedly applicable it was—stuck his face in her car window. Poppies suffused her cheeks and dewey violets swam in a sea of flame.

"All right?" he queried.

"Quite, thank you." The light was happily yellow, and she meshed her gears.

"What's the hurry?" He put a protesting hand on the wheel.

"I have an engagement!" She sped away frantically. Adonis whistled at the wabbling career of her little coupé down the street.

She saw him just ahead of her in the cafeteria line next evening at dinner time. She reached for her tray with hands that insisted upon trembling, though she shook them angrily. He smiled daringly back at her. He was even handsomer out of his taxi uniform than in it, and the absence of the cap revealed crisp auburn curls of undoubted pugnaciousness.

"You get a seat, I'll bring your dinner."

"But I—"

"Go on—"

There was a difference between Adonis' ordering of her movements and that of Logan's. A sureness of merry audacity against prim didacticism. She sat at a window table and meekly arranged silver napkins.

"But I could never eat all that," she protested at the tray, "Beef and potatoes and— and—all that food."

"I knew that's what's the trouble—diet of salads and iced tea and crackers, mentally, spiritually, physically."

Elise ate roast beef and corn on the cob and pie à la mode and laughed at Adonis' jokes, and his whimsical descriptions of man and his appetites. Over their cigarettes she chuckled at his deft characterizations of their fellow diners.

"Eat hay and think hay," he was saying, "thin diets and thin souls. You need a red-blooded chap like me to make you eat food, put flesh on your bones and reconstruct your thinking from New England inhibitions to New York acceptance and enjoyment of life."

Elise's world rocked. School principals used muddled English. Taxi drivers talked like college professors.

Adonis paused and regarded something on his shoulder as if it were a tarantula. Logan's hand quivered in rage, and veins stood up on its pallor "like long blue whips," Elise found herself thinking.

"Aren't you taking a lot of liberties with a young lady to whom you've not been introduced?" snarled the owner of pallor and veins.

Adonis brushed off the hand and the remark with a careless gesture. He arose and bowed elaborately. "Miss Stone and I have been introduced, thank you, by ourselves—and you?"

Elise looked perilously near tears, "Oh, er—Logan—Mr. Long—this is—er—Mr. McShane."

Logan looked stonily through Adonis, "I don't accept introductions to taxi drivers, even if you do eat with them, Elise."

"Oh, please—" she began.

"That's all right," Adonis gathered up the checks. "Just let me settle this with the cashier, and then if you don't mind, we'll go outside, and settle the physical difference between a taxi driver and—" He did not finish the sentence, but the sinister drawl and contemptuous pause made Elise's scalp prickle with shame for Logan.

"You would suggest a common brawl; quite true to type. I hope, Elise, you have seen enough of such ruffianly conduct to be satisfied."

"Quite the contrary," she answered cooly, "I am going out with Mr. McShane in his taxi." It was pure spite, and she had a sinking feeling that she might not be wanted.

"Terry to you," he retorted, "and let's be going. We've got a busy evening before us."

Logan was beside them on the sidewalk, blocking the way to the taxi parked at the curb.

"Elise, don't be a fool." He grasped her arm and wrenched it, so that she gave an involuntary cry of pain. Terence McShane's next three moves were so violently consecutive as to seem simultaneous. His right hand caught Logan neatly on the point of the chin, so that he went down with amazing swiftness; his left encircled Elise's waist and lifted her into the taxi, and both hands swung the machine with a roar and sputter in the general direction of the Washington bridge.

"But you're losing fares," Elise protested.

"Nonsense. If you can stand this bumpety-bump, what's the dif?"

"It's entrancing," she murmured at the river, the sky, the stars, the electric signs on the Jersey shore, at Terry's hatless curls.

"Police call," the radio protested, "calling all police cars. Look out for taxi license Y327D. Driver abducted summer school student. Watch for taxi. Arrest driver. Kidnapping charge."

From their leafy shelter, where somehow the taxi had parked itself—

neither could have told when or how it stopped under those particularly umbrageous trees, they stared at the radio's accusing dial.

"Well, I'll be—" Terry swore softly, "What do you think of that worm putting in such a charge at headquarters?"

"Oh, Terry, you'll be arrested and put in jail!"

"Will you go to jail with me?"

"You know I will—oh, what am I saying?"

"Words of wisdom, me darlin'. Let's go. Anyhow I'm glad we didn't cross the bridge and get into Jersey."

Through circuitous ways and dark streets, avoiding police, taxis, inquisitive small boys and reporters on the loose, they drew up in front of police headquarters.

Elise sat demurely on a bench, and began to repair damages to her hair, complexion, and neck frills. The little pocket mirror wavered ever so slightly as Logan stood accusingly in front of her, but her eyes did not leave the scrutiny of their mirrored counterpart.

"A pretty mess you've made of your life and reputation," he thundered. "Your chances for any position in my school are gone."

Elise put back a refractory curl behind her ear, then tried it out on her cheek again, surveying it critically in the mirror.

"Won't you recommend me for a job, Mr. Principal, after I've studied so hard all summer?"

Terry's gales of unrestrained mirth at the desk made them both look up in amazement. Laughter rocked the walls of the station house, rolled out into the summer street. Captain and Sergeant and Lieutenant and just plain officers roared lustily, all save one quiet plainclothes man, who laid an iron grip on Logan's arm.

"Terence McShane, you were always the best detective in the city," roared the Captain. "And you made him bring himself right into our outstretched arms."

The iron grip on Logan's arm terminated into steel bracelets.

"Okeh, Longjim Webb, alias Prof. Logan Long, the school principal, looking the summer students over for teaching material in his consolidated upstate school, we'll give you a chance in the Big House to meditate on the law against white slavery."

"Your zeal to corral this particular choice bit of femininity made you throw caution to the winds," suggested Detective Terrence McShane.

Increulity, disgust, anger swept the violet eyes. Elise flared into Terry's face.

"You—you—pretending to be a taxi driver. You just used me for a decoy," she raged.

Terry held her protesting hands tight as he whispered below the hubbub of Logan's protestations,

"Never a bit of it, my dear. I loved you the first day you stalled your car in the thick of things on 125th Street, before you even saw me, and I got in the habit of following you around while I was impersonating a taxi driver, to get a chance to know you. Then when I found this—" a wave towards the still-voluble Logan—"had marked you for another one of his prey—well you don't mind if I combined a bit of business with my pleasure?"

Elise's faint "No" was visible, rather than audible.

"It's all right then? Shall it be beefsteak for two?"

"Yes."

"And you won't take back what you promised up there on the Drive?"

"How can I," she laughed, "when my middle name is McBride?"

CA. 1928–1932, UNPUBLISHED

# M*asks*

## ELOISE BIBB THOMPSON

Paupet, an octoroon and born free, was a man of considerable insight. That was because, having brains, he used them. The cause of Julie's, his wife's, trouble was no secret to him. Although it never dawned upon him fully until after she died. Then he dictated the words to be placed upon her tombstone. The inscription proved to be unique, but not more than the cemeteries themselves of old New Orleans. The motto written in 1832 read as follows: "Because she saw with the eyes of her grandfather, she died at the sight of her babe's face."

This grandfather, Aristile Blanchard, had been an enigma to the whole Quadroon Quarter of New Orleans. But he was no enigma to Paupet although he had never lain eyes upon him. Seeing him had not been necessary for Paupet had heard his whole life's history from Paul, Julie's brother, whom he met in Mobile before he had known Julie. Paul, although a ne'er do well who had left the home-fires early, admired his grandfather immensely. Hence he had found delight even as a youth in securing from the old man those facts of his life which had proved so interesting to Paupet.

Now Paupet, among other things, was a natural psychologist albeit an unconscious one. He was accustomed to ponder the motives of men, their peculiar mental traits and their similarity to those of their parents whom he happened to know. No one was more interesting to Paupet than Julie, his wife. So of course he gave much thought to her. But the occasion is always necessary for the knowledge of a soul, and the opportunity for really knowing Julie came only when she was expecting her offspring. But even then Paupet would not have known where to place the blame for her peculiarity had he not known, as we have said, all there was to know about old Aristile Blanchard.

That Aristile was a man to be pitied Paupet felt there was no question. For what man does not deserve pity who sees his fondest dream fall with the swiftness of a rocket from a starlit sky to the darkness of midnight? No wonder that hallucination then seized him. With such a nature as his that was to be expected. But that the influence of such a delusion should have blighted Julie's young life was the thing of which Paupet most bitterly complained.

Aristile, Paul told Paupet, had been a native of Hayti. Coming to New Orleans in 1795 when the slave insurrection was hottest, he had set up an atmosphere of revolt as forceful as the one he had left behind him. Of course when Julie entered the world, the revolution had long been over; Toussaint L'Ouverture had demonstrated his fitness to rule, had eventually been thrown in an ignominious dungeon and been mouldering in the grave some five years or more. But the fact that distressed Paupet was that Aristile lived on to throw his baneful influence over the granddaughter entrusted by a dying mother to his care.

Of all the free men of color in Hayti at the time none were more favored than Aristile. A quadroon of prepossessing appearance with some capitol at hand, he had been sent to Bordeaux, France, by a doting mother to study the arts for which he was thought to show marked predilection. In reality he was but a dabbler in the arts, returning at length to his native land with some acquaintance with most of them, as for instance sculpture, painting, woodcarving and the like but with no very comprehensive knowledge of any one of them. There was one thing, however, that did not escape him—being there at the time when France was a hotbed of that revolt which finally stormed the Bastille— and that was the spirit of liberty. "Liberty, Fraternity, Equality" was in the very air he breathed. He returned from France with revolutionary tendencies that awaited but the opportunity to blossom into the strongest sort of heroism.

Although he burned to be of service to his race on returning to his native land he forced himself to resume his usual tenor of life. He sought apprenticeship to an Oriental mask-maker, a rare genius in his line where the rich French planters were wont to go in preparation for their masquerades and feast-day activities. Masks had always had a strange fascination for Aristile. He would often sit lost in thought beside their maker, his mind full of conflicting emotions. But when the French slave-owners assembled at Cape Haitien to formulate measures against the free men of color to whom the National Assembly in France had decreed full citizenship, he forgot everything and throwing down his tools immediately headed the revolt that followed.

With Rigaud, the mulatto captain of the slaves, he gave himself to the cause of France, offering at the risk of his life to spy upon the English when they came to the support of the native French planters bent upon re-establishing slavery upon the island.

Making up as a white man as best he could, he boldly entered the port of Jeremie where the English had but recently landed. His ruse would have succeeded had it not been for a native white planter all too familiar with his African earmarks, who standing by at the time readily spotted him out. Without warning, Aristile was seized, flogged unmercifully and thrown into a dungeon to die. But he was rescued after a time by a good angel in the form of an octoroon planter who identified with whites all his life because of a face that defied detection; not only rescued but shipped with his daughter in safety to New Orleans. Then the octoroon rescuer took up the work of spy upon the English which Aristile had been forced to relinquish. That he was successful is manifested in the subsequent work of Toussaint L'Ouverture who because of him was able before very long to drive in all the troops of the English, to invest their strongholds, to assault their forts, and ultimately to destroy them totally.

This incident had a lifelong effect upon Aristile. Full of despondency, disappointment over his failure in the work he had set himself to do with the enthusiasm and glow of a martyr, his mind dwelt wholly upon the facial lineaments that had brought about his defeat. "Cheated!" he would exclaim bitterly. "Cheated out of the opportunity of doing the highest service because of a face four degrees from the pattern prescribed for success. Fate has been against me.—Nature has been against me. It was never meant that I should do the thing I burned to do.—O, why did not Nature give me the face of my father?—Then all things would have been possible to me. Other quadroons have been so blessed. Hundreds of them—thousands of them! Save for a slight sallowness of the skin there was absolutely nothing to show their African lineage. But Nature in projecting my lips and expanding my nose has set me apart for the contumely of the world.—The ancients lied when they said the gods made man's face from the nose upwards, leaving their lower portion for him to make himself. Try as I may I will never be able to change the mask that Nature has imposed upon me."

Day and night these thoughts were with him. Paul described this state to Paupet declaring that his mother had feared for Aristile's mind. At length this mood suddenly changed to one of exultation and he rose from his bed a new man.

"I have found the formula for greatness!" he told those about him, "It reads, Thou shalt be seen wearing a white man's face.—But only a fraction being able to carry out this prescription it is left for me to create a symbol so perfect in its imitation of Nature that the remainder of mankind may likewise receive a place in the sun. My brothers and I shall no longer be marked for defeat. I shall make a mask that will defy Nature herself. There shall be no more distinct and unmistakable signs that will determine whether a man shall be master or slave. All men in future shall have the privilege of being what they will."

With this end in view he repaired to the Quadroon Quarter of New Orleans and set up a workshop that soon became the talk of the district because of the strange-looking objects it contained. Paupet could vouch for their strangeness for they were still in existence when he came to the place. Upon the walls of this room hung many attempts of the thing Aristile had set himself to do. There were masks of paper patiently glued in small bits together in a brave effort to imitate Nature in the making of a white man's face. Likewise masks of wood, of papier mache and of some soft, clinging, leaf-like material which it is very likely he discovered in Louisiana's wonderous woods. Interesting-looking objects they were, everyone of them, most of them, however, were far from the goal; but a few in their skin-like possibility of stretching over a man's face might have been made perfect—who knows—greater marvels have been seen—had their completion not been suddenly broken off. There was about the whole of this room an unmistakable depression, an atmosphere of shattered hope as if the maker of these objects had set out with high purpose toward their completion, then suddenly been chilled by some unforeseen happening that filled him with despair. And so it really had been. While Negro supremacy existed in his beloved country Aristile worked with ever-increasing enthusiasm toward his cherished dream. He had been unable, he told himself, to assist his brothers as a soldier because of the lineaments that Nature had imposed. But he would present them with a talisman like unto Aladdin's lamp that would work wonders for them in a world where to be blessed was to be white. But when the news reached him that Toussaint, the savior of his race had been tricked and thrown into a French prison to die, he was plunged into the deepest sorrow and turned from his purpose in despair. Laying aside his implements, for a long time he could not be induced to take interest in anything. At length when his funds began to dwindle, it was bourne in upon him that men must work if they would live. Then he turned to the making of those limp figures in sweeping gowns that when Paupet saw them were no doubt of his own distorted mind, designed for standing in the farthest corner of the room—grotesque figures wearing hideous masks, the reflection, clowns and actors of the comic stage.

It was not very long before the place began to be frequented by patrons of the Quadroon Masques and of those open-air African dances and debaucheries known as "Voodoo Carousals" held in the Congo Square. Later actors from the French Opera looked in upon him. Then he conceived the idea of having Clotile, his daughter, already an expert with the needle, prepare for his patrons of the masque and stage to be rented at a nominal fee, those gowns and wraps that were now fading behind the glass doors of yonder cabinets. But though he worked continuously it had no power, apparently, to change his usual course of thought. His mind ever dwelt upon the disaster that had blighted his life.

And then came Julie in this atmosphere of depression to take up in time the work which fate decreed Clotile should lay down. As apt with the needle as her dead mother had been she was able, when her grandfather through age and ill-health became enfeebled, to maintain them both. And those were formative years for the young Julie, obliged to listen to her grandfather's half-crazed tirade against Nature's way of fixing a man to his clan through the color of his skin. Unaccustomed to thinking independently she, however, could see something of the disastrousness of it all because of the stringent laws confronting her in New Orleans. As much as she longed to do so, for instance, she dared not wear any of the head-gear of the times, although much of it was made by her own fingers, because of the law forbidding it; a bandana handkerchief being decreed to all free women of color so that they might easily be distinguished from white ladies. And that was only one of the minor laws. There were others graver and more disastrous by far. So these conditions forced her to realize early that her grandfather had good reason for his lament. She too deplored the failure of his design— the making of a mask that would open the barred and bolted doors of privilege for those who knocked theron. Without anything like bitterness for these conditions, she began to reason that color and not mental endowment or loftiness of character determined the caliber of a man. For did not color determine his destiny? He was rich or poor, happy or unhappy according to his complexion and not according to his efforts at all. And so the words superior and inferior were invariably dependent upon the color of his skin. She, a brunette-like quadroon, the counterpart of her grandfather, was far superior to the black slave-peddlers who sometimes came into the Quadroon Quarter begging a place to rest. And that was why the Quarter guarded the section so jealously from all black dwellers, however free they might be, because they wanted only superior people in their midst.

One morning some months after her grandfather's death she awoke trembling with a great discovery. For years, she reflected in wonderment, her revered relative had tried to make a mask that when fitted to a man's face would change his entire future and had failed. And lo! the secret had just been whispered to her. "To me," she whispered to herself ecstatically, "to po' lil' me. An' I know it ees tr-rue, yes. It got to be tr-rue. 'Cause madda Nature, she will help in de work, an' w'at else you want?" For the life-mate she would choose for herself would be an octoroon, as fair as a lily. With her complexion and his she knew that she would be able to give to her children the mask for which her grandfather had yearned. She saw now why he had failed. No doubt it was never meant for men to know anything about it at all. It must be in the keepings of mothers alone. "Now we will see," she told herself exultantly. "Ef my daughter got to wear a head handgcher lak me. Fo' me it ees notting. I cannot help. But jes' de same a son of mine goin' be king of some Carnival yet. You watch out fo' me."

And so when Paupet, the whitest octoroon that she had ever seen, came to the Quarter, she showed her preference for him at once. When, after their marriage, in the course of time their first born was expected she was like an experimentalist in the mating of cross-breeds, painfully nervous and full of the greatest anxiety over the outcome of a situation that she had been planning so long. What preparations she made! She fitted up a room especially for the event. She was extravagance itself in the selection of the garments, buying enough material to clothe half a dozen infants. She literally covered the fly leaves of the Bible with male and female names in preparation for the Christening; and made so many trips to town for all sorts of purchases that Paupet became full of anxiety for the outcome of it all.

To him she talked very freely now of her readiness in marrying him—it was really good of the child that was about to come to them. Her trials would not be her infant's. She had seen to that. He would look like Paupet, and could therefore choose his own way in life unhampered by custom or law.

To the midwife too she communicated her hopes and expectations, dwelling at great length upon the future of the child the whiteness of whose face would be a charm against every prevailing ill. Such optimism augured ill to the midwife who rarely vouchsafed her a word. When at length the child was born, the midwife tarried a long time before placing it into Julie's arms. It was sympathy upon her part that caused the delay. But Julie could not understand it. In the midst of her great sufferings she marvelled at it, until at length she caught a glimpse of her child's face. Then she screamed. With horror she saw that it was identical with the one in the locket about her neck. It was the image of her chocolate-colored mother.

FROM *OPPORTUNITY,* OCTOBER 1927

# Mademoiselle 'Tasie

## ELOISE BIBB THOMPSON

It was all on account of that last Mardi Gras Ball. Mlle. 'Tasie felt it. Indeed she was absolutely sure of it. The night had been cold and damp and she had not had a wrap suited for such weather. So she had gone in a thin blue organdy dress, the best she owned, with simply a white scarf thrown over her shoulders. A "white" scarf, and a "blue" organdy. It was scandalous! And her "tante" but one year dead. No wonder bad luck in the shape of ill health had followed her ever since—putting off her mourning so soon to go to a Mardi Gras ball. Well, what was the use of thinking of it now? "De milk has been speel, so to speak," she mused, "eet ees a grat wonder, yes, as de doctah say, I deed not go into decline."

But try as she would Mlle. 'Tasie could not stop thinking of it. The heavy cold caught at that Mardi Gras ball was the direct cause of her being about to take the momentous step that she was planning to take to-day. And momentous it was, for a fact; there was not the slightest doubt about that. How it would all end, she was at a loss to comprehend.

Not that it counted so much with her now; for ill health and deprivation had forced her to accept with resignation many things that before had seemed unendurable. But her neighbors, ah! and her relatives who knew how thoroughly she had formerly hated the very thing that she was about to do. Mon Dieu! What were they not saying of her now?

217

Yes, there was a time in her life when Mlle. 'Tasie would rather have fainted, actually, than to even so much as have been seen on the street with a certain kind of individual, which she and her class designated as a "Negre Americain aux grosses orielles"—an American Negro with large ears. In a word, with a black American. How many times had she not said of such a contingency, "h-eet h-ees a thing not to be thought h-of h-at h-all." And now—O, now see what she was fixing to do!

For Mlle. 'Tasie was a Creole lady of much less color than a black American. Be pleased to know first of all, that there are colored Creoles as well as white Creoles, just as there are Creole eggs and Creole cabbages. Any person or article brought up in the French Quarter of old New Orleans, the downtown section across Canal Street, is strictly Creole. And to carry the thought to its final conclusion is, in the highest sense of the word, Superior. Mlle. 'Tasie was what was designated by her lightly colored contemporaries, in a whisper, as "un briquet," that is, she had a reddish yellow complexion, and very crinkled red hair. "In a whisper," because the hair of a "briquet" is usually so short and so crinkled that no one feels flattered at being called one. Yet in spite of all that, Mlle. 'Tasie was a Creole, came of a good family, and spoke "patois French" for the most part, sometimes English, and hence, thinking herself superior, had not mingled with English-speaking Negroes known as Americans. And being yellow, she had never been accustomed, until now, to even be on speaking terms with blacks.

It was a positive fact, Mlle. 'Tasie had come of an exceptional Creole family. Everyone with whom she came in contact knew that well. How could they help knowing it when they had heard it so often? As for the corner grocer from whom Mlle. 'Tasie bought charcoal for her diminutive furnace—she couldn't afford a stove—and various other sundries for her almost empty larder, why, had you awakened him from the soundest sort of sleep, he could have told you about her family, word for word, as she had told it, embellished it with glowing incidents, as she had done. In a word, he could have torn that family tree to pieces for you, from root to apex at the shortest possible notice. That was because, of course, so many circumstances had given rise there in his store, for the frequent telling of her history; having incurred, as she had, the hostility of her English speaking black neighbors, at whom she rarely ever glanced. By some strange trick of fortune, these black neighbors were much better off than she, and loved to put their little ones up to poking fun at her whenever she came to the store for the small purchases that she made—beans and rice, almost invariably, with a whispered request for meat-scrapings, thrown in by way of courtesy. Poking their heads in roguishly, thru the half-opened door, these taunting, little urchins were wont to scream at her, "Dere she goes, fellahs, look at 'er. A picayune o' red beans, a picayune o' rice, lagricappe salt meat to make it taste nice." Then Mlle 'Tasie would laugh loudly to hide her embarrassment. Pityingly she would say with up-lifted shoulders and outwardly turned palms, "Ow you ken h-expec' any bettah fum dem? My own fadda h-own plenty lak dat. —But h-I know, me. H-eet ees dey madda, yes, teach 'em lak dat. She ees mad 'cause h-I doan associate wid 'er. But 'er mahster wheep 'er back plenty, yes. Me—h-I nevva know a mahster, me. H-ask h-any one eef h-eet ees de trufe and dey will tell you."

None knew better of Mlle. 'Tasie's family than Paul Donseigneur, the clothier of Orleans Street. Paul had been owned by Mlle. 'Tasie's father, Jose Gomez, who belonged to that class of mulattoes known before the Civil War as free men of color. Escaping from the island of Guadaloupe, during a West Indian insurrection, Gomez had settled in New Orleans, purchased a number of slaves and a goodly portion of land, ultimately becoming a "rentier" of some importance. Paul, a tailor by trade, had been assigned to the making of his master's clothes. Because of his efficiency and estimable character, he had rapidly risen in favor. But Paul was aspiring also. He longed for his freedom and begged permission of Gomez to purchase it from him. After much deliberation, the latter surprised him one day with a gift of himself,—that is, with free papers showing a complete bestowal of Paul and all that he possessed upon himself.

Paul was deeply grateful. It was not in his nature, as it was with so many of his race, to hate the hand that lifted him, when that hand was black. He never forgot the generosity of his master, nor his subsequent assistance in the way of influence, immediately after the Civil War, toward the foundation of the very business in which he was still engaged.

But times had been precarious in New Orleans for any business venture during the early years of reconstruction. Especially so for Paul, efficient and alert though he was, yet an ex-slave, with no capital and no business experience. During the general upheaval, he saw nothing of his master who, like many men of his class, had kept well out of the way of all danger. When the smoke and powder of wrought-up feelings had at last cleared away, Paul again looked about for his old master, with the hope that things had not gone so badly with him. But alas! There was not the slightest trace of him to be found. Had he left the city, or had he only gone uptown? Either step would have been fatal for Paul's finding him. For people in the Faubourg Ste. Marie—the American quarter—

were as completely lost at any time, to the people of the French quarter, as if they had gone to New York.

Paul knew that out of that great family of many sons and daughters, only two remained. At least there had been two when last he saw them—his master and Mlle. 'Tasie, the youngest daughter. How had they fared during all those troublous times? Wherever they were, he knew that they were poorer; for the Civil War had stripped them of most of their possessions, and unprepared as they were for service, they would never be able to retrieve them, he was certain. It was all very sad. But there was nothing to be done, since he knew not where to find them.

Chance, however, some ten years later, just before the opening of our story, discovered to him one member of that family at least, Mlle. 'Tasie. He was crossing over to the French Market, one morning, from the old Place D'Armes, en route to his clothing store, when he heard the guttural tones of a Gascon restauranteur raised in heated discussion. Hastening to the spot he saw seated upon one of the high stools, before the oil cloth-covered counter of the "coffee stand," a shabby, little colored woman in a black calico dress, much-worn but speckless gaiters, and a long, cotton crepe veil thrown back from a faded straw hat—a perfect picture of bitter poverty trying to be genteel.

Thru the cracked and much be-scratched mirror that ran around the wall of the "coffee stand" in front of her, he saw reflected her small pinched face, courageously rouged and powdered, and recognized Mlle. 'Tasie.

Wonderingly, Paul took in the situation. The merchant's prices, it seems, were higher than some of the others in the market, or more, anyhow, than Mlle 'Tasie had been aware of. When the time came to pay for what she had eaten, small tho' it was, she was unprepared to do so completely. Hence the Gasconian war of words.

Mlle. 'Tasie's embarrassment at the turn of affairs was beyond description. With trembling fingers peeping out from cotton lace mittens that time had worn from black to green, she hurriedly lowered her veil, then fumbled about in her lace-covered reticule as if seeking the desired change with absolute fright. Going forward, Paul touched the enraged Gascon on the elbow. The sight of his proffered coin was like oil poured upon troubled waters. Mlle. 'Tasie was saved.

When she lifted her tearful eyes to Paul's pitying face, he saw even through the faded veil what privation had done for her. Gently he took her by the arm and led her to the Place D'Armes thru which he had but just passed. And there upon one of the benches, he coaxed out of her, her whole tragic story. She told him how their poverty becoming greater and greater, she and her father had hidden themselves as he had feared, in the American quarter across Canal Street, away from the people who had known them in brighter days; of her father's subsequent death, and her struggles to support herself with her needle; of her many failures at doing so, because of her complete unpreparedness. To his reproachful query as to why she had not appealed to him, she had answered, shoulders up-lifted and mitten-covered palms turned outward, "Ow h-I could do dat, my deah? Come wid my 'and h-open to you? Me? H-eet was h-impossible."

But he assured her that the success of his tailoring business, slow, to be sure, but very promising always, was such that he might have aided them at the time and was in a still better position of doing so now. She shook her head sadly at the suggestion, and her tears began to flow anew. "Me, h-I would die first!" she exclaimed passionately, "befo' h-I would come to dat."

When she grew calmer, he told her of an innovation that he was planning to bring into his business—the making of blue jeans into trousers for the roustabouts on the Levee, and for other workmen. She mopped her eyes and looked at him with interest. It was jean trousers, she had told him, that she had been attempting to make ever since she had been a breadwinner. But the factories from which she had taken work to be done at home had been so exacting, "docking" her for every mis-stitch, and every mistake in hemming so that there was always very little money coming to her when she finally brought her work back.

Paul surmised as much but had already thought out a plan to meet the situation. He would put her directly under the seamstress in charge, for supervision and instruction. And so, at length, Mlle. 'Tasie was installed into the business of her former slave. Her backwardness in learning to do the work set before her was, at first, disheartening. But for the sake of "Auld Lang Syne," Paul nerved himself into forbearance. When, at last, she gave evidence of beginning to "get the hang" of it, so to speak, she caught a dreadful cold at that Creole Mardi Gras ball.

For Mlle. 'Tasie was still young enough to long for pleasure with something of the ardor of her happier days. She was no "spring chicken" she confessed to herself sadly; she was thirty-seven "come nex 'h-All Saints Day," but that did not prevent her from wanting to "h-enjoy herse'f, yes, once een a w'ile h-any 'ow." Since Mardi Gras comes but once a year, she decided to forget everything and go to the ball. Closing her eyes at the horror of the thing—the laying aside of the mourning which she had worn for the past year for an aunt whom she had never seen—she went down into her trunk and pulled out an ancient blue organdy and a thin, white scarf. It had been years since she had seen these things, for some distant relative of Mlle. 'Tasie was always passing away, and custom compelled her to remember them during a long period of mourning.

Perhaps it was her act of rebellion against this custom, she kept telling herself, that had brought such disaster to her health. Oh, if she only had to do it again, how differently would she act. It had meant the almost giving up of her work at Paul Donseigneur's store, for most of her time was now spent at home trying to get well.

Calling one day to ascertain for himself the cause of these frequent absences, Paul became much disturbed at her appearance. She looked more frail than he had ever seen her. Certainly work, he decided, was not what she wanted now, but care and attention. She had already refused from him, in her foolish pride, everything but what she strictly earned by the sweat of her brow. How to help her now in this new extremity was indeed a problem. He must think it out. And Paul left her more perplexed than he had been before.

As he was about to enter his clothing store, he was stopped by a traveling salesman, Titus Johnson, from whom he bought most of the cottonade that he used. Titus was large and black, well-fed and prosperous-looking, with a fat cigar forever in his mouth and a shiny watch-chain forever dangling from his vest. Titus was the idol of his associates, likewise the idol of the "cook-shop" where he ate, for besides ordering the largest and most expensive steaks they carried, together with hot biscuits, rice, French fried potatoes, buck-wheat cakes and coffee, he tipped the waiter lavishly and treated him to a cigar besides. Not only generous, but full of good cheer was Titus, his hearty laugh resounding from one end of the street to the other. Especially so after he had told one of his characteristic jokes, which invariably brought as great a laugh from himself as from his listeners. Simple, whole-hearted and kindly, Titus Johnson met the world with a beaming face and received much of its goodwill in return.

"Hey dere, boss," he shouted to Paul from across the narrow street, as the latter stood upon the sill of his odd-looking suit-store. "I ben waitin' for you. W'at kep' you?" In a stride or two he was at Paul's side. "I hope you ain't gotten so prosperous," he continued, "dat you dodgin' us black folks and fixin' ter pass for white. Hya! Hya! Hya! Hya!" His great voice sounded to the end of the block.

"No danger," smiled back Paul, whose physiognomy forbade any such intention. "I been visitin' de sick. An'—"

"De sick? Whose sick?" Titus' face bespoke concern.

"Mlle. 'Tasie," replied Paul, "De lil' lady who use to sit at dat machine dere by de winda."

"Sho' nuff?" Titus knitted his brow. "I knows her. Leastwise, I mean, I seen her time and time again.—An' you say she's sick?—Very sick? You know, I uster lak ter look at dat lil' body. 'Pere lak dere wuz somepun' so pitiful lak, about her."

"Pitiful," reiterated Paul, his face wearing its troubled look, "Mais, it is worse yet. It is trageec."

"You doan say!—She ain' goin' die, is she?"

"Ah, I hope not dat, me.—All de same, she need right now plenty of care, yes. An'—you know, some one to see after her—right." He led the way thru a disordered room where women of various shades of color were bending over their work, some at machines, others at long cutting tables. When at length he reached his crowded little office in another wing of the building, he sank heavily into a chair, and motioned Titus to be seated also.

Why talk of business now, he mused, when his mind was so full of Mlle. 'Tasie, and her problems? She was downright troublesome, to say the least, he decided. Why had she let herself get into that weakened condition, just when she was beginning to earn enough to support herself decently? And she was so foolishly proud! It was absurd, it was ridiculous.

Before he knew it, Paul found himself telling the whole story to Titus Johnson—the history of Mlle. 'Tasie and of her remarkable family. Titus was astounded. He had heard that before the Civil War, New Orleans had held a number of men of his race who had not only been free themselves, but had owned a large number of slaves, but he had thought it only a myth. But here, according to Paul, was a representative of that class. He longed to meet her; to really be able, as he expressed it to Paul, to give her "his compliments." Never had he felt so much interest in any one before. When she got better, if Paul would arrange a meeting between them he would be glad to take her some evening to the Spanish Fort—the great, white way of New Orleans—or to see the Minstrel—some place where she could laugh and forget her troubles.

Titus, like most English-speaking Negroes, felt no inferiority to the better-born of his race, like Mlle. 'Tasie. Had anyone suggested it, he would have scoffed at the possibility of her looking down upon him. For was she not also a Negro? However low his origin, she could never get any higher than he. Her status had been fixed with his by the highest authority.

Paul pondered Titus' proposition. He knew Mlle. 'Tasie's prejudice to color, but he refrained from mentioning it. She was in great extremity and Titus was both prosperous and big-hearted. Suppose a match could be arranged between them in spite of her prejudices. Stranger things than that had happened. Paul was an old man, and had seen women, bigger than Mlle. 'Tasie let go their prejudices under economic stress. When insistently the stomach growls, he mused, and the shoe pinches, women cease to discriminate and take the relief at hand. The thing was worth trying.

Looking up into the eager face of Titus Johnson, Paul promised to arrange a meeting between him and Mlle. 'Tasie at the first possible opportunity. Titus went away highly pleased. Altho he would not have named it so the thing promised an adventure; and, approaching forty tho he was, it was nevertheless very pleasing to contemplate. As for Paul, that man realized with misgiving that there was much preparatory work to be done on Mlle. 'Tasie before the meeting could even be mentioned to her. He, therefore, planned to set about doing so without delay.

But strange to say, when he approached her on the subject, Mlle. 'Tasie was more tractable than he dared hope for. Undoubtedly she had been doing some serious thinking for herself. Here she was, she told herself, rapidly approaching forty, her health broken down, and no help in the way of a husband anywhere in sight. How different it was from what she had dreamed. Long before this, she had thought the "right one" would have turned up—and she would have been settled down for life. But alas! the men she had wanted, had all gone to handsomer and younger women. She had been too discriminating, too exacting. That was her trouble. But all that must stop now. She must feel herself blessed if some well-to-do man, even tho he met but half her requirements, should come along and propose to her.

And so when Paul, after dilating upon the prosperity and big-heartedness of the black "American," advised in the most persuasive of language that she permit him to call, instead of flaring up, as he had been sure she would do, she heard him out quietly and consented after a moment or two of sad reflection. Surprised beyond measure at the ready acquiescence, he sat looking at her for a full second in open-mouthed wonderment. Then he congratulated her on her good, common sense; shook hands with her heartily and left, promising to bring Titus as soon as he returned to New Orleans.

But Mlle. 'Tasie's cheerfulness after that seemed to have deserted her. Her health, tho far from being completely restored, enabled her, before long, to resume her duties at the store. And there she sat at her machine, perplexed and miserable, a dumb spectacle of defeat. Since necessity compelled an abandonment of her prejudices, she reflected, if only she could leave the neighborhood before this black man called, so that those who knew her sentiments might not have the pleasure of laughing in her face. But to be compelled to remain right there and receive with a pretense of welcome before a group of peeping, grinning back-biters, the very kind of "Negre aux grosses oreilles" whom she had been known to look down upon—Mon Dieu!—how could one be cheerful after that?

Yet in spite of this dread, the time came at last, when Titus, traveling agent that he was, again arrived in New Orleans. To say that he was eager to meet Mlle. 'Tasie, is far, very far, from the mark, for he fairly lived in the expectation. But Titus was a natural psychologist. On the day of his arrival, contrary to his usual custom, he remained away from Paul's store during the hours that he knew Mlle. 'Tasie was in it, altho he saw to it that Paul got a message that he had not only arrived in town, but would call on Mlle. 'Tasie that evening. For an adventure such as this must not be spoiled thru haste or lack of preparation.

"Ef you wants a lady to 'preciate you," Titus mused, "you must fust have de proper settin'; 'cause settin's everything. You mustn't on'y fix yo'self up for her, but you must git her all worked up fixin' up for you. Den w'en you comes in swaggerin' on yo' cane, a half hour or an hour after she expected you to come, you got her jes' as anxious to meet you, as you is her. All de rest den is clare sailin'.'"

Arriving in the morning, Titus spent the day shopping. Nothing but the newest apparel must meet her eye when first she beheld him. When Paul, therefore, rather falteringly presented him in the evening after having apprised Mlle. 'Tasie much earlier of his expected visit, Titus was resplendent in brand new "malakoff"-bottom trousers, well creased in the middle, a "coffin-back" shaped coat to match, creaking red brogues, lemon colored tie, and a deep red Camellia in the buttonhole of his coat.

To a man, less self-conscious than Titus was at the moment, the meeting would have been a dismal failure. For there was nothing of cordiality in Mlle. 'Tasie's subdued and rather mournful greeting. Paul was so impressed by the chilliness of it, that he beat a hasty retreat, leaving Romeo to the winning of his Juliet unaided. And Titus proved that he was not unequal to the task, for he soon had Mlle. 'Tasie interested in spite of herself. He told her of his travels up and down the state, described the dreary islands of Barataria with their secret passages, where smugglers and robbers nearly a hundred years before had hidden their ill-gotten gains. And had a world of news about the folks of Opoulousas and Point Coupee, places she had not visited since she was a girl. When at length he rose to go, she felt something very much like regret, and before she knew it, entirely forgetful of his color, she had invited him to call again.

Not only was Titus' "gift of gab" an asset to his courting but his frequent absences from town as well. For Mlle. 'Tasie could not help but feel the contrast between the quiet, uneventful evenings without him, and the cheer, the jokes, the kindly gossip that filled the hours when he was there. If only she had not to face the "pryers" with explanations as to why she had become suddenly so "cosmopel" as to bring into her home an American of his complexion. Relatives whom she hadn't seen for months hearing of the strangeness of her conduct, came way from Bayou Rouge and Elysian Fields Street to beg her with tears in their eyes not to disgrace them by allying herself with an American "Negre aux grosses orielles."

Mlle. 'Tasie became distracted. The opinion of these people meant much to her; but after long thinking she realized that the protection and assistance of a husband would mean vastly more. So she nerved herself to defiance. When at length, Titus proposed marriage to her, she accepted him, not with any feeling stronger than liking, it is true, but with a sense of great satisfaction that now she was for a truth, to have a protector at last.

But now that the marriage day had arrived she felt all the old hesitancy, the repugnance, the sensitiveness because of what the others had been saying, come back upon her, with painful intensity. Yet, nevertheless, she bravely prepared for the event. When, at length, evening came and her shabby, little parlor where the ceremony took place became enlivened by the cheery presence of Titus and the only two invited guests—Paul and the owner of the "cook-shop" where Titus ate—Mlle. 'Tasie felt herself grow calmer.

After partaking lavishly of her "wine sangeree" and her carefully-prepared tea-cakes, the guests finally took their departure, Titus went up to her and putting both his fat hands upon her shoulders, smiled reassuringly into her eyes. "Well ole 'oman," he said, "you an' me goin' ter make it fine! It's me an' you 'gainst de whole worl', you heah me? You po' lil' critter! You needs somebody ter take care o' you, an' Titus Johnson is de one ter take de job." Then Mlle. 'Tasie felt a sort of peace steal over her, the harbinger, she hoped of happier days.

FROM *OPPORTUNITY,* SEPTEMBER 1925

# John Redding Goes to Sea

## ZORA NEALE HURSTON

The Villagers said that John Redding was a queer child. His mother thought he was too. She would shake her head sadly, and observe to John's father, "Alf, it's too bad our boy's got a spell on him." The father always met this lament with indifference, if not impatience.

"Aw, woman, stop dat talk 'bout conjure. 'Taint so nohow. Ah doan want Jawn tuh git dat foolishness in him."

"Case you allus tries tuh know mo than me, but Ah ain't so ign'rant. Ah knows a heap mahseff. Many and manys the people been drove outa their senses by conjuration, or rid tuh deat' by witches."

"Ah keep on telling yur, woman, taint so. B'lieve it all you wants tuh, but dontcher-tell mah son none of it."

Perhaps ten-year old John was puzzling to the simple folk there in the Florida woods, for he was an imaginative child and fond of daydreams. The St. John river flowed a scarce three hundred feet from his back door. On its banks at this point grow numerous palms, luxuriant magnolias and bay trees with a dense undergrowth of ferns, cat-tails and rope-grass. On the bosom of the stream float millions of delicately colored hyacinths. The little brown boy loved to wander down to the water's edge and cast in dry twigs, and watch them sail away down stream to Jacksonville, the sea, and the wide world and John Redding wanted to follow them.

Sometimes in his dreams he was a prince, riding away in a gorgeous carriage. Often he was a knight bestride a fiery charger prancing down the white shellroad that led to distant lands. At other times he was a steamboat Captain piloting his craft down the St. John river to where the sky seemed to touch the water. No matter what he dreamed or whom he fancied himself to be, he always ended by riding away to the horizon, for in his childish ignorance he thought this to be farthest land.

But these twigs, which John called his ships, did not always sail away. Sometimes they would be swept in among the weeds growing in the shallow water, and be held there. One day his father came upon him scolding the weeds for stopping his sea-going vessels.

"Let go mah ships! you old mean weeds, you!" John screamed and stamped impotently, "They wants tuh go 'way, you let 'em go on."

Alfred laid his hand on his son's head lovingly. "What's mattah, son?"

"Mah ships, Pa," the child answered weeping. "Ah throwed 'em in to go way off an them ole weeds won't let 'em."

"Well, well, doan cry. Ah thought youse uh grown up man. Men doan cry lak babies. You mustn't take it too hard 'bout yo ships. You gotter git uster things gitten tied up. They's lotsa folks that 'ud go on off too ef somethin' didn' ketch 'em and hol' 'em!"

Alfred Redding's brown face grew wistful for a moment, and the child noticing it asked quickly, "Do weeds tangle up folks too, Pa?"

"Now, now, chile, doan be takin' too much stock of what Ah say. Ah talks in parables sometimes. Come on, le's go on tuh supper."

Alf took his son's hand, and started slowly toward the house. Soon John broke the silence.

"Pa, when Ah gets as big as you Ah'm goin' farther than them ships. Ah'm going to where the sky touches the ground."

"Well, son, when Ah waz a boy, Ah said Ah wuz going too, but heah Ah am. Ah hopes you have better luck than I had."

"Pa, Ah betcher Ah seen somethin' in th' wood that you ain't seen."

"What?"

"See dat tallest pine tree ovah dere how it looks like a skull wid a crown on!"

"Yes, indeed," said the father looking toward the tree designated, "It do look lak a skull since you call mah 'tention to it. You 'magine lotser things nobody else evah did, son."

"Sometimes, Pa, dat ole tree waves at me just after th' sun goes down, an' makes me sad an' skeered too."

"Ah specks youse skeered of de dahk, thas all, sonny. When you gits biggah you won't think of sich."

Hand in hand these two trudged across the plowed land and up to the house—the child dreaming of the days when he should wander to far countries, and the man of the days when he might have—and thus they entered the kitchen.

Matty Redding, John's mother, was setting the table for supper. She was a small wiry woman with large eyes that might have been beautiful when she was young, but too much weeping had left them watery and weak.

"Matty," Alf began as he took his place at the table, "dontcher know our boy is different from any othah chile roun' heah. He 'lows he's goin' to sea when he gits grown, and Ah reckon Ah'll let 'im."

The woman turned from the stove, skillet in hand. "Alf, you ain't gone crazy is you? John kaint help wantin' tuh stray off, 'cause he's got a spell on 'im, but you oughter be shamed to be encouragin' 'im."

"Ain't Ah done tol you forty times not tuh tawk dat low-life mess in front of mah boy?"

"Well, if taint no conjure in de world, how come Mitch Potts been layin' on his back six mont's an' de doctah kaint do 'im no good? Answer me dat. The very night John wuz born, Granny seed ole witch Judy Davis creepin' outer dis yahd. You knows she had swore tuh fix me fuh marryin' you 'way from her darter Edna. She put travel dust down fuh mah chile, dats what she done, to make him walk 'way fum me. An' evah sence he's been able tuh crawl, he's been tryin' tuh go."

"Matty, a man doan need no travel dust tuh make 'im wanter hit de road. It jes comes natcheral fuh er man tuh travel. Dey all wants tuh go at some time or other but they kaint all git away. Ah wants mah John tuh go an' see, 'cause Ah wanted to go mahself. When he comes back Ah kin see then furrin places wid his eyes. He kaint help wantin' tuh go 'cause he's a man chile."

Mrs. Redding promptly went off into a fit of weeping but the man and boy ate supper unmoved. Twelve years of married life had taught Alfred that, far from being miserable when she wept, his wife was enjoying a bit of self-pity.

Thus John Redding grew to manhood, playing, studying and dreaming. He attended the village school as did most of the youth about him, but he also went to high school at the county seat where none of the villagers went. His father shared his dreams and ambitions, but his mother could not understand why he should wish to go to strange places where neither she nor his father had been. No one in their community had ever been farther away than Jacksonville. Few, indeed, had ever been there. Their own gardens, general store, and occasional trips to the County seat—seven miles away—sufficed for all their needs. Life was simple indeed with these folk.

John was the subject of much discussion among the country folk. Why didn't he teach school instead of thinking about strange places and people? Did he think himself better than any of the belles thereabout that he would not go a courting any of them? He must be "fixed" as his mother claimed, else where did his queer notions come from? Well, he was always queer, and one could not expect the man to be different from the child. They never failed to stop work at the approach of Alfred in order to be at the fence to inquire after John's health and ask when he expected to leave.

"Oh," Alfred would answer, "yes, as soon as his ma gets reconciled to th' notion. He's a mighty dutiful boy, mah John is. He doan wanna hurt her feelings."

The boy had on several occasions attempted to reconcile his mother to the notion, but found it a difficult task. Matty always took refuge in self-pity and tears. Her son's desires were incomprehensible to her, that was all. She did not want to hurt him. It was love, mother love, that made her cling so desperately to John.

"Lawd knows," she would sigh, "Ah nevah wuz happy an' nevah specks tuh be."

"An from yo actions," put in Alfred hotly, "you's determined not to be."

"Thas right, Alfred, go on an' 'buse me. You allus does. Ah knows Ah'm ign'rant an' all dat, but dis is mah son. Ah bred an' born 'im. He cain't help from wantin' to go rovin' cause travel dust been put down on him. But mabbe we kin cure 'im by disincouragin' the idea."

"Well, Ah wants mah son tuh go, an' he wants tuh go too. He's a man now, Matty, an' we mus let John hoe his own row. If it's travelin', won't be for long. He'll come back to us bettah than when he went off. Anyhow he'll learn dat folks is human all ovah de world. Dats worth a lot to know, an' it's worth going a long way tuh fin out. What do you say, son,?"

"Mama," John began slowly, "It hurts me to see you so troubled over me going away, but I feel that I must go. I'm stagnating here. This atmosphere will stifle every bit of ambition that's in me. Let me go, Mama, please. What is there here for me? Give me two or three years to look around and I will be back here with you and papa, and never leave you again. Mama, please let me go."

"Now, John, it's bettah for you to stay heah and take over the school. Why won't you marry and settle down?"

"I'm sorry Mama that you won't consent. I am going, nevertheless."

"John, John, mah baby! You wouldn't kill yo' po' ole mama, would you? Come kiss me, Son."

The boy flung his arms about his mother and held her closely while she sobbed on his breast. To all of her pleas, however, he answered that he must go.

"I'll stay at home this year, Mama, then I'll go for a while, but it won't be long. I'll come back and make you and Papa oh so happy. Do you see, Mama dear?"

"Ah reckon t'ain't nothin' 'tall fuh me to do else."

Things went on very well around the Reddings home for some time. During the day John helped his father about the farm and read a great deal at night.

Then the unexpected happened. John married Stella Kanty, a neighbor's daughter. The courtship was brief but ardent—on John's part at least. He danced with Stella at a candy-pulling, walked with her home and in three weeks had declared himself. Mrs. Redding declared that she was happier than she had ever been in her life. She therefore engaged in a whole afternoon of weeping. John's change was occasioned feasibly by the fact that Stella was really beautiful, he was young and hot blooded, and the time was spring.

Spring time in Florida is not a matter of peeping violets or bursting tulips merely. It is a riot of color, in nature—glistening green leaves, pink, blue, purple, yellow blossoms that fairly stagger the visitor from the north. The miles of hyacinths are like an undulating carpet on the surface of the river and divide reluctantly when the slow-moving alligators push their way log-like across. The nights are white nights for the moon shines with dazzling splendor, or in the absence of that goddess, the soft darkness creeps down laden with innumerable scents. The heavy fragrance of magnolias mingled with the delicate sweetness of the jasmine and wild roses.

If time and propinquity conquered John, what then? These forces have overcome older men.

The raptures of the first few weeks over, John began to saunter out to the gate to gaze wistfully down the white dusty road, or to wander again to the river as he had done in childhood. To be sure he did not send forth twig-ships any longer, but his thoughts would in spite of himself, stray down river to Jacksonville, the sea, the wide world—and poor home-tied John Redding wanted to follow them.

He grew silent and pensive. Matty accounted for this by her ever-ready explanation of conjuration. Alfred said nothing, but smoked and puttered about the barn more than ever. Stella accused her husband of indifference and pouting. At last John decided to bring matters to a head and broached the subject to his wife.

"Stella, dear, I want to go roving about the world for a spell, would you stop here with Papa and Mama and wait for me to come back?"

"John, is you crazy sho 'nuff? If you don't want me, say so, an' I kin go home to mah folks."

"Stella, darling, I do want you, but I want to go away too. I can have both if you'll let me. We'll be so happy when I return."

"Now, John, you cain't push me off one side like that. You didn't hafta marry me. There's a plenty others that would hev been glad enuff tuh get me. You know Ah want educated befo han'."

"Don't make me too conscious of my weakness, Stella. I know I should never have married with my inclinations, but it's done now. No use to talk about what is past. I love you and want to keep you, but I can't stifle that longing for the open road, rolling seas, for peoples and countries I have never seen. I'm suffering, too, Stella, I'm paying for my rashness in marrying before I was ready. I'm not trying to shirk my duty—you'll be well taken care of in the meanwhile."

"John, folks allus said you was queer and tol' me not to marry yuh, but Ah jes loved yuh so Ah couldn't help it, an now to think you wants tuh sneak off an' leave me."

"But I'm coming back, darling. Listen, Stella—" But the girl would not. Matty came in and Stella fell into her arms weeping. John's mother immediately took up arms against him. The two women carried on such an effective war against him for the next few days that finally Alfred was forced to take his son's part.

"Matty, let dat boy alone Ah tell yah! Ef he wuz uh homeboddy he'd be drove 'way by you-all's racket."

"Well, Alf, dats all we po' wommen kin do. We wants our husbands an' our sons. John's got a wife now, an' he ain't got no business to be talkin' 'bout gon' nowhere. I 'lowed dat marryin' Stella would settle him."

"Yas, das all you wimmen study 'bout—settlin' some man. You takes all de get-up, out of 'em. Jes let uh fellah mak a motion lak gettin' somewhere an' some oman'll begin tuh hollah 'Stop theah! where's you goin'? don't fuhgit you b'long tuh me!'"

"My Gawd! Alf! What you reckon Stella's gwine do? Let John walk off and leave huh?"

"Naw. Git outer her foolishness an' go 'long wid him. He'd take huh."

"Stella ain't got no call tuh go crazy 'cause John is. She ain't no woman tuh be floppin' roun' from place tuh place lak some uh dese reps follerin' uh section gang."

The man turned abruptly from his wife and stood in the kitchen door. A blue haze hung over the river and Alfred's attention seemed fixed upon this. In reality his thoughts were turned inward. He was thinking of the numerous occasions upon which he and his son had sat on the fallen log at the edge of the water and talked of John's proposed travels. He had encouraged his son, given him every advantage his poor circumstances would permit. And now John was home-tied.

The young man suddenly turned the corner of the house and approached his father.

"Hello, Papa."

"'Lo, Son."

"Where's Mama and Stella?"

The older man merely jerked his thumb toward the interior of the house and once more gazed pensively toward the river. John entered the kitchen and kissed his mother fondly.

"Great news, Mama."

"What now."

"Got a chance to join the Navy, Mama, and go all around the world. Ain't that grand!"

"John, you shorely ain't gointer leave me and Stella, is yuh?"

"Yes, I think I am, I know how both of you feel, but I know how I feel also. You preach to me the gospel of self-sacrifice for the happiness of others, but you are unwilling to practice any of it yourself. Stella can stay here—I am going to support her and spend all the time I can with her. I am going; that's settled, but I want to go with your blessing. I want to do something worthy of a strong man. I have done nothing so far but look to you and papa for everything. Let me learn to strive and think—in short, be a man."

"Naw, John, Ah'll nevah give mah consent. I know you's hard headed jes lak you paw, but if you leave dis place ovah mah head, Ah never wants you tuh come back heah no mo. Ef I wuz laid on de coolin' board, Ah doan' want yuh standin' ovah me, young man. Doan never come neah mah grave, you ongrateful wretch!"

Mrs. Redding arose and flung out of the room. For once, she was too incensed to cry. John stood in his tracks, his eyes dilated with terror at his mother's pronouncement. Alfred, too, was moved. Mrs. Redding banged the bed-room door violently and startled John slightly. Alfred took his son's arm saying softly, "Come, son, let's go down to the river."

At the water's edge they halted for a short space before seating themselves on the log. The sun was setting in a purple cloud. Hundreds of mosquito hawks darted here and there, catching gnats and being themselves caught by the lightning-swift bull-bats. John abstractedly snapped in two the stalk of a slender young bamboo. Taking no note of what he was doing, he broke it into short lengths and tossed them singly into the stream. The old man watched him silently for a while, but finally he said, "Oh, yes, my boy, some ships get tangled in the weeds."

"Yes, Papa, they certainly do; I guess I'm beaten—might as well surrender."

"Nevah say die. Yuh nevah kin tell what will happen."

"What can happen? I have courage enough to make things happen, but what can I do against Mama! What man wants to on a long journey with his mother's curses ringing in his ears? She doesn't understand. I'll wait another year, but I am going because I must."

Alfred threw an arm about his son's neck and drew him nearer but quickly removed it. Both men instantly drew apart—ashamed for having been so demonstrative. The father looked off to the wood-lot and asked with a reminiscent smile. "Son, do you remember showing me the tree dat looked lak a skeleton head?"

"Yes, I do. It's there still. I look at it sometimes when things have become too painful for me at the house, and I run down here to cool off and think."

"You wuz always imaginin' things, John, things that nobody else evah thought on."

"Oh, yes, I'm a dreamer. I have such wonderfully complete dreams, Papa. They never come true. But even as my dreams fade, I have others."

The men arose without more conversation. Possibly they feared to trust themselves to speech. As they walked leisurely toward the house Alfred remarked the freshness of the breeze.

"It's about time the rains set in," added his son. "The year is wearin' on."

After a gloomy supper, John strolled out into the spacious front yard and seated himself beneath a China-berry tree. The breeze had grown a trifle stronger since sunset and continued from the southwest. Matty and Stella sat on the deep front porch, but Alfred joined John under the tree. The family was divided into two armed camps and the hostilities had reached that stage where no quarter could be asked or given.

About nine o'clock an automobile came flying down the dusty white road and halted at the gate. A white man slammed the gate and hurried up the walk towards the house, but stopped abruptly before the men beneath the China-berry tree. It was Mr. Hill, the builder of the new bridge that spanned the river.

"Howdy John, howdy Alf, I'm mighty glad I found you; I am in trouble."

"Well, now, Mist' Hill," answered Alfred slowly but pleasantly, "we're glad you foun' us too. What trouble could you be having now?"

"It's the bridge. The weather bureau says the rains will be upon us in forty-eight hours. If it catches the bridge as it is now, I'm afraid all my work of the past five months will be swept away, to say nothing of half a million of dollars' worth of labor and material. I've got all my men at work now and I thought to get as many extra hands as I could to help out tonight and tomorrow. We can make her weather tight in that time if I can get about twenty more."

"I'll go Mister Hill," said John with a great deal of energy. "I don't want Papa out on that bridge—too dangerous."

"Good for you, John!" cried the white man. "Now if I had a few more men of your brawn, I could build an entirely new bridge in forty-eight hours. Come on and jump into the car. I am taking the men down as I find them."

"Wait a minute. I must put on my blue-jeans. I won't be long."

John arose and strode to the house. He knew that his mother and wife had overheard everything, but he paused for a moment to speak to them."

"Mama, I am going to work all night on the bridge."

There was no answer. He turned to his wife.

"Stella, don't be lonesome, I'll be home at daybreak."

His wife was as silent as his mother. John stood for a moment on the steps, then resolutely strode past the women and into the house. A few minutes later he emerged clad in his blue jeans and brogans. This time he said nothing to the silent figures rocking back and forth on the porch. But when he was a few feet from the steps he called back, "Bye, Mama, bye Stella," and hurried on down the walk to where his father sat.

"So long, Papa, I'll be home around seven."

Alfred roused himself and stood. Placing both hands upon his son's broad shoulders he said softly, "Be keerful, son, don't fall or nothin'."

"I will, Papa. Don't you get into a quarrel on my account."

John hurried on to the waiting car and was whirled away.

Alfred sat for a long time beneath the tree where his son had left him and smoked on. The women soon went indoors. On the night breeze

were borne the mingled scents of jasmine, of roses, of damp earth, of the
river, of the pine forest near by. A solitary whip-poor-will sent forth his
plaintive call from the nearby shrubbery. A giant owl hooted and
screeched from the wood lot. The calf confined in the barn bleated and
was answered by his mother's sympathetic "Moo" from the pen.

Around ten o'clock the breeze freshened, growing stiffer until midnight when it became a gale. Alfred fastened the doors and bolted the
wooden shutters at the windows. The three persons sat about a round
table in the kitchen upon which stood a bulky kerosene lamp, flickering
and sputtering in the wind that came through the numerous cracks in
the walls. The wind rushed down the chimney blowing puffs of ashes
about the room. It banged the cooking utensils on the walls. The drinking gourd hanging outside the door played a weird tattoo, hollow and
unearthly, against the thin wooden wall.

The man and the women sat silently. Even if there had been no storm
they would not have talked. They could not go to bed because the
women were afraid to retire during a storm and the man wished to stay
awake and think of his son. Thus they sat: the women hot with resentment toward the man and terrified by the storm, the man hardly mind-
ful of the tempest, but eating his heart out in pity for his boy. Time wore
heavily on.

And now a new element of terror was added. A screech-owl alighted
on the roof and shivered forth his doleful cry. Possibly he had been
blown out of his nest by the wind. Matty started up at the sound but fell
back in her chair pale as death. "My Gawd!" she gasped, "dat's a sho' sign
of death."

Stella hurriedly thrust her hand into the salt jar and threw some into
the chimney of the lamp. The color of the flame changed from yellow to
blue-green, but this burning of salt did not have the desired effect—to
drive away the bird from the roof. Matty slipped out of her blue calico
wrapper and turned it wrong side out before replacing it. Even Alfred
turned one sock.

"Alf," said Matty, "what do you reckon's gonna happen from this?"

"How do Ah know, Matty?"

"Ah wisht John hadner went away from heah tuh night."

"Huh."

Outside the tempest raged. The palms rattled dryly, and the giant
pines groaned and sighed in the grip of the wind. Flying leaves and pine-
mast filled the air. Now and then a brilliant flash of lightning disclosed a
bird being blown here and there with the wind. The prodigious roar of
the thunder seemed to rock the earth. Black clouds hung so low that the

tops of the pines among them moaned slowly before the wind and made the darkness awful. The screech-owl continued his tremulous cry. The rain beat upon the shingle roof like buckshot and ran from the eaves in torrents. It entered the house through the cracks in the walls and under the doors. It was a deluge in volume and force, but subsided before morning. The sun came up brightly on the havoc of the wind and rain, calling forth millions of feathered creatures. The white sand everywhere was full of tiny cups dug out by the force of the falling rain drops. The rims of the little depressions crunched noisily underfoot.

At daybreak Mr. Redding set out for the bridge. He was uneasy. On arriving he found that the river had risen twelve feet during the cloud-burst and was still rising. The slow St. John was swollen far beyond its banks and rushing on to sea like a mountain stream, sweeping away houses, great blocks of earth, cattle, trees, in short, anything that came within its grasp. Even the steel framework of the new bridge was gone.

The siren of the fibre factory was tied down for half an hour, announcing the disaster to the country side. When Alfred arrived therefore he found nearly all the men of the district there.

The river, red and swollen, was full of floating debris. Huge trees were swept along as relentlessly as chicken coops and fence rails. Some steel piles were all that was left of the bridge.

Alfred went down to a group of men who were fishing members of the ill-fated construction gang out of the water. Many were able to swim ashore unassisted. Wagons backed up and were hurriedly driven away loaded with wet, shivering men. Two men had been killed outright; others seriously wounded. Three men had been drowned. At last all had been accounted for except John Redding. His father ran here and there, asking for him or calling him. No one knew where he was. No one remembered seeing him since daybreak.

Dozens of women had arrived at the scene of the disaster by this time. Matty and Stella, wrapped in woolen shawls, were among them. They rushed to Alfred in alarm and asked where was John.

"Ah doan' know," answered Alfred impatiently, "that's what Ah'm tryin' to fin' out now."

"Do you reckon he's run away?" asked Stella thoughtlessly.

Matty bristled instantly.

"Naw," she answered sternly, "he ain't no sneak."

The father turned to Fred Mimms, one of the survivors and asked him where John was and how had the bridge been destroyed.

"You see," said Mimms, "when dat turrible win' come up we wuz out 'bout de middle of the river. Some of us wuz on de bridge, some on de derrick. De win' blowed so hahd we could skeercely stan'; and Mist. Hill tol' us tuh set down fuh a speel. He's afraid some of us mought go over board. Den all of a sudden de lights went out—guess de wires wuz blowed down. We wuz all skeered tuh move for slippin' overboard. Den dat rain commenced—and Ah nevah seed such a downpour since the flood. We set dere an' someone begins tuh pray. Lawd, how we did pray tuh be spared! Den somebody raised a song and we sung, you hear me. We sung from the bottom of our hearts till daybreak. When the first light come we couldn't see nothin' but fog everywhere. You couldn't tell which wuz water an' which wuz lan'. But when de sun come up de fog began to lift, and we could see de water. Dat fog was so thick an' so heavy dat it wuz huggin' dat river lak a windin' sheet. And when it rose we saw dat de river had rose way up durin' the rain. My Gawd, Alf, it was running high—so high it nearly teched de bridge an' red as blood, so much clay, you know, from lan' she done overflowed. Coming down stream, as fast as 'press train was three big pine trees. De fust one wasn't forty feet from us and there wasn't no chance to do nothin' but pray. De fust one struck us and shock de whole works, an' befo it could stop shakin' the other two hit us an' down we went. Ah thought Ah'd never see home again."

"But, Mimms, where's John?"

"Ah ain't seen him, Alf, since de logs struck us. Mebbe he's swum ashore, mebbe dey picked him up. What's dat floatin' way out dere in de water?"

Alfred shaded his eyes with his guarded brown hand, and gazed out into the stream. Sure enough there was a man floating on a piece of timber. He lay prone upon his back. His arms were outstretched and the water washed over his brogans, but his feet were lifted out of the water whenever the timber was buoyed up by the stream. His blue overalls were nearly torn from his body. A heavy piece of steel or timber had struck him in falling, for his left side was laid open by the thrust. A great jagged hole, wherein the double fists of a man might be thrust, could plainly be seen from the shore. The man was John Redding.

Everyone seemed to see him at once. Stella fell to the wet earth in a faint. Matty clung to her husband's arm, weeping hysterically. Alfred stood very erect with his wife clinging tearfully to him, but he said nothing. A single tear hung on his lashes for a time, then trickled slowly down his wrinkled brown cheek.

"Alf! Alf!" screamed Matty, "Dere's our son. Ah knowed when Ah heard dat owl las' night."

"Ah see 'im Matty," returned her husband softly.

"Why is yuh standin' heah? Go git mah boy."

The men were manning a boat to rescue the remains of John Redding when Alfred spoke again.

"Mah po boy, his dreams never come true."

"Alf," complained Matty, "why doan't-cher hurry an' git my boy. Doan't-cher see he's floatin' on off?"

Her husband paid her no attention, but addressed himself to the rescue party.

"You all stop. Leave my boy go on. Doan stop 'im. He wants tuh go. Ah'm happy 'cause dis mawnin' mah boy is going tuh sea, he's goin' tuh sea."

Out on the bosom of the river, bobbing up and down as if waving good-bye, John Redding floated away toward Jacksonville, the sea, the wide world—at last.

FROM THE *STYLUS*, MAY 1921

# The Bone of Contention

## ZORA NEALE HURSTON

### I

Eatonville, Florida is a colored town and has its colored interests. It has not now, nor ever has had anything to rank with Brazzle's yellow mule. His Yaller Highness was always mentioned before the weather, the misery of the back or leg, or the hard times.

The mule was old, rawbony and mean. He was so rawbony that he creaked as he ambled about the village street with his meanness shining out through every chink and cranny in his rattling anatomy. He worked little, ate heartily, fought every inch of the way before the plow and even disputed with Brazzle when he approached to feed him. Sale, exchange or barter was out of the question, for everybody in the county knew him.

But one day he died. Everybody was glad, including Brazzle. His death was one of those pleasant surprises that people hope for, but never expect to happen.

The city had no refuse plant so H.Y.H went the way of all other domestic beasts who died among us. Brazzle borrowed Watson's two grey plugs and dragged the remains out to the edge of the cypress swamp, three miles beyond the city limits and abandoned them to the natural scavengers. The town attended the dragging out to a man. The fallen gladiator was borne from the arena on his sharp back, his feet stiffly raised as if in a parting gesture of defiance. We left him on the edge of the cypress swamp and returned to the village satisfied that the only piece of unadulterated meanness that the Lord had ever made was gone from among us forever.

Three years passed and his bones were clean and white. They were scattered along the swamp edge. The children still found them sufficiently interesting to tramp out to gaze upon them on Sunday afternoons. The elders neglected his bones, but the mule remained with them in song and story as a simile, as a metaphor, to point a moral or adorn a tale. But as the mean old trouble-making cuss, they considered him gone for good.

## II

It was early night in the village. Joe Clarke's store porch was full of chewing men. Some chewed tobacco, some chewed cane, some chewed straws, for the villager is a ruminant in his leisure. They sat thus every evening ostensibly waiting for the mail from Number 38, the southbound express. It was seldom that any of them got any but it gave them a good excuse to gather. They all talked a great deal, and every man jack of them talked about himself. Heroes all, they were, of one thing or another.

Ike Pearson had killed a six-foot rattler in a mighty battle that grew mightier every time Ike told about it; Walter Thomas had chinned the bar twenty times without stopping; Elijah Moseley had licked a "cracker"; Brazzle had captured a live catamount; Hiram Lester had killed a bear; Sykes Jones had won the soda-cracker eating contest; AND JOE CLARKE HAD STARTED THE TOWN!

Reverend Simms, the Methodist preacher, a resident of less than a year, had done nothing to boast of, but it was generally known that he aspired to the seat of Joe Clarke. He wanted to be mayor. He had observed to some of his members that it wasn't no sense in one man staying in office all the time.

"Looka heah," Clarke cut across whoever it was that was talking at the time, "When Ah started dis town, Ah walked right up to de white folks an' laid down TWO HUND'ED DOLLAHS WID DIS RIGHT HAND YOU SEE BEFO' YOU AN' GOT MAH PAPERS AN' PUT DIS TOWN ON DE MAP! It takes uh powerful lot uh sense an' grit tuh start uh town, yessirree!"

"Whut map did you put it on, Joe?" Lindsay disrespectfully asked. "Ah ain't seed it on no map."

Seeing Clarke gored to his liver, Rev. Simms let out a gloating snicker and tossed a cane knot to Tippy, the Lewis' dejected dog frame hovering about the group hoping for something more tempting to a dog's palate than cane chews and peanut shells might drop. He tossed the knot and waited for Clarke to answer. His Honor ignored the thrust as being too low for him to stoop to and talked on. Was he not mayor, postmaster, storekeeper and Pooh Bah general? Insults must come to him from at least the county seat.

"Nother thing," Clarke continued, giving Simms a meaning look, "There's a heap goin' on 'round heah under the cover dat Ahm gointer put a stop to. Jim Weston done proaged through mah hen house enough. Last Sat'day Ah missed three uh mah bes' layin' hens, an' Ah been tol' he buried feathers in his backyard the very next day. Cose Ah caint prove nothin', but de minute he crooks his little finger, he goes 'way from mah town. He ain't de onliest one Ah got mah eye on neither."

Simms accepted the challenge thrown at him.

"Fact is, the town ain't run lak it might be. We oughta stop dat foolishness of runnin' folks outa town. We oughta jail'em. They's got jails in all de other towns, an' we oughta bring ours up to date."

"Ah'll be henfired! Simms, you tries to know mo' 'bout runnin' de town than me! Don't you reckon a man thats got sense enough to start uh town, knows how tuh run it. Don't you reckon if de place had uh needed uh jailhouse Ah would have got one built 'long befo' you come heah?"

"We do so need a jail," Lindsay contended. "Jus' 'cause you stahted the town, dat don't make yo' mouf no prayer book nor neither yo' lips no Bible. They don't flap lak none tuh *me.*"

Lindsay was a little shriveled up man with grey hair and bow-legs. He was the smallest man in the village, who nevertheless did the most talk of fighting. That was because the others felt he was too small for them to hit. He was harmless, but known to be the nastiest threatener in the county.

Clarke merely snorted contemptuously at his sally and remarked dryly that the road was right there for all those who were not satisfied with the way he was running the town.

"Meaning to insult me?" Lindsay asked belligerently.

"Ah don't keer HOW yuh take it. Jus' take yo' rawbony cow an' gwan tuh de woods, fuh all I keer," Clarke answered.

Lindsay leaped from the porch and struck his fighting pose. "Jus' hit de ground an' Ah'll strow yuh all over Orange County! Aw, come on! Come on! Youse a big seegar, but Ah kin smoke yuh!"

Clarke looked at the little man, old, and less than half his size and laughed. Walter Thomas and 'Lige Moseley rushed to Lindsay and pretended to restrain him.

"That's right," Lindsay panted, "you better hold me offen him. 'Cause if I lay de weight uh dis right hand on him, he won't forget it long as he live."

"Aw, shet up, Lin'say, an' set down. If you could fight as good as you kin threaten, you'd be world's champeen 'stead uh Jack Dempsey. Some uh dese days when youse hollerin' tuh be let loose, somebody's gointer take you at yo' word, then it will be jus' too bad about yuh," Lester admonished.

"Who?—"

The war was about to begin all over on another front when Dave Carter, the local Nimrod, walked, almost ran up the steps of the porch. He was bareheaded, excited and even in the poor light that seeped to the porch from the oil lamps within, it was seen that he was bruised and otherwise unusually mussed up.

"Mist' Clarke, Ah wants tuh see yuh," he said. "Come on inside."

"Sholy, Dave, sholy." The mayor responded and followed the young man into the store and the corner reserved for City Administration. The crowd from the porch followed to a man.

Dave wiped a bruise spot on his head. "Mist' Clarke, Ah wants uh warrant took out fuh Jim Weston. Ahm gointer law him outa dis town. He caint lam me over mah head wid no mule bone and steal mah turkey and go braggin' about it!"

Under the encouraging quiz of the mayor, Dave told his story. He was a hunter and fisherman, as everybody knew. He had discovered a drove of wild turkeys roosting in the trees along the edge of the cypress swamp near the spot where Brazzle's old mule had been left. He had watched them for weeks, had seen the huge gobbler that headed the flock and resolved to get him.

"Yes," agreed Clarke, "you said something to me about it yesterday when you bought some shells."

"Yes, and thats how Jim knowed Ah was goin' turkey huntin'. He was settin' on de store porch and heard me talkin' to you. Today when Ah started out, jes 'bout sundown—dats de bes' time tuh get turkeys, when they goes tuh roost—he ups and says he's goin' long. Ah didn't keer 'bout dat, but when them birds goes tuh roost, he ain't even loaded, so

Ah had shot dat gobbler befo' he took aim. When he see dat great big gobbler fallin' he fires off his gun and tries tuh grab him. But Ah helt on. We got tuh pushin' and shovin' and tusslin' 'till we got to fightin'. Jim's a bully, but Ah wuz beatin' his socks offa him till he reached down and picked up de hock-bone of Brazzle's ol' mule and lammed me ovah mah head wid it and knocked me out. When Ah come to, he had done took mah turkey and gone. Ah wants uh warrant, Mist' Clarke. Ahm gointer law him outa dis town."

"An' you sho gointer get it, Dave. He oughter be run out. Comes from bad stock. Every last one of his brothers been run out as fast as they grow up. Daddy hung for murder."

Clarke busied himself with the papers. The crowd looking on and commenting.

"See whut you Meth'dis' niggahs will do?" asked Brazzle, a true Baptist. "Goin' round lammin' folks ovah the head an' stealin' they turkeys."

"Cose everybody knows dem Westons is a set uh bullies, but you Baptists ain't such a much," Elijah Moseley retorted.

"Yas, but Ah know yuh know," put in Lindsay. "No Baptis' ain't never done nothin' bad as dat. Joe Clarke is right. Jail is too good fuh 'em. The last one uh these heah half-washed christians oughta be run 'way from heah."

"When it comes tuh dat, there's jus' as many no count Baptists as anybody else. Jus' ain't caught 'em," Thomas said, joining the fray.

"Yas," Lindsay retorted, "but we done kotched yo' Meth'dis' niggah. Kotched him knockin' people ovah de head wid mule bones an' stealin' they turkeys, an' wese gointer run him slap outa town sure as gun's iron. The dirty onion!"

"We don't know whether you will or not, Joe Lindsay. You Baptists ain't runnin' this town exactly."

"Trial set for three o'clock tomorrow at de Baptis' church, that being the largest meetin' place in town," Clarke announced with a satisfied smile and persuaded the men to go back to the porch to argue.

Clarke, himself, was a Methodist, but in this case, his interests lay with the other side. If he could get Jim to taste the air of another town, chicken mortality of the sudden and unexplained variety, would drop considerably, he was certain. He was equally certain that the ambitious Simms would champion Jim's cause and losing the fight, lose prestige. Besides, Jim was a troublesome character. A constant disturber of the village peace.

## III

It was evident to the simplest person in the village long before three o'clock that this was to be a religious and political fight. The assault and the gobbler were unimportant. Dave was a Baptist, Jim a Methodist, only two churches in the town and the respective congregations had lined up solidly.

At three the house was full. The defendant had been led in and seated in the amen corner to the left of the pulpit. Rev. Simms had taken his place beside the prisoner in the role of defense counsel. The plaintiff, with Elder Long, shepherd of the Baptist flock in the capacity of prosecution, was seated at the right. The respective congregations were lined up behind their leaders.

Mutual glances of despisement and gloating were exchanged across the aisle. Not a few verbal sorties were made during this waiting period as if they were getting up steam for the real struggle.

Wize Anderson (Meth.) "Look at ole Dave tryin' to make out Jim hurt his head! Yuh couldn't hurt a Baptist head wid a hammer—they're that hard."

Brother Poke (Bapt.) "Well, anyhow we don't lie an' steal an' git run outa town lak de softhead Meth'dis niggahs."

Some Baptist wag looked over at Jim and crowed like a rooster, the others took it up immediately and the place was full of hen-crackling and barnyard sounds. The implication was obvious. Jim stood up and said, "If I had dat mule bone heah, Ahd teach a few mo' uh you mud-turtles something."

Enter His Honor at this moment. Lum Boger pompously conducted him to his place, the pulpit, which was doing duty as the bench for the occasion. The assembly unconsciously moderated its tone. But from the outside could still be heard the voices of the children engaged in fisticuffy trials of the case.

The mayor began rapping for order at once. "Cote is set. Cote is set! Looka heah, DIS COTE IS DONE SET! Ah wants you folks tuh dry up."

The courtroom grew perfectly still. The mayor prepared to read the charge to the prisoner, when Brother Stringer (Meth.) entered, hot and perspiring with coat over his arm. He found a seat near the middle of the house against the wall. To reach it, he must climb over the knees of a bench length of people. Before seating himself, he hung his coat upon an empty lamp bracket above his head.

Sister Lewis of the Baptist persuasion, arose at once, her hands akimbo, her eyes flashing.

"Brothah Stringah, you take yo' lousy coat down off dese sacred walls! Ain't you Methdis got no gumption in the house uh washup?"

Stringer did not answer her, but he cast over a glance that said as plain as day, "Just try and make me do it!"

Della Lewis snorted, but Stringer took his seat complacently. He took his seat, but rose up again as if he had sat on a hot needle point. The reason for this was that Brother Hambo on the Baptist side, a nasty scrapper, rose and rolled his eyes to the fighting angle, looking at Stringer. Stringer caught the look, and hurriedly pawed that coat down off that wall.

Sister Taylor (M) took up the gauntlet dropped like a hot potato by Stringer. "Some folks" she said with a meaning look, "is a whole lot mo' puhtic'lar 'bout a louse in they church than they is in they house." A very personal look at Sister Lewis.

"Well" said that lady, "mah house mought not be exactly clean. But nobody caint say *dat*"—indicating an infinitesimal amount on the end of her finger—"about my chaRACter! They didn't hafta git de sheriff to make Ike marry ME!"

Mrs. Taylor leaped to her feet and struggled to cross the aisle to her traducer but was restrained by three or four men. "Yas, they did git de sheriff tuh make Sam marry me!" She shouted as she panted and struggled, "And Gawd knows you sho oughter git him again and make *some* of these men marry yo' Ada."

Mrs. Lewis now had to be restrained. She gave voice and hard, bone-breaking words flew back and forth across the aisle. Each was aided and abetted by her side of the house. His Honor was all the time beating the pulpit with his gavel and shouting for order. At last he threatened to descend in person upon the belligerents.

"Heah! You moufy wimmen! Shet up. Ain't Ah done said cote was set? Lum Boger, do yo' duty. Make them wimmen dry up or put 'em outa heah."

Marshall Boger who wore his star for the occasion was full of the importance of his office for nineteen is a prideful age; he hurried over to Mrs. Taylor. She rose to meet him. "You better gwan 'way from me, Lum Boger. Ah jes' wish you would lay de weight of yo' han' on me! Ahd kick yo' cloes up round yo' neck lak a horse collar. You impident limb you."

Lum retreated before the awful prospect of wearing his suit about his neck like a horse-collar. He crossed the aisle to the fiery Della and frowned upon her. She was already standing and ready to commence hostilities. One look was enough. He said nothing, but her threats followed him down the aisle as he retreated to the vestibule to shoo the noisy children away. The women subsided and the Mayor began.

"We come heah on very important business," he said. "Stan' up dere, Jim Weston. You is charged wid 'ssaultin' Dave Carter here wid a mule bone, and robbin' him uh his wild turkey. Is you guilty or not guilty?"

Jim arose, looked insolently around the room and answered the charge: "Yas, Ah hit him and took de turkey cause it wuz mine. Ah hit him and Ahll hit him agin, but it wasn't no crime this time."

His Honor's jaw dropped. There was surprise on the faces of all the Baptist section, surprise and perplexity. Gloating and laughter from the Methodists. Simms pulled Jim's coattail.

"Set down Jim," he cooed, "youse one of mah lambs. Set down. Yo' shepherd will show them that walks in de darkness wid sinners and republicans de light."

Jim sat down and the pastor got to his feet.

"Looka heah, Jim, this ain't for no foolishness. Do you realize dat if youse found guilty, youse gonna be run outa town?"

"Yeah" Jim answered without rising. "But Ah ain't gonna be found no guilty. You caint find me." There was a pleasurable stir on his side of the house. The Baptists were still in the coma which Jim's first statement had brought on.

"Ah say too, he ain't guilty," began Rev. Simms with great unction in his tones. "Ah done been to de cot-house at Orlando an' set under de voice of dem lawyers an' heard 'em law from mornin' tell night. They says you got tuh have a weepon befo' you kin commit uh 'ssault. Ah done read dis heah Bible frum lid tuh lid (he made a gesture to indicate the thoroughness of his search) and it ain't in no Bible dat no mule bone is a weepon, an' it ain't in no white folks law neither. Therefo' Brother Mayor, Ah ast you tuh let Jim go. You gotta turn 'im loose, cause nobody kin run 'im outa town when he ain't done no crime."

A deep purple gloom settled down upon the Mayor and his followers. Over against this the wild joy of the Methodists. Simms already felt the reins of power in his hands. Over the protest of the Mayor he raised a song and he and his followers sang it with great gusto.

*"Oh Mary don't you weep, don't you mourn*
*Oh Mary, don't you weep, don't you mourn*
*Pharoah's army got drownded,*
*O-O-oh Mary, don't you weep"*

The troubled expression on the face of the Baptist leader, Elder Long, suddenly lifted. He arose while yet the triumphant defense was singing its hallelujah. Mayor Clarke quieted the tumult with difficulty. Simms saw him rise but far from being worried, he sank back upon the seat, his eyes half closed, his hands folded fatly across his fat stomach. He smirked. Let them rave! He had built his arguments on solid rock, and the gates of Baptist logic could not prevail against it!

When at last Long got the attention of the assembly, he commanded Dave to stand.

"Ah jus want you all tuh take a look at his head. Anybody kin see dat big knot dat Jim put on dere." Jim, the Rev. Simms and all his communicants laughed loudly at this, but Long went on calmly. "Ah been tuh de cote-house tuh Orlando an' heard de white folks law as much as any body heah. And dey don't ast whether de thing dat a person gits hurt wid is uh weepon or not. All dey wants tuh fin' out is, 'did it hurt?' Now you all kin see dat mule bone did hurt Dave's head. So it must be a weepon 'cause it hurt 'im."

Rev. Simms had his eyes wide open now. He jumped to his feet.

"Never mind 'bout dem white folks laws at O'landa, Brother Long. Dis is a colored town. Nohow we oughter run by de laws uh de Bible. Dem white folks laws don't go befo' whuts in dis sacred book."

"Jes' hold yo' hot potater, Brother Simms, Ahm comin' tuh dat part right now. Jes lemme take yo' Bible a minute."

"Naw indeed. You oughter brought one of yo' own if you got one. Futhermo' Brother Mayor, we got work tuh do. Wese workin' people. Don't keep us in heah too long. Dis case is through wid."

"Oh, naw it ain't" the Mayor disagreed, "you done talked yo' side, now you got tuh let Brother Long talk his. So fur as de work is concerned, it kin wait. One thing at a time. Come on up heah in yo' pulpit an' read yo' own Bible, Brother Long. Don't mind me being up heah."

Long ascended the pulpit and began to turn the leaves of the large Bible. The entire assembly slid forward to the edges of the seat.

"Ah done proved by de white folks law dat Jim oughter be run outa town an' now Ahm gointer show by de Bible—"

Simms was on his feet again. "But Brother Mayor—"

"Set down Simms" was all the answer he got. "Youse *entirely* outa order."

"It says heah in Judges 15:16 dat Samson slewed a thousand Philistines wid de jaw-bone of a ass" Long drawled.

"Yas, but this wasn't no ass, this was a mule" Simms objected.

"And now dat bring us to de main claw uh dis subjick. It sho want no ass, but everybody knows dat a donkey is de father of every mule what ever wuz born. Even little chillen knows dat. Everybody knows dat little as a donkey is, dat if he is dangerous, his great big mule son is mo' so. Everybody knows dat de further back on a mule you goes, de mo' dangerous he gits. Now if de jawbone is as dangerous as it says heah, in de Bible, by de time you gits clear back tuh his hocks he's rank pizen."

"AMEN!! Specially Brazzle's ol' mule," put in Hambo.

"An' dat makes it double 'ssault an' batt'ry," Long continued. "Therefo' Brother Mayor, Ah ast dat Jim be run outa town fuh 'ssaultin Dave wid a deadly weepon an' stealin' his turkey while de boy wuz unconscious."

It was now the turn of the Baptists to go wild. The faint protests of Simms were drowned in the general uproar.

"I'll be henfired if he ain't right!" The Mayor exclaimed when he could make himself heard. "This case is just as plain as day."

Simms tried once more. "But Brother Mayor—"

"Aw be quiet, Simms. You done talked yo'self all outa joint already." His Honor cut him short. "Jim Weston, you git right outa *mah* town befo sundown an' don't lemme ketch you back heah under two yeahs, neither. You folks dats so rearin' tuh fight, gwan outside an' fight all you wants tuh. But don't use no guns, no razors nor no mule-bones. Cote's dismissed."

A general murmur of approval swept over the house. Clarke went on, unofficially, as it were. "By ziggity, dat ol' mule been dead three yeas an' still kickin'! An' he done kicked more'n one person outa whack today." And he gave Simms one of his most personal looks.

CA. 1930–1935, UNPUBLISHED

# $S$*anctuary*

## NELLA LARSEN

### I

On the Southern coast, between Merton and Shawboro, there is a strip of desolation some half a mile wide and nearly ten miles long between the sea and old fields of ruined plantations. Skirting the edge of this narrow jungle is a partly grown-over road which still shows traces of furrows made by the wheels of wagons that have long since rotted away or been cut into firewood. This road is little used, now that the state has built its new highway a bit to the west and wagons are less numerous than automobiles.

In the forsaken road a man was walking swiftly. But in spite of his hurry, at every step he set down his feet with infinite care, for the night was windless and the heavy silence intensified each sound; even the breaking of a twig could be plainly heard. And the man had need of caution as well as haste.

Before a lonely cottage that shrank timidly back from the road the man hesitated a moment, then struck out across the patch of green in front of it. Stepping behind a clump of bushes close to the house, he looked in through the lighted window at Annie Poole, standing at her kitchen table mixing the supper biscuits.

He was a big, black man with pale brown eyes in which there was an odd mixture of fear and amazement. The light showed streaks of gray soil on his heavy, sweating face and great hands, and on his torn clothes. In his woolly hair clung bits of dried leaves and dead grass.

He made a gesture as if to tap on the window, but turned away to the door instead. Without knocking he opened it and went in.

II

The woman's brown gaze was immediately on him, though she did not move. She said, "You ain't in no hurry, is you, Jim Hammer?" It wasn't, however, entirely a question.

"Ah's in trubble, Mis' Poole," the man explained, his voice shaking, his fingers twitching.

"W'at you done done now?"

"Shot a man, Mis' Poole."

"Trufe?" The woman seemed calm. But the word was spat out.

"Yas'm. Shot 'im." In the man's tone was something of wonder, as if he himself could not quite believe that he had really done this thing which he affirmed.

"Daid?"

"Dunno, Mis' Poole. Dunno."

"White man o' niggah?"

"Cain't say, Mis' Poole. White man, Ah reckons."

Annie Poole looked at him with cold contempt. She was a tiny, withered woman—fifty perhaps—with a wrinkled face the color of old copper, framed by a crinkly mass of white hair. But about her small figure was some quality of hardness that belied her appearance of frailty. At last she spoke, boring her sharp little eyes into those of the anxious creature before her.

"An' w'at am you lookin' foh me to do 'bout et?"

"Jes' lemme stop till dey's gone by. Hide me till dey passes. Reckon dey ain't fur off now." His begging voice changed to a frightened whimper. "Foh de Lawd's sake, Mis' Poole, lemme stop."

And why, the woman inquired caustically, should she run the dangerous risk of hiding him?

"Obadiah, he'd lemme stop ef he was home," the man whined.

Annie Poole sighed. "Yas," she admitted, slowly, reluctantly, "Ah spec' he would. Obadiah, he's too good to youall no 'count trash." Her slight shoulders lifted in a hopeless shrug. "Yas, Ah reckon he'd do et. Emspecial' seein' how he allus set such a heap o' store by you. Cain't see w'at foh, mahse'f. Ah shuah don' see nuffin' in you but a heap o' dirt."

But a look of irony, of cunning, of complicity passed over her face.

She went on, "Still, 'siderin' all an' all, how Obadiah's right fon' o' you, an' how white folks is white folks, Ah'm a-gwine hide you dis one time."

Crossing the kitchen, she opened a door leading into a small bedroom, saying "Git yo'se'f in dat dere feather baid an' Ah'm a-gwine put de clo's on de top. Don' reckon dey'll fin' you ef dey does look foh you in mah house. An Ah don' spec' dey'll go foh to do dat. Not lessen you been keerless an' let 'em smell you out gittin' hyah." She turned on him a withering look. "But you allus been triflin'. Cain't do nuffin' propah. An' Ah'm a-tellin' you ef dey warn't white folks an' you a po' niggah, Ah shuah wouldn't be lettin' you mess up mah feather baid dis ebenin', 'cose Ah jes' plain don' want you hyah. Ah done kep' mahse'f outen trubble all mah life. So's Obadiah."

"Ah's powahful 'bliged to you, Mis' Poole. You shuah am one good 'oman. De Lawd'll mos' suttinly—"

Annie Poole cut him off. "Dis ain't no time foh all dat kin' o' fiddle-de-roll. Ah does mah duty as Ah sees et 'thout no thanks from you. Ef de Lawd had gib you a white face 'stead o' dat dere black one, Ah shuah would turn you out. Now hush yo' mouf an' git you'se'f in. An' don' git movin' and scrunchin' undah dose covahs and git yo'se'f kotched in mah house."

Without further comment the man did as he was told. After he had laid his soiled body and grimy garments between her snowy sheets, Annie Poole carefully rearranged the covering and placed piles of freshly laundered linen on top. Then she gave a pat here and there, eyed the result, and finding it satisfactory, went back to her cooking.

### III

Jim Hammer settled down to the racking business of waiting until the approaching danger should have passed him by. Soon savory odors seeped in to him and he realized that he was hungry. He wished that Annie Poole would bring him something to eat. Just one biscuit. But she wouldn't, he knew. Not she. She was a hard one, Obadiah's mother.

By and by he fell into a sleep from which he was dragged back by the rumbling sound of wheels in the road outside. For a second fear clutched so tightly at him that he almost leaped from the suffocating shelter of the bed in order to make some active attempt to escape the horror that his capture meant. There was a spasm at his heart, a pain so sharp, so slashing that he had to suppress an impulse to cry out. He felt himself falling. Down, down, down. . . . Everything grew dim and very distant in his memory. . . . Vanished. . . . Came rushing back.

Outside there was silence. He strained his ears. Nothing. No footsteps. No voices. They had gone on then. Gone without even stopping to ask Annie Poole if she had seen him pass that way. A sigh of relief slipped from him. His thick lips curled in an ugly, cunning smile. It had been smart of him to think of coming to Obadiah's mother's to hide. She was an old demon, but he was safe in her house.

He lay a short while longer listening intently, and, hearing nothing, started to get up. But immediately he stopped, his yellow eyes glowing like pale flames. He had heard the unmistakable sound of men coming toward the house. Swiftly he slid back into the heavy hot stuffiness of the bed and lay listening fearfully.

The terrifying sounds drew nearer. Slowly. Heavily. Just for a moment he thought they were not coming in—they took so long. But there was a light knock and the noise of a door being opened. His whole body went taut. His feet felt frozen, his hands clammy, his tongue like a weighted, dying thing. His pounding heart made it hard for his straining ears to hear what they were saying out there.

"Ebenin', Mistah Lowndes." Annie Poole's voice sounded as it always did, sharp and dry.

There was no answer. Or had he missed it? With slow care he shifted his position, bringing his head nearer the edge of the bed. Still he heard nothing. What were they waiting for? Why didn't they ask about him?

Annie Poole, it seemed, was of the same mind. "Ah don' reckon youall done traipsed way out hyah jes' foh yo' healf," she hinted.

"There's bad news for you, Annie, I'm 'fraid." The sheriff's voice was low and queer.

Jim Hammer visualized him standing out there—a tall, stooped man, his white tobacco-stained mustache drooping limply at the ends, his nose hooked and sharp, his eyes blue and cold. Bill Lowndes was a hard one too. And white.

"W'atall bad news, Mistah Lowndes?" The woman put the question quietly, directly.

"Obadiah—" the sheriff began—hesitated—began again. "Obadiah—ah—er—he's outside, Annie. I'm 'fraid—"

"Shucks! You done missed. Obadiah, he ain't done nuffin', Mistah Lowndes. Obadiah!" she called stridently, "Obadiah! git hyah an' splain yose'f."

But Obadiah didn't answer, didn't come in. Other men came in. Came in with steps that dragged and halted. No one spoke. Not even Annie Poole. Something was laid carefully upon the floor.

"Obadiah, chile," his mother said softly, "Obadiah, chile." Then, with sudden alarm, "He ain't daid, is he? Mistah Lowndes! Obadiah, he ain't daid?"

Jim Hammer didn't catch the answer to that pleading question. A new fear was stealing over him.

"There was a to-do, Annie," Bill Lowndes explained gently, "at the garage back o' the factory. Fellow tryin' to steal tires. Obadiah heerd a noise an' run out with two or three others. Scared the rascal all right. Fired off his gun an' run. We allow et to be Jim Hammer. Picked up his cap back there. Never was no 'count. Thievin' an' sly. But we'll git 'im, Annie. We'll git 'im."

The man huddled in the feather bed prayed silently. "Oh, Lawd! Ah didn't go to do et. Not Obadiah, Lawd. You knows dat. You knows et." And into his frenzied brain came the thought that it would be better for him to get up and go out to them before Annie Poole gave him away. For he was lost now. With all his great strength he tried to get himself out of the bed. But he couldn't.

"Oh Lawd!" he moaned, "Oh Lawd!" His thoughts were bitter and they ran through his mind like panic. He knew that it had come to pass as it said somewhere in the Bible about the wicked. The Lord had stretched out his hand and smitten him. He was paralyzed. He couldn't move hand or foot. He moaned again. It was all there was left for him to do. For in the terror of this new calamity that had come upon him he had forgotten the waiting danger which was so near out there in the kitchen.

His hunters, however, didn't hear him. Bill Lowndes was saying, "We been a-lookin' for Jim out along the old road. Figured he'd make tracks for Shawboro. You ain't noticed anybody pass this evenin', Annie?"

The reply came promptly, unwaveringly. "No, Ah ain't seen nobody pass. Not yet."

## IV

Jim Hammer caught his breath.

"Well," the sheriff concluded, "we'll be gittin' along. Obadiah was a mighty fine boy. Ef they was all like him—. I'm sorry, Annie. Anything I c'n do, let me know."

"Thank you, Mistah Lowndes."

With the sound of the door closing on the departing men, power to move came back to the man in the bedroom. He pushed his dirt-caked feet out from the covers and rose up, but crouched down again. He wasn't cold now, but hot all over and burning. Almost he wished that Bill Lowndes and his men had taken him with them.

Annie Poole had come into the room.

It seemed a long time before Obadiah's mother spoke. When she did there were no tears, no reproaches; but there was a raging fury in her voice as she lashed out, "Git outen mah feather baid, Jim Hammer, an' outen mah house, an' don' nevah stop thankin' yo' Jesus he done gib you dat black face."

From *Forum*, January 1930

# The Wrong Man

## NELLA LARSEN

The room blazed with color. It seemed that the gorgeous things which the women were wearing had for this once managed to subdue the strident tones of the inevitable black and white of the men's costumes. Tonight they lent just enough of preciseness to add interest to the riotously hued scene. The place was crowded but cool, for a gentle breeze blew from the Sound through the large open windows and doors, now and then stirring some group of flowers.

Julia Romley, in spite of the smoke-colored chiffon gown (ordered specially for the occasion) which she was wearing, seemed even more flamingly clad than the rest. The pale indefinite gray but increased the flaring mop of her hair; scarlet, a poet had called it. The satiny texture of her skin seemed also to reflect in her cheeks a cozy tinge of that red mass.

Julia, however, was not happy tonight. A close observer would have said that she was actively disturbed. Faint abstraction, trite remarks nervously offered, and uncontrolled restlessness marred her customary perfect composure. Her dreamy gray eyes stole frequently in the direction of Myra Redmon's party. Myra always had a lion in tow, but why that particular man? She shook a little as she wondered.

Suddenly, the orchestra blared into something wild and impressionistic, with a primitive staccato understrain of jazz. The buzz of conversation died, strangled by the savage strains of the music. The crowd stirred, broke, coalesced into twos, and became a whirling mass. A partner claimed Julia and they became part of the swaying mob.

"Some show, what?" George Hill's drawling voice was saying, while he secretly wondered what had got into Julia; she was so quiet, not like herself at all.

Julia let her eyes wander over the moving crowd. Young men, old men, young women, older women, slim girls, fat women, thin men, stout men, glided by. The old nursery rhyme came into her mind. She repeated it to George in a singsong tone:

*"Rich man, poor man,*
*Beggar man, thief,*
*Doctor, lawyer,*
*Indian chief."*

George nodded. "Yes, that's it. Everybody's here and a few more. And look, look! There's the 'Indian chief.' Wonder who he is? He certainly looks the part."

Julia didn't look; she knew what she would see. A tall, thin man, his lean face yellowed and hardened as if by years in the tropics; a man, perhaps, a bit unused to scenes of this kind, purposely a little aloof and, one suspected, more than a little contemptuous.

She felt a flash of resentful anger against Myra. Why was she always carting about impossible people? It was disgusting. It was worse—it was dangerous. Certainly it was about to become dangerous to her, Julia Romley, erstwhile. . . . She let the thought die unfinished, it was too unpleasant.

She had been so happy, so secure, and now this: Ralph Tyler, risen from the past to shatter the happiness which she had grasped for herself. Must she begin all over again? She made a hasty review of her life since San Francisco days: Chicago and the art school where she had studied interior decorating with the money that Ralph Tyler had given her; New York, her studio and success; Boston, and marriage to Jim Romley. And now this envied gay life in one of Long Island's most exclusive sets. Yes, life had been good to her at last, better than she had ever dreamed. Was she about to lose everything—love, wealth, and position? She shivered.

"Cold?" Again George's drawling voice dragging her back to the uncertain present.

"No, not cold. Just someone walking over my grave," she answered laughingly. "I'm rotten company tonight, George. I'm sorry; I'll do better. It's the crowd, I guess."

Her husband claimed her for the next dance. A happy married pair, their obvious joy in each other after five wedded years was the subject of amused comment and mild jokes among their friends. "The everlasting lovers," they were dubbed, and the name suited them as perfectly as they suited each other.

"What's wrong, Julie, old girl?" asked Jim after a few minutes' baffled scrutiny. "Tired?"

"Nothing, nothing. I just feel small, so futile in this crush; sort of trapped, you know. Why *do* the Arnolds have so many people to their things?" Quickly regretting her display of irritation, she added: "It's wonderful, though—the people, the music, the color, and these lovely rooms, like a princess's ball in a fairy tale."

"Yes, great," he agreed. "Lots of strangers here, too; most of them distinguished people from town."

"Who's the tall browned man with Myra, who looks like—well, like an Indian chief?" She laughed a little at her own pleasantry, just to show Jim that there was nothing troubling her.

"Doesn't he, though? Sort of self-sufficient and superior and a bit indifferent, as if he owned us all and despised the whole tribe of us. I guess you can't blame him much. He probably thinks we're a soft, lazy, self-pampering lot. He's Ralph Tyler, an explorer, just back from some godforsaken place on the edge of nowhere. Been head of some expedition lost somewhere in Asia for years, given up for dead. Discovered a buried city or something; great contribution to civilization and all that, you know. They say he brought back some emeralds worth a king's ransom."

"Do you know him, Jim?"

"Yes; knew him years ago in college. Didn't think he'd remember me after such a long time and all those thrilling adventures, but he did. Honestly, you could have knocked me over with a feather when he came over to me and put out his hand and said, 'Hello there, Jim Romley.' Nice, wasn't it?" Jim's handsome face glowed. He was undoubtedly flattered by the great man's remembrance. He went on enthusiastically: "I'm going to have him out to the house, Julie; that is, if I can get him. Small, handpicked dinner party. What say?"

She shivered again.

"Cold?"

"No, not cold. Just someone walking over my grave." She laughed, amused at the double duty of the superstition in one evening, and glad too that Jim had not noticed that his question had passed unanswered.

Dance followed dance. She wasn't being a success tonight. She knew it, but somehow she couldn't make small talk. Her thoughts kept wandering to that tall browned man who had just come back from the world's end. One or two of her partners, after trying in vain to draw her out, looked at her quizzically, wondering if the impossible had happened. Had Julia and old Jim quarreled?

At last she escaped to a small deserted room on an upper floor, where she could be alone to think. She groped about in her mind for some way to avoid that dinner party. It spelled disaster. She must find some way to keep Ralph Tyler from finding out that she was the wife of his old schoolmate. But if he were going to be here for any length of time, and Jim seemed to think that he would, she would have to meet him. Perhaps she could go away? . . . No, she dared not; anything might happen. Better to be on hand to ward off the blow when it fell. She sighed, suddenly weary and beaten. It was hopeless. And she had been so happy! Just a faint shadow of uneasiness, at first, which had gradually faded as the years slipped away.

She sat for a long time in deep thought. Her face settled into determined lines; she made up her mind. She would ask, plead if necessary, for his silence. It was the only way. It would be hard, humiliating even, but it must be done if she were to continue to be happy in Jim's love. She couldn't bear to look ahead to years without him.

She crossed the room and wrote a note to Ralph Tyler, asking him to meet her in the summerhouse in one of the gardens. She hesitated a moment over the signature, finally writing *Julia Hammond*, in order to prepare him a little for the meeting.

After she had given the note into the hand of a servant for delivery "to Mr. Tyler, the man with Mrs. Redmon," she experienced a slight feeling of relief. "At least I can try," she thought as she made her way to the summerhouse to wait. "Surely, if I tell him about myself and Jim, he'll be merciful."

The man looked curiously at the woman sitting so motionless in the summerhouse in the rock garden. Even in the darkness she felt his gaze upon her, though she lacked the courage to raise her eyes to look at him. She waited expectantly for him to speak.

After what seemed hours but was, she knew, only seconds, she understood that he was waiting for her to break the silence. So she began to speak in a low hesitating voice:

"I suppose you think it strange, this request of mine to meet me here alone; but I had to see you, to talk to you. I wanted to tell you about my marriage to Jim Romley. You know him?"

"Yes, I know him."

"Well," she went on, eagerly now, "you see, we're so happy! Jim's so splendid, and I've tried to be such a good wife. And I thought—I thought—you see, I thought—" The eager voice trailed off on a note of entreaty.

"Yes, you thought?" prompted the man in a noncommittal tone.

"Well, you see, I thought that if you knew how happy we were, and how much I love him, and that since you know Jim, that you—you—"

She stopped. She couldn't go on, she simply couldn't. But she must. There he stood like a long, menacing shadow between her and the future. She began again, this time with insinuating flattery:

"You have so much yourself now—honor, fame, and money—and you've done such splendid things! You've suffered too. How you must have suffered! Oh, I'm glad of your success; you deserve it. You're a hero, a great man. A little thing like that can't matter to you now and it means everything to me, everything. Please spare me my little happiness. Please be kind!"

"But I don't understand." The man's voice was puzzled. "How 'kind'? What is it you're asking?"

Reading masked denial in the question, Julia began to sob softly.

"Don't tell Jim! Please, don't tell Jim! I'll do anything to keep him from knowing, anything."

"But aren't you making a mistake? I—"

"Mistake?" She laughed bitterly. "I see; you think I should have told him. You think that even now I should tell him that I was your mistress once. You don't know Jim. He'd never forgive that. He wouldn't understand that, when a girl has been sick and starving on the streets, anything can happen to her; that she's grateful for food and shelter at any price. You won't tell him, will you?"

"But I'm sure," stammered the tall figure, fumbling for cigarettes, "I'm sure you've made a mistake. I'm sorry. I've been trying to—"

Julia cut him off. She couldn't bear to hear him speak the refusing words, his voice seemed so grimly final. She knew it was useless, but she made a last desperate effort:

"I was so young, so foolish, and so hungry; but Jim wouldn't understand." She choked over the last words.

He shook his head—impatiently, it seemed to the agonized woman. "Mrs. Romley, I've been trying to tell you that you've made a mistake. I'm sorry. However, I can assure you that your secret is safe with me. It will never be from my lips that Jim Romley hears you have been—er— what you say you have been."

Only the woman's sharply drawn quivering breath indicated that she had heard. A match blazed for a moment as he lighted his cigarette with shaking hands. Julia's frightened eyes picked out his face in the flickering light. She uttered a faint dismayed cry.

She had told the wrong man.

FROM *YOUNG'S MAGAZINE*, JANUARY 1926

# $F$*reedom*

## NELLA LARSEN

He wondered, as he walked deftly through the impassioned traffic on the Avenue, how she would adjust her life if he were to withdraw from it. . . . How peaceful it would be to have no woman in one's life! These months away took on the appearance of a liberation, a temporary recess from a hateful existence in which he lived in intimacy with someone he did not know and would not now have chosen. . . . He began, again, to speculate on the pattern her life would take without him. Abruptly, it flashed upon him that the vague irritation of many weeks was a feeling of smoldering resentment against her.

The displeasure that this realization caused him increased his ill humor and distaste. He began to dissect her with an acrimony that astonished himself. Her unanimated beauty seemed now only a thin disguise for an inert mind, and not for the serene beauty of soul which he had attributed to her. He suspected, too, a touch of depravity, perhaps only physical, but more likely mental as well. Reflection convinced him that her appeal for him was bounded by the senses, for witness his disgust and clarity of vision, now that they were separated. How could he have been so blinded? Why, for him she had been the universe; a universe personal and unheedful of outside persons or things. He had adored her in a slavish fashion. He groaned inwardly at his own mental caricature of himself, sitting dumb, staring at her in fatuous worship. What an ass he had been!

His work here was done, but what was there to prevent him from staying away for six months—a year—forever? . . . Never to see her again! . . . He stopped, irresolute. What would she do? He tried to construct a representation of her future without him. In his present new hatred, she became a creature irresistibly given to pleasure at no matter what cost. A sybarite! A parasite too!

He was prayerfully thankful that appreciation of his danger had come before she had sapped from him all physical and spiritual vitality. But her future troubled him even while he assured himself that he knew its road, and laughed ruefully at the picture of her flitting from mate to mate.

A feverish impatience gripped him. Somehow, he must contrive to get himself out of the slough into which his amorous folly had precipitated him. . . . Three years. Good God! At the moment, those three years seemed the most precious of his life. And he had foolishly thrown them away. He had drifted pleasantly, peacefully, without landmarks; would be drifting yet but for the death of a friend whose final affairs had brought him away. . . .

He started. Death! Perhaps she would die. How that would simplify matters for him. But no; she would not die. He laughed without amusement. She would not die; she would outlast him, damn her! . . . An angry resentment, sharp and painful as whiplash, struck him. Its passing left him calm and determined. . . .

He braced himself and continued to walk. He had decided; he would stay. With this decision, he seemed to be reborn, He felt cool, refreshed, as if he had stepped out from a warm, scented place into a cold, brisk breeze. He was happy. The world had turned to silver and gold, and life again became a magical adventure. Even the placards in the shops shone with the light of paradise upon them. One caught and held his eye. Travel . . . Yes, he would travel; lose himself in India, China, the South Seas . . . Radiance from the most battered vehicle and the meanest pedestrian. Gladness flooded him. He was free.


A year, thick with various adventures, had slid by since that spring day on which he had wrenched himself free. He had lived, been happy, and with no woman in his life. The break had been simple: a telegram hinting at prolonged business and indefinite return. There had been no reply. This had annoyed him, but he told himself it was what he had expected. He would not admit that, perhaps, he had missed her letter in his wanderings. He had persuaded himself to believe what he wanted to believe—that she had not cared. Actually, there had been confusion in his mind, a complex of thoughts which made it difficult to know what he really had thought. He had imagined that he shuddered at the idea that she had accepted the most generous offer. He pitied her. There was, too, a touch of sadness, a sense of something lost, which he irritably explained on the score of her beauty. Beauty of any kind always stirred him. . . . Too bad a woman like that couldn't be decent. He was well rid of her.

But what had she done? How had he taken it? His contemptuous mood visualized her at times, laughing merrily at some jest made by his successor, or again sitting silent, staring into the fire. He would be conscious of every detail of her appearance: her hair simply arranged, her soft dark eyes, her delicate chin propped on hands rivaling the perfection of La Gioconda's. Sometimes there would be a reversion to the emotions which had ensnared him, when he ached with yearning, when he longed for her again. Such moments were rare.


Another year passed, during which his life had widened, risen, and then crashed. . . .

Dead? How could she be dead? Dead in childbirth, they had told him, both his mistress and the child she had borne him. She had been dead on that spring day when, resentful and angry at her influence in his life, he had reached out toward freedom—to find only a mirage; for he saw quite plainly that now he would never be free. It was she who had escaped him. Each time he had cursed and wondered, it had been a dead woman whom he had cursed and about whom he had wondered . . . . He shivered; he seemed always to be cold now. . . .

Well rid of her! How well he had not known, nor how easily. She was dead. And he had cursed her. But one didn't curse the dead. . . . Didn't one? Damn her! Why couldn't she have lived, or why hadn't she died sooner? For long months he had wondered how she had arranged her life, and all the while she had done nothing but to complete it by dying.

The futility of all his speculations exasperated him. His old resentment returned. She *had* spoiled his life; first by living and then by dying. He hated the fact that she had finished with him, rather than he with her. He could not forgive her. . . . Forgive her? She was dead. He felt somehow that, after all, the dead did not care if you forgave them or not.

Gradually, his mind became puppet to a disturbing tension which drove it back and forth between two thoughts: he had left her; she was dead. These two facts became lodged in his mind like burrs pricking at his breaking faculties. As he recalled the manner of his leaving her, it seemed increasingly brutal. She had died loving him, bearing him a child, and he had left her. He tried to shake off the heavy mental dejection which weighed him down, but his former will and determination deserted him. The vitality of the past, forever dragging him down into black depression, frightened him. The mental fog, thick as soot, into which the news of her death had trapped him, appalled him. He must get himself out. A wild anger seized him. He began to think of his own death, self-inflicted, with feeling that defied analysis. His zest for life became swallowed up in the rising tide of sorrow and mental chaos which was engulfing him.

As autumn approached, with faint notice on his part, his anger and resentment retreated, leaving in their wake a gentle stir of regret and remorse. Imperceptibly, he grew physically weary; a strange sensation of loneliness and isolation enveloped him. A species of timidity came upon him; he felt an unhappy remoteness from people, and began to edge away from life.

His deepening sense of isolation drove him more and more back upon his memories. Sunk in his armchair before the fire, he passed the days and sometimes the nights, for he had lost count of these, merged as they were into one another.

His increasing mental haziness had rejected the fact of her death; often she was there with him, just beyond the firelight or the candlelight. She talked and laughed with him. Sometimes, at night, he woke to see her standing over him or sitting in his chair before the dying fire. By some mysterious process, the glory of the first love flamed again in him. He forgot that they had ever parted. His twisted memories visioned her with him in places where she had never been. He had forgotten all but the past and that was brightly distorted.

He sat waiting for her. He seemed to remember that she had promised to come. Outside, the street was quiet. She was late. Why didn't she come? Childish tears fell over his cold cheeks. He sat weeping in front of the sinking fire.

A nameless dread seized him; she would not come! In the agony of his disappointment, he did not see that the fire had died and the candles had sputtered out. He sat wrapped in immeasurable sadness. He knew that she would not come.

Something in this thought fired his disintegrating brain. She would not come; then he must go to her.

He rose, shaking with cold, and groped toward the door. Yes, he would go to her.

The gleam of a streetlight through a French window caught his attention. He stumbled toward it. His cold fingers fumbled a moment with the catch, but he tore it open with a spark of his old determination and power, and stepped out—and down to the pavement a hundred feet below.

FROM *YOUNG'S MAGAZINE*, APRIL 1926

# BIOGRAPHICAL NOTES

For some of the writers in this collection, biographical information was difficult to come by. Some of them did not write much other than one or two stories in *The Crisis* or *Opportunity*, and only rarely did the journals provide biographical headnotes.

## Gwendolyn Bennett (1902–1981)

Educated as both an artist and a writer, Gwendolyn Bennett was born in Giddings, Texas and educated in both Washington, D.C. and Brooklyn, New York. The daughter of a lawyer and a teacher, she went on to study fine arts at Teachers College at Columbia University and graduated from the Pratt Institute in 1924. While studying at Pratt she wrote two class plays. In 1925 Bennett won a sorority scholarship from Delta Sigma Theta to study art in France. In France she found other artists and painters who supported her artistic endeavors. Upon returning to New York, she became assistant editor for *Opportunity* magazine, during which time she wrote her own column, "Ebony Flute," a review of current literary, artistic, and social news. Bennett also coedited the controversial publication *Fire!!*, in which her first short story, "Wedding Day," appeared. Later, Bennett taught water color, design, and crafts at Howard University. After her marriage she abandoned her artistic career, but continued to teach. In 1935, after her husband's death, Bennett returned to Harlem. Back in the artistic community, Bennett became the director of the Harlem Community Arts Center, a position that she held until 1940. She eventually married a second time and retired to Kutztown, Pennsylvania, where she and her husband owned and operated an antique store, until her death.

## Marita [Odette] Bonner [Occomy] (1899–1971)

Marita Bonner was born and educated in Brookline, Massachusetts. She graduated from Radcliffe in 1922 with a degree in English and comparative literature. After graduation Bonner moved to Bluefield, Virginia, where she taught at the Bluefield Colored Institute. She then relocated to Washington, D.C., where she taught English at Armstrong High School. Bonner first gained acclaim for her writing when she won *The Crisis* literary contest in 1925 with her essay, "On Being Young—A Woman and Colored." The following year she won a prize in *The Crisis* contest for her story "Drab Rambles." Bonner frequented Georgia Douglas Johnson's S Street Salon and became a member of the Krigwa Players through contacts made with Johnson. Johnson encouraged Bonner to become a playwright, and in 1927 her "Purple Flower" won the *Crisis* award for best play. When Bonner married William Occomy in 1930, she moved to Chicago, where she continued to teach (at Phillips High School and the Doolittle School for developmentally impaired children) and where her three children were born. The literary works that she produced while living in Chicago set the model for the next generation of African-American writers, including Richard Wright. Bonner's death was precipitated by a fire in her Chicago apartment.

## Anita Scott Coleman (1890–1960)

Anita Scott Coleman was a poet, short story writer, and essayist. She was born in Guaymas, Sonora, Mexico to a Cuban father who bought her mother as a slave and who later fought for the Union in the Civil War. Educated in Silver City, New Mexico, Coleman began teaching school in Los Angeles. Later she operated a boarding house for children and wrote stories for children as well. Although she sometimes wrote under the pseudonym Elizabeth Stapleton Stokes, stories and essays that she wrote under her own name were well received in the African-American literary community. In 1926, Coleman won second prize in the *Opportunity* literary contest for her nonfiction sketch "Dark Horse." That same year she won second prize in an Amy Spingarn contest in literature and art, sponsored by *The Crisis*, for her essay "Unfinished Masterpieces" and third prize for her short story "Three Dogs and a Rabbit" in *The Crisis* literary contest. Coleman published two books of poetry: *Reason for Singing* in 1948 and *Singing Bells* in 1961.

## Alice Moore Dunbar-Nelson (1875–1935)

As is evident in much of her early short fiction, Alice Dunbar-Nelson grew up in New Orleans in a middle-class family. She studied at Straight College (now Dillard University) and graduated in 1892. Following graduation, Dunbar-Nelson began teaching in New Orleans, but she began to further her education in 1896 at Cornell University, Columbia University, and the University of Pennsylvania. *Violets and Other Tales* (1895), a collection of poetry and sketches, was her first published work; it was followed by her short story anthology *The Goodness of St. Rocque* in 1898. Her other published writings include *Masterpieces of Negro Eloquence* (1914) and *The Dunbar Speaker and Entertainer* (1920). Poet Paul Lawrence Dunbar read some of her poetry in a Boston magazine and became steadfastly interested in her; they married in 1898. Her career as a political activist began when she became secretary of the National Association of Colored Women in 1897. Dunbar-Nelson's marriage to Paul Lawrence Dunbar was short-lived: they separated in 1902, and he died shortly thereafter in 1906. Dunbar-Nelson relocated once again, to Wilmington, Delaware, where she taught English at the all-black Howard High School. She remained there for eighteen years and eventually became head of the English department. While teaching and writing, she remained active in politics, and became the first African-American woman to be a member of the Delaware Republican State Committee, to which she was elected in 1920. She married journalist John Robert Nelson in 1916 and together they edited and published the *Wilmington Advocate*, a paper dedicated to the advancement of African Americans. Through her later work in education, she cofounded the Delaware Industrial School for Colored Girls and volunteered as a teacher and parole worker. She eventually succumbed to a heart ailment and died in Philadelphia in 1935.

## *Jessie Redmon Fauset (1882–1961)*

Jessie Fauset was born in Camden County, New Jersey, the seventh child of an African Methodist Episcopal minister; she grew up in Philadelphia, Pennsylvania. Her mother died when she was very young, and her father remarried. Fauset was the only African-American student in her high school. After graduating, she tried to attend Bryn Mawr College but was rejected because of her race. She went on to study classical languages at Cornell University, from which she graduated in 1905, as one of the first African-American women to graduate with Phi Beta Kappa honors. In her first attempt to teach after graduation, Fauset came once again face to face with racism in Philadelphia, so she moved to Baltimore and taught Latin and French at the all-black Douglas High School and later at M Street High School in Washington, D.C., which later became Dunbar High School. She decided to continue her education at the University of Pennsylvania, where she graduated with a master's degree, and also studied for one year at the Sorbonne in Paris. Eventually taking up residence in New York City, Fauset became literary editor of *The Crisis* magazine. Throughout her tenure there her short stories, novelettes, poetry, translations, reviews, critiques, and essays were published in the magazine. She simultaneously edited *The Brownie's Book*, a magazine for black children. During this period she also traveled abroad. In 1921, Fauset was sponsored by Delta Sigma Theta sorority to attend the second Pan-African Congress in Paris, and while in Europe she traveled to London and Brussels as well, where she lectured on the condition of African-American women in the United States. Fauset traveled to Africa for the first time in 1924; after this visit she returned to Paris again. The most prolific woman writer of the Harlem Renaissance, she wrote four novels in the space of a decade: *There Is Confusion* (1924), *Plum Bun* (1929), *Chinaberry Tree* (1931), and *Comedy: American Style* (1933). She eventually left *The Crisis* in 1926, over a skirmish with DuBois. She went back to teaching French at DeWitt Clinton High School in New York and married Herbert Harris in 1929. Together they eventually settled in Montclair, New Jersey. Fauset died in her home town of Philadelphia, of heart failure.

## Angelina Weld Grimké (1880–1958)

The child of Archibald Grimké, a former slave, and Sarah Stanley, a wealthy white woman, Angelina Weld Grimké was born and brought up in Boston. Her mother left shortly after her birth, and Grimké was raised primarily by her father. Grimké's famous abolitionist and feminist aunts, Sarah Grimké and Angelina Grimké Weld, strongly influenced her as well. Throughout her education, Grimké was the only African-American student in the schools she attended. She graduated from Boston Normal School of Gymnastics in 1902 and moved to Washington, D.C., where she taught English at Dunbar High School. While teaching, she wrote poetry, short fiction, and plays for various periodicals. In 1916 she wrote the play *Rachel*, which was first produced at Myrtilla Miner Normal School the same year, and later produced elsewhere. Grimké was attracted to other women, especially to her contemporary poets, such as Clarissa Scott Delany, Georgia Douglas Johnson, and Mary Burrill; much of her writing, especially her poetry, contains lesbian subject matter. When her father died in 1930, Grimké was devastated; she subsequently gave up teaching and moved to New York, where she lived in seclusion until her death in 1958.

## Zora Neale Hurston (1901–1960)

Zora Neale Hurston's home town, the all-black Eatonville, Florida, became the backdrop for her stories and novels, which are steeped in the African-American folklore of the South. Hurston grew up with seven siblings and went to school at Morgan Academy in Baltimore. She later attended Howard University and studied with Alain Locke. Hurston wrote her short story "John Redding Goes to Sea" for the Howard University campus magazine *Stylus* in 1921. While studying anthropology at Barnard College, from which she graduated in 1928, Hurston became involved with the literary community in Harlem and began to publish her short stories and folklore in African-American periodicals. Her short story "Spunk" won second prize in the 1925 *Opportunity* magazine literary contest. The following year her play "Color Struck" won second prize in the same contest. After graduating from Barnard, Hurston was awarded a fellowship from the Association for the Study of Negro Life and History to collect folklore throughout the South, but even while she conducted her anthropological research, she still involved herself in the literary world. With Gwendolyn Bettett, Langston Hughes, and Wallace Thurman, she became a cofounder and coeditor of *Fire!!* In 1934 she was awarded a Julius Rosenwald Fellowship to study anthropology and folklore; and in 1936 and 1937 two Guggenheim Fellowships to study magical practices. During and after the Renaissance, Hurston published several novels, including *Jonah's Gourd Vine* (1934), *Mules and Men* (1935), *Their Eyes Were Watching God* (1937), *Moses Man of the Mountain* (1939), and *Seraph on the Suwanee* (1948). Despite her success, she died obsure and penniless in her home state of Florida.

## Georgia Douglas Johnson (1886–1966)

Georgia Douglas Johnson was born in Atlanta, Georgia but later came to call Washington, D.C. her home. She studied music and literature at Atlanta University and Oberlin Conservatory of Music in Oberlin, Ohio. Johnson became a teacher as well as a poet and playwright and later worked for the government. During her lifetime she published four volumes of poetry: *The Heart of a Woman* (1918), *Bronze: A Book of Verse* (1922), *An Autumn Love Cycle* (1928), and *Share My World: A Book of Poems* (1962). Her "Plumes: Folk Tragedy" won the award for best play in *Opportunity* magazine's contest for 1927. Johnson made her home available to many other African-American writers during and after the Harlem Renaissance. Her S Street Salon in Washington, D.C. was a meeting ground where writers could share their work with each other. Johnson continued writing until her death in 1966.

## Nella Larsen [Imes] (1891–1963)

Larsen was born in Chicago to a white Danish mother and a black West Indian father. When her father died, Larsen's mother decided to marry a white man. Brought up with this mixed-racial heritage, Larsen became preoccupied with the theme of marginality, and through her novels, *Quicksand* (1928), and *Passing* (1929), she explored what it means to belong simultaneously to the black and white communities. When she was sixteen, Larsen traveled through Denmark to discover her matrilineal heritage. She studied at both white and black institutions: first at Fisk University, then later at the University of Copenhagen, still later at the Lincoln Hospital Training Program in the Bronx, from which she graduated in 1915. Larsen then became a nurse at Tuskegee Hospital in Alabama. Still not satisfied with her work, Larsen moved to New York and entered the New York Public Library Training School and became a children's librarian at the 135th Street branch library in Harlem from 1922 to 1929. While working at this library, Larsen made many contacts and found a community that encouraged her writing career. She married physicist Elmer Imes in 1919, but divorced him in 1933. Her novel *Quicksand* won the bronze medal from the Harmon Foundation in 1929. In 1930 Larsen became the first African-American woman to win a Guggenheim for creative writing. It was intended to assist her in writing her third novel, but this novel never became a reality, because of the scandal over her story "Sanctuary." Even though Larsen successfully refuted the charge of plagiarism, she felt impelled to disappear from the literary scene. For a short time she worked as assistant secretary for the Writers League Against Lynching, a racially mixed organization combating murder and violence. She spent most of her later life as a nurse at Bethel Hospital in Brooklyn, New York and died in obscurity of heart failure.

## Eloise Bibb Thompson (1878–1928)

Poet, short story writer, journalist, and playwright, Eloise Bibb Thompson resembled Alice Dunbar-Nelson not only in the diversity of her writing abilities but also in her middle-class upbringing and place of birth, New Orleans. In 1895, when she was only seventeen, her first book, *Poems*, was published by Boston's Monthly Review Press, who published Dunbar-Nelson's first book that same year. Thompson attended Oberlin College's Preparatory Academy from 1899 to 1901 and subsequently taught for two years in New Orleans. She eventually graduated from Howard University's Teacher's College and became head resident of the Social Settlement House at Howard from 1908 to 1911. In 1911 she married Noah Davis Thompson and together they moved to Los Angeles. While in Los Angeles, Thompson wrote for the *Los Angeles Tribune* and the *Morning Sun*. She wrote three plays—*Caught*, *Africans*, and *Cooped Up*—all of which were produced. She moved to New York City in 1927 when Noah became the business manager for *Opportunity*. The following year she died, ending a short but brilliant career.

## Dorothy West (1912–     )

Dorothy West was the only child of Isaac Christopher West, an ex-slave, and Rachel Pease Benson. She grew up in Boston and attended Girls Latin High School and, later, Boston University and the Columbia School of Journalism. At eighteen, West won second place in the *Opportunity* literary contest with her first short story, "The Typewriter." In 1927, to help support her writing, West auditioned for and landed a small part in the original stage production of *Porgy*. When the show went to London in 1929, West accompanied the cast and crew for its short three-months run. She became a member of Boston's Saturday Evening Quill Club and wrote short stories for their magazine of the same name. (This group of African-American writers financed the magazine themselves in order to publish their work.) West joined a group of Harlem Renaissance artists, including Langston Hughes, who went traveling to Russia to make a propaganda film about African Americans, entitled *Black and White*, but it was never filmed. As one of the youngest of the Harlem Renaissance writers, she continued writing after the Renaissance, as a social and cultural phenomenon had ended, and, with money left over from the film venture, became editor of *Challenge* magazine in her efforts to keep African Americans still writing and publishing. She managed to get Claude McKay, Zora Neale Hurston, and Countee Cullen, as well as other writers, to contribute to her magazine. West was initially the sole editor and financial backer for the magazine; when the name changed to *New Challenge*, Richard Wright and Marian Minos joined the editorial board. She wrote under the pseudonym Mary Christopher in some of the issues of *Challenge*. In 1948 West published her novel *The Living Is Easy*, which has made an important contribution to the African-American literary tradition. Currently, she lives in Martha's Vineyard and continues to write short stories as well as a column, "Oak Bluffs," for the *Martha's Vineyard Gazette*.

# BIBLIOGRAPHY

Ammons, Elizabeth. *Conflicting Stories*. New York: Oxford University Press, 1991.

———. "New Literary History: Edith Wharton and Jessie Redmon Fauset." *College Literature* 14 (1987): 207–218.

Anderson, Jervis. *This Was Harlem 1900–1950*. New York: Farrar Straus & Giroux, 1981.

Baker, Houston A., Jr. *The Journey Back: Issues in Black Literature and Criticism*. Chicago: University of Chicago Press, 1980.

———. *Modernism and the Harlem Renaissance*. Chicago: University of Chicago Press, 1987.

Bell, Bernard W. *The Afro-American Novel and Its Tradition*. Amherst: University of Massachusetts Press, 1987.

Bone, Robert. *The Negro Novel in America*. New Haven: Yale University Press, 1965.

Bonner, Marita. *Frye Street and Environs: The Collected Works of Marita Bonner*. Boston: Beacon, 1987.

Bontemps, Arna, ed. *The Harlem Renaissance Remembered*. New York: Dodd, Mead & Co., 1972.

Bowen, Angela. "The Literary Tradition of Black Women." *Sojourner*, June 1984, 20–21.

Carby, Hazel. *Reconstructing Womanhood*. New York: Oxford University Press, 1987.

Christian, Barbara. *Black Women Novelists*. Westport, Conn.: Greenwood, 1980.

Cohee, Gail and Leslie Lewis. *Sisters of the Harlem Renaissance: A Photographic Postcard Series*. Bloomington: Helaine Victoria, 1991.

Cullen, Countee. *My Soul's High Song*. Ed. Gerald Early. New York: Anchor, 1991.

Davis, Arthur P. *From the Dark Tower: Afro-American Writers 1900–1960*. Washington, D.C.: Howard University Press, 1981.

Draper, Muriel. *Music at Midnight*. New York: Harper & Row, 1929.

Dunbar-Nelson, Alice. *The Goodness of St. Rocque and Other Stories.* New York: Dodd, Mead, & Co., 1899.

————. *Violets and Other Tales.* Boston: Monthly Review, 1895.

Fabre, Michel. *From Harlem to Paris: Black American Writers in France, 1840–1980.* Urbana: University of Illinois Press, 1991.

Fauset, Jessie Redmon. *The Chinaberry Tree.* New York: Frederick A. Stokes, 1931.

————. *Comedy American Style.* College Park, Md.: McGrath, 1969.

————. *Plum Bun: A Novel without a Moral.* Boston: Beacon, 1990.

————. *There Is Confusion.* Boston: Northeastern University Press, 1989.

Feeney, Joseph J. "Black Childhood as Ironic: A Nursery Rhyme Transformed in Jessie Fauset's Novel *Plum Bun.*" *Minority Voices* 4 (1980): 65–69.

Ferguson, Sally Ann. "Dorothy West and Helen Johnson in *Infants of the Spring.*" *Langston Hughes Review* 2 (1983): 22–24.

Fisher, Rudolph. *The Walls of Jericho.* New York: Arno, 1969.

Gates, Henry Louis Jr., ed. *Reading Black, Reading Feminist.* New York: Penguin, 1990.

Giddings, Paula. *When and Where I Enter: The Impact of Black Women on Race and Sex in America.* New York: William Morrow & Co., 1984.

Grimké, Angelina Weld. *Rachel: A Play in Three Acts.* College Park, Md.: McGrath, 1969.

Hemenway, Robert. *Zora Neale Hurston: A Literary Biography.* Urbana: University of Illinois Press, 1977.

Hernton, Calvin C. *The Sexual Mountain and Black Women Writers.* New York: Anchor, 1990.

Honey, Maureen., ed. *Shadowed Dreams.* New Brunswick, N.J.: Rutgers University Press, 1989.

Huggins, Nathan Irvin. *Harlem Renaissance.* New York: Oxford University Press, 1971.

Hughes, Langston. *The Best of Simple.* New York: Hill and Wang, 1961.

————. *The Big Sea.* New York: Thunder's Mouth, 1940.

————. *Five Plays By Langston Hughes.* Bloomington: Indiana University Press, 1968.

————. *I Wonder as I Wander.* New York: Thunder's Mouth, 1940.

————. *The Selected Poems of Langston Hughes.* New York: Vintage, 1990.

————. *The Ways of White Folks.* New York: Vintage, 1990.

Hughes, Langston and Zora Neale Hurston. *Mule Bone: A Comedy of Negro Life.* New York: HarperCollins, 1991.

Hull, Gloria T. *Color, Sex, and Poetry.* Bloomington: Indiana University Press, 1987.

————. "Shaping Contradictions: Alice Dunbar-Nelson and the Black Creole Experience." *New Orleans Review* 15 (1988): 34–37.

————, ed. *Give Us Each Day: The Diary of Alice Dunbar-Nelson.* New York: W. W. Norton, 1984.

Hurston, Zora Neale. *Dust Tracks on A Road.* New York: HarperCollins, 1991.
———. *Jonah's Gourd Vine.* New York: HarperCollins, 1990.
———. *Mules and Men.* New York: HarperCollins, 1990.
———. *Sanctified Church: Folklore Writings of Zora Neale Hurston.* Berkeley, Calif.: Turtle Island Foundation, 1981.
———. *Seraph on the Suwanee.* New York: HarperCollins, 1991.
———. *Spunk: The Selected Short Stories of Zora Neale Hurston.* Berkeley, Calif.: Turtle Island Foundation, 1985.
———. *Tell My Horse.* New York: HarperCollins, 1990.
———. *Their Eyes Were Watching God.* New York: HarperCollins, 1990.
Ikonne, Chidi. *From DuBois to Van Vechten: The Early Negro Literature, 1903–1926.* Westport, Conn.: Greenwood, 1981
Jenkins, Wilbert. "Jessie Fauset: A Modern Apostle of Black Racial Pride." *Zora Neale Hurston Forum* 1 (1986): 14–24.
Johnson, James Weldon. *Along This Way.* New York: Penguin, 1990.
———. *Autobiography of an Ex-Coloured Man.* New York: Penguin, 1990.
Kellner, Bruce. *Carl Van Vechten and the Irreverent Decades.* Norman: University of Oklahoma Press, 1968.
———, ed. *The Harlem Renaissance: A Historical Dictionary for the Era.* New York: Methuen, 1987.
———. *Letters of Carl Van Vechten.* New Haven: Yale University Press, 1987.
Kinney, James. *Amalgamation!* Westport, Conn.: Greenwood, 1985.
Kramer, Victor A., ed. *The Harlem Renaissance Re-Examined.* New York: AMS, 1987.
Larsen, Nella. *Quicksand and Passing.* Ed. by Deborah E. McDowell. New Brunswick, N.J.: Rutgers University Press, 1989.
Lewis, David Levering. *When Harlem Was in Vogue.* New York: Oxford University Press, 1979.
Locke, Alain., ed. *The New Negro.* New York: Atheneum, 1968.
Lupton, Mary Jane. "Bad Blood in Jersey: Jessie Fauset's *The Chinaberry Tree.*" *College Language Association Journal* 27 (1984): 383–392.
———. "Black Women and Survival in *Comedy American Style* and *Their Eyes Were Watching God.*" *Zora Neale Hurston Forum* 1 (1986): 38–44.
———. "Clothes and Closure in Three Novels by Black Women." *Black American Literature Forum* 20 (1986): 409–421.
McKay, Claude. *Home to Harlem.* Boston: Northeastern University Press, 1987.
———. *A Long Way from Home.* New York: Harcourt, Brace Jovanovich, 1970.
McKay, Nellie. *Jean Toomer, Artist.* Chapel Hill: University of North Carolina Press, 1984.
Osofsky, Gilbert. *Harlem: The Making of a Ghetto.* New York: HarperCollins, 1963.
Ovington, Mary White. *Portraits in Color.* New York: Viking, 1927.
———. *The Walls Came Tumbling Down.* New York: Harcourt, Brace, 1947.

Perkins, Kathy A., ed. *Black Female Playwrights: An Anthology of Plays before 1950*. Bloomington: Indiana University Press, 1990.

Perry, Margaret. *Silence to the Drums: A Survey of the Literature of the Harlem Renaissance*. Westport, Conn.: Greenwood, 1976.

Pryse, Marjorie and Hortense J. Spillers, eds. *Conjuring: Black Women, Fiction, and Literary Tradition*. Bloomington: Indiana University Press, 1985.

Ramsey, Priscilla. "Freeze the Day: A Feminist Reading of Nella Larsen's *Quicksand* and *Passing*." *Afro-Americans in New York Life and History* 9 (1985): 27–41.

———. "A Study of Black Identity in Passing Novels of the 19th and Early 20th Century." *Studies in Black Literature* 7 (1976): 1–7.

Roses, Lorraine Elena and Ruth Elizabeth Randolph. "Marita Bonner: In Search of Other Mothers' Gardens." *Black American Literature Forum* 21 (1987): 165–183.

Russell, Sandi. *Render Me My Song*. New York: St. Martin's, 1990.

Schockley, Ann Allen. *Afro-American Women Writers 1746–1933*. New York: Penguin, 1988.

Schuyler, George. *Black No More*. Boston: Northeastern University Press, 1989.

Scott, Bonnie Kime, ed. *The Gender of Modernism*. Bloomington: Indiana University Press, 1990.

Studio Museum in Harlem. *Harlem Renaissance Art of Black America*. New York: Abrams, 1987.

Sylvander, Carolyn Wedin. *Jessie Redmon Fauset: Black American Writer*. Troy, N.Y.: Whitston, 1981.

Thorton, Hortense. "Sexism as Quagmire: Nella Larsen's *Quicksand*." *College Language Association Journal* 16 (1973): 285–291.

Thurman, Wallace. *The Blacker the Berry* . . . . New York: MacMillan, 1970.

———. *Infants of Spring*. Boston: Northeastern University Press, 1992.

Toomer, Jean. *Cane*. New York: W. W Norton, 1975.

Van Vechten, Carl. *Nigger Heaven*. New York: Alfred A. Knopf, 1926.

Walker, Alice, ed. *I Love Myself When I Am Laughing . . . And Then Again When I Am Looking Mean and Impressive*. New York: Feminist, 1979.

Wall, Cheryl A. "Passing for What? Aspects of Identity in Nella Larsen's Novels." *Black American Literature Forum* 20 (1986): 97–111.

Washington, Mary Helen. *Invented Lives: Narratives of Black Women 1860–1960*. New York: Anchor, 1987.

———. "I Sign My Mother's Name." *Mothering The Mind: Twelve Studies of Writers and Their Silent Partners*. Ed. by Ruth Perry and Martine Watson Brownley. New York: Holmes & Meier, 1984.

———. "Nella Larsen: Mystery Woman of the Harlem Renaissance." *Ms.*, December 1987, 44–50.

West, Dorothy. *The Living Is Easy*. New York: Feminist, 1982.

————. "The Living Was Easy: A Memoir by Dorothy West." *Boston Review*, August 1983, 7–10.

Wintz, Cary D. *Black Culture and the Harlem Renaissance*. Houston: Rice University Press, 1988.

Youman, Mary. "Nella Larsen's *Passing*: A Study in Irony." *College Language Association Journal* 18 (1974): 235–241.